Murder at Duffy Hall Castle

A Nora Duffy Mystery

Babs L. Murphy

NEWMAN SPRINGS PUBLISHING
320 Broad Street
Red Bank, NJ 07701

First originally published by Newman Springs Publishing 2019

ISBN 978-1-64531-571-1 (Paperback)
ISBN 978-1-64531-573-5 (Digital)

Printed in the United States of America

For Peg and Doug

Thanks for all your love and support; to my husband, Don, and to Donald, Monica, Douglas, Maureen, David, Melissa, and my extended family; and to Sister Catherine Siena, OP, and her many colleagues who spent their lives teaching us to love God, each other, words, and music.

All shall be well, all shall be well,
For there is a Force of Love
Moving through the Universe
That holds us fast and will never let go.
—Saint Julian of Norwich (circa 1342–1416)

INTRODUCTION

P lease do come in and enjoy the story! I didn't mean to get in your way, but I'm searching for a girl named Nora Duffy, and I'm not having much luck yet. My name is Bridie, and I'm the resident ghost at Duffy Hall Castle in a town called Sneem on the southwestern coast of Ireland. I haven't left Sneem for more than 200 years, and this place called the USA, where Nora lives, seems to be awfully far away, and I understand it's very big.

Nora is scheduled to have business at Duffy Hall down the road, but dark forces are at play. I've been assigned to watch over Nora by Angel Christopher so that I'll be able to help her when she needs it most. Christopher told me that Nora looks a lot like I used to when I was alive, pale and thin, with long red hair, although she's much shorter than I was.

I wasn't very effective when I was alive, and that hasn't improved much. Most ghosts can scare people by making rooms icy cold, uttering horrible moans, or clanking their ponderous chains. I try hard not to do any of those things, since I remember only too well how afraid I was most of my life because of my harsh father.

I've tried to warn people of danger over the years, but the best I've been able to come up with is whispering. The current owner of my castle, Mr. Cyrus Duffy, doesn't seem to hear me at all. He probably thinks the sound he hears is just the wind blowing through the cavernous halls of the Castle. I can sometimes incline people to smell honeysuckle, my favorite flower, but I doubt it works with him.

My father was Lord Rupert Fitzpatrick, and I heard people say that he was responsible for my mother's early death. I grew up with a very old woman, Justine, as my governess, and I rarely saw my father. He was always off hunting some woman or animal. He gave me money but very little love, so I was pretty mixed up by the time I thought about boys.

I was a vain and vacuous young woman, and I loved fancy dresses and parties (I wish I had one of those gowns now, since this white sheet thing I have to wear is so very plain). I used to be known as Bridie the Beautiful, and I tried my best to live up to it. I used pomegranate juice to redden my lips and cheeks and I wore scent jewelry filled with rose petals on my neck and both hands. I was quite pretty, if I do say so myself.

I had a number of suitors, but Father wanted me to marry Lord Jeffrey McMahon, because he was rich. Jeffrey was old, at least thirty, and he was too much like my father for my liking. I fell in love with Brendan, a groom at our stables, who took special care of my father's huge black steed, Satan. Just looking at Brendan's curly brown hair and cornflower blue eyes gave me that fluttery feeling all over, if you know what I mean. Brendan made me realize how poor and miserable the people on our estate were because of my father's ruthlessness. If a person or an animal tried to resist his power, Father found a way to crush them.

We knew there was no use trying to talk to Father about our love for each other, so we planned to run away to Brendan's people who lived in Dublin. My father had spies everywhere and found out about our plans. He resolved to lock me up and get rid of Brendan permanently.

We tried to leave the castle one fateful night. We waited until sundown, and then we mounted our horses and were ready to cross over the drawbridge, but Father's archers were waiting for us. I thought Brendan had said to turn to the left, but he turned to the right, and before we could sort the situation, both of us were killed with arrows. That hurt a lot, I can tell you. I've been wandering around the castle ever since, and I haven't seen my sweet Brendan since that night.

My father didn't last too long after that. He caught a case of the black death when he went on a trip, which is a terrible way to die. I should have felt a sense of justice, but I was sad, because even the worst of men does something nice occasionally. I couldn't help remembering the pretty doll and her flowered dress that he gave me for my fifth birthday. I think that doll is probably still there somewhere at the castle.

Angel Christopher assigned me to another case a few years ago, but I failed miserably. I learned then that one of the keys to helping people is patience. Christopher told me that if I'm successful this time, I have a very good chance of receiving Angel status and being reunited with Brendan, so I'm trying hard to follow his instructions.

I'm not sure exactly what to do, so please stay with me. You've come in just as I've found Nora, and I can see that she is in real danger, but I'm not sure how much I can intervene now. Please wish me good luck. I'll need it!

Tuesday, September 11
Chicago, 4:00 p.m., CDT

Nora lay on the concrete platform, dazed and gasping for breath, and knew that she was in big trouble. Pain. Dizziness. Light flickering up and down like an ancient television set. She tried to think of a prayer, but instead, her mind conjured up the famous lines from Shakespeare in *As You Like It*:

> All the world's a stage,
> And all the men and women merely players;
> They have their entrances and their exits…

Amazing organ, the brain. So small, about three pounds, yet holds the memories and dreams of a lifetime. Spits out things in an instant that you haven't thought about in years. Was Nora about to make her exit tonight? She didn't think she had that imminent feeling of dread that people report when they know they're about to die, but as an intern, she was around death so often, she knew that it was always lurking nearby.

Nora had developed a habit of picking out appropriate music for any situation, and Chopin's "Funeral March" came to mind, but she remembered her harp teacher, Mrs. McGee, saying that it was too funereal for most funerals. That made her try to laugh, but any movement made her headache worse. She tried humming Pachelbel's

"Canon in D" instead, played at a million weddings and renowned for making people feel calm, but soon gave it up as a bad job.

She tentatively moved her fingers and toes after taking a few shallow breaths and was relieved that they seemed to respond well enough. She was looking up at a crowd of concerned faces around her and was still clutching her phone. As her mom would say, "That's the good news."

On the other hand, her vision was clouded by blood and the kind of vertigo that makes things spin upside down. She was shivering so much, and the pain in her head and her side was getting more intense. She wanted to get up, but she knew that the first rule for head injuries was "don't move." She was used to being in control, but now, her "fight or flight" hormones were running the show. She groped to think logically, but the pain in her head kept getting in the way.

Nora went through her mental checklist for assessing the onset of shock and knew that she was experiencing some classic symptoms—dizziness, confusion, blood loss, thirst. Just yesterday, she had attended Professor Gratz's seminar about psychological shock and recalled his pithy warning: "If you wait, you'll be too late." Someone told her that an ambulance had been called, which was good, because time was of the essence. She tried to assess the size of the bump on her head, but her hand came away covered in blood—not good!

Nora wondered if she could have avoided this predicament if she had only taken an earlier or later train. She fondly recalled an old saying her practical great-grandmother, Peg, used to tell her about accidents and "if only." "If stands in the corner, stiff. Plans change, and you have to change with them."

She tried to recall some details about how this had happened. She had taken the Rock Island train from 103rd Street in Beverly to the end of the line. Then she walked across LaSalle Street to the LaSalle subway entrance, carefully walked down the many stairs in her heels, inserted her ticket in the automatic machine, and sat down to wait for the train. She got in line as she heard the train coming into the station and was absentmindedly looking at her phone and waiting for the train's wheels to stop screeching. Somehow, she had dropped her phone, so she bent down fast to pick it up. The next thing she remembered was being knocked off her feet so hard that her head hit the cement platform.

She hoped that she hadn't scuffed her flowered Jimmy Choo heels when she fell. She had saved for several months to buy them. Her stomach was doing flip-flops, and she had a sinking feeling that she was going to throw up on her new dress. She had bought the yellow one with the flowered insets because Tommy told her that it made her look like a pretty canary. She hadn't cried yet, but when she thought of Tommy being so far away, the tears started to flow.

A young man knelt next to her and asked if he could help. Nora asked him to use her cell phone to send an "urgent help" text to her "Family" contact and explain that she was hurt and was at the LaSalle Blue Line subway platform. "Please tell them to come here fast," she managed to blurt out. He assured her that he would take care of it.

Lying on the subway platform, looking at the gray walls and dreary ceiling, gave Nora an interesting perspective on things she'd never noticed down here before. *Uncle Joe could help out the City of Chicago with some good paint down here*, she thought. She saw a tiny bird way up at the top who was chirping away. *He must have gotten trapped down here*, Nora thought to herself. *I hope both of us can see daylight soon.* As she looked sideways, she saw a tiny gray mouse daintily chewing on something and wondered how many other critters lived down here and what they found to eat. She was sure there must be rats down here too, and she hoped to be off this platform before they spotted her.

A Humphrey Bogart-type man told her that his name was Lieutenant Matthew Braxton from the Chicago Police Department, and he encouraged her to tell him what had happened. She tried to concentrate on what he was saying, but between her head hurting so much and the echo down here, it sounded as though he was speaking under water. She could see that his mouth was moving, but all she heard was "Waaa, waaa, waaa, waaa."

"First, I need to get this blood out of my eyes," she sputtered out. A bystander tried to help by wiping the blood off her right eye but realized that it would require a much bigger box of tissues, since small rivulets of blood kept dripping down her face. A watchful Chicago Transit Authority person told them she would try to find more tissues.

Nora recovered some of her doctor-layman manner and told the lieutenant that she hoped he wasn't afraid of blood. She asked him to push down on her wound with tissues and keep applying pressure, which could slow the bleeding. It would be best if he had on plastic gloves, but beggars can't be choosers. She noticed that the cuffs of his shirt were very white, and she hoped that they wouldn't be ruined by the blood. Nice silver cufflinks too.

"All I know is that I was waiting to board the train and looking at my phone. Then I suddenly dropped the phone and bent down fast to pick it up. The next thing I knew, something hit me with such force that I fell on the ground and hit my head really hard. I heard some screams. That's about it. Has an ambulance been called? I'd like to get this bleeding stopped."

Lieutenant Braxton assured Nora that an ambulance was on its way. He wasn't sure at first about the age of the injured girl, but she assured him she was an adult. She didn't seem to be as big as his ten-year old niece. With her mop of curly red hair, she did remind him of a movie character, but he couldn't think of who it was.

He asked her how she thought it was that the man behind her had plunged to his death while she had survived. The only answers that came to her mind were fate or divine intervention. She hadn't even been aware that it was a man who had knocked her down, but she felt sorry for anyone who had died so violently.

"By the way, where's my purse?" Nora asked. Lieutenant Braxton found the purse and put it next to her, and it made her feel better to know that the green leather purse was safe, since she had taken out $200 from the ATM just before she came down to the subway. She obviously wasn't going to make it to the dinner and play she'd planned with Mrs. Barry and her soon-to-be sisters. That reminded her of Tommy, and a fresh set of tears ran down her cheeks, mixing with the blood.

She usually enjoyed the pungent odors that came from Barney's hotdog stand at the end of the platform, but today, those smells were making her nausea worse. Marty, the blind accordionist, was trying hard to play a cheery tune, but the discordant sounds were jangling her nerves. It was a good sign that she was aware of these sensory things, but she knew that she needed immediate medical attention. Her parents were at a party a few blocks from here, and they would know just what to do. She prayed they had received the text.

Hail Mary, full of grace...pray for me now and at the hour of my death... The ancient words swirled in and through Nora, and she had a sudden spurt of energy. She was able to tell the lieutenant that her name was Nora Duffy and her father was a doctor who should be on his way here.

A man leaned over her and told her that the ambulance should be here any minute. "That bump on your head is getting very large and purple," he said, which didn't make her feel any better.

A woman from the CTA came running over with a blanket and asked if she wanted it under her head. "No," Nora responded. "Don't move my head until my parents have a chance to examine me. I would appreciate it if you'd put that blanket over me, though. It's freezing down here."

The CTA had sent out word that all Blue Line trains bound for O'Hare Airport were canceled for now and no trains bound for Forest Park were to stop at LaSalle. However, the latter trains continued to run past the station, and the amorphous woman's voice still made announcements, so it was as noisy as usual in the confined space.

Nora was thinking how easily we dismiss the many potential dangers in the subway because our awareness of them gets muted by our familiar routines. Today, those dangers had become only too real for her, and especially for the man who lay on the tracks below.

She wished that she would see her parents very soon.

Tuesday, September 11
Chicago, 5:00 p.m., CDT

Nora suddenly heard the voices she'd been waiting for, shouting, "Bitsy, Bitsy, we're here!" She felt herself relaxing a bit as she heard her parents calling her by her nickname, and she smiled as she saw the elegant, formally dressed couple running down the platform. Whenever someone complimented Nora on how good looking her family was, she always remarked that "the apple doesn't fall far from the tree." Dr. Duffy had chiseled features with a streak of white in his dark blond hair, and Eileen Duffy bore a striking, albeit shorter, resemblance to the movie star Rita Hayworth, with her wreath of dark red hair framing her face. The Duffys were older now, but good genes and good habits helped them retain a youthful appearance.

"Bitsy, we're coming," yelled Nora's mother.

"Mom, don't break your ankle in those high heels," wheezed Nora. "You'll ruin your dress if you fall."

"Oh, don't worry about us," responded Mrs. Duffy, trying to distract Nora by making light of the situation. "We were just about to start dancing at the hotel. I'm glad I heard the text beep when I did, since the orchestra was just about to launch into 'Celebration.'"

Nora's parents looked at each other in dismay. They couldn't believe that their beautiful daughter's body was just inches away from the stopped train. It was a miracle that she hadn't either lost a foot or been pushed off the platform. She only had one pretty shoe on, and presumably, the other one had fallen the five feet to the tracks below. Eileen Duffy breathed a prayer of thanks to Nora's guardian angels that she was still alive. Now they had to keep her that way.

Tuxedo coat, sequin jacket, and high heels were quickly shed, and plastic gloves were put on. They joined in their usual prayer when they were about to treat someone in danger of death: "Remember, O gracious Virgin Mary, that never was it known that anyone who fled to thy protection, implored thy help, or sought thy intercession was left unaided..." They had worked together on hundreds of patients in serious condition without "turning a hair," but Eileen's hands were shaking as she pushed Nora's matted hair up and wiped the blood away from her eyes. Dr. Duffy's snap diagnosis told him that they had to act quickly to prevent shock from setting in, since blood leaking out and not enough blood getting in to the internal organs was potentially life-threatening.

Nora's usually pale complexion was now almost sheet white. She was shivering violently, and there was a small but steady stream of blood oozing out of the very large cut and bump on the right side of her forehead. And why was her body lying in such a strange way? They realized that she had fallen on the huge canvas bag slung over her right shoulder. That had probably saved her life, but it was now putting too much pressure on her head and ribs.

"Bitsy, tell me what's going on," insisted her father.

"Daddy," she moaned, "my head hurts so much. I can feel the blood running down my face, and I think I might be bleeding internally too. My ribs feel like someone is hitting them with a hammer. I'm awfully cold, and I lost consciousness for a minute. It's a good thing I had my big bag we bought in London last year with me. It kept me from hitting the cement full force. I'm worried about my right wrist hurting so much. I'm supposed to play at Barry's on Wednesday. I'm so thirsty too."

Nora called out to her sister, Maureen, who had come from the party with her parents. She was standing behind her mother and was shaking almost as much as Nora was. "Reenie, call the Barry's and let them know what's happening," directed Nora. "I was supposed to go

17

to a play with them tonight. And stop sobbing so hard, I'll be okay. If the twins are here, don't let them see me. They'll be scared."

Maureen nodded but didn't seem too reassured. Bitsy was so very pale, and there was a small pool of blood under her head. *I'm the one who's scared*, she thought, *let alone the twins.*

Molly and Caitlan, the young teenage twins, were there along with their other siblings, but their brothers were keeping the young girls at a distance so they couldn't see how badly Nora was injured. That just made the girls worry even more. Their aunt, Holly, was there too, and she had taken them in her arms in an attempt to soothe their fears. She assured them that her mom and dad were with her now and they would make sure that Nora would be fine. The girls felt frantic and said they still wanted to hold Nora's hands, but Holly convinced them not to get in the way for now.

"Bits," Dr. Duffy asked Nora, "what's in the bag over your shoulder?"

Nora suddenly felt like she should go to sleep right now and started to go limp and close her eyes. Dr. Duffy pulled out a bottle of sterile water from his case and poured some on Nora's face, which made her somewhat more alert. He didn't want to give her any medication until he knew more about her condition.

Right about then, Nora heard a sound like loud whispering in her ears, and that seemed to snap her out of her faint. She also smelled honeysuckle flowers, which she'd always loved. Strange that she would smell honeysuckle down in the subway. She knew that her mother always used Chanel No. 5.

Nora suddenly recognized the tune that the blind accordionist was trying to play, and she launched into singing the verse of the Frank Sinatra hit as she looked at her sweet parents:

"You're just too marvelous
Too marvelous for words
Like glorious, glamorous,
And that old standby amorous."

That made her parents smile warily. It was a good sign that she remembered the lyrics, but there was a long way to go before Bitsy would be marvelous.

"Bitsy, I need to know right now what is in your bag," shouted her father.

"Besides my fiddle, there are a lot of large tablecloths to use for Tommy's birthday party. Mom, tell Tommy that I need to see him right now."

Eileen Duffy glanced at her husband with a new sense of alarm. "Bitsy knows that Tommy is out of the country. I'm concerned about her confusion. If that ambulance doesn't get here very soon, we're going to have to rig up an IV for her."

"Jim!" shouted Dr. Duffy to his son. "See if you can get Nora's fiddle out of her bag that she's lying on and slowly pull out the tablecloths one by one. Do it quickly but as gently as you can." Dr. Duffy and Eileen tried to hold Nora's body steady while her brothers removed the contents of the bag underneath her.

After a few minutes, Jim and younger brother, Jack, were able to retrieve the fiddle. Grandpa Burke had made the case, which must have been very sturdy, and they hoped that the treasured violin hadn't been damaged. They also pulled out four large tablecloths. As the bag got gradually smaller, Nora's body laid flatter. Dr. Duffy put the tablecloths under Nora's feet to raise them higher to help balance her internal blood flow.

Mrs. Duffy took Nora's vital signs. Her blood pressure was low, and her heart rate was high. Her green eyes weren't as focused as they should be. Eileen covered her daughter with their suitcoats to try to warm her up.

"Mom, try to keep the blood off my new dress."

"Bitsy, *a stor*, I'm sorry, but your lovely yellow dress is a goner," said Mrs. Duffy as she stroked Nora's hair. Eileen Duffy only resorted to using the Irish phrase *a stor*—my treasure—when she was terribly worried about one of her children, but now she repeated it over and over. Nora's brightly colored dress was already stained with many splatters of blood. Hospital personnel would be working fast and would just cut it off in the emergency room anyway. That was the least of their worries now.

Mrs. Duffy removed Bitsy's beautiful engagement ring from her finger and made sure it was safely stored in her purse. She knew that the ring was a little big, so she wanted to be sure it hadn't gotten lost in the chaos.

The tall policeman introduced himself to them. "My name is Lieutenant Matthew Braxton, and I'll likely be heading the investigation as to what happened here. My partner and I were at a nearby restaurant when the alert went out about an emergency in the LaSalle Blue Line stop, and we rushed over here. You are her parents?" he queried.

Mrs. Duffy explained to Lieutenant Braxton that her name was Eileen Duffy, and Nora/Bitsy was their eldest daughter. Her husband, Dr. Michael Duffy, was a cardiac surgeon at Holy Savior, and she was his head nurse. They had been at a hospital party at the Conrad Hilton when she saw the urgent text message on her phone, and they came as quickly as they could.

"I'm assuming that Bitsy must be your daughter's nickname," asked Lieutenant Braxton.

"Yes, you can see how very small she is, and we've called her Bitsy since she was born. Anyone who knows her well calls her that."

"Which hospital will you be going to?" the lieutenant asked.

Dr. Duffy responded they'd be at the emergency room at Holy Savior where he was on staff.

"I'm going to need to talk to all of you some more," Lieutenant Braxton said, "so I'll see you at the hospital later."

Soon they saw the ambulance attendants running down the platform. Dr. Duffy instructed the paramedics to put a collar around Nora's neck and to gently roll her onto their spinal board as a precaution. The four men couldn't believe how light Nora was and how easy it was to lift her. They transferred her to the stretcher and began the trip up the stairs and into the waiting ambulance on LaSalle Street.

There was some momentary confusion about the hospital destination. The Chicago paramedics were always instructed to go to the nearest hospital, and they would have to pass up that hospital to go to

Holy Savior. Dr. Duffy assured them he would take responsibility for it, and they raced over to Savior as fast as possible with sirens blaring.

Chicago police had closed off the subway's entrance stairs next to the Eisenhower Expressway due to the fatality of the unknown man and Nora's injuries. However, Lieutenant Braxton told them they could let Nora's relatives come down. Jim and Jack Duffy told their parents that they would stay at the subway stop for now to talk to worried family and friends and would meet them at the hospital soon. One after another of Nora's family and friends who had been downtown and had seen the urgent help text came running down the stairs to get the news from the Duffys.

Lieutenant Braxton and his team had herded the other people who had been on the train to the exits and told the disgruntled passengers to find alternative transportation. CTA representatives told the passengers that buses would be coming to take people to O'Hare, but that would take some time to arrange. If they were in a hurry, they should take a cab. Their last line was the usual, "Sorry for the inconvenience," which made the passengers feel even more inconvenienced.

Sergeant Laura Belsky, Lieutenant Braxton's partner, yelled out that everyone should give their names and phone numbers to her, and then they could leave the station unless they had more information about the accident.

A few passengers that had been awaiting the train came forward to explain what they had seen, but their stories were similar. They'd all been wrapped up in their own thoughts or had been using their phones. They hadn't noticed much until they realized that the man in black was falling off the platform, and people began to scream, but it was too late to do anything about it. A few people relayed that they saw the diminutive young woman in the yellow dress drop her phone, lean down quickly to pick it up, and then get knocked to the floor, but they didn't know much more.

A CTA crew had begun the very unpleasant task of gathering up what was left of the man who'd fallen beneath the incoming train. Lieutenant Braxton asked them to look for any identification on him. He would need it since he had nothing else to go on.

Lieutenant Braxton and Sergeant Belsky had more questions than answers about what had happened. Everyone agreed that there had been a crowd of people waiting to board the train. Could someone behind him have pushed the man in black so hard that he fell against Nora and then landed on the tracks? That didn't seem likely since everyone they had talked to mentioned how large he was. Could he have fainted and fallen forward? Again, that probably wasn't the case, because he would have been too far from the edge of the platform to just fall off. Besides, everyone they had talked to mentioned that he had screamed as he fell, so he was aware of what was happening. Could he have intended to commit suicide and Nora happened to be in his way as he did it? That seemed to be the prevailing scenario. So far, no one had given him other information to contradict that notion. He talked to a harried CTA representative and told him the little he knew.

Lieutenant Braxton was getting ready to leave when a young woman approached him and asked if he was the person in charge. "I have some information about the incident that might be helpful," she began.

"I thought I asked anyone who knew something to stay behind," grumbled Lieutenant Braxton. "Where were you?"

"I had a very important test at school," explained the earnest young woman with the large silver book bag strapped to her back, "and I started to leave. But I couldn't stop thinking about that pretty girl who'd been hurt so badly, so I came back to talk to you."

"Well, what's this information you have?" asked the lieutenant as he pulled out his notebook. He didn't expect to hear much new; people sometimes just wanted to get their fifteen minutes of fame when they talked to the police.

"I know you're probably thinking that the man in black committed suicide," said the woman in blue, "but I think he was trying to push the girl in the yellow dress onto the tracks and accidentally ended up killing himself. I took pictures of them both on my cell phone."

"That's very interesting," exclaimed Lieutenant Braxton, trying to suppress his excitement. "I don't know why you know more than anyone else I talked to, but tell me more."

Tuesday, September 11
Chicago, 5:30 p.m., CDT

"My name is Elsie Young," said the young woman in the blue jacket, "and I was on my way to DePaul University. I had just missed the previous train, so I had a few minutes to relax. I'm a buyer of better dresses for Macy's. I don't usually pay much attention to what other people are doing down here, but then I don't think I've ever seen anyone dressed in Chanel and Jimmy Choo's in the subway, so the girl caught my attention right away. I only saw her from the back at first and almost thought she was a kid dressing up in her mother's clothes because she's so little. Her long curly red hair went so well with the color of the dress too. She reminded me of that Disney movie character of a few years ago, the Scottish princess."

"Ah," thought Lieutenant Braxton, "that's the movie character I was trying to think of."

Elsie continued, "Then I started to notice this man all dressed in black with a big black mustache who looked like a generic movie villain. I realized that he appeared to be shadowing yellow dress. No matter where she walked or sat, he was standing behind her, although she didn't seem to be noticing him at all. I thought at first that he might have been planning to steal her Kors purse, so I started to watch him more carefully. Yellow dress appeared to be waiting for an important call and kept glancing at her phone. I had the impression that it would be a happy call. She was standing right across from me, and I could see that she had a smile on her face. Her happy dress and happy smile made this whole dismal place seem brighter."

Elsie continued to relate details as she explained that they heard the train coming and everyone got into position to board. She had lost track of what the man in black was doing for a minute, but then she noticed that he was standing directly behind yellow dress and had his big hands out right behind her back.

"I started to get scared about what he planned to do and even yelled out to yellow dress, but the train was screeching so loudly, and the PA voice told us that the train was arriving. It looked to me as though yellow dress suddenly dropped something and bent down very fast to pick it up. Then the man in black was flying past her and falling off the platform.

"I'll never forget his scream. The more I think about it, I believe he had planned to push her onto the tracks, but he got carried away by his forward momentum when she bent down so quickly. That's all I know, but at one point, I did take a picture of them, just in case he did steal her purse. Look at this," she gestured as she showed Lieutenant Braxton a very clear picture on her phone of both the small girl in yellow and the very large man in black.

Lieutenant Braxton asked Elsie to forward that picture to his phone and wrote down her contact information. He then thanked her for coming forward and told her she was free to leave but to expect his call soon. "And good luck with your test," he added. *And good luck to me*, he thought. *At least I have something to work with now.*

Tuesday, September 11
Chicago, 6:00 p.m., CDT

D r. Duffy and Eileen rode in the ambulance to Holy Savior and guided the paramedics. Dr. Duffy had alerted the hospital en route and greeted the waiting ER attendants who whisked Nora into an examining room. The nurses had been alerted that the patient was Dr. Duffy's daughter. They were curious as to what had happened to her, but they didn't waste time now. Most of them knew Nora already and worked quickly on their friend. They carefully adjusted her position on a bed, reluctantly cut off her silk dress with practiced fingers, and replaced it with a generic hospital gown.

They hooked her up to various monitors that began to whirr and beep as they monitored various bodily functions. Her initial readings were cause for concern, so they carefully watched them. Amy was called upon to insert the IV line and was able to find a good vein right away. Dr. Duffy worked with the doctor in charge of the ER, his friend, Dr. Hal Fong, who had given instructions for the IV meds, and the life-giving fluids began dripping into Nora's arm.

The nurses from Dr. Duffy's office had heard the news and rushed down to the ER to see how Nora was. Nora was happy to see some familiar faces: Diane and Amanda, the charge nurses; Keisha, the lab tech; and Sue, the scheduling secretary. Dr. Whiteside and some nurses from the pediatric cancer unit where Nora worked also came down. Her friend, Therese Cummings, who always had a funny story to share, tried to smile at Bitsy through her tears and told her that all the parents and kids in the oncology clinic were keeping her in their prayers.

The friends had to stay out of the way as the ER nurses cleaned and treated the large cut and bump on Nora's head and looked for other injuries, but just knowing they were around her was a comfort to Nora.

An intern asked her the usual questions to ascertain mental acuity to see if she knew where she was, what date it was, and more. He also took her medical history, which was very brief. Nora's mom helped her to answer the series of "Have you ever had this disease or that" questions. She had always been extremely healthy, and the answer to the many questions was "No."

A lab tech came in and drew several vials of blood. After the IVs did their work for a while, the color started to return to Nora's cheeks, and her other numbers improved. Dr. Fong ordered a full set of X-rays, since Nora was complaining about pain from her head to her toes.

Nora had always thought it would save time and confusion in these tech-savvy days if a baby were fitted with a chip when it was born that would update medical information throughout life. However, many people seemed to think it would violate the person's privacy, and there would be too many technical issues to overcome. It would surely help the doctors and nurses in the ER, though. It was amazing how many people lost track of what they'd been treated for and why, when the treatment had occurred, and who the doctor was. People might remember the medications they were taking, but they rarely remembered the dosage. They also had trouble remembering their blood type and when they'd last had a tetanus or flu shot. Having that information available right away would save valuable time in case of a real emergency, especially if the patient were unconscious or confused.

Doctors Keith Marlowe and Patma Patel, Dr. Duffy's partners, and other team members came in to see if they could help. Other visitors appeared from the business office and the chaplain's office. Nora realized that she was in the hospital almost every day, but she hadn't ever been a patient. This would be a good opportunity for her to see things from the other side of the bed.

Dr. Fong finally got the head bleeding under control, and a nurse shaved a good-sized patch on the right side of her scalp so that the doctor could insert stitches. There was some initial concern about the need for plastic surgery, but they decided against it, since almost all the stitches would be hidden by her copious hair. They would decide whether Nora needed a transfusion after they got the results of the blood tests.

When the X-rays were read, it was confirmed that she did have a concussion, but it appeared to be minor. She had two broken ribs on her right side. Her left wrist was bruised, but no fracture was seen. The blood tests were slightly abnormal in some areas, but Nora preferred not to have a transfusion unless she really needed it. She was a lucky girl, although her head injury and resulting eye bruise that would certainly turn purple made her look as though she'd been in a prize fight. Her regimen of daily running and dancing had contributed to her overall excellent health, but she would have a whopper of a headache and sore ribs for a few days.

Nora's siblings and many other family members arrived at the hospital and met in the ER waiting room. Dozens of other people had gathered at the hospital to support Nora and her parents—including her family in and near Chicago—neighbors, and friends. The youngest Duffys, Molly and Caitlan, brought the group frequent updates and were cheered to learn that Nora's injuries were painful but probably not too serious. Sister Mary Cecilia Clark, the chair of the hospital, visited the crowd, and the cafeteria provided sandwiches and drinks for all.

PJ and Cathy Barry, Nora's future in-laws, rushed over to the hospital after hearing the news from Maureen. They arrived with four of their children and were happy to receive the news that it appeared that Nora had not been seriously injured.

Nora was finally able to talk to Tommy in London, which helped her mood considerably. Tom was horrified to hear about her accident and asked if she wanted him to come home right away. She assured him that she was feeling a little better now, was being looked after well, and would probably stay overnight at the hospital. Nora told Tom to stay for the three days until his conference was over, although she wouldn't have minded if he appeared at her bedside right now.

Father Benedict MacNamara, or Father Mac, the disabled hospital chaplain, asked Nora if she would like to receive the Sacrament of the Sick, and she gratefully asked him to go right ahead. Father Mac began the prayers for healing and health, anointed her hands and head with blessed oils, and family and friends joined in, asking God to grant Nora a full recovery.

Nora asked about the man who knocked her down and had possibly committed suicide. She murmured the prayer for him that she usually said for those who had died: "May the angels lead you into paradise." She had done some research on suicide after one of their friends took his own life, and she knew that people weren't in their right minds when they got that desperate. If the man had been so unhappy in this life, she felt sure that God would be merciful to him.

Lieutenant Braxton and Sergeant Belsky arrived at Nora's room and asked to speak to Dr. Duffy. He told them that Nora was still receiving medical treatments and wouldn't be able to speak with them until the next day. Dr. Duffy told them that Nora would likely go home the next afternoon, and they could come to their home to speak with her then. The two policemen told Dr. Duffy they were glad to hear that Nora's condition was not worse, and they assured the Duffys that they would be pursuing their investigations starting the next day.

A number of reporters and media members with television cameras also arrived at the hospital and wanted an interview with someone from the Duffy family. Nora's brother, Jim, met with them and gave them a brief overview of the little they knew about the night's events and Nora's status. They absorbed what he had to say and wanted to know more details, but Jim told them in the famous words of the *Wizard of Oz* to "come back tomorrow."

In these days of almost instantaneous communication, Jim felt certain that their reports of the subway incident would soon be available to the public on their phones, computers, and televisions, perhaps before they could even get home from the hospital. He had no doubt that the media would indeed be pestering them for many days to come.

Nora wanted to go home, but Dr. Fong insisted that she stay overnight, just to be sure there were no serious effects from the concussion. Nora thanked Dr. Fong and the other people in the ER for their expert care. She was assigned to a room, and the orderlies pushed her cart through the long maze of corridors, carrying the heart monitor with her. She joked with them that she had often walked these long corridors, but she might call on them in the future for a ride.

Tuesday, September 11
Chicago, 9:00 p.m., CDT

The floor nurses came in to meet her and get her settled in the hospital bed. Her RN was Evelyn and her CNN was Carey. They got her hooked up to the various machines and offered her some Jell-O and soup, but Nora said her stomach didn't want any food right now. The nurses explained that they would be just outside the room and she should push her red button on the bed control if she needed them. They helped her go to the bathroom, but they asked her to call them if she had to get up later, just in case she was dizzy. They encouraged her to drink water out of the pink plastic glass and put ice in the matching pitcher. They turned on the television, and an old episode of the *Seinfeld* show was on that provided some much needed laughter in the background. Nora took mental notes about it all for her future patients.

Nora noticed that the recent rehabilitation efforts at the hospital had resulted in attractive rooms that looked as though they could be photos from a magazine like *Traditional Home*. The earth tone paint colors and décor looked sophisticated, and the new furniture appeared to be as comfy as they could make it. However, a little new paint and fancy furniture couldn't disguise the fact that these rooms held hundreds of sick people, and hope and despair alternated as though on some cosmic teeter-totter. Nora was very much aware of the tenuous state of life and death that existed around her. When the voice on the intercom proclaimed "Medical Alert," which happened with some regularity, you really knew that you weren't at a Holiday Inn.

Dr. and Mrs. Duffy and the many family members finally left for the night but assured her that she should call them at any time. She received many hugs and kisses, and then she was alone for the first time since the accident. Normally she would be reviewing the events of the past few hours over and over in her mind, but the pain medication started to take effect, and she fell asleep easily. Alas, the old phrase that "there's no rest in a hospital" appeared to be only too true. The nurses came in to check on her and her vital signs several times during the night, especially since she had a head injury.

There was a change of nursing staff at 7:00 a.m., and the new nurses came in and introduced themselves and took her vitals, which were all good. They helped her to get up and walk up and down in the hallway and then get to the bathroom. She was relieved that she felt almost normal again and looked forward to going home.

Wednesday, September 12
Chicago, 7:00 a.m., CDT

Dr. Duffy arrived to check on Nora in the morning, chatted with her for a while, and said he thought she could go home a little later. A series of other doctors came in to look at the results of the X-rays where Nora could have other possible injuries—eyes, hands, back, hips, and knees—but all those areas appeared to be fine. She laughed when she thought about her Aunt Ellen's comments about doctors who come in to see you in the hospital. "If he says good morning to you and asks how you are, you can be sure you'll receive a bill for $500, whether you know him or not." Nora thought that Aunt Ellen had exaggerated, but there did seem to be a number of men and women in suits or white coats whom she'd never seen before, asking her questions.

Mr. Kostka, the minister of care from St. Mary's, came by with Communion for her, and they said a prayer together. She recalled that yesterday was the anniversary of the September 11 attacks on the World Trade Center, but with all the chaos surrounding her, she'd forgotten about it. Everyone in the room said a prayer for the victims of those horrendous attacks and asked God for help for their families.

Nora had a breakfast tray delivered to her room, but she could only eat a few spoons of oatmeal and take a few swallows of apple juice. Her head felt a little better, but those cracked ribs were making her feel nauseated every time she moved. She was very relieved that her wrist felt a lot better. It wouldn't do for a musician or an aspiring brain surgeon to have problems with her hands.

Nora's mom and dad and other family members appeared, the nurses printed out a list of instructions for her, and by noon, she was cleared to go home, provided she followed directions to be inactive. Her sisters brought a fresh outfit for her and helped her to get dressed. Nora gratefully thanked the healthcare team and said goodbye to them. She wondered what had been going on at home that she had missed and was eager to find out how the kids were doing at the cancer clinic. Tommy had promised to call her tonight, and she looked forward to his loving chatter and always wise observations.

Wednesday, September 12
London, 3:00 p.m., GMT

Tom Barry, Nora's fiancé, was trying to pay attention to the seminar on international cooperation among law firms he was attending in London, but he kept wondering how his Bitsy was doing. He normally didn't think of Nora as small because of her powerful personality, but she didn't have much to fight with if she were seriously hurt. Dr. Duffy had sent him a disturbing text about Bitsy having a concussion after her fall.

Tom usually enjoyed these conferences, but he was already tired of the endless lectures and presentations. Representatives from each country talked to each other in their native languages outside of the conference room, but the official language of the conference was English. The immaculately groomed and coiffed participants certainly made a lot of noise as they tried to impress each other with their expertise and their expensive gadgets.

One of the main reasons to go to these conferences was to meet and greet other lawyers and get new ideas for problem solving in other countries. He'd talked to two men from Australia and a very knowledgeable woman from France last night. This morning, he'd had breakfast with a group from Germany and Brazil that he'd met last year in Frankfurt. It was almost comforting to hear that some vexing problems were the same the world over, especially today's challenges posed by social media.

Networking like this was valuable, and everyone had exchanged business cards and promised to stay in touch. Tom thought he had accomplished most of the work he'd been expected to do already. He'd accumulated many pages of notes to accompany the four-color documents that most people had distributed about their firms.

An intense young man, whose name tag said he was from Facebook in San Francisco, approached him and asked what his firm was doing about protecting the confidentiality of its clients. Tommy was about to turn the question around and ask him what Facebook's latest moves were to protect their many clients, but then the gong sounded, and they were summoned to the next lecture.

Tom was supposed to stay until Saturday because his boss, Mr. Kornan, wanted him to learn new methods for international cooperation as they expanded their firm's reach to other countries. This had certainly been helpful last year when they opened an office in Birmingham, England. Tommy had been able to make contact with Max Golden, a lawyer he had met at the Frankfurt conference, and Max had offered Tom his expertise as he attempted to navigate the complex rules of British law. Nora's Uncle Cyrus in Ireland had told him they needed more international representation too. Tom was feeling more confident now about working in the international realm, and Mr. Kornan had hinted that he might want Tom to head up their international department soon.

Tom didn't think he could keep his mind engaged for three more days since he was so worried about Nora. He was trying to formulate an excuse that would allow him to leave the next day. Besides, he'd tried to eat some Indian food last night that smelled delicious but had given him indigestion. He'd been attempting to develop his international cuisine taste buds, but Barry's chicken soup and a good strip steak would be a treat right now.

He had talked to his mom and dad and Nora's brother, Jim, yesterday, and they told him that Nora was doing well, but he'd like to see for himself. He couldn't imagine anyone wanting to hurt Nora, so he certainly hoped it was just an accident. There weren't many truly good people in the world, but Nora would have to be numbered among them. He never failed to be surprised that he was lucky enough to be her fiancé. He just wanted to hold her in his arms and give her a kiss and see that she was doing as well as they thought. He wished for the tenth time that their wedding was going to be next week and not six months from now. There were so many things to discuss about the wedding, their honeymoon, and finding a house. It was past time for them to start their lives together.

"I'll call Nora and talk to her myself after dinner," Tom decided. "If I know her"—he laughed to himself—"she had the hospital staff hopping to it until they let her go. She looks small, but she's more like an Irish warrior princess when her mind is made up."

6

Wednesday, September 12
Chicago, 1:00 p.m., CDT

Nora was happy to transfer to her dad's black Ford Explorer from the hospital wheelchair, and she was surrounded by a crowd of hospital personnel clapping for her. A crowd of media and TV cameras were also there to record the scene, but hospital security personnel were keeping them at a distance. Nora smiled at them and gave them a thumbs up sign. The reporters loved it and snapped as many photos as possible of her and her large family.

The family drove past the tree-lined streets and familiar homes and businesses to Longwood Drive where another crowd was gathered to welcome her. The St. Mary's band was lined up in front of their house and was playing the old alma mater tune, "Remember St. Mary's Forever," while the choir and the crowd loudly sang out the stirring words. The church bells were ringing lustily, and Nora was visibly moved.

She could almost picture Sr. Bernadette in first grade reminding them that the world could hold a wealth of troubles, so they should always remember to say the prayer: "St. Michael, the Archangel, defend us in battle. Be our protection from the malice and snares of the devil…"

St. Michael must have been working overtime for me last night, she mused.

She looked up and smiled back to old Monsignor Callahan who was waving enthusiastically to her from his second floor window across the street. *He knows what it's like to be confined to a wheelchair, but he's the cheeriest person I know,* thought Nora. She just kept thinking what a lucky person she was to be alive today. God must have had other plans for her on this earth.

As the family approached the house, they were confronted by a crowd of reporters and television cameras. The scenario of "brave but small victim in a wheelchair, large family, crowds of friends accompanied by a band, and the question as to whether an attempt had been made on her life" had the reporters energized. They were able to interview a few people in the crowd and learned a little more about the Duffy family, but the Chicago PD finally shooed them away.

Mr. Majszak from the hardware store had provided a ramp so it was easier to get the wheelchair into the back door of their house. Her brothers were finally able to push her inside to the kitchen, and Nora breathed a sigh of happy relief that she was sitting in her own house. Mrs. Jesse Meyers, their loving housekeeper, turned on the CD player, and The Chieftains blared out the tunes Nora loved the best. Listening to Van Morrison playing and singing "Ragland Road" with such a pulsating beat was a sure way to restore her energy.

Nora chuckled as she noticed the huge poster that Molly, Caitlan, and their eighth-grade friends had made saying "Welcome Home, Bitsy," accompanied by a cartoon of a sick-looking canary being smiled at by a cat with long whiskers and a wolfhound with big teeth. "Gosh, it looks like a conservatory in here with all the flowers too," she exclaimed. "It's wonderful to know that so many people are thinking of me."

Nora was indeed grateful for the many kindnesses of family and friends, but it was hard to forget that last night, she had almost been killed, and there was the possibility that it wasn't an accident. She thanked everyone for their assistance, but she had the very strong feeling that this was just the start of a long ordeal.

Wednesday, September 12
Reflections by the Killer

*W*hat a disaster! All my plans of the last six months down the drain.

I was hiding behind a post down in the subway station last night and gave the "famous assassin" the thumbs up that he had correctly identified his victim. She practically had a target painted on her back with that bright yellow dress she was wearing, so he could hardly miss. I thought all I had to do was wait a few minutes until that simpering goody two-shoes, Nora, was dead, but what happened instead? She's alive, and the "famous assassin" is dead!

What a stupid schmuck that guy was! He told me over the phone that he'd been successful all over the world, he'd get the job done in no time, and no one would ever be able to connect him with me. Instead, he ended up killing himself while that Nora got away with just a head injury.

She weighs about as much as my Labrador puppy! How hard could it be to knock her off a subway platform? I probably should have done it myself, but I thought it would be safer to have an expert do it. Some expert! I didn't think that the subway idea was a good plan from the beginning, and now I know I was right.

"Mr. Jones," the assassin, has my $5,000 too! I wonder where that's at? At least I don't have to give him the remaining $5,000 "upon completion," but how frustrating to know that I'll get nothing for all that money! My inheritance came in handy, but I don't want to squander it

all away. I'm going to give Nick, the Russian guy I talk to at the hospital, a piece of my mind for recommending that loser to me and ask for a refund.

I suppose the Chicago PD could identify "Mr. Jones" quickly enough, if there's enough left of him to recognize. Maybe they won't realize that he was supposed to kill Nora, but they will surely be curious as to why he was operating in Chicago. Luckily, there's no paperwork that I know of to connect him to me, but I hope he didn't have anything on him with my information. Even if he did, it probably got destroyed along with the rest of his miserable body.

I want that Dr. Duffy to suffer as much as I have over the last year. He doesn't deserve to have such acclaim at the hospital. He won't have his beloved daughter, and his "likes" on Facebook will plunge dramatically because he won't be able to work by the time I'm through. Then he'll know what it's like to be wrongfully ignored and cheated out of a successful future.

I'll have to think up a new plan that will really work. It won't be long now before the Duffy family realizes they can't get away with their arrogance! They'll be so sorry!

It's a good thing that I'm able to hear most of their plans without anyone suspecting me. I've been careful, and they have no idea how much I hate them, but they're going to find out. I'll be looking for the next available opportunity to get rid of Nora, and this time, no one is going to stop me!

Wednesday, September 12
Chicago, 1:30 p.m., CDT

Lieutenant Braxton and Sergeant Belsky from the Chicago PD came to Nora's house after she got home to ask her more questions and to return her flowered shoe that the CTA workers had recovered.

They both admired the very large home that was painted bright white with black shutters and had a wrap-around porch, complete with a swing and rocking chairs. A large American flag hung on a flagpole in front of the house, and two smaller flags for Ireland and the Chicago Police Department hung next to the red double front doors with stained glass panels on both sides. The doors were also flanked by tall pots of red and white geraniums, and planters with multicolored impatiens adorned the porch railings. Tall evergreens of various heights and shapes stood in front of the wide porch. A plaque next to the doors proclaimed that this was a historical home that was built in 1907.

They rang the bell and were warmly welcomed by a sturdy handshake from a smiling middle-aged woman who introduced herself as Jesse Meyers, the housekeeper. They passed through a spacious entranceway with black and white floor tiles, a full-length mirror on a large closet, a tall antique-looking armoire, two chairs covered in bright green damask, and a formidable-looking plant with orange flowers. Portraits of many children adorned the walls. Jesse gave them a warning to avoid tripping over the floor divider and then ushered them into the living room.

The very large room made a statement by having several points of interest that attracted the eye. The walls were painted a pale colonial blue, and the ceiling and embellished crown molding were a bright white. An old heavily carved piano covered with sheet music stood against the far wall, a stately wooden harp had pride of place in the bay windows, and a wide red brick fireplace had a fire going on this chilly day. A huge oil painting of a white thatched cottage overlooking crashing ocean waves onto a shore filled with giant boulders hung above the fireplace, and two large red leather wing chairs looked welcoming. Someone in the family must like modern art since Sergeant Belsky recognized several colorful Paul Klee paintings above the piano.

Books were everywhere, on the many tables and in the shelves on either side of the fireplace. Polished wooden woodwork and matching floors shone, and a very large navy and red oriental rug covered the dark floor. Many wide windows were graced by filmy white curtains and drapes of golden cloth. Comfortable couches and chairs with puffy pillows filled the room and proclaimed that many people called this place home. One end table held an oversized chess set that appeared to be still in play. They could see a television set peeking out from an armoire next to the piano as though it were only there in case of need. An opened laptop computer stood on the large cherry wood desk, and a tall ficus plant grew in a rococo planter.

Jesse turned off the CD player and brought the police persons over to visit with Nora who was sitting in her wheelchair since she had promised to stay quiet. Her imposing companion was her very tall grayish dog with a wooly coat, an Irish wolfhound who was growling somewhat quietly but steadily as they approached. Reilly kept his large head on Nora's lap and looked as though he dared anyone to touch her. Sergeant Belsky was afraid of dogs, especially enormous ones like Reilly, but Nora assured her that he was only concerned about her safety and was normally very gentle. "Once Reilly gets used to you, you'll be able to pet him too, and then he'll be your slave forever."

Just then a tiny little dog with bright eyes and lots of black and white unruly hair and a briskly wagging tail came trotting into the room. Nora introduced them to Billy and said he liked to be petted at any time and that he is Reilly's best friend. The two policemen smiled as they thought of the very tall and the very small dogs being best buddies.

Billy hopped over to them, barked out a few tiny sounds, licked Sergeant Belsky's new shoes, and seemed very happy to be a part of the group. He settled down at Reilly's feet after Nora slipped him a few treats. A large ginger-colored cat looked at the dogs with disdain and jumped over to the window seat behind the harp. Nora told them her name was Cheshire, and she believed they were all trespassers in her house. She didn't have a wide smile like her literary namesake, but she had kept them company for many years.

Nora introduced the policemen to Mrs. Duffy's parents, John and Marie Burke, and Dr. Duffy's parents, Conor and Deirdre Duffy. The two sets of grandparents were there to keep an eye on Nora, since Dr. and Mrs. Duffy had to be at the hospital this afternoon. Lieutenant Braxton wished he had grandparents like this friendly bunch. The Burkes and Duffys shook hands with the policemen and thanked them for all they were doing to find the culprit who had hurt their Nora. Mr. Duffy's right hand was in a cast, since he'd just had hand surgery. The Burkes had a pronounced Irish brogue, which resulted in words like "three" sounding like "tree" and was charming. The more Lieutenant Braxton talked to them, however, he realized that this group was not to be taken lightly and didn't much care as to what he thought about them. They just wanted action taken to protect their darling girl, and they wanted to hear some specifics about how this would happen.

Nora suggested that the grandparents wait until after lunch for an answer to their questions. Nora asked the lieutenant and the sergeant to be seated close to her so they could chat. Sergeant Belsky asked Nora if she played the harp.

"Yes, I've been playing since I was small, and most of my siblings do too. I also play the piano, but my hands are rather small for those bigger instruments. I prefer the violin. I used a smaller violin when I was younger, but, fortunately, my hands are big enough now for a full-size instrument. My parents love to have music around the house, and they've always encouraged us to play. My siblings play a variety of other instruments, and we have a Ceili band, where each one of us plays a different instrument."

The lieutenant asked what the delicious smell was, and Nora explained that Jesse was a master bread maker and was baking many loaves of bread, scones, and a raisin coffeecake. "Jesse knows that I love homemade bread and butter, and she's doing all she can to make me feel better. You're welcome to stay for lunch when we're finished here." Both policepersons thought that sounded like a tempting invitation, since their ordinary lunchtime fare would be something from McDonald's.

Lieutenant Braxton handed a package to Nora and said that it was her missing shoe. He said that he hadn't known anything about Jimmy Choo's and how much they cost, but Sergeant Belsky had filled him in. He couldn't imagine spending $700 or more just for shoes. His sister, Donna, had spent $150 on her last pair of shoes, and he thought that was too much. "I'll have to apologize to Donna," he said. "I just hope she doesn't develop a liking for these finer things."

Sergeant Belsky said, "This is such a large house. It must take a lot of work to maintain it."

Nora explained that they all pitched in, and early on, their parents ran the house rather like a barracks. Each person was expected to keep their space neat and clean and to either do their own laundry or sort it out for Jesse. They had a longtime cleaning lady, Ellen, who came in three times a week to do normal cleaning. Nora continued, "Before holidays or special occasions, she brings in a crew to wash as many surfaces as they can, inside and outside. Ellen's husband, Jake, takes care of the lawn, bushes, and flowers, and his partner, Ed, does house repairs and painting."

Nora said, "My mom and dad just don't have the time for all that now. They're doing their best to preserve what is literally 'this old house.' Mom is a great cook when she has time, and dad is too. Mom does love to garden, and she grows a lot of herbs in the backyard, which Jesse uses in her delicious food."

"I hope your shirt wasn't ruined when you were putting pressure on my bleeding cut," said Nora. "Thanks, by the way, for doing that. It really helped."

Lieutenant Braxton responded that it was an old shirt and he had thrown it away. He asked Nora how she was feeling today, and she responded that she felt better, but she still had a headache and had to be careful how she moved because of the broken ribs.

"Well, let's get started then for my report. Sergeant Belsky will take notes while we have a conversation. By the way, I will need photos of you and your family members for our investigation as soon as possible, please. Nora, it's very important that you tell me as much as you can remember about why you were in the subway, how long you were down there waiting for the train, where you planned to go, and anything else you can think of that would be useful to our investigation. Sergeant Belsky tells me that the clothes and shoes you had on in the subway were expensive. Were you going somewhere special? I recall that you mentioned that you were daydreaming about having twenty bridesmaids."

Nora smiled at that; she hadn't remembered that she told him about the bridesmaids. She noticed that Lieutenant Braxton was a great dresser and not at all like the rumpled policemen of fiction. He didn't have a raincoat, but if he did, she imagined that it would be white and wrinkle-free. Nora liked men's fashion and admired his black suit coat and striped blue and white tie. It was easy to feel comfortable talking to him.

Sergeant Belsky wore her navy business suit well, and her high heels looked like a pair Nora had admired on Zulily. Laura's light red lipstick matched what must have been a recent manicure. With her curly blond hair, wide blue eyes, and thin figure, Laura was "a dish," and Nora wondered if the two partners were an item off the force as well as on.

Nora began to tell them about her and her family. "I'm a last year medical student at Holy Savior and often take the subway to meet my fiancé, Tommy Barry, who lives on the north side. His parents own Barry's Pub on Irving Park. Tommy is out of the country in London on a business trip. I was on my way to Barry's to meet

Tommy's mother and sisters. We were going downtown to have dinner and then attend a play. I had my fiddle in the large bag I had slung over my right shoulder as well as four large tablecloths that would be used for Tom's birthday party next week.

"I had just missed the previous train, so I had time to sit down on a bench and wait for the next one to arrive. I was expecting a text from Tommy, so I was checking my phone frequently. As to the comment about the bridesmaids, we're going to get married next St. Patrick's Day, March 17. We could easily have twenty bridesmaids or more. I have to make a decision about that soon, so I was trying to focus on that knotty problem while I had a few minutes of free time."

Nora said that she had been imagining what it would be like to have so many people as part of the bridal party. She didn't want to get swallowed up in the wedding photos surrounded by twenty girls in fluffy dresses, but it could also be fun. She was also trying to decide if the dresses should be tied to a St. Patrick's Day theme, although green was not her favorite color. "I have five sisters, Tommy has four, and together we have about fifty female cousins. We both have many friends from school and work. The extended family is huge. I could easily have a very large wedding party, but it's a lot to figure out so that no one feels left out."

Nora explained that she had been wearing good clothes since she was supposed to attend a play at the Cadillac Theater after she had dinner with Tommy's mom and sisters. She said that her mother always told the girls that they should save up to buy one nice dress rather than three cheaper ones, since the good ones looked better and lasted longer. "I wait for sales, but usually, I have to special order because of my small size. Shoes are my one weakness. I like all the Jimmy Choos, but I especially loved the flowered pair I was wearing yesterday." She patted the package with her missing shoe and said she was so glad to get it back. "I'm so short that I almost always wear high heels when I'm going out."

Lieutenant Braxton noticed that Nora was speaking much better today, although she was wearing sunglasses to ward off dizziness. He told her that a witness had come forward to say that a very large man dressed all in black, the one who later fell off the platform,

seemed to be watching her carefully the whole time they were waiting for the train. "Didn't you notice him?" questioned Lieutenant
Braxton.

"No," responded Nora, "I didn't see him at all until I heard his
scream and felt his body knocking me down. I saw the story about it
on my phone this morning, but that's all I know. Have you been able
to figure out why he was down there?"

Wednesday, September 12
Chicago, 2:00 p.m., CDT

Lieutenant Braxton told Nora they were still working on trying to identify the man in the subway. "Please tell me more about the members of your family, Nora. Since we have nothing to work with on this case so far, we have to be thorough in gathering as much information about you as we can."

"Well, as you know, my dad, Michael, is a heart surgeon at Holy Savior. He grew up in this house, which belonged to his parents, Conor and Deirdre Duffy, whom you've just met. They live in Long Beach, Indiana. Dad met my mother, Eileen, in Dublin, Ireland, at a party at Trinity College where Mom was attending college with her friend, Nan, and Dad was there on a vacation with his family. They've always said that it was love at first sight, although there are some inconsistencies in that story, depending on who's doing the telling.

"Mom decided to come home after her first year abroad since she wanted to be closer to Dad. Dad completed college at Notre Dame University, and Mom went to nursing school at nearby Saint Mary's College. After Dad graduated from medical school, they dated for about a year and then got married. They lived in an apartment downtown until Mom got pregnant with me. Then Dad's parents told them they wanted to retire and move to Long Beach where they had many friends. They wanted my parents to have this house, and Mom and Dad have been here for the last twenty-seven years. My dad is fifty-two and mom is fifty, and they just celebrated their twenty-eighth wedding anniversary."

Nora continued, "There are ten of us children. I'm the oldest. I'll be twenty-six in two months. I'm engaged to marry Tom Barry. Then there are two boys—Jim is twenty-five, and Jack is twenty-four. Jim works for a big technology firm, and Jack is a stock trader. Jim is engaged to a fun and brilliant girl, Trish Morgan, who goes to Northwestern and is a champion fencer, so he'd better watch his step. We think that Jack is close to being engaged to Sally Doerr. Sally teaches fifth grade right across the street at St. Mary's.

"My sister, Mary Ann, is twenty-three. She's married to Al O'Rourke, and they are expecting a baby in the spring, which is wonderful news. Mary Ann teaches math at a high school, and Al works at a downtown law firm. Maureen is twenty-one, and she is about to graduate from St. Xavier. She's going to be a surgical nurse. She's spent a lot of time watching our parents at the hospital, so she'll be a natural. Siobhan is nineteen, and she's a freshman at Notre Dame. Not sure what she's going to be yet, maybe an actress. She has been in plays since she was five, and she has that natural spark she needs to be a great actress.

"Kevin is seventeen and a senior, and Brian is fifteen and a sophomore at St. Ignatius College Prep. They are dedicated soccer and rugby players, and they work hard at their studies. The twin girls are Molly and Caitlan, and they are thirteen and will graduate from eighth grade at St. Mary's across the street next June."

Sounds like a lot of time and tuition, thought the lieutenant. "Your mother must be a remarkably healthy and energetic woman," said Lieutenant Braxton, "to have had all those children so close together and become a talented nurse besides."

"It would have been eleven, but she had a miscarriage two years after the twins. She never stops grieving for that baby," said Nora. "If you're a loving person like she is, no matter how many children you have, the one who died is still missed terribly."

"I heard your mother saying '*a stor*' to you while she was taking care of you at the train platform. What does that mean?"

"It's Gaelic or Irish for 'my treasure.' She only uses it when she's very worried about one of us. Her Irish grandmother used it a lot, and we love hearing it."

"Your father must have people working for him at his office."

"I'm not around Dad's office as much as I used to be, but the last I knew, there are six full-time employees who have all been with him for years, plus a number of other people who come in when they are needed. And, of course, my mom is the head nurse."

"Tell me about the six, please."

"Amanda Carlson is a nurse and has been with my dad for about ten years. She's probably in her early thirties. She is extremely good with the patients and has an encyclopedic memory about each case. She's a health food nut and a runner. She has a naturally bubbly personality. She was close to getting married about five years ago, but her boyfriend was tragically killed in a car accident. I believe she lives alone, but I heard that she's been dating someone for a while now.

"Diane Kaputis is the other nurse, and she's been with Dad almost as long as Amanda. They are like two sides of a coin and work together well. Diane is the X-ray technician, and she's about the same age as Amanda. She lives with her sick mother and cares for her. She is a natural comedian and keeps a happy tone going in the office, which is very helpful.

"Keisha Adams is the best lab tech I've encountered. I believe she could get blood out of a mosquito if she had to. The patients appreciate that she is usually able to take their blood with just one stick, which is not always an easy feat. She's married and has a three-year old daughter, Chelsea, and we see new pictures all the time, which the patients love.

"Sue Bonner is the scheduling secretary and is excellent at her complex job of keeping straight the schedules of the surgeons, the hospital departments, and the patients. We never hear a complaint about anything she does. My dad had to do emergency surgery on her fiancé last year, but Jim was in such poor shape that he did not survive. Sue was always reserved, but she doesn't smile much these days.

"Jason Reynolds is probably in his mid-twenties and is in charge of physical therapy. Many of the patients say he's a miracle worker.

He's good looking and has the outgoing personality he needs to help the patients do things with their bodies they didn't think they could do. He used to have a different date every month, but recently, he seems to be sticking to Belinda, so perhaps it's a real romance this time.

"Carly is the receptionist and hasn't been with Dad too long, but she has a pleasant voice and is very efficient. There's also Mary Beth Rivers and her sister, Cathy, who welcome the patients and keep the computers going, but they are part-time.

"Those are the regular employees, and then there are the fill-ins who come in when we need them. Each one of them is efficient, but together, they make a very good team. Finances at a medical office today are so complex with Medicare and the various insurance plans, so Dad uses a professional firm to keep track of finances, but they are in a different building."

Lieutenant Braxton told Nora that it was important that she compile a list of as many people as she could who had some relationship to her. The Chicago PD would be doing a check on all of them. He also told her it would be helpful to have photos of the workers at Dr. Duffy's office and at her office. She agreed and said she could have the list and the photos for them by the next day.

As they were talking, a constant stream of visitors arrived at Nora's home. A happy voice shouted, "Yoo-hoo, Bitsy Boo, I love you!"

Nora explained that the unmistakable voice came from her next-door neighbor, Connie Carroll. "We've grown up together since we were babies, and she's like another sister and another certain bridesmaid."

"I made that chicken soup that you like with the extra carrots and brown rice," yelled Connie. "Jeanie is with me too." Jean, Connie's younger sister, explained that she had brought some colcannon, another Nora favorite.

The door barely closed when the Murrays, a couple from the end of the block, came in with fish and chips from Fox's. Cousins Tess and Jennie arrived with a lemon fluff cake from Wolf's Bakery. They were soon followed by Father Ted Ahearn from St. Mary's who brought a bottle of white wine and said that he had come for Jesse's cooking and to "get the lowdown" from Bitsy. He also brought along Monsignor Callahan who was delighted to get out in his wheelchair.

"Kudos to Mr. Majszak for the ramp to the back door," said Father Ahearn. "That makes it much easier for us."

The phone kept ringing with calls of concern, and younger sister, Siobhan, offered to take down the messages. Bitsy gave her a grateful hug and asked Sibby to make sure to get phone numbers so she could eventually call them back.

10

Wednesday, September 12
Chicago, 2:30 p.m., CDT

After Lieutenant Braxton had all the notes he needed, he
and Sergeant Laura did accept the invitation to lunch. He
thought it would be instructive to observe Nora in familiar
surroundings. The first thing he noticed was that the kitchen was
huge and shiny and immersed in delicious smells. Two large windows
faced the street, and a set of glass doors led out to a patio filled with
colorful chairs. The windows filled the room with dappled light as it
reflected off the giant oak trees out back.

The appliances didn't look new, but they were super-sized.
There were two refrigerators and two very long tables with twelve
chairs around each, most of which were filled already. A large Black
Forest clock sat on the wall next to the tables, and a cuckoo ducked
in and out every fifteen minutes. Everything looked spotlessly clean,
but there were two holes in the wall over the stove that looked as
though someone started to fix them but never finished. That made
the lieutenant feel right at home since he frequently started projects
but didn't quite finish them.

Some artistic person had put plaques decorated with flower borders above the doors that read "Play Like a Champion Today" and
"God Has a Path in Mind for You Today—Look for It."

Jesse told them that the younger children would normally be
in school on a weekday, but they were up so late last night at the
hospital that their parents agreed that they could stay home. Many

51

teachers from St. Mary's had stopped in early this morning to see how Nora was, and Principal Brodie told the twins they could make up any work they missed the next day.

Everyone waved and shouted out a welcome to the two policemen. Lieutenant Braxton sat down next to Father Ahearn, but the twin girls motioned Sergeant Belsky to sit next to them at their table. There wasn't too much of a choice anyway, since the "grown-ups" table was already filled. Caitlan explained that they had been given a school assignment to find out how first responders felt about their jobs. Molly said she was especially interested in this from a woman's point of view. She said she didn't think she would want to have such a dangerous job when she grew up.

Sergeant Belsky told them that her father had been a policeman, so she'd known a lot about it before she started. She enjoyed most aspects of her job, although she still didn't like arresting people but knew that it was necessary to keep the public safe. It was a difficult time to be a policewoman, but it was probably always that way.

Laura told them that she had always wondered what it must be like to be a twin. The young girls were surprisingly articulate and had no problem telling her the mostly positive things about having another person in the world who looked just like you, but there were also a few drawbacks. They said they loved it when they were little, but now they were both trying to develop their own identities. They were so used to thinking alike that it was hard to separate from each other. They giggled as they explained that boys needed to be able to tell them apart too. They had always dressed alike when they were younger, but now they'd been experimenting with wearing different outfits.

They were most likely going to go to different high schools too, which kind of scared them, but they saw it as a necessary choice. Molly said she had always been interested in the serious study of music and wanted to become an orchestra conductor. She spent hours watching the technique of various conductors, and her favorite was Leonard Bernstein since he looked like he was having fun while having such a connection with the music and the musicians. There are very few women conductors, but Molly said she understood that the key to becoming a good conductor was to know the music better than anyone else in the orchestra, and she intended to do that. She'd seen illustrations of the complicated musical score that the conductor had to follow, and it looked daunting, but she was determined to learn.

Caity said that she had always been more interested in science and hoped to eventually work for the Center for Disease Control in Atlanta so she could experiment with cures for different diseases. "Ugh," said Molly. They realized that even though their intended high schools were not that far apart, the girls would make different friends, which would affect their later paths through life.

The girls also told Laura that they were practicing hard now for the Irish dancing Mid-America Oireachtas or Irish Dancing Competition. It's always held just around Thanksgiving in a different Midwestern city each year. When Laura inquired as to the significance of the competition, the girls explained that the top ten girls in each age group were then invited to go to the World's Oireachtas, usually held in Ireland but this year in the US, where they would compete against the best dancers from all over the world. The twins had been able to go the last two years, but there was always so much competition, so they couldn't take anything for granted. Their cousin, Lizzie, ended up in eleventh place last year, so she wasn't eligible for the World's, and she cried for weeks. There was always the possibility that she could go if someone in the top ten got sick, but of course, no one did.

Laura thought that the twins were much farther along the path of realizing what it meant to be a grown up than she had been when she was their age. Thirteen was an awkward age when you alternated between clinging to the better aspects of childhood and the dreaded world of adult responsibilities. It seemed to Laura that the Duffys had prepared these children well for the time when they would have to leave the protection of the nest. She felt the eyes of the older boys on her and knew that the twins were well-protected by all their siblings.

The girls asked Laura if she would come and speak to their class, and she said they should let her know when it would fit in with their teacher's schedule, and she would be happy to do that.

Jesse asked Father Ahearn to lead them in saying grace, and everyone chimed in, asking blessings on the food and for those who didn't have any food today, and especially thanking God that Nora's life had been spared.

Jesse served Connie's soup from an oversized blue and white tureen into pretty bowls accompanied by the homemade bread with Kerry butter. This was followed by a salad, the fish and chips, colcannon, and homemade apple sauce. Lieutenant Braxton had to inquire what was in the colcannon, and it was explained to him that it consisted of mashed potatoes, cabbage, cooked bacon, and Jesse's special spices. Anyone who didn't like fish got homemade chicken strips served with copious amounts of water filled with lemonade ice cubes, which was Jesse's specialty. The meal was followed by generous slices of the lemon fluff cake, homemade chocolate chip cookies, and Barry's tea and coffee. Delicious food and good conversation led to an air of conviviality that was infectious.

The boys had begun a heated debate over which team would get the nod for the college football championships this year. It would most likely be Alabama again, but they hoped that Notre Dame would do well. Mr. Askew, pastor of Trinity Methodist and Dr. Duffy's golf partner, suggested that Tiger Woods might regain his momentum and win another major soon. Grandpa Duffy was a big fan of Phil Mickelson, but he liked many of the younger players too.

Lieutenant Braxton asked who was going to play in the World Series next month, and that drew a heated argument about the merits of the Cubs versus the White Sox. Mrs. Askew said she thought it might be the New York Yankees, but she was scoffed at as a pessimist.

Father Ahearn, a native of Milwaukee, said that he thought Aaron Rodgers and the Green Bay Packers would be going to the Super Bowl. Monsignor Callahan didn't hear much, but he heard that well enough. As a longtime Bears fan, he thought Father Ted's comments were the ravings of a "cheese head," the Chicago expletive used for Packers fans. The high school boys were more interested in the rivalry that was ever-present among the local high schools' football teams.

It was clear that anyone who wanted to be heard around this table had to know what they were talking about and how to defend their position. The comradery that existed within this lively family and their friends was palpable, and that made it difficult for Lieutenant Braxton to remain objective.

The "elephant in the room" was ignored as much as possible, but the Murrays finally asked Lieutenant Braxton how the police were going about trying to solve if someone had deliberately tried to kill Nora. The lieutenant gave them a generalized answer and said that "every possibility was being investigated." They hoped to have answers "soon" to that question.

Life goes on during any emergency, and Jesse consulted the huge wall calendar and reminded Kevin and Brian that they had soccer practice after school the next day, and band practice after that for Saturday's football game. The twins had volleyball practice after school the next day and Irish dancing after that at 7:00 p.m. "You'll have to try to fit in your homework between volleyball and dancing," reminded Jesse. "Don't forget that the family September birthday party is a week from Sunday at Aunt Betty's, so think about presents. If anyone has special laundry needs for school over the next week, now is the time to let me know," instructed Jesse. "Poppy and Ann," Jesse reminded the young cousins, "your mother must be wondering if you've left home by now. You'd better go check in with her after lunch. You too, Tim."

Jesse spoke with a quiet but authoritative voice, and Lieutenant Braxton could see that she was used to giving orders and having them obeyed. It was obvious that she was well-loved by all the Duffy family members.

Nora explained that there were so many neighbors and cousins who felt at home at their house they never knew exactly who would be there for any meal. "We have first cousins living across the street and at the end of our block as well as at three more houses nearby, and each one of us has friends who are frequent guests. Jesse is a marvel at producing enough to feed everyone from the original 'loaves and fishes.'"

Nora continued to relate the story about her family. "Jim, Jack, and Mary Ann have moved out, but all the rest of us still live here since the Rock Island train and the CTA bus lines are so close to us. And our parents would be lost without us," she laughed.

"As you can see, this is a big old Victorian house with lots of rooms, but whoever is in the house usually congregates in the living room or the kitchen. We only use the big dining room for special occasions. My parents have their 'master' bedroom on the first floor, although it's not very big by today's standards. There's another small room that serves as Jesse's occasional bedroom and a storage room. We girls have bedrooms on the second floor, and the boys have rooms in our large attic. There's been many a night when I've fallen asleep on the couch in the sunroom, especially when I've been at the hospital all night. There's not much privacy, but we're all used to that. We have our share of sibling rivalry, and an occasional fight flares up, but we generally like each other and adore our parents.

"By the way, you'll notice that the family calls me Bitsy. When I was born, I only weighed about three pounds. I wasn't premature, just very small, and I never grew very much. At my last doctor's appointment, they measured me at four-foot five and seventy-four pounds. People sometimes think I'm a dwarf. I'm used to it, but there are times when being so short is a disadvantage, and I keep step stools and grabbers around. My size three feet are a real problem. I usually buy kids' shoes, but adult high heels cost me more money since I have to special order them."

Lieutenant Matt and Sergeant Laura enjoyed the lunch and thanked Nora and Jesse for the hospitality. The lieutenant told Nora they would be in touch if their investigation revealed any more answers.

As they were leaving, they encountered more friends and relatives coming in to see how Nora was doing. Lieutenant Braxton had arranged for a police guard from District 22 to be stationed at the front and back of the Duffy home, and he checked with those officers to see if they had any observations so far. He warned them to clear any visitors with the family before letting them enter the house.

The lieutenant would have been even more concerned if he'd known what his comrades had discovered after they'd examined the wallet of the dead man from the subway.

Wednesday, September 12
Chicago, 4:00 p.m., CDT

L ieutenant Braxton and Sergeant Belsky decided to return to
their office, and Sergeant Alonso Rodriguez brought them fascinating news. The wallet belonging to the dead man on the
subway tracks survived most of the impact of the train running over
him. The cards were a bit crinkled and stained but were still readable.

They had found no less than three driver's licenses, all with different names and from different countries: Paul Allons from Canada,
Eduard Vanderhoven from South Africa, and Miles Godfrey from
London. The picture on each license revealed that they were all for
the same man, the large man with the large black mustache. There
were also Visa and MasterCard credit cards imprinted with the names
of all three men.

Lieutenant Braxton called the chief of the Chicago PD and
filled him in on this discovery. The chief told the lieutenant to notify
the FBI, and he did that and explained the situation to them. They
began the task of searching for the three names. It didn't take long
to discover that Paul Allons was a well-known terrorist, and many
countries were looking for him on a variety of charges. One of those
charges was that he worked as an assassin for anyone who had the
money to hire him.

Bingo, mused Lieutenant Braxton. He realized that the search
for Nora's would-be killer had taken on new dimensions. "This
changes the trajectory of the investigation enormously," he declared,

and he asked himself a number of questions. Why would an international terrorist assassin be involved with trying to kill an apparently sweet young woman from the south side of Chicago? Who paid him to do it? Did Paul Allons target the wrong person? Or is there more about the Duffy family that we don't know? Could they be involved with drugs or other crimes? He'd grown somewhat attached to these fun and interesting people, but his experience over the years bore out the old saying that you couldn't tell a book by its cover.

Sergeant Rodriguez also told him that the CTA had confirmed that the cameras at the LaSalle Street subway station were not working at the time of the incident, so they were no help. The lieutenant wondered if Paul Allons had purposely disabled the cameras, so it was even more important that Elsie Young had taken those pictures on her cell phone.

There was also a business card that was tucked into a somewhat hidden compartment in the wallet of the dead terrorist. That business card was the only thing that could possibly be treated as a clue. It read: "Philip Warriner, seller of fine used cars." Part of the telephone number was missing, but the street address was 4485 South Ashland.

He and Sergeant Belsky decided to get into their squad car, and they drove south on Ashland to see if they could spot Philip Warriner, since a check of the telephone records did not show any such business.

They saw a number of small used car businesses that did not appear to contain "fine" used cars. Sergeant Belsky said she wondered if some of those cars would even make it off the lot. The majority of the surrounding population seemed to consist of those living on the edge of poverty, so perhaps cars like these were all they could afford.

Although the name of Philip Warriner was not present on the large outdoor sign, a small building at 4485 surrounded by a few sad-looking cars and a high chain-link fence did advertise "Fine Used Cars." From the threadbare appearance of the place, they thought the sign was misleading at best.

They entered the miniscule building through a narrow dirty door and saw a young man sitting at what passed as a desk who sullenly asked them to come in. When he saw the two well-dressed people, his eyes opened wide, and he backed away from them. "Hello, my name is Georg. What do you want?"

Lieutenant Braxton knew that the surrounding area was mostly populated by Hispanics and African-Americans, but this fellow appeared to have some sort of Eastern European accent, perhaps Russian. He approached the young man and told him he was looking for Philip Warriner, which appeared on a business card they had found. Georg responded that Philip Warriner was a name his uncle used, and he owned this property.

"We're from the Chicago PD, George, and we have a few questions for you about your uncle. Where is your uncle now?"

"He is only here on Saturdays. I don't know where he is today."

"Well, George, here's the deal. We have reason to believe that your uncle may have some ties to a known terrorist. We need to know more about your uncle and need you to tell us where he is right now. If you refuse, we might have to arrest you for obstruction of justice. Let's start by having you give us your full name and address."

George was trying to maintain a brave front, but the mention of "arrest" had taken a lot of the air out of his bravado. "My name is Georg Popov. I live in Burbank with my mother. I could call her and ask her if she knows where her brother is."

"Where does your mother live, George?"

The young man's complexion had gone from pasty white to a most unbecoming shade of gray, but he did tell them his mother's address. Lieutenant Braxton warned him that he'd better have told them the truth, and then he sent a number of Chicago PD cars to the mother's address with the instructions that she should be brought to 4485 S. Ashland. If she refused to come, they could assure her that her son would be arrested and brought to jail and she would be joining him.

While they were waiting, Lieutenant Braxton took a better look around the tattered room and did not see a posted State of Illinois license to sell automobiles. That was a violation of Illinois law that could start criminal proceedings. Georg told them that he was nineteen years old and lived at home with his mother. He'd only been working there for two months. His uncle's name was Gregor Popov and he lived at various places. Georg didn't know where the name of Philip Warriner came from. Georg sounded very convincing, but Lieutenant Braxton had been a cop long enough to know that people could cook up phony stories at a moment's notice.

Shortly afterward, a squad car pulled up with Mrs. Katrina Popov. It would have been an understatement to say that she was upset. She was using what they presumed to be swear words very fluently in a foreign language. Sergeant Rodriguez ushered her over to Lieutenant Braxton, and they asked her to be seated. "Why am I being brought here like a criminal?" she kept demanding. Lieutenant Braxton tried to mollify her, but her face was turning purple with rage.

Sergeant Belsky was good at defusing situations, and they asked her to initiate the conversation with the agitated woman. Laura handed the woman a tissue from her purse and got her a drink of water from the water fountain, which she hoped would soften her mood. "Mrs. Popov, ordinarily we would not be in such a hurry in our investigations, but we think that time is of the essence. We have reason to believe that your brother, Gregor, may be acquainted with a known international terrorist who recently appeared in Chicago. Can you tell us how we can reach your brother? We just want to ask him a few questions. It could be a matter of life and death."

Mrs. Popov kept glancing at the heavily armed policemen around her and at her frightened son. Laura tried to reassure her by saying, "You know how men are when they are worried. They're always so aggressive, but we women understand that in uncertain situations, we're the ones who keep our heads and make wise choices. Please tell me how we can reach Gregor before this situation gets worse for you and your son."

Mrs. Popov started to open her purse, and several of the policemen surged forward, but Sergeant Belsky assured them the situation was under control. Mrs. Popov gave a piece of paper to Sergeant Belsky and told her it was Gregor's address and phone number at his north side apartment. "Thanks so much, Mrs. Popov," Laura responded as she patted her shoulder.

Lieutenant Braxton called the captain and told them to get over to the address on the piece of paper and to bring Gregor and anyone else at the address into the downtown station as soon as possible. He warned them to use extreme caution in case Gregor or other associates were armed.

Now that Laura had established a thin relationship with Mrs. Popov, she asked her more about Gregor.

Katrina responded that her brother had come to Chicago about five years ago and had sent for her and her son, Georg, four years ago. He had always been very helpful to her, but she had always suspected that his car business and the other businesses he wouldn't talk about were probably not very legitimate. She worked as a cleaning lady downtown, and Gregor gave her and Georg extra money. She had tears in her eyes as she asked them to be good to her brother.

Gregor was at his apartment and was not expecting to be accosted by the police. He came with them somewhat willingly once he heard that they were holding his sister and nephew. Once they got him downtown, they told him about the man in the subway who was a known terrorist and asked what his relationship was to him. At first, he said he didn't know anything about it, but he eventually relented and told them that he and his friend, Dimitri, had gone to school together in Russia, and Dimitri had contacted him and told him he was coming to Chicago for business and needed a place to stay for one night. He didn't know what the business was that had brought Dimitri to Chicago.

"Where did the card come from with the name Philip Warriner?"

Gregor responded that the car lot used to be owned by a man with that name about forty years ago. It sounded like a classy name, so he'd been using it. The police grilled him more to see if Gregor would tell them about the business that Dimitri was involved in, but after several hours, it seemed pretty clear that Gregor wasn't going to be changing his story anytime soon. They would continue questioning the Popovs to see if the story about "just helping a pal" was true or if the Popovs had been running a safe house for terrorists. If the latter were true, Gregor might be more afraid of the terrorists than the Chicago PD.

They told the Popovs they were going to hold them in jail for forty-eight hours, the allowable time for persons thought to be connected to a crime could be held, and they encouraged them to think about giving them the truth about their connections to Dimitri/ Paul Allons.

Finding Gregor Popov had seemed like a promising lead as to who had hired the man in black to try to kill Nora, but Lieutenant Braxton had to admit that they were back to square one as far as a motive and the person responsible for bringing Dimitri here.

Lieutenant Braxton called the Duffy home and said that he would be coming back to their home around dinner time and that he would want to talk to Dr. and Mrs. Duffy and Nora at that time so they should be sure to be there. He thought that things were getting "curiouser and curiouser" as Alice said in her *Adventures in Wonderland*.

12

Wednesday, September 12
Chicago, 4:00 p.m., CDT

Siobhan Duffy answered the phone at the Duffys home and passed it on to Nora saying that the call sounded important and was from a Miss Kitty Lloyd from Ireland. Nora took the phone and talked to Kitty who said that she had a message for her about her great uncle, Cyrus Duffy. Kitty would not elaborate further, but she said that she and her companion, Mr. Sean Duffy, were staying at the Marriott Hotel in downtown Chicago and wanted to come and visit her today. Nora said she would be glad to have them come to the house and assured them they would be most welcome whenever they arrived. Uncle Cyrus had always been one of her favorite people in the world, and Sean must be her Uncle Kevin's son, so another cousin.

Nora was excited that they were coming and asked Jesse to have the girls straighten up the living room as quickly as they could and make sure there were some refreshments available for their visit. She also asked Jesse to help her apply some cover-up on her black eye.

About an hour later, the doorbell rang, and an attractive young woman dressed in a gray business suit and a smiling young man with flaming red hair and a navy suit were at the door. Jesse greeted them and ushered them into the living room to meet Nora. Experts say that it only takes seven seconds to make a first impression, and Nora took even less time than that to feel a kinship with them.

She easily recognized Sean as another red-haired cousin. Kitty Lloyd said that Nora had probably met her father, Duncan Lloyd, Uncle Cyrus' legal solicitor. Sean said he remembered meeting Nora a few years ago and apologized for not keeping in touch. He explained that he was representing the family, especially Uncle Cyrus' sister, Great Aunt Lavinia. That phrase "representing the family" sounded a bit ominous, and Nora became apprehensive as to why they were there. They both seemed nervous and reluctant to get to the reason for their visit.

Kitty and Sean accepted a cup of tea and a piece of Jesse's soda bread, which they proclaimed was delicious. They told Nora they had heard about her accident and were glad that she wasn't seriously injured. After more pleasantries were exchanged, Kitty explained that they had both bad and good news to impart.

The bad news was that Uncle Cyrus had died the day before yesterday. Nora stifled a scream, and Sean saw the tears start in her eyes. He assured her that Uncle Cyrus had only been ill for a few days, had died relatively peacefully in his own bed, and was surrounded by family, business associates, friends, several priests, and his beloved dogs.

Sean continued that the funeral for Uncle Cyrus would take place on Saturday at Duffy Hall Castle in Sneem, Ireland, and they sincerely hoped that Nora and her parents would be able to attend.

Kitty explained that the good news was that Uncle Cyrus had remembered Nora, her parents, and his brother, Conor, in his will, and they hoped that everyone mentioned in the will could be there to hear the official reading, just prior to the funeral. Uncle Cyrus' company, Duffy Medical, had already paid for their airfare, and they would have no expenses once they were at the hall. "Aunt Lavinia has extended a very personal invitation to you, and she does hope you'll be there," assured Kitty.

"By the way," explained Sean, "please do not think of sending flowers for the funeral. Uncle Cyrus specifically mentioned that he wanted people to donate any money to the orphan's home he has supported for years. The company will provide a few large bouquets of yellow daisies, Cy's favorite flowers, but that's all he wanted."

Nora said that was good to know and they would do that. Her parents wouldn't be home for a few hours, but she thought they would almost surely want to attend. However, Grandpa Conor had just had hand surgery a few days ago, so he would not be able to fly. "Cyrus has been good to us over the years. He remembered all of our birthdays and sent us lovely gifts for Christmas."

She pointed to a photo that sat on the piano across the room.

Sean brought it over, and Nora said that it was a picture of her and Cyrus when she was five-years-old and first visited him at Duffy Hall. "I loved him right away," said Nora, "and I've always admired his brilliance and determination. I know there are people who thought he was an old curmudgeon, but they didn't take the time to really know him."

Just then, the thirteen-year-old Duffy twins came bursting into the room dressed in their blue and white cheerleading outfits. "Hi, Bitsy!" they intoned. "Oh, sorry, we didn't realize you had company."

"Kitty and Sean," replied Nora, "these are the babies of the family, Molly and Caitlan. They are cheerleaders for our football team at St. Mary's." Nora then explained to them about Uncle Cyrus, and the girls both expressed their sorrow to their Irish guests.

"We didn't know Uncle Cyrus very well," Molly said. "We did meet him once, but we've always heard such wonderful stories about him and his castle." Caitlan added that they would ask their class at school to say a prayer for him and his family.

Nora asked the girls to go and change their clothes and help Jesse prepare supper. "Okay," they agreed, "but we'll talk to you more later about our assignment to be flyers for the next game against St. Thomas. We're going to be practicing even more now." The girls pounded up the stairs as only young teenagers can, laughing and shaking their pom-poms as they ascended.

"Oh to be young again," laughed Kitty. "They are beautiful girls, Nora, and so precocious. Your mom and dad must be so proud of them. They are so identical," she observed. "How do you tell them apart?"

"Many people have trouble doing that, and we often get a call asking that question when they get a new teacher. A few times, the girls have tried to switch places on us, but we know their few unique characteristics too well. Molly has a spate of freckles on her nose that Caitlan doesn't, and Caity has a streak of red hair mixed in with the blond," responded Nora. "We'll have a little more trouble with them when they both start using makeup and hair dye. Life has been kind to them so far, and they haven't experienced too many adversities yet. We're doing our best to keep it that way."

"Back to the report on your Uncle Cyrus," said Kitty. "I'll tell you a little about his recent activities. He was at the office last Friday, and Dad tells me that he was as cantankerous as ever. He wanted a full accounting of our new office in Dublin and wasn't at all happy with the figures he saw. He was having a little trouble walking long distances, but his mental powers seemed not to be lessened at all. He insisted that my father go to Dublin personally to make sure they knew what they were doing. He had always wanted Duffy's medical supplies to be known for the highest quality and he wasn't about to see any reduction in that goal.

"He had been talking about putting more effort into expanding into the US markets and wanted to know what the holdup was in those plans. We have a small office in New York, but most of our activities there involve imports rather than having a main US presence. He'd been talking about expanding more and more recently, so he had not lost his competitive instincts. One thing he mentioned in his detailed will was that he hoped that your parents, as experienced surgeon and nurse, would join the board of directors of Duffy Medical."

Kitty continued, "Cyrus' doctor had urged him to slow down, but that just seemed to spur him to go even faster. I think he knew that he was fighting an uphill battle with his health and that time was not on his side, but if he suffered, he gave no outward sign of it. He was only sick about three days. As he slipped into a coma, he said just a few words. Emily and Nora were two of those words, so he was thinking of you as he died."

Nora showed them pictures of her family and a photo of her fiancé, Tom Barry, and they all agreed that he was, indeed, very handsome. She explained that he was currently in London on business for his company, so he would probably not be able to join them for the funeral, although Nora would see if he could cut short his business trip.

Nora asked Kitty and Sean if they would like to stay for dinner, but they explained that they were going back to Ireland early the next day to prepare for the funeral, so they were returning to the hotel now. Sean handed Nora airplane tickets for her parents and herself for the next afternoon and said that there would be someone to meet them at Dublin Airport.

"Please let us know if there will be any problems with you attending the funeral, Nora," said Sean as he handed Nora his business card. "Uncle Cyrus would want you there, so does Aunt Lavinia. And so do we."

Sean and Kitty left with hugs and kisses, and Nora sat back down in her rocker to mull over what they had told her. Her head still hurt, but she felt there was no way that she could stay away from paying her last respects to the man she had admired so much. She always looked forward to the trip to Ireland too, but she wished it were to talk to Uncle Cyrus and not to be at his funeral.

Wednesday, September 12
Chicago, 6:00 p.m., CDT

When her parents arrived home, Nora explained what she had learned about Uncle Cyrus' death and the very strong request for them to attend the funeral. Her parents were sad to hear the news, but Uncle Cy had lived a long and productive life. Dr. Duffy said he had a few important appointments in the next week, but fortunately, no scheduled operations. Eileen Duffy agreed that they should definitely be there for Uncle Cyrus. A lot of arrangements would need to happen before they could leave, but it should work out.

It was nice to know that they were remembered in Uncle Cy's will, but Dr. Duffy said he couldn't imagine that it would amount to anything substantial for them. As to joining the board of directors of Uncle Cyrus' company, they would wait and see, but it sounded like more than they could take on. It would be nice to get to Ireland more often, but their schedules were already so busy.

Just before supper was ready, Lieutenant Braxton and his perky partner, Sergeant Belsky, arrived and said they had more surprising news for them. They explained what they'd discovered so far about the big man with the black mustache being a known international assassin and that he apparently had intended to kill Nora. The family was understandably shocked and upset by this news. They couldn't think of any possible reason why someone like him would want to do this to Nora.

After Nora had processed the news that the man who knocked her down may not have committed suicide but was trying to kill her, she didn't know what to think. She had come to realize over the years that she usually had an initial advantage in most relationships. Most people tended to treat her the way they do babies and pets because of her small size: they thought she was cute and they liked her. The fact that someone disliked her so much they wanted to destroy her was a novel and scary thought.

"Does your family interact with many people outside of the United States?" queried Lieutenant Braxton.

Dr. Duffy explained that their only international contacts were Uncle Cyrus and the others who lived at Duffy Hall, his cousins in Killarney, and Eileen's Aunt Tilda and her family who ran a bed and breakfast in Cork. "Last year, some of us went to London, which was a combination medical seminar for Eileen and me and a brief vacation. We visited a colleague of mine there who does cardiac research. I do have a distant cousin who's a professor and lives outside of Oxford, and we occasionally keep in touch via Facebook, but I last saw him about ten years ago. About five years ago, Eileen and I went on a pilgrimage to the Holy Land with some friends. I believe those are the only times we've been out of the US in recent years since we went to Rome, Venice, and Florence on our honeymoon many years ago. We have enough going on here to keep us busy enough."

Lieutenant Braxton thanked him for the information and told them that he would like them to compile a list of those names, addresses, and phone numbers so that he could check them out. He also told them that the Chicago PD had done a trace on everyone in the Duffy family. Nothing out of the ordinary had shown up, but he wanted them to stay available, if needed.

Nora told Lieutenant Braxton that she should have those pictures of the family and work contacts he was waiting for later today.

Lieutenant Braxton said, "I did see that your 'acceptable surgical mortality rates' are less than 2 percent, Dr. Duffy, which seems to be less than the standard number. You must be very good at your job."

Dr. Duffy explained that those actuarial rates represented not only the skill of the individual surgeon but also the excellent team of doctors, nurses, and staff members that assisted him. "We aspire to get those mortality rates even lower, and they do keep declining across the US as our knowledge and experience get better, which is a great thing. Believe me that none of us wants to tell a family that their loved one has fallen into the 2 percent category, no matter how ill the patient was." His wife, Eileen, had been his senior nurse for many years, and he had many skilled doctors and nurses in his practice. "That kind of expertise takes years to build up, and we work together very well. Holy Savior is one of the top cardiac hospitals in Chicago, and they provide us with great support."

Dr. Duffy told the lieutenant that they would be leaving tomorrow afternoon for his Uncle Cyrus' wake and funeral in Ireland and they would probably be gone for five days. He explained the situation about Uncle Cyrus' death and the need for them to be there for the reading of the will. Lieutenant Braxton said that would be acceptable, but he asked them to leave all their contact information with him. He said he would keep in touch with them by phone or e-mail and wanted them to keep him updated.

Lieutenant Braxton addressed Nora and asked her to think about whether she could think of anyone who might have wanted to kill her by hiring an assassin. "Is there some person you've ticked off or some knowledge you have about a crime or something you saw or any reason why you were targeted?"

Nora told him that she'd been trying to think of this but without success so far.

They gathered in the kitchen, and Jesse served them her famous meatloaf, mashed potatoes, and green beans with bacon, followed by apple cobbler. Lieutenant Braxton and Sergeant Belsky wished them a safe flight and told them that they would be back frequently for Jesse's meatloaf. Sergeant Belsky said she would ask Jesse for her recipe, but she was a terrible cook and was sure her attempt would fall far short of Jesse's delicious meal.

The family talked about what they would need to do for the coming trip. Dr. Duffy asked Siobhan to make out a list and print out the pertinent information about their credit cards and to take pictures of their driver's licenses and passports. They'd never had a problem with anything being stolen on other trips they'd taken, but now was not a time when they would want to deal with any of that. The surprises just kept coming, and they hoped to keep them to a minimum.

Wednesday, September 12
Chicago, 9:00 p.m., CDT

Nora moved to her dad's recliner chair in the living room and started to doze off. She thought about what it meant that someone had apparently hired an assassin to deliberately kill her. Everyone had some acquaintances who liked you less than others, but disliked to the point of killing and even paying for it was rather terrifying. Was it someone she had somehow offended? Was it a family member? A neighbor? Someone from work? A patient's family? She tossed and turned as she tried to make sense of it all. Her ribs were better, but she was still experiencing twinges when she moved the wrong way.

It was hard to fight against an enemy you couldn't see. In a seminal movie like *Jaws*, the music by a genius like John Williams created an overall frightening mood right from the first frame. You always knew the terrible danger was imminent when you heard the warning of the horns and the back and forth of the strings playing the "dum-dum, dum-dum, dum-dum" theme faster and faster. That kind of handy clue didn't seem to be happening for her, and she was still just mystified as to who would be doing this and why...and if they were going to try again.

Lieutenant Braxton had asked her to think of possible people she might have offended or who might be angry with her, so she gave it a try:

Richard Snodgrass? A fellow intern at Holy Savior. *Three words came to mind almost immediately when I first met him—tall, handsome, and smart. But a fourth followed quickly—obnoxious. Most of the women in our class think his last name should be changed to Snobgrass. His father is the chief of Internal Medicine, but other than that, it's a mystery as to why he even wants to be a doctor. He doesn't like weakness or women, and his attitude toward patients is patronizing. If someone were to question his decisions about their care, I'm sure he would say, 'Because I said so.' He certainly has never liked me, but would he carry that to the point of killing?*

Mickey Hurley? A name from the past. *He tried many times to ask me for a date, but he just didn't appeal to me, and I always turned him down. I thought I'd done it nicely, but maybe he was still angry about it? That doesn't seem likely, but the newspapers are full of stories about people who want revenge for having their affections spurned.*

Georgia Franco? My competitor for a spot in the children's cancer research project. *When they gave the appointment to me, Georgia made no bones in saying she thought I was chosen because of my father's influence. Maybe that was still bothering her?*

Mrs. Hartnet? The woman who rammed into my eleven-year old bright red Chevy, my "red robin." *Mrs. Hartnet had backed up into the front fender and put a big dent in it, and I was so upset that I swore at her. I apologized to her later, but Mrs. Hartnet's insurance premiums had risen after that. Maybe she wanted to get back at me?*

Mrs. Mitchell? The mother of little Amelia who died a few months ago of liver cancer at the clinic. *Mrs. Mitchell hated everyone at the hospital after that and said she was going to get even with us. Could she have blamed me for it?*

This is silly, thought Nora, *and the medication is making me loopy. I may not be their BFF, but none of these people seem like they would hate me so much they would have gone through the process of finding and paying an international assassin.*

Nora went upstairs, and her mom helped Bitsy pack for their five-day trip. They didn't want to bring too many suitcases, so Eileen gathered several dresses, suits, and daytime outfits for Bitsy as well as a good coat and jacket, underwear, and shoes, plus a raincoat and umbrella for the Irish weather. They wouldn't leave until the next afternoon, so they could finish up in the morning.

Eileen helped Nora to get to bed and gave her two pain pills, which would help her sleep. They said a few prayers together for protection and safety, and Eileen recited the favorite Stevenson poem that Bitsy used to love when she was little:

> And now at last the sun is going down
> behind the wood,
> And I am very happy, for I know that I've
> been good.
> My bed is waiting cool and fresh,
> With linen smooth and fair.
> And I must off to sleepsin-by,
> And not forget my prayer.

As Michael and Eileen prepared for bed, they shared their feelings that this had to have been one of the worst weeks they'd had in a very long time. Besides Nora being almost killed, Michael was still angry that someone in his office had mixed up the phone messages, and he had missed a very important meeting at the hospital this morning.

"Sue Bonner has been with me for years as my scheduler and claimed that our relatively new receptionist, Carly, didn't pass on the message to her that Sister Cecilia had called an unexpected meeting of all the department directors for today. Carly swears that she remembers putting the pink paper on Sue's desk in the usual box, although the message was later discovered under a pile of papers on Carly's desk. Regardless of whose fault it is, the result is that I wasn't there, and Sister Cecilia was not happy. She was counting on my support as they discussed the possibility of a merger.

"Jack Cassidy was looking as pleased as the cat that stole the cream that I wasn't there. Ever since I was appointed Director of Cardiology six months ago, Jack never misses an opportunity to show me up and hint that he should have had the promotion rather than me. He seems to have developed a sardonic attitude lately, which is not good for a surgical team that needs to have unity."

Michael continued, "I had a meeting with my whole staff about how serious this was, and I put Amanda in charge of all communications and told her to e-mail me at the end of every day we're gone, but I don't need this kind of distraction. This is not the best time for me to be away for almost a week."

Eileen told him she was sorry about the meeting, but she was sure that Sister Cecilia would still rely on his help. She also said that Jack's wife, Marion, had not been very pleasant to her either. "Watch out for Jack, Michael," Eileen urged. "I sense controlled violence underneath that polished exterior."

Eileen continued, "I know that Carly hasn't been there very long, but she strikes me as being very conscientious, and I'm sure she's upset. You know that Sue is not one of my favorites. Amanda is so efficient that she'll get everyone to do things right while you're away."

"I also feel bad for our Kevin," said Michael, "since he's worried that he might not be able to avoid getting a D in chemistry this quarter. Kevin tries hard, but science is not his thing. I've asked Jim to give him some tutoring help before the upcoming tests. Also, Skip Jenson looked at our very large roof on the house and said the whole thing should be replaced. And now we have this unexpected trip to Ireland."

Eileen told Michael that she was very sorry about Cyrus' death. He responded that he hadn't always liked Cyrus much when he was younger since he appeared to be such a grouch, but in recent years, he seemed to have changed. "I think our Nora had something to do with that. She always seemed to be able to get him to laugh."

"They said that we had been mentioned in the will. What do you suppose Cyrus could have left us?"

"I don't know, but I doubt it's anything to get too excited about. I'm sure that Aunt Lavinia will get the most, and my cousin, Kevin, in Dublin was always visiting him, so he'll probably get a nice sum. I'll be happy if he just left us enough to get the roof fixed."

"How do you think Nora is doing now?"

"She seems to have recovered well so far, but head injuries can be funny things, so I don't think we can really say for a few months yet. How's Mary Ann feeling now?"

"She seems fine, but she's worried because she hasn't gained much weight with her pregnancy."

"Every woman is different, and if she's eating and drinking enough and taking prenatal vitamins, she and the baby should be fine. She's always been thin, and she'll be glad afterward that she won't have to lose so much weight. I'm sure her OB, Dr. Childers, is watching her carefully."

Jesse had assured them she would be glad to stay at the house during the day to act as chaperone for the "darlings" as she called the Duffy bunch. She was so competent and caring and knew the children well, so they were sure that their family would be in good hands. Maureen would be there at night to keep an eye on her younger siblings, and Jim and Jack had promised to stop in every day.

Michael and Eileen whispered a prayer for their family and for Uncle Cyrus. Finally, they were able to fall asleep, but Eileen kept "one ear open" in case Nora called out for them. Head injuries sometimes play havoc with the person during sleep, and she didn't want to miss her call.

Wednesday, September 12
Reflections by the Killer

Well, well! I thought I'd have to wait longer to try again to get rid of Nora, but as fate would have it, now Nora and her parents are going to Ireland, and I may have found another method.

I contacted a guy via the Internet in Ireland who said that he knew the area well where the Duffys will be staying. He said there were any number of dangerous things that Nora could encounter at the castle such as auto accidents, falling down the steep stairs, fire, being locked in the dungeon, game shooting, and more. Eamon said he knew one of the wives of the Duffy Medical Board members, Valerie, and she had impressed him as being willing to do almost anything to get money. She also hates Americans.

It will be fun trying to figure out the next part of my plan. Of course, I'll have to pay Eamon quite a bit for his services, but he tells me the woman he knows is smart and cunning and would be capable of thinking up any number of ways to injure Nora or even kill her. We should know shortly what the uncle's will has to say, and then I think I'll be able to work with her.

Wouldn't Dr. Duffy be surprised to know that it's me behind all of this? He'll become very aware of me soon!

Thursday, September 13
Chicago, 8:00 a.m., CDT

Everyone at the Duffys went to St. Mary's for the morning mass and visited with Father Ahearn. He wished them well on their trip and again expressed his sorrow about their Uncle Cyrus' death. Dr. Duffy said it would be most appropriate if Father Ahearn could find a way to come to the funeral and said he'd be glad to pay for his ticket. Uncle Cyrus had given a generous donation to St. Mary's last Christmas, and there would undoubtedly be many international priests at the funeral that Father Ahearn could host. Father Ahearn said he would see if he could get someone to cover for him at the parish and that he would call them shortly to let them know.

The family then took a short drive to eat a quick bite at their favorite breakfast restaurant, Beverly Bakery. As usual, the place was packed, and they had to wait for a table. The owners had heard about their trip and wished them well. Their usual waitress, Megan, greeted them with a hug, and Michael and Eileen ordered one of their famous omelet dishes accompanied by their favorite Monsoon Malabar coffee, and Nora chose the ham and cheese quiche with Earl Grey tea so they would be well-fortified for their trip. They took some cranberry scones and blueberry muffins to go for the plane ride.

Michael and Eileen made sure that all the arrangements had been made to cover their absence at the hospital. Eileen went to County Fair market and stocked up on the food the children liked.

She also stopped at the ATM and withdrew a sufficient amount of money for Jesse to use in case of any emergency while they were gone. Nora took care of things on her end at the oncology clinic and she went to the bank and converted enough dollars to euros to cover the first part of their trip. Nora stopped in at her friend Maggie's shop and asked her to give her hair a quick trim and also had a quick manicure. "That's about as beautiful as I'm going to get," Nora laughed.

The suitcases were checked to make sure they had enough clothes for five days and that nametags were inserted into the name plates. They made sure their phones were charged and the European chargers were with them. They checked to see that their passports were safely zipped up in their bags and did one last check of all their belongings.

Nora sent the photos and contact information she'd gathered of family and other acquaintances to Lieutenant Braxton's e-mail address and told him she hoped that would be sufficient.

Father Ahearn called and said he was able to get Father Martini from the neighboring parish to cover for him, so Siobhan called Aer Lingus and made flight arrangements for him for tomorrow. Nora said she'd make sure that someone would be there to pick him up at Dublin Airport.

They left the list of their schedule and contact information for Jesse, and then they were finally ready. Goodbyes and hugs were given all around, and suitcases were carried out to Dr. Duffy's SUV, and they left for their adventure.

Jim and Jack had taken the day off to make sure they could help their parents and Nora prepare for their trip. Jim drove them out to O'Hare Airport via I-294, and he maneuvered the large SUV through the jam-packed lanes to the Aer Lingus entrance. The ever-vigilant traffic control ladies warned them that they had to promptly move their car, so they quickly grabbed their suitcases, gave Jim a quick kiss, said goodbye to their world, and entered the airport doors.

The very long line waiting to be checked in looked imposing, but since they were frequent flyers and had pre-check status, they got to the front of the line rather quickly. They provided the requisite identification, checked in their bags and obtained their boarding passes, and they stopped at a restaurant for a quick snack. It was always amazing how much a salad, coffee, and a bottle of water cost at any airport. They walked around the airport as much as possible since they would be sitting for a long time once they got on the plane.

Dr. Duffy did another check of his e-mails, and Amanda assured him that she would alert him if anything needed his immediate attention. Eileen and Nora visited the appealing Barbara's Bookstore and bought a book. Nora normally used her Kindle on plane trips, but Eileen liked to browse through the many books and pick an author with whom she was not familiar. Today, Eileen was in the mood for a little serious learning, so she chose a book that told her it would show her how to "boost her brain power dramatically." She'd pass it on to Nora when she finished it since the brain was Nora's area of expertise. Nora felt like she needed a break from anything too heavy today and definitely didn't want to read about murders, so she chose what appeared to be a light romance story set on Cape Cod.

They rejoined Dr. Duffy and went through the security area and passed their carry-on bags and purses through the detectors, then walked the long way to their departure gate. Dr. Duffy couldn't help thinking how much easier this whole process used to be before the world became menaced by terrorists. Their flight was finally called, and they entered their home for the next eight hours. They were seated in Choice seats where the seats reclined and were not too cramped. That was never a problem for Nora since she had such short legs, but Dr. Duffy appreciated the extra leg room.

4:00 p.m.

Nora had always admired the green and blue outfits worn by the stewardesses, and they enjoyed a brief chat with them while so many people continued to board the large plane. A stewardess named Lucy introduced herself and said that they were aware of why the family was traveling to Ireland, and they all wanted to express their condolences to them on the death of such a great and generous man. The family looked forward to the trip across "the pond," but they certainly wished it was for a different reason.

Dr. Duffy and Eileen sat together, and Nora sat behind them. A very nice old gentleman sat next to her, and after exchanging a few words with her, he promptly fell asleep. Nora always experienced a few minutes of concern when the plane took off, but today, all went smoothly, and they quickly reached their traveling height of 35,000 feet. She had looked up the reason for that, and it was because flying at least that height or more enabled the plane to experience less drag, so it saved money and time.

The family opened their laptops once they were cleared to do so. Dr. Duffy and Eileen checked on their patients, and Nora had homework to do.

Dr. Duffy told his wife and daughter that he had been thinking about a possible person who might have been behind Nora's "accident." Nora and Eileen stared at him, and he said that he'd thought about Ben Durant, one of his interns that he'd had to fire last year.

"As you recall, I hadn't been happy with him for a while. He was consistently late for rounds, he didn't hand in reports on time, and patients reported that he was rude to them. Then one of our younger female interns accused him of trying to force his attentions on her. Mrs. Samuels from HR had someone investigate this thoroughly, and their subsequent report indicated that the young woman was clearly right, and eyewitnesses substantiated her claims. That was the last straw for me, and I called Ben in and told him he would have to leave the internship.

"He was livid and tried to make every excuse he could find. He realized that my negative reference would jeopardize him finding another position elsewhere. As he was leaving, he knocked my favorite Turner painting off the wall and vowed to get even with me. I thought at the time that he was just angry, but now I'm wondering if Ben might have been following up on his threat by trying to hurt you. I lost track of him after he left, but I wonder where he is now."

Eileen and Nora said they remembered what Dr. Duffy told them about Ben at the time, but they'd forgotten about him. Once they got to Sneem, Nora said she would try to find out more about him and what he was doing now.

The stewardesses came by to take their food and drinks orders. They offered them champagne, wine, or soft drinks. Dr. Duffy asked for champagne, Eileen had Magners cider, and Nora settled for water. Her stomach was rebelling against the pain meds, so she wanted to keep that in check. In about an hour, the family was served tasty meals of steak for Dr. Duffy, chicken for Eileen, and Nora's favorite, salmon. Her parents ordered wine, but Nora asked for hot Barry's tea with lemon.

The backs of each seat had an HD screen so that passengers could choose movies or TV shows to watch. Nora selected several episodes of *Game of Thrones*. She had mixed feelings about this wildly popular show. She appreciated the acting by the many characters and the overall story and loved the dragons, but the almost constant violence was not something she wanted to watch in her current mood. She switched to *The Great British Baking Show* and wondered why her baking attempts didn't turn out as well as their delicious-looking creations. She thought that the pretty young woman who consistently turned out unusual treats would win, but the winner turned out to be the older man who was so meticulous.

Nora was getting sleepy, so she pulled out her new book, which was easy to read and painted a pleasant picture of boy meets girl on a beach in a lovely village on Cape Cod, just the kind of distraction she needed today. She had been wanting to finish the Jonathan Kellerman book she had started on her Kindle, but his vivid descriptions of killers and their motivations were more than she wanted to think about right now. How she wished that Tommy were here right now, instead of old Mr. Kenny who was peacefully snoring next to her.

The pain medications started to catch up with her, and Nora succumbed to taking a nap. She woke up and saw that it was still dark out. She loved to see the sky about halfway through the flight, dark night at the bottom, a sliver of light in between but growing ever brighter, and sometimes a bright star or two at the top. The eight-hour flight commenced at 4:00 p.m. and Dublin was six hours ahead of Chicago time, so they would arrive at Dublin about 6:00 a.m. After someone from the castle picked them up, it would be another four hours of driving before they arrived at their destination of Sneem. They had thought about taking a connecting flight to Shannon and driving from there, but the total time would be about the same, and if they missed a flight connection, even longer.

Nora dozed again and thought that the number one reason she was so happy to go to Ireland was that she would be away from the potential killer.

She recalled when she first met Uncle Cyrus and saw his castle and all the animals on his estate. He was so large and imposing a figure in those days. She probably should have been afraid of him, but she always just found him immensely interesting. They thought alike about many things, and he always tried out his latest joke on her to see her smile. She recalled the last time she'd been with him, he asked her, "Why did the Irish pig cross the road?"

When she answered that maybe the pig just wanted to get to the other side, he had laughed uproariously and said, "Because he'd heard they had better Guinness over there."

Soon the sky got lighter, and the stewardesses came around with a small breakfast meal and advised the passengers to gather up their belongings and get ready for landing. The temperature in Dublin was moderate, and no surprise, there were rain showers.

The Duffy's exited the plane and proceeded to the baggage carousel to look for their luggage. Nora had received a set of purple luggage decorated with fleur-de-lis when she left for college, which she still used. She was always happy about that when she was able to easily identify her purple among the black suitcases spitting out of the luggage chute.

They procured their suitcases and went through customs and immigration, which was crowded, as usual, but the line seemed to be moving along pretty well. They were getting tired out about now and looked forward to arriving at their destination and being able to relax.

Friday, September 14
Chicago, 9:00 a.m., CDT

Lieutenant Braxton called the Duffy home and asked to speak to Jesse, the housekeeper. He told her that he had left his jacket in their closet. He realized that the Duffys were out of town, but he would like to come to the house to pick it up. Jesse said that would be fine and she would be expecting him. She told him that there was a lot of fall housecleaning going on inside and out but he should just ring the bell.

When Lieutenant Braxton arrived at the Duffys, he saw a crew of people doing yard work, painting the front porch, and putting up Halloween lights on the evergreens. Jesse greeted him at the front door and bade him to step carefully since the curtains and draperies were all being taken down so the windows and the curtains could be washed.

Jesse asked him if he could stay for a while, and she ushered him into the kitchen where some of the cleaning crew were taking a break and enjoying some of Jesse's baked goods. She introduced him to Ellen Butler and her husband, Jake, and Tanya Wisowata and her helpers, Jan and Ted.

While she got Lieutenant Braxton some breakfast treats, she explained that all the Duffys were away today for work or school, so it was a good time to get things done.

Lieutenant Braxton had just taken a few bites of a tasty raisin scone when his phone rang. The caller was Sergeant Rodriguez who sounded worried. He told him that he should get back to the office as soon as he could since they had some disturbing news.

"I just heard from the lockup downstairs that both Popovs—the uncle and his nephew—have been shot in the head and are dead."

"OMG," Lieutenant Braxton almost screamed, "how did that happen? Were the cameras working down there? Lock that place down and look for any clues. Don't let anyone touch anything. Call Doc Merrill and tell him to get over there right away so he can examine the bodies."

"They never got around to installing cameras in that cell area, so we don't know how it happened."

"Where's the sister?" demanded Lieutenant Braxton.

"I believe she's still in the women's short-term cells."

"Get over there right now and take some backup with you. Bring her to my office and don't let her out of your sight. You don't have to tell her anything. I'll take care of that when I get there. Remember, don't leave her alone for a minute. Someone may try to get rid of her too."

Lieutenant Braxton wiped his fingers and thanked Jesse for her hospitality but said he had to leave right away. He would call back later. He jumped into his car, put the siren on, and drove as fast as he could to his downtown office. While he was driving, he called Sergeant Belsky and told her what had happened and said he would need her help in dealing with Mrs. Popov who would undoubtedly be very upset.

Lieutenant Braxton made the trip downtown as fast as could be and ran into the building. He was glad to see that Laura had already arrived, and he brought her with him to talk to Mrs. Popov. The agitated woman was aware that something had gone wrong and was demanding answers. Lieutenant Braxton had weighed his options for how he would handle her but decided that the best choice would be to tell her the truth to see if he could get any more answers from her. Obviously, this had gone beyond the "pal helping pal" situation they had heard from the Popovs earlier.

After explaining to her about the death of her brother and her son, Sergeant Belsky took over and said they wanted to keep her safe but didn't know what they were dealing with. She would have to help them if she didn't want to end up like they had. They could see the fear and uncertainty in her eyes, but Mrs. Popov finally told them that whenever they were going to have one of these visitors from Russia, Gregor would talk to a friend named Nick. She didn't know his last name, but she believed that he worked at a hospital. She thought the hospital was Holy Savior.

Alarm bells started to jangle when Mrs. Popov mentioned Holy Savior and Nick. Lieutenant Braxton had met the head of the hospital, Sister Cecilia Clark, the night of Nora's accident, and he dialed the number for Holy Savior and asked to speak to her. He explained as briefly as he could what had happened and said he needed to speak to someone who could look up an employee there named Nick, last name unknown.

Sister Cecilia was as sharp as she was nice, and in seconds, he was transferred to the head of Human Resources, Mrs. Samuels. She was a computer whiz and looked up any employee with the name of Nick. There were only three, and she thought that Nick Chernoff was a good fit for what he was looking for. Mrs. Samuels put Matt on hold while she talked to the head of Maintenance. He said that Nick Chernoff had only been there about six months. He had been relatively reliable, but he hadn't reported for work in three days now. They had tried to call the phone number he'd given them but were told that no such number existed. Mrs. Samuels then got on the line and gave the information to Lieutenant Braxton, but he suspected that the address they'd been given would probably not be accurate either.

He asked Mrs. Samuels to check with Nick's supervisor to see if they could tell them who Nick talked to at the hospital while on duty or on breaks. She said she would do so and would get back to him as soon as possible.

They had secured a search warrant for Mrs. Popov's house, but nothing new was discovered. Lieutenant Braxton couldn't help but feel a bit sorry for her, but it was obvious that she and her family had made a very poor decision when they thought they could handle partnering with international terrorists.

He also asked for a complete report on how it was that the two Popov's had been assassinated under the very noses of his officers without anyone noticing someone who clearly didn't belong there. He hoped that they would be able to find Nick Chernoff, and perhaps he would be able to shed more light on things since he sounded like the top link in the chain.

Lieutenant Braxton also remembered that in all the excitement, he still didn't have his jacket, which was still in the Duffys' closet.

18

Friday, September 14
Dublin, 8:00 a.m., GMT

The Duffys looked for their driver outside the airport, and their chauffer turned out to be no one less than Old Tim McMahon who had been Uncle Cyrus' driver for forty years. He greeted them with a warm nod and led them to his waiting car. Tim said he was sad about Cyrus but was relieved that he didn't suffer long and knew that he would be so happy to be with his Emily again. Tim told them that he was glad that they were coming, since Lavinia seemed to be in a bad way and would welcome their presence.

Dr. Duffy helped Tim to stow away the luggage, and then Tim pointed out to them that Mrs. O'Hara had sent along a good assortment of scones, breads, and biscuits—"Cookies to you Yanks"—and coffee and tea to tide them over until they reached the hall.

Old Tim pulled out of the airport and said the light rain was supposed to clear up later. After a few hours, they stopped for a brief rest in the town of Tipperary about halfway to Sneem and famous for the WWI song "It's a Long Way to Tipperary." Once they were approaching Killarney, they knew they were getting closer to the castle.

Nora knew they wouldn't have time today for a tour of the Ring of Kerry on the Iveragh Peninsula, part of the Wild Atlantic Way, but she fondly recalled when the family had taken that delightful tour last summer. This famous tourist road had always been much renowned for its wild beauty of forty shades of green hills, silvery lakes and rivers, and expansive blue coastline. The weather could change quickly from romantic blue skies with white puffy clouds to misty rain to an Irish gale with strong enough winds to blow the tourist buses back and forth. On bad days like that, the blustery weather obscured the view of anything but the rain. Experienced travelers carried an umbrella and raincoat, just in case, while others risked getting soaked.

Nora remembered thinking that it was a challenge to drivers who just wanted to get somewhere and weren't taking the Ring of Kerry tour, but Old Tim had skillfully maneuvered around the rows of tour buses that made stops in the various town centers. The tour began in Killarney and continued through towns with enchanting names like Beaufort, Killorglin, Glenbeigh/Rossbeigh, Kells, Cahirciveen, Portmagee/Valentia, Ballinskelligs, Waterville, Derrynane/Caherdaniel, then Sneem, and finished at Kenmare. Each town had its own attractions, ranging from castles to mountains to golf courses and magnificent scenery everywhere. Passengers could buy everything in the towns from Irish crystal and linen to candy bars like Nora's favorite, Maltesers.

Numerous pubs and restaurants painted in a variety of colors offered tasty food and drink. The architecture ranged from traditional thatched cottages to the nineteenth-century mansion of Muckross House with its gardens and traditional farms in Killarney National Park. During "the season," the narrow roads in Kerry were completely swamped with traffic.

The Duffys always enjoyed seeing the stone walls that lined the roads in Kerry. The foundation of the island of Ireland was comprised of limestone, and in order to farm the land, the farmers had to dig up the stone in pieces. They used these rocks to construct waist-high walls without mortar. The walls were not very sturdy, and the people and animals within them learned quickly that if they hit the walls too hard, they collapsed on them. The fragile walls required constant maintenance.

An aerial view of Kerry showed the extent of these low stone walls that divided the various properties. Many of the walls were covered in wildflowers, and it was a picturesque sight to delight the eye, but Nora couldn't help but think of the backbreaking labor that it must have taken to dig out these stones. Then the farmers still had to go about the business of plowing, planting, and harvesting. It always made her feel a bit guilty when the most work she had to do to procure a vast array of food was to drive to the supermarket.

Noon

They arrived in the town of Sneem, and the Duffys asked Tim to maneuver the car through the narrow streets so they could say hello to the folks at Dan Murphy's Bar. Nora delighted in seeing the array of paint colors on the various shops and restaurants, but her favorite was Dan Murphy's, which stood out in hot pink. A huge black stone sat in front of the bar, and the chorus of the poem written about the pub could be seen on the external wall of the building:

> Those days in our hearts we will cherish
> Contented although we were poor
> And the songs that were sung
> In the days we were young
> On the stone outside Dan Murphy's door

The proprietor of Murphy's was standing outside his establishment, sweeping the narrow sidewalk, and the Duffys asked Old Tim to stop so they could say hello to him. He recognized them and greeted them warmly. He told them he was very sorry to hear about the death of Uncle Cyrus and invited them to come for a free dinner whenever they could find the time. Nora told him that they hoped he would be able to come for the funeral.

Nora recalled the fun they had last spring when they watched the Irish dancers at Murphy's. When they found out she had been a dancer in Chicago as well as in Ireland, they asked her to join them. One of the dancers had a younger sister, and they let Nora use her purple performance dress and hard shoes. Nora was happy to see that her years of training hadn't failed her. She was almost able to keep up with the younger dancers just fine. Everyone had given her a rousing cheer, and that had been a very happy day. One of the women said she remembered seeing her at the World's competition when it was in Limerick, and Nora came in second in hard shoes. She thought that was a wonderful compliment that with all the dancers in Ireland, they remembered her.

Nora was permanently reminded of her dancing days because both her big toes were bent from standing on her toes in the hard shoes so often when she was little. Ballet shoes accommodated such standing better than Irish dancing hard shoes. Her toes didn't bother her now, but someday, she might develop arthritis in them. Most athletes were reminded of the toll their younger endeavors took on their bodies when they got older, but the good memories made good compensation.

They arrived at the gates of Duffy Hall shortly, and Old Tim carefully negotiated the twisting road that led uphill to the castle. Nora wondered what it would be like without its loving owner of so many years.

Nora delighted in just looking at the building, which always reminded her of the Hollywood version of the castle in *Robin Hood*. She almost expected to see Errol Flynn and Basil Rathbone swinging long swords at each other in the stairwells and Olivia De Havilland peeking out at them in her white silk outfit.

It was exhilarating to see the flags representing all the countries that do business with Duffy Medical lining the entrance under the portico. The life-sized silver leprechaun sculpture was shining in the sun, and the replica stones decorated with ancient Irish swirls looked enormous as they flanked the entrance stairs. Nora had loved just looking at the hall as a small child, and each time since, the sight of it brought a song to her heart. She used to love reading about castles when she was little, and now this fairytale place was part of her heritage.

She alighted from the car and was almost knocked over by Cyrus' devoted wolfhound, Liam, who seemed happy to be welcoming Nora home. She noticed that Liam was even bigger than her Reilly, and she could look him in the eye. His speckled coat was a lighter color than Reilly's, almost white. Liam's companion, Bran, a magnificent Irish Setter, trotted gracefully beside him, but as befitted his noble heritage, he was more reserved in his greeting.

Aunt Lavinia's much smaller spaniel, Lady, brought up the rear and barked a happy greeting to them. Chief Herlihy's German Shepherd, Dusty, joined in the welcoming party, but the Chief had to restrain him from jumping on the visitors. The Duffys petted all the dogs and then turned their attention to the humans who were waiting for them.

Aunt Lavinia held her arms open wide to give them a hug, and many officers of Duffy Medical were there to greet them and welcome them to Duffy Hall. Nora whispered to Aunt Lavinia that she was so very sorry to hear about Uncle Cy's death, and Lavinia gave her a hug and said they would talk about it later. Nora was saddened to see that Aunt Lavinia seemed to have aged since she last saw her six months ago. Nora always remembered Lavinia as having such excellent posture, but today, she couldn't seem to manage her usual straight and tall deportment.

Dr. and Mrs. Duffy expressed their heartfelt condolences to everyone on the loss of Cyrus. They seemed in their element and warmly embraced Lavinia and the others who had patiently waited for their arrival. Aunt Lavinia suggested that they enter the hall and get settled. Sean O'Keefe, the butler, and Mrs. Sheila Doyle, the housekeeper, awaited their instructions.

They greeted Enda, the ebullient and always pleasant receptionist who said she was so delighted that they were there. She whispered to Nora that Lavinia really needed them.

The family climbed the steep flight of steps to their rooms on the upper floor, and two young men followed them with their luggage. They had given Dr. and Mrs. Duffy Uncle Cyrus' bedroom with the huge four-poster bed and gigantic fireplace where a peat fire was burning "to take off the chill." Sean O'Keefe assured them that, although Uncle Cyrus had died in this bed, they had since replaced not only the bed linens but also the mattress. Dr. and Mrs. Duffy responded that they appreciated all this concern for their comfort.

Nora was happy to see that her bedroom across the way, which used to belong to Aunt Emily, overlooked the lake and the deer park.

It was a pretty room with flowered chintz curtains and chairs, and the snowy white bedcover looked thick and inviting. Nora unpacked her suitcase and put the clothes in the sturdy mahogany wardrobe. She noticed, as always, that old Irish bathrooms were extra-large, and she had plenty of room for her personal products on the shelves. She looked forward to soaking in the big tub and settling down in the comfy bed. Jet lag was beginning to set in; it would be dinner time at home.

She took her laptop and went down to the library where she thought an Internet connection might work and she searched for the man her father had talked about on the plane, Ben Durant. She tried Facebook first but found no mention of him. Then she just typed in his name on an Internet search, and several listings came up. Ben Durant was a chef in Maine and renowned for his farm-to-table food. That would have meant quite a change of occupations. She would look for more about him soon.

Nora ran back upstairs, put her laptop in her bedroom, and told her parents that she was going to take Liam for a walk outside. Liam seemed only too happy to be prancing about his familiar territory, and Nora's mood was enlivened by his vital presence. Bran came with them, and Nora reflected that his was an ancient name. Bran the dog had belonged to the giant, Fionn Mac Cumhaill, in the stories of the ancient *Fenian Cycle*, and Finn and Bran had many adventures together.

Enda saw Nora heading to the door and reminded her that lunch would be served soon, and then Mr. Lloyd was going to start the reading of the will, so she shouldn't take too long outside. Nora responded that she would just take the dogs for a quick run and would be back soon.

What a perfectly beautiful day, she thought as she watched the attractive sights and sounds of the men cutting the grass and tidying up the grounds. She admired the reds, purples, and golds of the many fall flowers in their well-manicured beds. Mr. Gilbert, the groundskeeper, was doing his best to keep the lawns and gardens trimmed and in immaculate condition since so many guests were expected for the funeral.

Nora was always surprised that the world went on its merry way the same as usual when someone you loved so much had died. When Nora returned to the Hall, she guided the dogs to the care of Tim Taylor, the animal keeper for the estate. She saw that many of the friends and guests had already gathered in the front hall. She ran up the stairs quickly, freshened up, and changed into her favorite white sheath dress with the black satin ribbon trim and her favorite black patent heels with the little bows on the side. She completed her outfit with her antique Claddagh necklace and earrings that Tommy had given her for their engagement. She wore her engagement ring with the square diamond with emeralds on each side in an antique platinum setting.

Her mother and father also changed into more formal dress. Her mother was a handsome woman, and her silvery dress and shoes complemented her stylish red hair. The Duffys loved the view of the staircases and the hall below and walked down slowly to prolong their enjoyment.

Kitty Lloyd and Sean Duffy greeted Nora and her parents warmly at the door, and the group entered the dining hall for brunch. Anticipation was half the fun, and they all wondered where things would stand for each of them by the end of this important day.

She knew that her dad was a little concerned about the bill to replace the whole roof on their old house, so she hoped that Uncle Cy had left him at least enough money to cover that. She had no expectations for herself and would much rather reverse events so she could find Uncle Cy seated in his favorite old maroon chair, waiting to give her a hug and tell her a joke. Listening to the reading of his will would make his death only too real.

19

Friday, September 14
Sneem, 12:30 p.m., GMT

Nora took a moment to look around the huge stunning dining hall with the gray walls constructed of immense blocks of stone. It could easily be the place where knights were gathered for a medieval feast. She was glad that the renovations that had occurred over the years had left intact the wooden roof beams and the intricately carved minstrels' balcony where the musicians used to entertain while the feasting was going on. She was happy to see a large golden harp sitting there now, and she resolved to play it later.

Nora knew that the role of harpist had been revered in Ireland for centuries, and troubadours used to travel from castle to castle, providing entertainment on their beloved instruments. Some historians thought they might have also passed on messages about rebellion. Ireland is perhaps the only country in the world to have a musical instrument like the harp as its symbol.

The massive stone fireplace against the far wall could easily hold a whole pig turning on a spit, although today, there was just a peat fire burning and filling the room with its distinctive homey odor. Above the fireplace mantel was a large painting of Duffy Hall Castle, accompanied on each side by a plaque with the Gaelic greeting of *Céad míle fáilte!*—a thousand welcomes—and a St. Brigid's cross constructed from the rushes that grew along the banks of the lake on the grounds. Nora did welcome the modern additions of central heating and the marble flooring that had replaced uneven flagstones. She'd always wondered if there were spy holes in the walls. Some of the old castles used to have this convenient way for the Lord to find out what his enemies might be plotting.

Many small tables and chairs had been set up for today's brunch. Sean accompanied Nora and her parents to their places, and the autumn-themed floral centerpieces and table settings were a treat for the eyes. At each place, a large white lace placemat with the Duffy crest was adorned with cream-colored Belleek china with its signature green shamrocks around the borders accompanied by Waterford silverware and glassware. Nora used to think that the Belleek china might break easily because it was so translucent, but it must have been surprisingly sturdy to be used as the dinnerware for large groups of people. She was happy to see that the water and wine glasses were in her favorite Waterford pattern, Colleen. Magnificent candleholders shaped like the Waterford seahorse graced each table, and the burning white tapers added a cheering touch.

They could see a spectacular array of breakfast foods and drinks on the massive table in front of the fireplace. Mrs. O'Hara and her staff had outdone themselves in preparing a selection of various kinds of eggs, meats, potatoes, boxties, black and white pudding, smoked salmon, colcannon, cheeses, baked apples, whortleberries, pancakes, waffles in the shape of shamrocks, soda bread, brown bread, oatmeal with brown sugar and raisins, heavy cream, butter, and several varieties of juices, mead, and wines. This was, indeed, a feast.

Neal, Johnny, Biddy, and Mary—Mrs. O'Hara's helpers—orchestrated the movement of diners to the waiting line in front of the food table, and Nora and her mother took dainty portions of a few of the delicious foods. Nora's weakness was brown bread and butter, and she enjoyed two slices with her colcannon, which was a combination of mashed potatoes, kale/cabbage, and Irish bacon. Dr. Duffy enjoyed a taste of almost everything. After the main meal, the helpers were on hand to clear the dinner plates and replaced them with small crystal plates adorned with cream puffs and chocolate mints. After the glass chargers and small plates had been cleared, they then removed every crumb from the tables and served coffee and tea.

After everyone had their fill, Mr. Duncan Lloyd, the solicitor, called them all to attention and said he would be reading Cyrus Duffy's will in fifteen minutes, so they could visit the washrooms or take a walk and then gather in the library next door.

Nora's parents decided to take a walk after all the food and said they wanted to call home and see how everyone was doing there. Nora said that she would go right to the library. She sat next to Kitty and Sean in the last row of the chairs that had been set up. The atmosphere reminded her of a scene from an Agatha Christie novel with the greedy relatives of the deceased lord of the manor anxiously waiting to see how much they would get. She didn't know most of the people there, but she found it surprising that no one looked very sad when she could feel her tears welling up and waiting to emerge at any minute.

Friday, September 14
Sneem, 1:30 p.m., GMT

Nora closed her eyes and dozed for a few minutes. She couldn't help thinking about the conversation she'd had with Uncle Cyrus in this beautiful room last fall. She told him she liked the new addition of the various countries' flags of the customers of Duffy Medical that one had to pass before coming into the front doors of the castle.

"Ah, that was Duncan's idea. He thought it would bring a more international character to the headquarters of Duffy Medical. I do like the flags too, but my da would not be best pleased to see a Union Jack out there. Times change, and England and Northern Ireland are two of our best customers," Uncle Cyrus explained.

"I think Duncan was right," said Nora, "and I was pleased to see the Stars and Stripes right next to the Irish green, white, and orange. By the way, Uncle Cyrus, I've heard a few people say that they've heard that your castle has a ghost. Have you ever seen or heard any signs of one?" asked Nora.

"Well, child, Emily used to say that she sometimes heard strange sounds like whispering near Vinnie's rooms, but I have not heard it myself. I think Em was so attuned to the supernatural that she might have had more of an ear for folks like that, if they are here. I suppose it's possible that most old houses may still harbor the spirits of their past inhabitants. You remind me of Emily in many ways, so if there is a ghost, you might hear the whispering too. I think it must be a good ghost since no one has reported negative feelings about it."

Uncle Cy asked her what she thought of the library that he had amassed over the years and added that the walnut-lined walls, Art Deco furniture, decorations, and the stained-glass windows were all Em's ideas.

Nora told him that she was awed by his brilliant library, including the collection of Irish china and crystal that were everywhere in the room. Waterford chandeliers, bowls, and vases twinkled in the sunlight, and the tables received additional lighting from Belleek lamps imprinted with green shamrocks and pink flowers. She'd never seen large statues of the Sacred Heart of Jesus, the Madonna, and St. Patrick in Belleek anywhere else, but there they were, right in front of her in glass cases. The windowsills were enhanced by the shiny green leaves of potato plants growing in Belleek pots, and a few of the plants were blossoming with pink flowers.

Nora was especially impressed by the large collection of important books from all over the world sitting on the walnut shelves and asked Uncle Cy how he had started his collection.

"I didn't aspire to have a 'real' library. One of the first things a town of any size does is to do that. I just started with the books that I had grown to love and added new ones all the time. I have some historical books about most of the countries in Europe and North America. Recently, I've started to add more about the great cultures of the rest of the world, from Egypt to Africa to other Asian and American countries. I have a small collection about the history of the Jewish people. The persecution of these people has always mystified me. I find them to be like anyone else. Some are good, some are bad, most are in-between. They are smart and hardworking and talented. Even in the concentration camps, they organized orchestras. But every so often, this hatred starts up again. I've never been able to figure it out, and it must surely be difficult for them to explain to their children.

"Most of my collection is about Ireland and related subjects. Various strong peoples have persecuted us over the years too. The Vikings conquered Dublin—or Dubh Linn, which means black pool—in about 900 AD. They killed off many of the original inhabitants, but then many of them must have decided that our fair lasses were worth staying for. Your red hair probably comes from them."

Uncle Cyrus continued, "There's always existed a love-hate relationship with our neighbors, the English. We admire their many amazing accomplishments and that 'the sun never sets on the British Empire,' but over the centuries, they've tried to subjugate, starve, or kill us. So we've tried, with our limited means, to fight back with periodic 'risings,' usually without much success Neither island is very big. All of Ireland is about the size of your Indiana, and England is about the size of Montana, but between us, we've had quite an influence on the world.

"I'm sure you've sung the song 'Four Green Fields,' about the four provinces of Ireland. You know that the Republic of Ireland has twenty-six counties in three provinces, Connacht, Munster, and Leinster, while Northern Ireland has the other six counties in Ulster. Northern Ireland wanted to remain loyal to England in 1921 when the Republic of Ireland was officially recognized. That has caused violence and heartaches in places like Londonderry, but since the Peace Accords in 1998, there's been a relative state of calm, so we thank God for that."

Nora saw books by many famous authors: W. B. Yeats, James Joyce, C. S. Lewis, G. Bernard Shaw, Brendan Behan, Shakespeare, Marlowe, Ben Jonson, Samuel Johnson, Chesterton, J. R. Tolkien, Dickens, Churchill, Maeve Binchy, Mark Twain, Edgar Allen Poe, Walt Whitman, Robert Frost, and many more. She also saw a section of books about the Great Famine of 1845–49.

"Yes," Cyrus said, "the complete failure of the blighted potato crops from a plant disease led to a million deaths, and millions more left for places like America and Australia. They called it the Great Diaspora. The population of Ireland has never really recovered. Queen Victoria's answer to the Irish starvation problem was to send maize, which was almost inedible."

Cyrus asked Nora to look at the glass case on the wall behind her at one of his greatest treasures. In the case was a letter that had belonged to his grandmother and had been written by her great-great grandfather, John Duffy, during the famine. He had written the letter to his five-year-old son, Eamon. It explained that John was one of those who couldn't pay his rent since he no longer had a potato crop to sell, so the English landlord forced the family to leave their home. Then they put a giant log through the house from the front to the back door and used chains and horses to tumble the cottage so the family could never return.

Cyrus explained that the starving family had to take to the road. They tried eating shellfish when they could find it, but eventually, they ate grass. The family's one saving grace was that John was a talented carpenter and blacksmith, and a church in Ennis let them live in an old shed and gave them as much food as they could in return for his services. Many of his neighbors died from starvation and disease. Compounding their troubles, the failure of the potatoes was followed by an extremely cold and snowy winter.

"Somehow the family managed to live through this. How the letter survived all these years is a mystery, but my ancestors must have thought of it as a great treasure, because it's in relatively good shape."

Nora read the letter that had been written in a cramped hand and had tears in her eyes as she thought about what this family had to endure, but she was so glad that the letter had survived. It added enormously to the value of this incredible room and the hall itself. It also explained a little of where Uncle Cyrus had gotten his traits of stubbornness and determination.

Another glass case contained a good-sized very old-looking doll with a china face that had a few cracks. Its dress had been white with blue flowers and it still had both white shoes. Cyrus said the doll was found in the old section of the castle under a small bed. An antiques dealer had told him he thought the doll was easily 200 years old or more. The dealer offered to buy it from him, but Cyrus said he thought it was a valuable part of Duffy Hall history and was not for sale at any price.

Cyrus pointed out to her another glass case that contained a number of very old-looking books. He explained that they were illuminated manuscripts that had been bound in vellum or calf skin and probably dated from the twelfth century. One of the books was opened so that the artistic writing and colored illustrations could be viewed. Irish monks had saved Western Civilization during the Dark Ages by laboriously writing down the wisdom of the centuries. Trinity College in Dublin had a huge collection of these priceless manuscripts, including one of the most famous books in the world, the *Book of Kells*. Cyrus said that he'd like to let Nora hold one of these books, but the case was specially designed to be airtight and lightproof.

On the shelves to the left of the door behind lightproof glass were quite a few first editions. Cyrus explained that James Joyce was considered to be the most influential author of the twentieth century, so he numbered *Ulysses* and *Finnegan's Wake* among his books. Cyrus said that he'd tried reading them a few times but decided that the man, though brilliant, must have wanted the whole world to know how intelligent he was and didn't care a bean about whether most people grasped his meaning.

"Who starts and ends a book with a sentence like this?" Cyrus asked as he opened *Finnegan's Wake.* "'Riverrun, past Eve and Adam's, from swerve of shore to bend of bay, brings us by a commodius vicus of recirculation back to Howth Castle and Environs.' I know that literary experts spend much of their lives trying to interpret what he meant, but that holds no appeal for me," said Cyrus. "Although he owed much of his education to the Irish Jesuits, Joyce left Ireland at a young age and never came back. He must have needed a good woman like Emily too, because he was surely mixed up about how to love a woman."

Nora responded, "People say that libraries are no longer needed in these days of the phone and Internet, but just think what people would be missing if they couldn't see this tactile feast for all our senses."

Cyrus knew that Nora admired Charles Dickens and numbered many of that genius' fascinating stories among his treasures. "I think Dickens must have had some Irish in him somewhere. He certainly could tell a long and complicated tale, fill it with a huge number of amazing characters, and have all the threads of a complex plot come out right at the end."

Nora said she knew that Dickens had visited Ireland a few times to do readings from his novels, and those visits had been very successful.

Cyrus pulled out a handsome red-bound volume of *Great Expectations*. He grinned and said that he loved this fascinating Dickens story, but he also kept a bottle of *poitín*—potcheen, 90 percent alcoholic content whiskey—and two glasses behind it for special occasions. Cyrus asked if she'd like to taste it, but she declined. Nora said the powerful vapors were enough to get her drunk as soon as he removed the cap from the bottle.

Cyrus took a sip and gulped. He explained that no matter how experienced a drinker you were, ninety proof whiskey packed a hearty wallop on your innards. Many homeowners still gave visitors a shot of poitín as a sign of hospitality, but it was not always a welcome surprise. Cyrus said that after his mother had visited several houses on Christmas Day, she used to pour the poitín on the plants to get rid of it. She swore that some of the plants had withered on the spot.

"Those old potato farmers discovered a long time ago that they could produce more than just vegetables," he laughed. "There are lots of fishermen out here on the west coast of Ireland, and a shot of poitín keeps them from freezing in the Atlantic gales. It's like antifreeze for a car."

He said he was pretty sure that Lavinia didn't realize his indulgent treat was there, but he asked Nora to keep his stash a secret.

"What's the special occasion today?" asked Nora.

"Well, it's not every day that I get to entertain a pretty and accomplished young woman," replied Cyrus. "People think that I have everything I could want, but I get lonely in this big old place with just my sister for company, wonderful woman though she is. Em and I had just one pregnancy, but that wee one never had a chance to be born. The doctor wasn't sure why she lost the baby, but to save her life, he had to do things that meant we were never able to have children. It was a misery to Em all her life. If she'd been able to have the baby, it would be just about your mother's age now. I hope I'm not boring you," Cyrus queried. "Old people sometimes talk too much."

"I find you and everything about your home fascinating," assured Nora. "And I'm so sorry to hear about your lost child." Nora was once again struck by what a handsome man he was with his sky-blue eyes and full head of white wavy hair.

"Let's sit down here on these fancy gold chairs that Em purchased that never get used, and I'll tell you something more about my life and my business," Cyrus said.

Friday, September 14
Sneem, 1:30 p.m., GMT

Uncle Cy continued, "I started life not far from here. My da was a potato farmer, and Ma made fancy lace tablecloths that the shops in town sold to the tourists. We weren't poor, but we certainly weren't rich. We only had three rooms in the house—a gathering room with a fireplace and two bedrooms. All five of us children were in the one small bedroom, Lavinia, Ann, Jack, Conor, and me. The kitchen was outside to prevent fires from spreading, and the outhouse was set far back on our land. Da surprised ma one day and told her that he was going to build a kitchen and a bathroom in the house. Ma felt very modern to think that we would have these handy improvements.

"Our priest wanted me to go to a Jesuit college and become a businessman, but I had a hankering to be an artist, which I probably got from my mother. When I got a little older, I added to the family income by working as a caddy at the local golf clubs and as a shepherd in the lambing season, which I really enjoyed.

"Mr. Kilroy, the blacksmith, made all kinds of metal things to sell to the tourists—shamrocks, leprechauns, ponies, wind chimes, and more. I asked him one day if he could teach me how, and he hired me as his apprentice. That's where I got my experience working with metals. You've seen the big silver leprechaun sculpture that sits in front of the castle. That was one of my first pieces. I was good at it, and I seriously thought about becoming a metal sculptor.

"Then one day, my oldest brother, Jack, died after a botched appendicitis operation. There was some question that it could have been because the town doctor didn't have sterile, good quality knives. Jack and I were very close, and I was devastated by his death. At first, I was just mad, and then I thought about producing superior tools for doctors so this wouldn't happen again.

"My Uncle Willy lived in Dublin, and I stayed with him a few weeks while I talked to different doctors and found out what they thought they needed in their tools. I had a friend outside of Dublin who was a manager at a steel plant, and he helped me with practical suggestions along the way. I asked Mr. Kilroy for his help in producing scalpels and other surgical implements and opened my first small Duffy Medical factory outside of Cork. That gradually became quite successful and profitable.

"Irish hospitals bought our wares, but gradually, we became well-known, and other European countries began to be reliable customers. Em and Vinnie helped me at the beginning, but as we got bigger, we had to hire people to run the business and keep track of distribution. From the first, we had doctors on our board who gave us wise advice. So I ended up becoming the businessman that my parents had envisioned for me after all."

Uncle Cyrus continued, "We kept getting requests to produce more and more supplies, and little by little, we added all the lighting and receptacles and furniture a hospital would need, and then we added medicines. Today, we are a first-class hospital supply company all over Europe and in parts of Asia. It hasn't been easy since there is so much competition in our field, but I've still done very well. I'd like to expand to the American market, but there is serious competition there, so it might be more difficult than I think.

"After we got married, we lived in Galway and we did love it there. Our house was close to Emily's family, and we enjoyed the beauty of the Cliffs of Moher and Galway Bay. I know you've sung the famous song that talks about seeing 'the moon go down on Galway Bay.' It certainly is a beautiful sight.

"We went on a vacation a few years later and found this old castle in Sneem. It was on a very large piece of property and close to the Atlantic Ocean and the Coral Beach, which is pink because of a unique kind of dried algae. The mountain range you see includes Knockmoyle, which is more than 2,000 feet high. The whole area was filled with beautiful trees and plants, including palms, fuchsias, and rhododendrons. We loved to walk and found great vistas of beauty, no matter which way we looked. The fishing in the River Sneem was great, and there were large colonies of seals to be seen near the beaches. It all felt like a too-good-to-be-true home.

"They told us that the castle had been built in the sixteenth century by a Fitzpatrick family, but it had been abandoned for about eighty years. There were red deer in the woods and salmon and sea trout in the Sneem River. The property was for sale, but nobody seemed to be interested in it because the house and the grounds were so dilapidated.

"We fell in love with it right away. We hired an architect to draw up plans and we dreamed a lot about how we wanted it to look. Emily had the artistic sense you need when you're thinking about restoring a big old place, and I had the desire to find not only a beautiful home but a fitting place for my company's headquarters. We hired the best craftsmen to tear down and build up. We used attractive high-quality materials for the restoration, which is still going on.

"We were very happy here until Emily got sick suddenly and died within two days. She's been dead a long time now, but when I close my eyes, I still see her how she was—beautiful and talented and loving. I got sick myself after she died, and it took me years to recover."

Whether it was the poitin or just the memories of Emily, Nora could see that Cyrus was on the verge of tears. She said she would like a better look at the leprechaun with the big smile and led him outside. The silver sculpture was shining in the sun and was a true work of art, done by the man who had been enjoying himself as he had coaxed forth the happy figure from the metal.

There was a beautiful bench next to the sculpture, and she suggested they sit there for a few minutes and enjoy the view. They could see a herd of red deer in the distance, and a small rainbow hovered over the duck pond. Glints of light sparkled on the lake and the river.

It was amazing that a man who had come from such humble origins had achieved all this.

"And you, Nora dear, how are things going for you with the sick children?"

"You've asked the big question, Uncle Cyrus, that I wonder about myself. In the beginning, I thought about quitting about once a week. It was their eyes that got me—the suffering eyes of the children and the desperate eyes of the parents. But we have a motto on the wall of our office that helped me: 'God provides the life; with his help, we keep it going.'"

"After a while, I got more resigned to knowing that some of these kids were not going to survive, but it never gets easy. The children endure treatments that are painful and frightening too. Chemotherapy and radiation should be words in a book for these kids, but instead, they are treatments that make many of them very ill. I'm confident that someday, more cures for cancer will be found, but in the meantime, we slog along. I thank God for those children he spares and I pray for those he doesn't. Many of those who do survive still face an uphill battle."

"I'll be graduating from medical school next summer, but before I begin doing brain surgeries, I want to get even more experience, so I'm going to stay on at my hospital as an assistant for another year. The brain is an awesome organism, and I feel it is a real privilege to be able to understand more about it. We take it so for granted, but every day, we all process many millions pieces of information. That's true for the smartest as well as the humblest people on earth. I find that amazing. So I guess the short answer to your question is, I love it!"

Nora took out her cellphone and showed Cyrus a few pictures of the children she had worked with recently. Joel had been in and out of the hospital since he was born and had just had his first birthday. They were hopeful that this beautiful boy with the flashing dark eyes might be able to stay at home more often soon. Samantha was a gorgeous seven-year-old who had so many treatments that she'd forgotten how to smile. Her future was not very bright, but she'd been alive much longer than her original diagnosis called for. For children like her, length of days was counted as success. The prospect of more cures for cancer kept parents and caregivers motivated to keep going. Cyrus thought Nora was right about their uncertain and pleading eyes, and he admired her immensely for being willing to take care of them as she did.

When Nora left the next day, Cyrus asked that she come and visit him as often as she could. She thanked him for sharing his stories and told him that she would come back soon. However, she'd been so busy recently with school and work and family that the best she'd been able to do was to call him every Sunday. It was always delightful to hear his voice with the Gaelic lilt, and they kept each other apprised of their news. It gave her a jolt to think that she would never hear that mellifluous voice again in this life, and she fought to keep her tears from falling.

Friday, September 14
Sneem, 2:00 p.m., GMT

Nora was brought back to the present by Sean Duffy who appeared at her side and was tapping on her shoulder. He said that Aunt Lavinia asked if she would sit with her during the reading of the will. Sean explained that the elderly woman said she was feeling a bit faint and thought that having Nora close to her would be a help. Nora wiped away her tears with some tissues and waved goodbye to her mom and moved up to the first row in the seat next to Aunt Lavinia who smiled and reached for Nora's hand with a tight but shaky grip.

This has got to be so hard for her, thought Nora, *but she looks so nice today in her Duffy plaid suit of greens, yellow, and black. Her Connemara marble pendant goes well with it too. She's going to miss Cyrus so much, but I sense that there's more to her than we see on the outside.*

Mr. Lloyd banged his gavel on the podium and then began speaking in his richly modulated voice:

"Ladies and gentlemen, thank you for being here today. Without further ado, I'm going to read to you just the summary of what Cyrus J. Duffy had in mind as his last will and testament. I'll pass out copies to all of you after this is completed. There is a much wordier legal version in English and another version in Irish, the official language of the Republic of Ireland, which anyone who requests it can see.

"Technology is a wonderful thing, and I want to be sure that all of you can see what I'm going to be reading, so I've asked my daughter, Kitty, to prepare a PowerPoint video for us. You'll be able to see the words I'll read on the raised screen behind me."

The large blue screen clicked to life, and the title "Last Will and Testament of Cyrus John Duffy" appeared with the Duffy Medical logo. Kitty sat next to her father so that she could click through each page.

Mr. Lloyd continued, "Cyrus was a generous man, and I think most of you will be well-pleased. Cyrus was also an innovative man and was always good for a few surprises. Here's what he had to say just a few months ago on the fifteenth of May. He began with the traditional Irish greeting:

"God bless all here! My name is Cyrus John Duffy, Owner and President of Duffy Medical, Ltd., of Sneem, Ireland, and this is the shortened version of my last will and testament. My solicitor, Mr. Duncan Lloyd, has the more detailed version that contains all the legal language.

"I, Cyrus John Duffy, affirm that I am of sound mind, and I make this will without any kind of duress being placed upon me. I don't want anyone to try to say later that I was an old fool who didn't know what I was doing. I've spent many days and months thinking carefully about it and I've taken wise counsel from my sister, Lavinia, and some of the officers of my company.

"To be sure that no one will question my sanity and my complete understanding of what I'm doing, I also had my personal physician, Dr. Rod McGarry, who has known me for much of my adult life, conduct a comprehensive mental examination of me, and he said that I passed the tests with flying colors. If anyone has questions about this, Dr. McGarry can provide more details.

"Now, on to the good stuff, which I know is what you are anxious to hear. I am making the following testamentary gifts to those whom I believe will use the money and property wisely and well in the future. I wish I could be there to talk this over with you, but God had other plans for me. So let's get started.

"I designate my solicitor, Mr. Duncan Lloyd, to be the executor of my estate. I affirm that this will, dated 15 May, 2018, is the will that should take precedence, and I abrogate any other older wills that I might have made over the years.

"To my dearest sister, Lavinia 'Vinnie' Mary Duffy, I leave the sum of one million euros and her section of Duffy Hall, which she has inhabited much of her life. Lavinia has been a devoted companion to me and is the only person who has really cared for me since I was born. She contributes to many charities, and now she can easily continue to do that. I also direct that Lavinia should be a permanent member of the board of directors of Duffy Medical, Ltd. She was there at the beginning and knows what I have in mind for the company better than anyone. I trust her judgment implicitly.

"To the Chief Executive Officer of my business, Duffy Medical, Ltd., Mr. John O'Malley, I leave the sum of 500,000 euros for him personally and five million euros to be used at his discretion to keep the firm growing and as a fund for worthy and aspiring employees. Duncan Lloyd can provide the detailed financial sheets I asked to be drawn up. I ask John to remain as CEO so that he can assist in my other future wishes—see more below.

"I leave the sum of 500,000 euros each to my longtime solicitor, Mr. Duncan Lloyd, who has helped my money grow through wise investments, and to my physician, Dr. Rod McGarry, who has kept my heart going for more years than it should have.

"I leave the sum of 100,000 euros each to my devoted secretaries, Kitty and Maryann Condon; my batman/butler, Mr. Sean O'Keefe; my housekeeper, Mrs. Sheila Doyle; my stable director, Tim Taylor; and my talented groundskeeper, Donald Gilbert. All these individuals have supported me in various ways through the years and have kept me, my business, and my homes in good shape.

"My dear wife, Emily, had only one surviving brother, Allen Butler of Waterford, Ireland, and I leave him the amount of 100,000 euros. Allen was always a good friend to us and helped us in so many ways.

"I leave the sum of 500,000 euros to the International Jesuit Fund with Father Matthew Tooley S. J. as executor. Father Matt has helped me personally many times, and I know he'll see that the money is put to good use in the Jesuit schools.

"I leave the sum of 500,000 euros to my nephew, Mr. Kevin Duffy of Dublin, Ireland, and 500,000 euros each to my brother, Mr. Conor Duffy and my nephew, Dr. Michael Duffy of Chicago, Illinois, USA."

Michael, Eileen and Nora exhaled deeply.

"These three good men represent the best of the Duffy family, and I know they will use the money wisely. They can give some of it to their children in the manner they decide best.

"I leave the sum of 50,000 euros to my great-nephew, Alan Fitzpatrick. Alan has never

shown me the slightest affection and only contacts me when he needs money, but I loved his
mother, my sister, Ann, and I make this bequest
to him in her name. I ask God to grant him wisdom in the future.

"I leave the sum of 50,000 euros each to the
other members of the board of directors of Duffy
Medical, and I thank them for their service.

"I leave the sum of 1,000 euros each to the
administrative staff members at Duffy Hall.

"I leave 500 euros each to all the other
employees of Duffy Medical at our various
locations.

"I leave the sum of 100,000 euros to the
Town of Sneem, Ireland, to be used for the work
needed to protect the shoreline, and I thank them
for their help over the years."

Hmm, thought Nora, *I'm happy for Grandpa, Dad and Uncle
Kevin, but so far I haven't heard my name mentioned. Maybe I'll get
that Great Expectations book that Cyrus showed me, and I'd love to
have Liam.*

Mr. Lloyd resumed reading after stopping to take a sip of water,
and Nora felt his eyes on her with a large smile on his face. Nora felt
the pressure on her hand from Aunt Lavinia increase. She seemed to
have recovered her strength nicely.

"All the rest of my personal and business
property and money, lands, buildings and their
contents, the animals, and all the rest of my
company, Duffy Medical, Ltd., I leave to my
great-niece, Miss Nora Eileen Duffy, of Chicago,
Illinois, USA."

A collective gasp went up from the audience, especially from
Nora!

"She will not know what to do with it all at first, but she will quickly learn, and I have no doubt she will administer it with zeal and good-will. She will have the assistance of my solicitor, my CEO, and other board members. The money amounts will run into the billions of US dollars; Mr. Duncan Lloyd will have the details.

"I am also designating Nora Duffy as chairman of the board of Duffy Medical. I realize that this will be a surprise to her and I know she is very much an American and may not wish to spend much time in this role. Mr. Duncan Lloyd will explain to her that the only real requirement of her will be to spend two weeks in Ireland every year in the fall at the company's annual meeting. In these days of the Internet, most business can be conducted via computer. Whether she wishes to live at Duffy Hall or to be active in this business role or not, my devoted officers of Duffy Medical will be there to guide her. Nora has many brothers and sisters, and I know she will give them a share of the money.

"There will be people who wonder why I am leaving the bulk of my estate to a young woman whom I've only seen a few times in my life. Em and I were never able to have children, and I've always thought of Nora as the daughter I never had. She's visited me and called me frequently over the years, and I know she loves me. Also, although she doesn't yet realize it, Nora saved my life at a critical time so that I would have all this money to leave to the people I love.

"On 15 July, 1985, I had all my plans made to take my own life. Life had been losing its grip on me for some time, and it was the fifth anniversary of my darling wife's death. I had become a hard and bitter man and was in pain most of the time from the back injury I'd sustained when I fell off a horse. No one except my sister loved me, and I felt the same about them. I wasn't even interested in my company anymore. I knew my home and my business would be in good hands. I should have had a few qualms about taking my own life for religious reasons, but I didn't care enough that day, even about God, if there was one.

"I had a quick-acting poison and a bottle of Jameson's in my one pocket and a note of instructions for my solicitor in the other. I had walked down to the chairs at the edge of the lake where Emily and I used to sit as we watched our ancient home being restored. It was dusk, the sky was a lovely color, and the birds and the trees were making a racket, just the kind of evening we enjoyed together so much. I could feel Em's presence so vividly, and I longed to be with her again. I sat down and toasted Em with the Jameson's.

"I was reaching in my pocket for the poison when a little but strong voice said so very clearly, 'Uncle Cyrus, I've been looking all over for you. We're going home today, and I wanted to thank you for the lovely time I've had at your very nice house. I'm glad you're having it fixed so it will be even better than it is now. Will you let me come back and see it when it's done?'

"I opened my eyes, and there was that tiny little girl from America standing next to me with her mop of red curls, big green eyes, and a huge smile on her face. She started to talk and tell me all about herself. She said that day was her fifth birthday, and the present she liked the best was being here with me and her family. She told me about all the things they'd done while they were

116

visiting in Ireland and all about her friends and her dog at home. She was excited that she would be going to kindergarten.

"I asked her what she liked about my house, and she went on and on about the castle with the big rooms and how pretty they were, the big yard, the lake, all the animals she'd seen in the woods, and Donal, my big wolfhound. As she was talking, I noticed that Donal had put his massive head on her very small feet. They seemed very comfortable with each other. She then gave me a picture she had drawn of Donal standing next to me with Duffy Hall in the background and a rainbow in the sky. The perspective was a bit off, but both the dog and I had smiles on our faces.

"Nora was a chatterbox, and as she talked, I started to relax for the first time in ages. I only caught a few things she said, but I realized that this funny little child liked me and felt comfortable with me. I asked her if she wasn't scared of me, and her answer was, 'Mommy says that you're just grumpy and sad because you have a pain in your heart and you need to do something different. I came to tell you that I think you should come and visit us in Chicago. Our house is nice and big, although it's tiny compared to your castle. I have a nice bedroom with two beds, and you could stay in my room. I have two little brothers, but they don't make too much noise. You'd feel better right away after you spend some time with me and my friends and my dog, Peanut. No one can stay grumpy with Peanut when she gives you kisses. She's much smaller than your big wooly dog, but she's awfully cute. I know you'd have a good time.'

"Just then, her worried parents came running toward us. They'd been looking all over the grounds for her. Nora told them that she'd invited me to come to visit them at home, and my nephew, Michael, and his pretty wife, Eileen, said that would be fine with them. Nora then gave me a hug and kissed me on the cheek. What a turn of events! I felt very much like that character, the Grinch, whose small and icy heart had started to grow and melt because of the touch of a loving child. I wasn't even noticing my back hurting.

"I asked the family to return to the house and told them I'd be there to say goodbye to them shortly. I knew that Emily was smiling as I threw the bottle of poison and the suicide note in the lake. I replaced them with the picture Nora had drawn. I couldn't be as bad as I had thought if this charming child wanted me to spend time with her, even to sharing her bedroom! I then asked God to guide me as to what I should do next—the first prayer I'd uttered in a very long time.

"I bade little Nora and her family a fond farewell and I did get to Chicago during a business trip the next year. Nora was right that it was impossible to be grumpy around her frisky little dog and her friends. The family had made a number of trips to visit me, and I received frequent cards and letters from Nora and regular phone calls reminding me that she missed me.

"During the last twenty years, I've had more energy to expand my company and my circle of friends and I've had my back fixed. I've had more business success than ever before. I'm now a very wealthy man, and I've learned to value each day.

None of this 'return to life' would have occurred if I had died on that long ago day, and it all happened because of the love and joy emanating from Nora Duffy. I keep the picture she drew for me on my office wall to remind me of this.

"I'd like to explain all this to Nora in person, but if she's hearing this, I am dead. I hope my plans will be a pleasant surprise for her. She gave me back my life, and now I'd like to help make her life a little easier. I'd especially like her to have the house that she admired so much when she was little. I know she'll enjoy having Liam and the other dogs. I hope she'll want to keep Finnbar too, my beautiful black racehorse. Her small size would fit better on one of our bog ponies, but even though Finn is too big for her, she is a horse whisperer and she'll find a way to work with him. I know they'll like each other.

"I've kept track of her over the years. She is young, but she is talented and ambitious and is still spreading love all around her. She also has a double degree in hospital and business administration as well as about to have a medical degree, so this bequest is not entirely sentimental. I'm convinced that she will figure out how to use the money and the influence it brings in a way that will enhance the lives of everyone she touches.

"Human nature being what it is, a few people in the company may resent her at first, but I hope she will soon win them over. I am adding a clause to the will as a safeguard for Nora and for the company stating that any major changes she might suggest will not be binding for the first year, unless they are unanimously agreed to by the board. This will give her time to understand the business and for the company officers to get to know and trust her. Mr. John O'Malley and Mr. Duncan Lloyd will help her all along the way.

"Nora is engaged to be married to a young man who appears to be an ideal match for her. Together, they may find innovative ways to change and increase what Em and I started. I've been thinking about expanding Duffy Medical in America, and Nora may help with that.

"I don't think Nora has been aware that I've been asking her questions for some time now as to how she feels about Duffy Medical, and now I'm more convinced than ever that she will love it as much as I always have. She's told me for years that she loves me, and I believe that to be the case. Love is the key in life and in business, and I'm sure that my legacy will be safe with Nora Eileen Duffy since I consider her to be the daughter I never had.

"I know Emily would approve, and that's all that really matters to me. Years ago, we started our medical supplies business as a way to help people everywhere, and Nora will keep that going.

"I thank God for my long life, and I thank everyone here again for all you have done for me. I ask Jesus, Mary, and Joseph to bless Nora as she deserves and to guide her coming decisions.

"With my love and best wishes to all,
"Cyrus J. Duffy

"P.S. I want a modern funeral, none of those old customs of covering up mirrors and stopping clocks at the minute of death, and especially no keening. If some of the boys want to have a Guinness or two, that's fine, but no staying up all night with the deceased. Send my body to Mr. Dowling in the village so he can do what he does before returning me for the wake and mass. Have the reading of the will one day and a few hours for a wake the next, followed by a mass, and then plant me next to Emily. If you don't follow these wishes, expect me to haunt you."

Mr. Lloyd stopped for a moment and then said, "The will is dated 15 May, 2018, and has been signed by two witnesses—Mrs. Alice O'Hara, the cook, and Mr. Tim Taylor, the stable director."

Friday, September 14
Sneem, 3:00 p.m., GMT

The crowd sat stunned for a few minutes while the impact of the testamentary gifts from Cyrus Duffy sank into everyone. A buzz of excited conversation soon filled the room.

Aunt Lavinia embraced Nora, said that she knew what was in the will, and assured her she was thrilled by it. Nora and her parents hugged each other but had puzzled looks on their faces. They found it hard to believe that Uncle Cyrus had left them so much when it seemed like they'd done so little for him. Nora was thinking that she wasn't even sure she wanted it. It sounded like it would require a lot more time and energy than she could give to it. She didn't need so much money since she already had everything she wanted.

And how much would the IRS and the Irish tax system want out of "billions?" And she could just imagine that every person she ever knew would now want to become her friend and ask for money. She always did have a hard time saying no to people in need, so how would she handle that? And she was thinking of the passage in Matthew: "It's easier for a camel to go through the eye of a needle than for a rich man (or, presumably, woman) to enter the kingdom of God." If the person who'd been trying to kill her wanted to have Uncle Cy's money, maybe he'd try even harder now.

Kitty Lloyd and Sean Duffy smiled broadly at Nora and said they too knew what was in the will, and they were certainly glad that she and her parents had decided to come. "We're not sure what we would have done if you'd said no," they declared, "since we were told in no uncertain terms that Uncle Cyrus wanted your inheritance to be a surprise."

Mr. O'Malley announced that they were free to do whatever they wished now but that they should return for a full dinner served in the dining room at 8:00 p.m. "Then I suggest everyone get a good night's sleep before the funeral tomorrow. You'll be receiving a formal letter before you leave here, outlining the provisions of the will and when you can expect to receive your inheritance. If anyone has questions about the will, please see me or Duncan. Miss Nora, would you kindly meet with Duncan and me in about fifteen minutes so we can discuss things in more detail?"

Nora agreed that she would, and then she went upstairs to change her clothes. She was still so astonished by the contents of the will. She had to go for a short run while she tried to process it. She put on her comfortable gray jogging suit and replaced her black patent heels with her favorite pair of pink Skechers.

The first thing she had to do was call Tommy and tell him about this incredible turn of events. She rehearsed in her mind for a minute what she would tell him. "We're rich. We're really, really rich. We'd never have to work again if we didn't want to." What actually occurred when she heard his voice was to break down in tears.

"Bitsy, what in the world is the matter?"

"Oh, Tommy, the most wonderful and most awful thing has just happened," Nora cried out. She gradually recovered some of her composure and relayed what she'd just heard about inheriting billions of dollars and how scary the whole thing was.

At first, Tommy thought she was joking, but when he heard the tears in her voice, he realized this was actually the case and he became serious and empathetic. "Bits, darling, you know what you are always telling me. Perspectives and expectations are everything. We'll figure it out together. Just think of all the good we could do with that much money. It won't change anything between us, and we know enough smart people to get us through this. I know I wouldn't be running off and buying a Lamborghini—it would be much too impractical on the streets of Chicago—and I can't see you doing anything silly, so we'll be fine. I've been wanting to get out of this conference for two days now. I'll get the first plane to Shannon and I'll be there with you as soon as I can. I love you so very much, you poor little rich girl!"

That made Nora laugh, and she felt better right away after their conversation. Of course, Tommy was right as he usually was. She was so glad that he was coming to be with her. She really needed him. She quickly skipped down the stairs so she could run for a few minutes before her meeting with John and Duncan. She realized for the first time that this gorgeous filigree staircase was going to be hers. It was an exciting but sobering thought.

As soon as she began to run, she realized that she'd already had a bunch of ideas for using the billions she was supposed to get. Ever since she'd been a little girl, a thought placed in her mind seemed to fast-forward to limitless possibilities.

She remembered seeing a PBS special about an English mansion that helped to support itself by having tenant farmers produce many products that were sold in a store on the property. The English farmers received a good share of the profits, and the mansion received the rest. People in the surrounding towns loved to come and shop. Duffy Hall could do all that and add peat turves, lavender bunches, and Irish crosses made from the reeds that grew next to the lake as well as greeting cards and calendars with picturesque scenes of the castle and grounds. They had the talented and experienced farmers and business people to make such a thing possible. She could just imagine the kind of creative brochures her talented sisters would make for such a venture. She was sure it would be huge success. One questionable thing was that the visitors also got to tour the English castle. She wasn't too sure about that part yet for Duffy Hall.

They could also add another building that could serve as a medical research and technology center and perhaps a theater and music center. It would be best if this additional building could be connected to the hall by some kind of passageway. They could make a movie about the castle and Cyrus, Emily, and Lavinia.

Wow! she thought. *For not wanting the money, I've certainly found a way that I could spend a lot of millions very quickly. These things might be possible. We'll have to see.*

She ran down as far as Aunt Emily's tombstone and then turned around to get a view of the hall from there. It was a larger building than she remembered from this perspective, and with a few renovations, it would indeed look like a castle from a fairy-tale. Maybe they could add a drawbridge and a moat to emphasize the castle connection but populate the surrounding water with swans rather than alligators. The castle's whitewashed stones and the silver leprechaun were glinting in the sun. She thought the happy little man in the sculpture had been keeping good watch over her "pot o' gold." The two giant stones outside the front porch looked immense with their Celtic knot circles carved on them, like the stones found at the ancient burial site of Newgrange on the River Boyne that dated to 3200 BC, predating even the Pyramids.

She was impressed by the six gigantic tents that had been set up for the funeral the next day. Duncan had told her that one was for the priests and musicians, and the other five held 500 people each. They were expecting many important personages to attend from Ireland, the US, the UK, Canada, Australia, India, and other countries as well as townspeople. One never knew what kind of weather would show up in Sneem, and their property was the biggest place to have the funeral; thus the tents. Father Keane from the village agreed that it would be the most fitting plan.

Nora's head was hurting a bit, and she'd forgotten to take her pain pill, so she slowly jogged back. As she was about to go up the steps, she thought she saw a man watching her from the corner of the building. Since her subway incident, she was always on the lookout now for anything that appeared out of the ordinary; but he did not approach her, so she kept going.

She savored the experience of jogging up the twenty-eight steps to the massive front doors embossed with the beautiful Celtic carvings. Messrs. O'Malley and Lloyd met her and ushered her into a small office outside of the dining hall. They were joined by a small group of others wearing Duffy Hall badges. "Nora, first I'd like to introduce you to Mr. John Herlihy who is our head of security. He will arrange to have you accompanied most of the time by his officers in a similar way that your Secret Service protects your president.

Don't be surprised if you see a man following you. They know the house and grounds well."

Ah, thought Nora, *that explains the man who was watching me.*

"The lovely twins are Kitty Condon and her sister, Maryann. They will be your secretaries and personal helpers. You'll see that they are identical, so to help us distinguish between them, they wear different-colored suits, although they could fool me if they wanted to. They also served your Uncle Cyrus in this capacity and are experts in knowing the things you'll need in your new role. They'll tell you about the people you'll be expected to meet, make travel arrangements, and explain the various meetings you might be expected to attend. John Cahill will be your chauffeur when Old Tim is otherwise occupied. Mrs. O'Hara is our talented cook, and she will work with you to make the healthy kind of food I hear you like. You've met Dr. McGarry last night. He will be your personal physician whenever you are in Ireland."

Nora shook hands with everyone and assured Kitty and Maryann that she was very experienced in dealing with identical twins and was sure they'd get along fine. Nora noticed that Maryann had more freckles on her cheeks, and Kitty's dark hair was curlier, features which she could use to distinguish them. The group exchanged a few pleasantries. Then Duncan thanked them all and said they would see them later at dinner.

Duncan asked Nora to sit down and explained why they wanted to meet with her. "Nora, I'm sure you are still reeling a bit from the announcements in Cyrus' will. I helped him to make those arrangements, and he had such a look of happiness when they were done. I only wish that he could be here to enjoy his surprise."

John continued, "You have been promised that you'll receive a lot of money, but that will not take place for a few weeks while we complete an audit of all the company finances. In the meantime, we want you to have some money in advance. If you'll give me your bank account information, we'll deposit $50,000 in your account today. This envelope contains US$5,000 to help tide you over on the trip home. I'll put it into the safe in this office for now.

"I'll ask you to sign this agreement saying that you agree to become the chairman of the board of Duffy Medical as of today's date. You'll have no duties yet, other than to read some materials we've prepared for you, which you can do when you get home. And we both want to say that we are delighted that you will be serving in this role."

Nora signed the agreement, although her hands were trembling a bit. John and Duncan witnessed her signature. "I estimate that the remaining money should be available to you in about three weeks. We can help you to make any financial arrangements you'd like. We'll also help you with understanding the tax regulations for both countries—the Irish Tax and Customs and your Internal Revenue Service."

Nora retrieved her checkbook from her purse and gave her bank information to Duncan. "This is all such a mystifying turn of events," said Nora. "I'll definitely be needing your assistance. Money has never meant much to me. I live in the house of a well-off man, so I guess that's easy for me to say. When there's a time that I can pay my bills, save a bit, go out to restaurants a few times, and make a few charitable donations, I think of that as a very successful month. I occasionally buy a few clothes and a pair of shoes, but most days, I live in my hospital whites. Our family has been influenced by our great-grandparents who remembered how miserable it was during the Depression and encouraged us to be as frugal as possible.

"I can't imagine having so much money that I wouldn't have to worry about paying bills and tuition. That alone would be wonderful. Tommy and I and our siblings have a Ceili band, and our instruments are old. It would be great to replace some of them. We have an old upright piano in our living room that now has a few keys that stick. We've had a lot of fun with it, but it would be brilliant to see a Steinway grand in that corner. And maybe we can have steak at our wedding rather than just chicken. I suppose I'd like to have a charitable foundation like I hear about on our PBS TV stations. It all seems too good to be true, and I've always been suspicious when that's the case."

Duncan laughed and assured Nora that it was all very true and very safe.

Nora's face took on a more serious look as she explained, "My views on having a lot of money are also very much influenced by my profession. I regularly deal with children's brain tumors. No amount of money can save some of these babies' lives, so money isn't everything. The wealth I value most is knowing that my family and friends are healthy. I guess I'll just go along day by day while the enormity of Cyrus' bequest becomes more real to me."

John said, "That's all for now. Go and talk this over with your parents, and then we'll see you at dinner."

"I'm going to go for a run," said Nora. "It's such a beautiful afternoon, and I'd like to have another look at the lake where I first met Uncle Cyrus and bring some flowers to put on Aunt Em's grave. Thanks for all your help."

Kitty said she would get her some flowers, and Johnny Moreland introduced himself as her security man for the afternoon and explained that he would follow her around the grounds but at a distance in a golf cart.

Before she did anything else, Nora stopped in Uncle Cyrus' office and sadly looked at his maroon chair where she'd often found him. She would make sure that the entire office was saved, just as it was. She also noticed the painting on the wall that she'd drawn as a five-year-old of him and his wolfhound, Donal. Nora silently thanked Uncle Cy for his great gift to her, and she asked him for his help in the future.

Then she snuck upstairs to the minstrel's gallery above the dining hall. She'd been longing to try her hand at playing the beautiful harp that seemed to be calling her name. She ran up the steps and entered the gallery, sat down on the waiting chair, and the beautifully carved full-sized harp fell comfortably into her hands. She thought that it would probably be dusty, but some conscientious person had been keeping it not only cleaned but tuned. She wondered how many other people had played this harp or other instruments up here, and she pretended she was entertaining at a medieval gathering. She began playing softly at first and then increased the volume as she got into playing and singing one of her spirited childhood favorites, "The Irish Rover." She remembered her mom playing and singing that for them.

The kitchen staff had heard Nora playing and all clapped when she was finished and said it was so good to hear the harp being played, and they had enjoyed her beautiful voice. Nora acknowledged them with a happy grin, ran back down the stairs, and out the front door.

Friday, September 14
Sneem, 3:30 p.m., GMT

Nora skipped down the front stairs and was about to start running when she saw a young woman that she didn't recognize standing underneath one of the massive oak trees near the entrance of the hall. The woman came toward her indicating that she wanted to talk to her. Johnny Moreland quickly came up behind her and asked her what she was doing here.

"I'd like to talk to Miss Nora Duffy," she said. "Someone from this location just sent a message to the Associated Press saying that the bulk of Cyrus Duffy's estate has been left to his American niece. Is that true?"

"We're not talking to reporters today," said Johnny, indicating that she should leave.

"That's all right," said Nora. "I'll talk to her. What's your name, Miss?"

"I'm Ann O'Shea from the *Ennis Tribune*," she responded.

Nora admired her midnight blue outfit with the tangerine trim and noticed that her stylish blue high heels matched the color of her suit. Nora liked her manner and her shoes and decided to talk to Ann.

Liam, the wolfhound, was keeping a close watch on the young woman and was quietly growling at her. "As long as you don't make any sudden moves toward me, the dog should be fine," instructed Nora, "but you wouldn't want him to bite you. He's usually gentle, but his teeth are very sharp.

"I'm surprised that you were able to get this far onto the estate. Here's the deal," said Nora. "Duffy Medical has a Communications Director who will be putting out an official press release, and I'm not at liberty to tell you anything more yet. I can tell you that Uncle Cyrus was generous to me and my parents. I'm going to ask you to leave now before the Garda discover you. Please give me a business card. If I can, I'll make sure that you are one of the first to receive the press release. As you can imagine, this is a time of mourning for all of us. We loved Uncle Cyrus very much." Nora made sure that Johnny guided Ann to the exit gate.

Great, Nora thought and shook her head. *Now we have someone here leaking information to the press already. So easy to do when everyone has a cell phone—or mobile phone as they would say here—but who would do that? I was hoping we'd be able to wait until after the funeral to have to deal with the details of Cy's will. If the news is on the AP, the media will be salivating to find out more any minute.*

Nora turned to Johnny and told him that she was going to visit the chapel and asked him to keep an eye on Liam.

Cyrus and Emily had built the chapel shortly after they moved to the hall. It was built of the same stones as the hall and looked much older than it was. They also added an adjacent stone tower. In former days, tall stone towers were built all over Ireland as a place of protection in case of a military siege. The Duffy version contained a large telescope at the top to accommodate Uncle Cyrus' love of astronomy and stargazing. Nora shared his interest and hoped to spend some time up there before she had to go home.

The chapel was small and had seats for about 200 people. It was decorated in the old style with lots of wood and stucco, and it had gorgeous stained-glass windows in the dark hues that Nora loved. The front of the beautiful alabaster altar was decorated with carvings of many Irish saints, and the crucifix was in the traditional style, which Nora was glad to see. The chapel was named after St. Patrick and St. Brigid, and there were two tall windows honoring each of those saints to the right and left of a magnificent round rose window on the back wall. Emily had made sure that the chapel had a small pipe organ, and many silver pipes stood across the wall in back of the altar. Nora vowed that she'd experiment with playing that beautiful instrument soon.

Nora sat down in one of the pews and talked to the man on the cross. Theirs had been a sketchy relationship for the last few years. Ever since she was a child, her mind had asked too many "why" questions. She stopped believing in Santa very early since the feat of visiting every home on the planet—let alone getting through their chimneys—in one night was beyond scientific plausibility. When she first heard about Adam and Eve, she couldn't help asking why Eve was always blamed for giving the famed apple to Adam. *Typical male behavior*, she thought when she got older. He wanted the apple, especially since it had the added appeal of being forbidden, but when he got caught eating the fruit of the one tree he was warned to stay away from, his first thought was to throw Eve under the bus. Women had been getting the short end of the stick ever since. Nora generally liked most men, but some of them still exhibited the same tendency to avoid responsibilities for their actions as Adam had.

A few years ago, she had stayed overnight at her Aunt Honey's who asked if she needed help with her homework. When she told her about her questions as to why we are put on this earth, Honey told her that she didn't much care about why we are here, the figuring out of which she saw as a big waste of time. "All I know is that I am here and I'm determined to make the most of the time I have on this earth for me and those I love, like you."

Aunt Honey hadn't gone to college, but Nora thought that she was very wise.

"So Lord, enough of these old philosophical questions I've been bugging you about for years, but I feel so sad today since I just received a text saying that Leon McClay, four-years-old, died of bone cancer last night. We tried so hard to keep him alive, but he just couldn't keep up anymore. That is a *big* why. There's so much sadness in the world as well as so much happiness. Does the happy outweigh the sad? Sometimes I wonder. Please hold this poor baby in your arms and do the same for his mom, Evelyn. I tell myself that I can deal with the deaths of these children, but when I get home, there will always be more and more kids like Leon. Give me the strength to deal with that.

"I hope you're taking good care of Uncle Cyrus. He tried to be tough, but he was so sentimental underneath. I hope he wasn't scared when he died. Please help Aunt Vinnie. She's going to miss him so much and she seems so alone. What am I supposed to do about all this money they want to give me? I guess I could turn it down, but Uncle Cy seemed so intent on giving it to me, I would feel disloyal to him if I did. What would you like me to do with it? It scares me just thinking about it, so please show me the best way to deal with it.

"And what can you do about the person who's trying to kill me? I really have no idea why it's happening and I don't want anybody else in my family to get hurt because of me. Thanks for bringing Tommy here early. I really appreciate it. Help all my brothers and sisters and everyone in my family. Well, I told you last week that I didn't know what it meant to pray, but I guess I've given you a laundry list today. I do love you and thank you for this day and every day of my life, and I ask your blessings on all the people I've promised to pray for. And please let us have good weather tomorrow for Uncle Cy's funeral. And let peace begin with me."

She could almost hear her mother saying, "That's enough now, Nora, *a stor*."

With that, Nora genuflected to the tabernacle, made the sign of the cross with the holy water sitting in the angel statue's hands, and left to continue her run. She indicated to Johnny that he could let Liam go so he could join her for the run down to Aunt Emily's tombstone. She could tell that Liam felt happy today, and Nora had to lengthen her stride to keep up with him.

Friday, September 14
Sneem, 4:00 p.m., GMT

Nora could tell that the news about her inheritance must have gotten out since she suddenly heard her phone ringing constantly. She recognized a few of the callers—Aunt Janet from California, cousin Larry from Ohio, Marina from Notre Dame, and so many others. She let the calls all go into voice mail and decided to try to call them back later. What a pain in the neck this was going to be! She was going to need more time to decide what to say to these people. Aunt Janet was such a sweetheart, and she was sure that she'd ask her to come out to Sonoma to see her now that she was going to have all this money.

She did stop to answer a call from Lieutenant Braxton. He told her that the Chicago PD had used the pictures she'd sent to construct a "storyboard" about her case, but so far, they didn't have much new information. He told her that he'd heard the news about her inheritance and was happy for her, but he suspected that she would find it difficult to deal with. He said that Laura Belsky sent her best wishes to her and her family.

Lieutenant Braxton did not tell her about the Popovs or Nick; he thought she had enough to think about now. He hoped he'd be able to give her more information when they returned home.

Nora gave Liam a treat, and they ran down the hill toward Aunt Em's tomb about two blocks away. It was a beautiful afternoon, but gray clouds were trying to overwhelm the puffy white ones, and there was a hint of rain in the air. Since Ireland was an island and Kerry was so close to the ocean, not too many days were completely rain free.

When she got to the tombstone, she looked closely at the picture of Emily as a young woman with a look of wonder and determination on her face and a circlet of white roses on her wavy brown hair. She was so very beautiful. No wonder Uncle Cyrus had been so lonely without her for these many years. *I wonder what she would think of Duffy Medical today and her beloved Cy's plans*, mused Nora.

Nora placed the bouquet of white roses just underneath the inscriptions on Emily's tombstone that had been pounded into the mauve granite:

> Beloved Wife and Partner
> Emily Mary Butler Duffy
> 1935–1980
> Love You Forever
> Cyrus John Duffy
>
> Golden lads and girls all must,
> as chimney-sweepers,
> Come to dust

Nora once again admired the ubiquitous Shakespeare who had something to say about almost everything. Those words from *Cymbeline* reminded us that no matter how golden our days appeared to be, eventually we all came to an end, regardless of our state in life. She prayed that Emily and Cyrus were reunited now and would be together for eternity.

Nora had planned to run in a circle around the hall, but she decided to stop at the stables to see Finnbar and the bog ponies. She'd had a few thoughts about how to tackle the Finn problem. Many horses loved music, so as she entered the stable, she began singing "Danny Boy." Sometimes horses also formed a bond with dogs, so she thought that bringing Liam along might help her to break the ice.

She nodded to Tim Taylor, the stable director, and passed by the stalls of Star, Aunt Vinnie's white horse with the black star on her head, and the horses that belonged to the staff. She stopped outside Finn's stall for a minute until she knew that he had seen her. Then she walked right by, still singing, until she got to the stall with the four bog ponies.

She knew their names were Billy, Milly, Paddy, and Tilly, but she didn't know which name matched each pony. She hadn't seen them since last summer, but they were still the very small size they were. She had grabbed some apples as she came in and held them out to the cream-colored ponies who gobbled them up quickly. She was glad that Mr. Taylor was just outside, because they could become aggressive if they didn't get what they wanted. They were small, but so was she.

They were so cute that most people didn't realize they were also very useful, a conundrum that Nora had experienced in her own life. A larger horse would get mired down in the squishy soil of the bog ponds on the edge of the estate, but these little ponies' small size and broad feet were ideal for the task of gathering peat. Peat was composed of decayed vegetation that was not yet coal, and the men dug it out of the earth in long rectangular slices with special tools for the job. After a few days of drying, the workers placed the sliced peat into the holders that lay over the ponies' backs and brought it back to the keeping rooms to dry.

The many fireplaces of Duffy Hall usually burned dried peat or turves, and that's why the hall had that distinctive smell that couldn't be duplicated with a wood fire. There was also a market for international customers who longed for the smell of home and bought packets of peat for their own fireplaces.

She then turned back to Finn's stall and admired this magnificent but very large animal who towered over her. *He must be about eighteen hands*, thought Nora. Uncle Cyrus had explained to her one time that the hand measurement equated to four inches each and was taken from the base of the horse's hoof to a point on his "withers" or back just behind his mane. That meant that Finnbar would be at the top of the chart for height, imposing for any rider, but very difficult for someone as short as Nora. The magnificent horse didn't appear to have a strand of white hair anywhere on his ebony black coat. He had been thrashing about in his stall and snorting impressively while she was busy with the ponies.

Nora pretended not to notice him at first, kept singing, and held an apple out for him while she stood perfectly still. She thought that Finn had beautiful eyes, although he was trying to send her a message that wasn't very positive now.

She waited until they were both looking into each other's eyes, and then she said, "Finnbar, we're going to be great friends, but I'll give you more time to get to know me."

Finn wanted her to know he was still upset by her presence, and he began kicking the door of his stall.

"Okay, boy, I'll try this another time," she said. "I don't want you to get hurt while you're trying to prove to me how fierce you are. I know you miss your master, and so do I."

Liam had been barking and trying to get Finn's attention, but the huge horse had paid no attention to him. Nora dropped the apple onto Finn's hay, gave an apple to Star and the other two horses, and headed out to her next stop.

Friday, September 14
London, 4:00 p.m., GMT

Tommy would have liked to have seen more of London, a city he loved, especially the Parliament buildings and the Churchill War Rooms, but he was anxious to leave and get to Nora. He called Aer Lingus and was able to get a seat on the next plane to Shannon Airport. He called Nora with the details, and she said that she would arrange to have John Cahill pick him up at the airport.

Tom and Nora had always loved classic movies, including some of the original Disney movies. *Pinocchio* had always been one of their favorites, and Tom had seen a clock shop on the next street that reminded him of Geppetto's enchanting shop with the many clocks and music boxes all keeping time and dinging each one's particular mechanical specialty. He had time before his flight, so he stopped at the shop to look around at their fascinating merchandise. He wanted to get something for Nora to cheer her up.

Most of their clocks were the traditional type of carved dark wood with impressively carved birds and beasts. Tom told the owner that he would like to buy something special for his fiancée but in a more modern style. The owner led him to another room containing clocks that not only had a more modern appearance but also had chimes and tunes that were technology driven.

Tom looked over the huge selection and zeroed in on a medium-sized clock that looked like a charming English countryside home with flowers, trees, and a boy and girl sitting at a table in the forefront with a little brown dog at their feet. An English sparrow popped out every fifteen minutes, and his appearance also coincided with the various musical phrases from "Greensleeves" that played at fifteen-minute intervals. The owner explained that the volume of the music could be regulated and even turned off, if desired. Tom pictured Nora's happy smile when she saw the clock, and he could imagine them dancing to the music in their kitchen to be. He complimented the owner on his marvelous shop and told him that he would definitely take the clock.

He also purchased an attractive pocket watch and chain for Dr. Duffy that had modern innards and a similar one for his dad that required old-fashioned winding. He got two crystal wristwatches, one for his mom and one for Mrs. Duffy. He also bought attractive phone cases for all of his siblings and Nora's. *There. Family Christmas shopping done!* He asked the owner to ship it all to his house in Chicago, and then he headed out to Heathrow Airport. He was fortunate to get a cab right away, and the driver typically complained about the infernal traffic and the infernal government, common complaints among cab drivers everywhere.

Heathrow was one of the busiest airports anywhere, and it was awesome to see the paint colors and decorations on planes from all over the world. It was also incredibly crowded. They found the Aer Lingus entrance, and Tommy entered the airport and looked forward to the short flight to Shannon. Soon he would be with his Bitsy, and they could begin to plan their future all over again after these new developments. He thought that Bits had been exaggerating to say that she was scared about having lots of money, but the more he thought about it, he could see that the siren song of great wealth could completely skew one's perspective on what's important in life. He doubted that would happen to them, but it would be good to be aware of possible unwise temptations.

When he boarded the plane, he sat next to an attractive older woman who introduced herself as Dr. Christine Weller who told him that she was on her way to the Cyrus Duffy funeral in Sneem. Tommy and Dr. Weller had an informative conversation about how her hospital started using implements from Duffy Medical and how much they appreciated the excellence of the instruments and Duffy's prompt service.

Tommy offered to drive Dr. Christine to Sneem once they arrived at Shannon. John Cahill met them with a sign saying "Duffy Hall Guests" and maneuvered his Volvo on the crowded roads until they neared Sneem. They drove Dr. Weller to the Sneem Hotel where she had a reservation and made sure she got to the front desk. Tommy said he would look forward to seeing her tomorrow at the funeral, and then they were off to Duffy Hall.

John sensed that Tommy was anxious to arrive at the hall, so he negotiated the streets of Sneem and the drive to Duffy Hall as quickly as he could. Tommy had only been at the hall once before, and he admired it from a distance, but rain clouds were threatening so the view was not the best. He didn't care as long as he could be with his Bitsy. He couldn't wait to see the expression on her face when she realized that he had arrived sooner than expected.

Friday, September 14
Sneem, 4:30 p.m. GMT

Nora asked Johnny to keep a good hold on Liam and she then jogged over to the bench by the lake where she had first talked to Uncle Cyrus as a child. She walked up the incline and sat down on the beautifully carved bench Uncle Cy had placed there. He'd even thought to include a large stone at the bottom of the bench where she could rest her feet. She could see all the way across the lake to the forest of massive oak trees and a large clump of weeping willows.

Today, a trio of red deer were enjoying the sphagnum moss that grew along the lake's banks. Ducks and geese aplenty were splashing up and down, searching for something good to eat, and two imperial-looking white swans were serenely gliding back and forth between lily pads. Flocks of a wide variety of birds were flying and chittering away nearby. She saw many bubbles in the lake and determined that she would go fishing for lake trout as soon as she could. She was sure that Mrs. O'Hara would do something wonderful with them.

A light rain started to fall, and Nora put up her hood and zipped up her Patagonia insulated jacket, which she was so glad she'd brought along. The wind had whipped up, and she was chilly. Memories came flooding back of that day when she first gave Cyrus a kiss and asked him to come and visit them in Chicago. She asked God again to take good care of Cyrus. *What a beautiful spot this is,* she thought, *and it smells so good too with all the flowering plants. Whenever I'm at Duffy Hall, this is where I'll come when I need to think.*

She could hear Liam barking for her, but Johnny was keeping a tight hold on his leash. Suddenly, Liam could stand it no more, broke free, and came bounding toward her at the bottom of the incline. Something like whispering in her ears told Nora to lean down quickly to pet Liam's head, which was near her feet. She also thought she smelled honeysuckle, which was strange since she hadn't noticed any growing nearby (Bridie the ghost was whispering frantically and trying hard to emit honeysuckle perfume).

At the same time, Nora smelled gunpowder from a rifle shot and felt a sharp pain in her scalp. A second shot hit her in the right arm just above her elbow. Blood pumped furiously out of the scalp wound and clouded her eyes. "Ow," Nora screamed and dropped to the ground at first. Then she jumped up and hid behind the oak tree behind her. "Not again," she cried in anguish. "Who could be doing this and why?"

She heard Johnny's shrill whistle and cry for help to his phone. Johnny and his partner, Sean, came running to where Nora was hiding and tried to rescue her, but Liam was wildly barking at them and wouldn't let them get close to her. Johnny and Sean were finally able to convince Liam that they were trying to help her and they half-dragged Nora to the golf cart to get her back to the hall. Johnny drove the cart while Sean wiped up some of the blood that was dripping down Nora's cheek. He called the local Garda and urged them to come to the hall immediately.

Chief Herlihy came running down the steps of Duffy Hall to meet them. Michael and Eileen Duffy were alerted that Nora had been hurt, and they rushed out the front door with his medical bag.

Pandemonium reigned for a while as everyone figured out what to do. Dr. Duffy and Eileen looked Nora over, and Johnny and Sean helped to get her inside the hall to a small room that Dr. McGarry used as his surgery. They had to cut off her beautiful silver jacket to see where she'd been hit, the second time in a week that one of her favorite garments was headed to the trash bin. They began to clean up the wounds and had to cut off a large patch of beautiful red curls on the crown of her head.

The wail of sirens and flash of blue lights told them that many cars of the Garda had arrived. Nora's mom told her through her tears that she brought along a cute hat that she could use to cover the wound on her head. "This is getting very dangerous and repetitive," cried Eileen. It began to sink into them that the subway incident was no accident and that someone had to be deliberately trying to kill Nora.

Chief Herlihy strode into the surgery and wanted to know if Nora had any clues as to where the gunfire came from. She explained that she thought that it came from the patch of willow trees on the far right side of the lake. Chief Herlihy talked to Chief Brennan of the Garda and sent out a platoon of Gardai to search the area.

The news about Nora being hurt swept through the hall quickly, and a large group of people all waited outside the surgery until Dr. Duffy had completed his ministrations. Lavinia pulled out her rosary beads and tearfully asked the Blessed Mother to intercede for her darling Nora. Everyone prayed that Nora had not been seriously hurt. Also waiting for her were Liam, the wolfhound, and Bran, the Irish Setter, and they kept up a steady racket of barking and whining.

Dr. Duffy explained to the group that he had cleaned up the wounds and put eighteen stitches in Nora's scalp and eight in her arm. He also gave her a shot for pain. He explained that several things had occurred to prevent the bullets from being deadly. Nora had tightened her thick jacket and hood, which had helped just a little to protect her scalp, and she told him that something had warned her to put her head down to pet the dog and she had twisted her body to the left. The bullets had only grazed her scalp and her arm, but the wounds and the stitches would still be painful.

"I'm going to let Nora rest for a while, and then she said she still wanted to attend the dinner tonight. Johnny, please let the dogs get to Nora before they drive us all crazy with that barking."

Nora snuggled with the dogs as they ran over to her, but they all had trouble settling down. Nora prayed that Tommy would get here soon. She also wondered if it had been the Duffy Hall ghost who had warned her to put her head down. If so, she muttered a thank you to her.

28

Friday, September 14
Sneem, 5:30 p.m., GMT

D r. Duffy pushed Nora in the wheelchair into a small room near the front entrance of the hall. It was dark in there, and he hoped that Nora could rest for a few hours before they had to go into dinner. Chief Herlihy assured them that he would have two officers stand guard outside the room. Liam put his head on Nora's lap, and after a while, the pain shot took effect, and she dozed off to sleep.

Shortly before 7:30 p.m., Dr. Duffy and Eileen pushed Nora into the dining room in her wheelchair. Nora asked Johnny to hang onto Liam at the back of the room. She arrived in her running outfit and bandages. A crowd of about thirty people sat around a highly polished mahogany table. Mr. O'Malley introduced Nora and her mother and father. Nora thanked everyone from the Duffy Hall board for the warm welcome and said that she would like to say a few words to them before the dinner.

"Hello, everyone. As Uncle Cyrus would say, God bless all here! We met briefly yesterday during the reading of the will, but that was before Uncle Cy's surprise announcement. I wanted to say a few words to you before the dinner tonight and the funeral tomorrow since I imagine that you were probably very surprised at Uncle Cy naming me as Chair of the board and leaving me much of his estate. I assure you that I was also very much surprised.

"I apologize for my informal apparel. This is my favorite old jogging outfit. I know there's some blood on the front, and Dad had to cut off one of the sleeves to treat my arm. I bought a new dress for this occasion, but I didn't want to get blood on it and didn't want to keep you waiting for dinner, so I'm just going to stay as I am tonight.

"I am feeling a bit under the weather at the moment since I was shot at several times with a high-powered rifle a few hours ago. I owe my life to this very lovely wolfhound, Liam. I had jogged down the green earlier to place flowers on Aunt Emily's tombstone, and then I decided to sit on the bench where I first talked to Uncle Cyrus many years ago, next to the lake. I recall sitting up rather straight while I was saying a prayer for him, but Liam came bounding up to the slope, so I put my head down to tousle his ears. If I hadn't done that, you'd be seeing me alongside Uncle Cyrus.

"My dad is a surgeon, and he put many stitches in my scalp and more in my arm. He tells me that the wounds are grazes and aren't serious, but frankly, they hurt like heck. We'll be going home tomorrow since Dad wants to have more X-rays taken to make sure that my concussion from last week was not made worse.

"Uncle Cyrus was my great uncle—my father's uncle. My parents and I came here to pay our respects to Uncle Cyrus and to offer our condolences to Aunt Lavinia and to you who knew him much better than we do.

"I am in my last months of medical school at Loyola University in Chicago and I'm about to become a pediatric oncology surgeon, which means I'll be treating very young children with brain tumors. I have lived in Chicago all my life, except for the time when I was away at Notre Dame University in South Bend, Indiana. I have a degree in business and a master's degree in hospital administration. I have nine siblings: five sisters and four brothers. I'm the oldest, then two brothers, three sisters, two more brothers, and two more sisters.

"I am engaged to be married to Tom Barry, the son of a well-known pub owner in Chicago. His parents are PJ Barry and his wife, Cathy. They run a happy place called Barry's Pub on the north side of Chicago and they have eight children. Tommy wanted to be here today, but he's a lawyer for an international legal firm and is currently in London for a major meeting. He sends his condolences and promises to come with me for the next meeting. We plan to be married on next St. Patrick's Day in Chicago and we had planned to spend some time with Uncle Cyrus for our honeymoon.

"It appears now that last week's incident in the subway was not accidental. It's very disheartening to realize that someone is trying to kill me. I'm assuming it has something to do with Uncle Cyrus' bequest to me, although I don't know that for sure. Perhaps someone doesn't want me to have this money. The Garda is currently looking for clues as to where the person was when he was aiming at me. It feels rather like I've wandered into a James Bond novel. If any of you has any information that you think would be helpful, I'd ask you to share it with our head of security, Chief Herlihy.

"Some of you might think that two attempts on my life might make me frightened enough to just cry and run away. Don't forget that I'm from Chicago where we're tough, and I'll keep fighting until we find out who is doing this. I have the good example of Uncle Cy and generations of stouthearted Cork and Kerry men and women to inspire me. I don't know why this is happening, but I'm not about to hide out. I hope I can count on your support."

Nora continued, "One of your great leaders, Michael Collins, before he was killed, said that even though he was unable to achieve the unity of all thirty-two of the Irish counties, he viewed the twenty-six and six as 'the freedom to achieve freedom.' That's how I feel about this opportunity that Uncle Cyrus has given me.

"I have no suggestions for the business side of Duffy Enterprises, since I hardly know much about it yet. Besides, Uncle Cyrus wisely stated that nothing I suggest now will be legally binding for at least a year, giving me a learning curve time and you an opportunity to get used to me.

"I believe you all have a copy of the will he signed leaving much of his estate to me. I want to assure you that the first I heard about Uncle Cyrus making me his heir was today. I used to talk to him by phone almost every Sunday, and he never mentioned anything about it. I didn't know anything about his planning to commit suicide years ago or any of the rest of it. I will accept his bequest because I loved him and thought he was one of the smartest people I've ever known, so he must have had good reasons, but I'm going to need help from all of you.

"I do have a few suggestions that I hope you will take into consideration for the future as to renovations that appear to be needed for the house and grounds, but I'll put all of that into an e-mail that I'll be sending out to all of you.

"I want to assure you that I am a proud American, but I have dual citizenship and also love Ireland. I would like to see Duffy Medical become more global, a goal which I understand Uncle Cyrus shared. It seems to me that it would be good to have Duffy Medical become an openly traded company on the New York Stock Exchange and to open an office in Chicago. My brother and several of my cousins are traders, and they would know just what to do. That seems like a good idea to me, but there could be reasons why it isn't. I would suggest a committee of your members be formed to examine this. Now, let's enjoy the wonderful meal that Mrs. O'Hara has prepared for us."

Maryann took notes of Nora's talk and assured them that she would distribute the notes in an e-mail after the funeral.

All during the time Nora was speaking, Liam never took his chin off her shoes, which comforted Nora. Liam had been Uncle Cyrus' constant companion and wouldn't leave his side when he was sick, even though the doctor kept trying to push him out in the hallway. Liam thought that the doctor was just a fat human with no fur on his head, but he now recognized Nora as his true mistress.

A huge round of applause greeted Nora as she finished speaking, although Nora thought she noticed a few people that looked rather sour.

Mrs. O'Hara and her helpers had prepared even more of a feast than they had for brunch. They could see many soups, a variety of meats like beef, turkey, ham, pork, shepherd's pie, several kinds of potatoes, vegetables, salads, cheeses, fruits, breads, beer, wine; and alcohol like Bailey's, Jameson's, scotch, brandy, and soft drinks. Nora was only able to stomach some grapes, a salad, and Barry's tea. She chuckled a bit as she noticed the absence of one alcoholic drink— Uncle Cyrus' potcheen. She would make sure that Uncle Cy's bottle and glasses from the library would be saved and protected as precious relics.

After the dinner, many of the group spoke to Nora and her parents and assured them of their concern and support. Nora's dad encouraged her to go to bed early so she'd be ready for the morning's busy schedule. Eileen assured Nora that there was an extra twin bed in their room, and she wanted her to sleep there tonight so they could keep an eye on her to make sure that she wasn't exhibiting any bad effects from her earlier concussion.

Friday, September 14
Sneem, 9:00 p.m., GMT

Aunt Lavinia asked for a few minutes of Nora's time before they retired for the night. She suggested they have tea in the garden outside her bedroom, and Johnny Moreland pushed her chair into the pretty space. Lady, Lavinia's molasses and white spaniel, stayed close to her side, and Nora petted Lady's silky head.

Nora noticed that Aunt Lavinia's purple dress and cape were made of fine Irish wool, but the muted color was a bit drab. However, her necklace had a fabulous amethyst as its centerpiece.

As they were sitting there, they admired the work of a good-sized spider and his web of considerable height and breadth. Lavinia said her pet name for the spider was Harry and that the interconnected strands he wove reminded her of the tangled and complex webs that existed within Duffy Medical.

"I wanted to talk to you about a few things before the funeral tomorrow, Nora," Lavinia began. "I know you had quite a shock today to hear that Cy had left you most of his estate, but I wanted to assure you that this was not a sudden impulse on his part. He told me several years ago that he was thinking about doing that, and I agreed with his decision. You'll figure it all out as you go along, so don't be too concerned about having a lot of money. He knew that you would find ways to use it wisely.

"Even I was a bit surprised to hear that Cy had tried to commit suicide, but then it fits with his character at the time. As a young boy,

Cy was always so intelligent and creative, and those traits continued throughout his life. But he was interested in so many things that when it came to getting things done, he tended to be a bit lazy.

"Emily was the perfect companion for him. They met at a dance in Galway, where she lived, and he was smitten with her that first night. When he got home, all he could talk about was how beautiful and sweet she was and how she had a sense of style that set her apart from other young women. She was also the perfect antidote to his lack of focus. She was a voracious reader and smart in practical ways too. When he first suggested that he'd been thinking about starting his own company, she helped him to think through each step of the process until the paperwork was signed and Duffy Medical became a reality.

"He often told me that God had given him his greatest blessing when Em came into his life. He was so very happy when they got married. They lived in Galway for a few months, but then they found this abandoned castle on a trip and began the work of restoring it enough to become livable, a work that has continued until now. Emily's dreams can be seen in every room, especially the library. When she died of cancer, it took Cy months to be able to recover enough to function, but the light had gone out of him as he explained in his will. He never fully recovered from Em's death, but when you came into his life, he had someone to work for again."

Nora told Lavinia that she had talked to Uncle Cyrus last spring, and he had shown her the library that he was so proud of.

"Did he also show you where he had his potcheen hidden?" inquired Lavinia.

Nora laughed and said that Uncle Cy had assured her that his sister wouldn't know that he had the whiskey there.

"I knew most of his secrets," Lavinia assured her. "I was his big sister and looked out for him. Cy hired many capable men to help him run his company, but he was also naïve in many ways about the people that work for him," she continued. "I know he thought he was doing a good thing to leave you all his money, but there are those on the board who are like the people who worked in the heat of the day and won't approve at all of someone coming in at the last minute to 'reap the reward of their labors.'

"I want to especially caution you about two couples on the board that could create problems for you. The tall dark-haired woman, Valerie, wife of our chief accountant, is ambitious and probably not at all happy about your bequest. I think her husband, Fred, would probably prefer to retire and run a bookstore, but she has other plans for him. Valerie's friend, the short plump blond woman, Ellen, is the wife of our Treasurer, Ben. She seems to do whatever Valerie wants her to do. Ben thinks the chairman of the board position should have gone to him since he's been here such a long time.

"They think I'm just a prissy old lady who relied on her brother for her living, but I've been watching them carefully for a long time now and believe I know them well. Perhaps they will come around, but I wouldn't count on it. John and Duncan are aware of them too, so if those two witches start to cause you trouble, rely on those two good men for help."

Aunt Lavinia continued, "I'm a Shakespeare lover and I often think of Valerie as Goneril and Ellen as Regan, two of Mr. Shakespeare's more powerful but unlikeable women who smile on the outside but compose horrible plots on the inside. I don't want to worry you too much, but I don't want you to be like Cordelia who went through so much injustice and pain.

"I'm not sure how far those women are willing to go, but just to make sure we are both protected, I suggest that when writing letters or sending e-mails to each other, we use code names. I'll be Mortimer Lear, and you will be Cordelia. To confirm this, I've written this arrangement down and I'm putting it in my safe, which is hidden behind that rather ugly picture of the painted Irish sheep over my fireplace. I'm pretty sure Goneril and Regan have no idea that I would even have a safe. If ever we need to produce proof of our arrangement, it will be in here. I have a key to the safe and I want you to have one too, but I'm going to hide the key under the unicorn statue in the garden that's partially hidden by the red rose bushes."

Aunt Lavinia said all this as if it were the most normal thing in the world, but it appeared to Nora to be a mysterious plot out of a book.

"Drink up your tea, dear. It will help you sleep," advised Lavinia. "It has some of Mrs. O'Hara's chamomile herbs in it."

Nora did as she was told and thought that Lavinia was right about there being many complex webs being spun by the inhabitants of Duffy Hall. It was a fortuitous thing that Lavinia had been watching how they were all interconnected. She must have been a much smarter woman than people thought.

Friday, September 14
Sneem, 9:30 p.m., GMT

"Now for some more things you need to know," continued Vinnie. "It was very generous of Cy to leave me so much money in his will, but I wanted you to know that I have quite a bit of money of my own. My old fiancé, Mortimer O'Brien, died many years ago in a boating accident, just a month before we were to be married, and I've never met another man who could take his place. Someday I'll tell you more about Mort.

"I was very lonely and frightened then and I needed a hobby. I had gone to university with a dear friend from France, and her family owned a flower farm. We decided to merge our talents and start a perfume company. Monique is dead now, but I bought that farm. And that's where my headquarters is."

Nora listened to her with a puzzled look on her face. *Headquarters for what?* she thought. *I thought she was just a sweet old lady.*

"Producing and selling perfume for the mass market is not an easy thing to do with all the competition, but it's worked quite well for me." Lavinia looked around to make sure no one was nearby, and she continued, "Not many people know this and I ask you to keep my secret, but I'm Carol of Carol Cleary's Seasons."

"Wow," Nora said after she could close her open mouth, "this is the second big surprise I've had today. I just read an article recently that said no one knew who Carol was. My mom gave me some

Shivery last Christmas, and I receive compliments whenever I use it. I can't believe that you're Carol!

"Yes, we've managed to keep my identity a secret pretty well," laughed Lavinia. "Maintaining the headquarters in a small town in France helped with that as does having trusted employees. I pay them well, and they work hard to protect me. I make a few trips every year to the factory, but I tell everyone here that I'm going to visit Monique's family, which is partially true.

"I'm glad you like Shivery. We decided from the first to focus on creating only four perfumes, one for each season of the year. Springy is a combination of the most-loved spring flowers, lily of the valley, and lilac. For Summery, we used the old-fashioned rose scent and other summer flowers. Harvesty has hints of lavender, cranberry, and the fall spices, cinnamon and nutmeg. Shivery has the musky smell of the sea winds for winter. We color the scents appropriately and put them in pretty bottles and boxes with appealing colors and artwork. My company name, Carol Cleary's, uses a tiny iridescent green shamrock as the apostrophe. I don't know if you noticed it, but the front of Duffy Hall and the surrounding landscape are featured on all the boxes.

"For years, these four perfumes have sold very well around the world, and about five years ago, we added lotions and soaps too that have added to our profits considerably. I am now quite a wealthy woman."

"Now I'll let you in on another secret," Lavinia said with an impish grin on her face.

Nora noticed that when she smiled, Lavinia was quite a beautiful woman, and when she was happy, her brogue increased its lilt. "No one knows this yet except a few people at Carol's, but at Christmas time this year, we'll be introducing a new perfume, Holly & Ivy. My chemists have been diligently working to combine just the right scents for it and it should be coming out next month. The box will feature the two old holly trees that grow just outside our front door. The brilliant berries are small now, but they will become huge in November, and the wall ivy never quite dies. We're also going to introduce colognes for young children, which seems to be growing in popularity, and a scent for men called Danny Boy."

"To use an American phrase," giggled Nora, "I'll be a monkey's uncle! You certainly have everyone fooled with the old-lady look. You are a genius and you've made so many women happy with your products. How did you decide to use seasonal names?"

"It was just a fluke," answered Lavinia. "We figured that women might be likely to buy a new scent four times a year. There are already so many perfume names for the seasons, so Monique and I just came up with names for seasonal feelings that we thought would be unique. Some women like to stick with one signature perfume, but we thought that others would like to change off. It's worked so far."

"Anyway, I can see that you are getting tired," Lavinia observed, "but I wanted to warn you that not everyone on the board can be trusted. I believe that most all of the members of the board will probably support you all the way, but 'Beware the Jabberwock' as Lewis Carroll said.

"I heard you say that you want to improve Internet access for the whole building. I pay extra to have high-speed Internet in my bedroom, but you're right that most of the rooms don't have it, and it would be so helpful.

"Cy told me about his plans a few weeks ago, and he was so thrilled to think that you would be the primary owner of Duffy Hall. I just know you'll think of a lot of innovations. I'm so happy you're feeling better so far. Captain Brennan and the Garda are usually very efficient, so I hope they find this cowardly person soon that hurt you again. Please know that you can always call on me for anything. And I'll be sending you and your family cartons of Carol Cleary's. I understand that you have many sisters and cousins.

"By the way, Nora—or if you'd like, Bitsy—I've remade my will too, and if anything happens to me, I'd like you to take over the helm at Carol's. My colleagues are wonderful people, but they will need leadership and direction. Duncan has all the details about that."

Lavinia added, "One more thing before you go to bed. The castle is our home as well as the headquarters of Duffy Medical. Every month, we host an event here for the village with a different theme.

In October, we'll have the annual Art Fair. In November, we celebrate the end of World War I, and in December, there's a craft fair where people exhibit and sell their works. Now that you'll be the owner of Duffy Hall, we should ask you if you want these events to continue."

Nora responded that while her name might be listed as the owner of the castle, Lavinia would always be the mistress. If she thought these events were good to have, then by all means they should continue. "They sound like fun," said Nora, "and I only wish I could be here for more of them."

Lavinia told her to get up to bed since they were all going to need their energy for tomorrow. "And please call me Vinnie. I was named after some ancestor, but I've always hated the name Lavinia."

Nora stood up and gave Lavinia a warm hug. "Aunt Vinnie, I've heard that the hall might have a ghost that whispers in the hallways. I think I might have heard something like that myself a few times. Are you aware of this?"

"Yes, I've heard it too, and lately, it seems I'm hearing it more often. There's a wonderful painting hanging over there above my bed of a young woman who looks a lot like you. The picture was painted by an experienced craftsman, and the young girl stares out at us at the height of her beauty in her willowy pink dress and picture hat. I believe her name was Bridget Fitzpatrick, the daughter of a former owner of Duffy Hall. The legend I've heard is that Bridget was in love with one of the servants, and Lord Fitzpatrick had both of them killed. Perhaps Bridget is a good ghost who has been trying to warn us about dark deeds that might be planned close to us."

Nora responded, "I'm not sure I believe in the concept of ghosts, but if Bridget is whispering more often now, I feel as though she's a good influence and I'm thankful for her presence. I do believe in angels and saints interceding for us, so I suppose a ghost might be a similar good spirit, although they're not usually portrayed that way."

Nora thanked Aunt Vinnie and told her she couldn't take any more surprises today. Johnny Moreland escorted her to her parents' room, and Chief Herlihy also came with them and assured them they would be safe during the night. Eileen helped Nora remove her bloodstained outfit and get washed up with the Duffy Hall lavender soap that was made from the clumps of lavender that grew profusely around the grounds. The attractive odor was very calming and eliminated the need to count sheep.

Just as they were about to get into bed, Enda called them and said that a nice young man named Tom had arrived and would like to see Miss Nora. Dr. Duffy talked to Tom and told him that he would be right down to meet him. He ran down the stairs and explained to Tom that Nora had been shot again but she appeared to be out of danger. Tommy was horrified to hear the news and said he'd like to see Nora right away. Dr. Duffy grabbed some of Tommy's luggage, and they made their way upstairs quickly.

Dr. Duffy knocked on the bedroom door and said that he had a surprise visitor. Nora screamed in wonder that Tommy had arrived somewhat early, and they were both so thrilled they couldn't stop hugging each other. Tommy examined her most-recent stitches and thanked God that she had survived this latest assault. What miserable coward would be doing this to this wonderful girl? Mrs. Doyle helped Tommy get settled in the room across from the Duffys and showed him where everything was.

Tommy finally had a chance to spend some time with Nora alone and he gently grabbed her hands and greeted her with one of their favorite movie lines: "Of all the gin joints in all the towns in all the world, she has to walk into mine." *Casablanca* from 1942 was the classic movie they loved the best, and Humphrey Bogart's Rick uttered that famous line with such conviction. *Casablanca* had the perfect balance of entertainment and life or death moral dilemmas.

The music was so memorable, whether it was Sam playing "As Time Goes By," the love song in the background as they drove down the Champs-Élysées, or the two famous national anthems "Deutschland Uber Alles," stridently sung by the Germans, and "La Marseillaise," sung so passionately by the French, and both strangely harmonizing so well. Nora knew what was expected of her, and she responded to Tommy, "We'll always have Paris." Then both of them laughed and hugged each other for a long time.

Mrs. Duffy finally intervened and told them that Nora should get some rest while she could. Nora finally fell asleep and only woke up twice to drink more water and take another pain pill. Perhaps it was the medication, but she had an uneasy sleep and dreamt of being chased by ghouls menacing her with the atomizers on huge black perfume bottles.

Dr. Duffy didn't want Liam in the room, so the devoted dog slept next to the door where he could be the closest to Nora. Bran was lonely these days and slept next to Liam. The two pets would have busy jobs in the coming days.

31

Saturday, September 15
Sneem, 8:00 a.m., GMT

In the morning, Nora showered and smiled as she squirted herself with Shivery shampoo, being careful not to get much on the top of her head. She was feeling strong enough to walk without the wheelchair, and Tommy would be next to her, so that was a step in the right direction.

Nora again thanked God for sparing her life. She put on her comfortable underwear, the kind she used to use on dancing performance days since she knew it fit her perfectly. She donned a casual outfit this early in the morning. She opened the bedroom door and was almost run over by Liam and Bran who were so glad to see her. She glanced into Tommy's room, but he was still asleep.

The dogs joined her as she ran downstairs for a cup of tea. Nora passed the front doors on her way back from the kitchen, stuck her head outside, and realized that it was going to be a beautiful day. She enjoyed seeing the men setting up the scaffolding yesterday where the presiders and orchestra would be sitting today and admired their expert work.

Nora went back upstairs and gave Tommy a glass of juice, and then she donned her black suit-dress, decided to wear her comfortable flats in case she felt dizzy, and covered her butchered scalp with an emerald green lacey hat. She usually wore her long hair down, but today, her mother helped her to put it into a bun at the back of her head.

She warmed up herself and her violin by playing the "Irish Jig" several times and adjusted the instrument's strings so it would be ready to play at the funeral mass. She felt as though the day would be sad but fine and hoped that it would be pleasing to Uncle Cy. She felt tears behind her eyes every time she thought of him, so she tried to distract herself. She didn't want to start the day with red and swollen eyes.

Nora joined her parents and Tommy and they went down to the small dining room, but she was feeling a bit woozy from the pain medication, so she had her usual performance day breakfast that usually agreed with her stomach: a small bowl of oatmeal with one teaspoon of brown sugar with half a cup of milk and a small glass of orange juice. Mrs. O'Hara had provided a repeat of the delicious repast of yesterday morning for the rest of the group, and Dr. Duffy and Tommy enjoyed it all. Eileen kept a close watch on her wounded daughter.

After breakfast, Nora asked Johnny Moreland to give her and Tommy a ride around the grounds in his golf cart. Tommy had seen it once before, but he recalled that the weather that time was rainy. This time, it all seemed much bigger and prettier. He could see why Nora loved it so much, and they resolved to come back later on a happier day.

Both of them were apprehensive, thinking that the killer could be lurking nearby. With all the people expected for the funeral, it might be a good opportunity for the killer to try again, but Nora and Tommy tried to help each other by keeping their conversation light and upbeat.

They returned to the hall and made last minute preparations for the busy day in front of them. They could see that cars were already starting to arrive in the parking lot and the tents were beginning to fill up.

Saturday, September 15
Sneem, 11:30 a.m., GMT

Maryann knocked on Nora's door and said that a special delivery letter had arrived for her. Nora gingerly accepted the letter, but past experiences had made her wary of its contents. Sure enough, it was from the would-be killer. She read through it and dropped it on the floor, exclaiming, "Holy Mother of God!"

Tommy glanced through the letter and held Nora in his arms.

The letter said that Nora shouldn't think she was safe because she was not in the US. She would be killed sooner rather than later. Nora was shaking at first, but she told Tommy that she saw that there were only two choices. "I can fall apart and hide out in my room or I can keep on with my usual routine and hope that the killer continues to have bad luck. I'm pretty good with God, and there are too many things I have to do to hide out. If someone is bound and determined to kill me, it will either happen or it won't. We only have fifteen minutes before we have to leave for the funeral, so help me finish getting dressed, and I'll be like Scarlett O'Hara and worry about things tomorrow—assuming I'll be here tomorrow."

Tommy wanted to tell her that everything would be fine but realized he couldn't do that. He told Nora that he would be right back, but he went to find Chief Herlihy, showed him the letter, and demanded more police protection for Nora. Chief Herlihy directed two of the gardai to stay close to Nora for the entire day and to be alert for any threatening behaviors in the crowd.

Even though it was only 5:30 a.m. in Chicago, Nora sent a text to Jim and asked him who was going to Notre Dame today for football and how everyone was doing. It wasn't long before she received a response from Jim saying that eight of them would be heading out in about an hour. It was a beautiful day in Chicago, so the traffic would probably be heavy, but they hoped to make it in time to go to breakfast at Perkins Restaurant and still get to the band concert in front of the Golden Dome before heading over to the stadium.

Notre Dame was considered a slight underdog, but they hoped for a good game. The girls wanted to get there in time to buy this season's Fighting Irish tee shirt at the bookstore, but he was sure that they would find a number of other things to purchase as well. Jim said he promised Trish that next week, he'd go with her to the Northwestern game, but she'd be with him today.

Jim added, "Everyone else at home seems to be fine, and Jesse is going to stay home with the twins who will be spending a big portion of the day with their many friends. Aunt Ellen and her family are going to Grant Park today for a fall festival. The whole family sends you their best, and they hope that everything goes well at the funeral."

Nora greeted the two gardai who had been assigned to "stick with her like glue," and the family headed downstairs. Nora was once again surprised to smell a strong odor of honeysuckle in the lobby and she sent positive thoughts to the Duffy Hall ghost, if there was one, and asked her to do what she could to help them all. Nora put herself in God's hands and stepped out the door to face this historic day.

Saturday, September 15
Sneem, Noon, GMT

The entire group departed from the front doors of Duffy Hall for the funeral mass and burial ceremony. The weather was perfect at the moment, about 15.5 degrees Celsius and 60 degrees Fahrenheit. No rain was in the forecast, and the sun was peeking out from behind the clouds. Aunt Lavinia was pushed in a wheelchair to the chapel while the rest of the party followed on foot. Johnny followed with the dogs, and this time, he had them securely harnessed to the golf cart.

Nora could see a group of reporters and television cameras waiting for them, but a very large group of gardai motioned for them to stay at a distance, so they contented themselves for now with taking pictures.

A large crowd of townspeople and dignitaries were expected from governments, companies, the town of Sneem, and many locations in northern and southern Ireland. There would be a large contingent of representatives from Chicago, including several stand-ins for the mayor and the cardinal's office. The US Ambassador to Ireland was expected to attend. The archbishop would be the main celebrant, and many other priests from Ireland would participate. Father Ahearn would act as host for the priests from Chicago, Boston, New York, and other cities who were expected.

Uncle Cy's body had been well-prepared by Mr. Dowling and he looked as though he were just taking a nap in his Duffy plaids.

The sturdy-looking casket was a simple wooden affair, handmade by the Trappist monks. The visitation had been well-organized so that the crowds would enter in one door of the chapel, say a prayer at the casket, and then proceed out the back door to the tents that had been set up for the mass. Many ushers were there to guide people to their places and hand them a program that had been carefully prepared by the talented twins, Kitty and Maryann. Television cameras and reporters abounded from many countries. Tommy spotted Mrs. Weller in the crowd, whom he'd met yesterday on the plane, and they waved to each other.

The tent for the presiders had been decorated in a green and gold theme and was filled with flowers, especially yellow daisies, Cyrus' favorites. The archbishop presided over the mass and was joined by twenty-two priests on the altar. The music was provided by the combined orchestras and choirs of many towns. While they were waiting for everyone to get into place, the choir sang several pieces in Gaelic.

When everything was ready, a cantor encouraged the congregation to refer to the program and join in singing the opening hymn of "Amazing Grace." Nora recalled the story about this now-standard hymn being composed by a desperate British sailor who needed God's help to survive. The bagpipers led in the procession, the presiders took their places, and then the opening prayers of the mass were begun.

Kevin Duffy read the first reading from Isaiah in the Old Testament: "Like a shepherd he will tend his flock, in his arms he will gather the lambs." The choir responded with the refrain of the same theme. Dr. Duffy read the second reading from Luke in the New Testament: "If a man has 100 sheep and one of them is lost, he leaves the 99 in open pasture and goes after the one which is lost until he finds it." Father Tooley read the Gospel from John 10: "I am the good shepherd; the good shepherd lays down his life for his sheep."

Father Tooley gave the homily and explained that those readings about the Good Shepherd were more than just pleasant and comforting. They represented an important part of Cyrus' firsthand experiences when he worked as a shepherd to help support his family. Father Tooley did a good job of weaving the theme of shepherd throughout Cyrus' life as he began and developed his company into one of the premier medical supply firms in the world.

At the offertory, the children of Duffy Medical employees and the orphans Cyrus had supported brought up the symbolic gifts, and more glorious music was played and sung. The sacred parts of the mass ensued, and at the Communion, a coterie of priests and Eucharistic ministers helped to distribute the consecrated hosts.

Nora thought how interesting it was that this poor boy from a small farm had all this pomp and circumstance at his death. She thanked God for his life and asked him to bless all these people and to bless her and Tommy and to protect them from whoever it was that had been trying to kill her.

John and Duncan from Duffy Medical and Aunt Lavinia gave brief and very moving eulogies for Cyrus. The theme in all of their talks essentially focused on how Cyrus J. Duffy saw hardships as opportunities for growth rather than as insurmountable troubles. They pointed out that success in life for him meant that he felt obligated to use his money and his talents to make other people successful too. Nora was proud of Aunt Lavinia that she made it through her heartfelt talk without succumbing to maudlin tears. She knew Cy better than anyone, and Nora thought that Uncle Cy would surely feel proud to hear such words of praise from his big sister.

John explained that about 5,000 memorial tributes had come in for Cyrus, and they had to assemble them all in a huge book, which anyone could see at the back of the chapel. These memorials came from the Vatican and religious leaders, kings and queens, presidents of countries and companies, family and friends, and thousands of people who had encountered Cyrus J. Duffy somewhere on the road of life and found that he embodied his motto, "He cared." "Perhaps the one letter that Cyrus would have appreciated the most can be found on the back of your program from the children at St. Brigid's Orphanage to their Uncle Dan-O, as they called him."

"As you know, we have a new chairman of the board at Duffy Medical, Miss Nora Duffy from Chicago, Illinois, in the USA. I asked Nora if she wanted to say some words about the man who considered her to be his daughter, but she said she preferred to express her thoughts with music. Nora, please come up to the podium."

Nora told the crowd that she had selected the following music for several reasons: "First, because I love it and find it completely inspirational. And second, because Beethoven reminds me of Uncle Cy in many ways. By the time Beethoven composed this masterpiece, he was already getting quite deaf. Can you imagine how frustrating it must have been for a master composer to think up this glorious music but then have to struggle to hear it? And I love the cadence of the music. I think of Uncle Cy just relentlessly moving forward no matter what his challenges were. As we're playing this, I ask you to reflect on the persistence of the human spirit that Uncle Cy embodied and how he might inspire us to follow his example.

"I am so honored to be playing this with the incredibly talented members of our combined orchestra. I usually keep my eyes closed when I'm playing this piece at home so that I can internalize the music, but I promise to keep my eyes open and watch the baton of the eminent conductor, Mr. Derek Gleeson."

Mr. Gleeson waved his baton and the orchestra began to play the opening notes of the Allegretto movement from Beethoven's "7th Symphony in A Major." Nora joined them on her violin as her testament to Uncle Cyrus. She did her best to stop herself from crying, but fortunately, she knew the music well, because eventually, tears streamed down her face and clouded her vision. The television cameras and photographers caught it all. When she finished, she went over to the catafalque, kissed the casket, and placed a huge bouquet of yellow daisies and white lilies on it.

At the conclusion of the mass, Nora sang one verse of "Danny Boy" a cappella and then encouraged the congregation to consult their program and join her in singing the remaining verses:

> Oh Danny boy, the pipes, the pipes are calling
> From glen to glen, and down the mountain side
> The summer's gone, and all the flowers are dying
> 'Tis you, 'tis you must go and I must bide.

But come ye back when summer's in the meadow
Or when the valley's hushed and white with snow
'Tis I'll be here in sunshine or in shadow
Oh Danny boy, oh Danny boy, I love you so.

As the music died away, the priests and attendants led the way down the aisle, and Mr. Dowling and his assistants guided the congregation to the place where Cyrus's body would be entombed.

More blessings were said over the coffin, and then it was left there, next to Emily's tombstone, for the cemetery attendants to do their work.

The inscription on Cyrus' tombstone read:

Cyrus John Duffy
1933–2018
HE CARED
May flights of angels sing thee to thy rest

Nora knew that Aunt Lavinia had chosen that lovely quote from *Hamlet* for her "sweet prince," but she thought Uncle Cy would probably think it was too highbrow for someone like him. He most likely would have preferred something like "Do not go gentle into that good night" by Dylan Thomas. If there were any truth to the story about the golden gates of paradise, Cy was likely looking them over to see if they needed refurbishing and making his recommendations to St. Peter.

While the congregation was busy at the gravesite, assistants set up tables and chairs in the tents. Everyone was then guided back to the tents to partake in a luncheon. Mrs. O'Hara and a variety of caterers from the local towns had prepared a delicious meal, which was easily served to everyone in prepackaged containers that had been heated to just the right temperature. Trays of delicious sweets were passed out, and the servers provided drinks.

It took several hours for the crowds to leave, and afterward, Nora had agreed to a televised interview with Ann O'Shea, the reporter from the *Ennis Tribune*. Ann asked her a number of general questions about her relationship with her uncle and Duffy Medical, and Nora did her best to answer her questions, but she found that she was getting very tired.

Nora received a text back from Jim who said that many in the family were going to a festival at Grant Park today, but they had made it to South Bend and were now heading to the band concert. They had met Uncle Joe, Aunt Honey, and their kids. They hoped they would be able to stay for the whole game since they liked to join the team at game's end in singing Notre Dame's Alma Mater, "Notre Dame, Our Mother." Many of the fans only remembered the last four words—Love Thee, Notre Dame—but the Duffys enjoyed singing it all.

They would then head over to Sacred Heart church afterward and hoped they would get in before it got filled up. They loved the organ concert in Sacred Heart that always followed the game. They enjoyed seeing the stone tablets outside the church doors that proclaimed: "God, Country, Notre Dame."

Jim continued, "Saw you on television. If you don't want your billions, we can find plenty of ways to use them—ha, ha, LOL. Jesse is keeping everything going fine at home. Good luck today at funeral. Can't wait to see you."

Dr. Duffy called home and talked to Jesse who said that they turned on the O'Connor radio show this morning, which was full of news and gossip about Cyrus, Nora, and the family. The far south Irish facility, Gaelic Park, and the north side Irish facility, The Irish American Heritage Center, were both abuzz with speculation and gossip. *The Irish American News* had a whole column on the family and wondered what the future would hold for Nora and Duffy Medical.

Jesse had been flustered since TV cameras and reporters had been camped out in front of the house, but they had been trying to shoo them away. Dr. Duffy told them they should advise the reporters to wait until they got home and they would give them more information then.

Dr. Duffy also called his office and talked to Dr. Marlowe who said there was the usual busyness, but no emergencies, and they would be glad to see him when he returned. He said that Jack Cassidy was sowing his usual negative comments about the state of cardiology at Holy Savior.

Nora and Tommy passed the Stone Tower on their way back to the castle, and Tommy said he thought they should go inside and check out the astronomy objects up at the top. Nora hesitated. She didn't want to be like the teenagers in those slasher movies that went out into the woods when they knew the monster was out there, and the inside of a stone tower would be very dark. She finally decided that Tommy was right and they gave the long winding stairway a try. They didn't see any sign of electric lighting, but their phones gave off enough light to at least see the stairs.

The walls of the interior were very rough and they heard various squeaking sounds; Nora hoped it wasn't rats. She couldn't help but think of the terrifying classic radio *Escape* episode *Three Skeleton Key* where the starving rats swarmed the lighthouse and the men inside. When they arrived at the top of the tower, they marveled at the panoramic view of the whole area. No wonder Uncle Cy liked to come up here. They pulled off the covering from a large telescope and realized it was probably in good working condition. Nora told Tommy she thought they should come back some evening to do more investigating when they could bring along more lighting and more protection.

Just then, they heard the entrance door slam shut below them. They were already feeling apprehensive from being in there and hoped that someone hadn't deliberately locked them in. They soon heard the voices of Johnny Moreland and Chief Herlihy who had been frantically looking for them. Nora and Tom went down the rough steps as quickly as they could and apologized to the frightened men. The chief pointed out to them that the door didn't have a lock, so they couldn't have been locked in, but he agreed that if Nora wanted to use this tower, they should put more efforts into making it safe and functional.

Nora and Tommy joined the Duffys and Father Ahearn at the hall and had a cup of tea and rested, but then they decided they wanted a change of pace before they had to head back to Chicago the next day.

Saturday, September 15
Sneem, 7:00 p.m., GMT

Nora, Tommy, her parents, Father Ahearn, and Chiefs Herlihy and Brennan went to the Sneem Hotel for dinner to discuss what they knew so far and to make plans for the next few days. The two chiefs explained that they had been working on some leads about the shooter that seemed promising. As soon as they had definite information, they would let the Duffys know what they'd found. They want them to be aware that they are also keeping in touch with Lieutenant Braxton in Chicago.

They enjoyed a delicious dinner and followed it up with the hotel's signature drinks. The Duffys and Father Ahearn went back to the Hall to finish packing and to say their goodbyes to Lavinia and the staff. Nora and Tommy walked out to the stables and spent some time with the horses, accompanied by the dogs—Liam, Bran, and Lady. Nora and Tommy enjoyed a last walk through Duffy Hall, and then they went to their rooms and attempted to get to sleep so they would be ready for the return plane trip tomorrow.

Sunday, September 16
Sneem, 10:00 a.m., GMT

In the morning, John O'Malley and Duncan Lloyd came to bid farewell to Nora and the Duffys and gave Nora the $5,000 from the safe, plus a packet of materials they asked her to review when she could. The Duffy Medical directors told the family that Mrs. O'Callahan, the communications director, had sent out a bulletin about Uncle Cy's bequests in his will to all the news outlets. Nora sent a text to Ann O'Shea from the *Ennis Tribune* and reminded her to look for the bulletin.

Mrs. O'Hara and staff prepared a full Irish breakfast for the Duffys. Tommy loved the bangers and mash, which translates to sausages and mashed potatoes. Dr. Duffy and Father Ahearn also had a full plate, but Eileen and Nora contented themselves with an omelet and blueberries.

Nora brought Tommy to say a final goodbye to Finnbar and the bog ponies. Nora mounted Finnbar, Tim Taylor saddled one of the staff's mounts for Tommy, and they enjoyed a picturesque ride around the hall. Tommy was a talented photographer, and by the time they returned to the stables and Tim Taylor, he had taken more than 200 pictures on his phone of Duffy Hall, its people, grounds, and animals. Nora and Tom looked forward to making quite a collage of photos for their new home.

With no warning, a shot rang out, and Finnbar went from a leisurely canter to a full gallop within seconds. Nora was a very small and inexperienced rider sitting on the huge and terrified horse, and she screamed in fear. She hung on to the reins for dear life, but she could see that Finn was headed toward the deer enclosure that was surrounded by a wire fence. She realized she had to divert Finn before he ran right into it. She tried yelling various commands to the thoroughly spooked horse, without success. She thought about possibly falling off the horse to protect herself, but he was going too fast, and the ground was very uneven. She might hurt herself even worse if she fell off.

As the fence got closer and closer, she recalled a conversation she had with Uncle Cy last year when he told her his secret signal to Finn. She suddenly remembered it and shouted out, "Slainte, slainte!" to Finn several times. Finally, she felt the great horse reduce his speed and she attempted to steer him to the right. At the last second, Finn pulled up and switched to a canter alongside the fence instead of running straight into it. Nora felt the poor horse shaking

171

underneath her and she tried to bring him to a complete stop so she could see if he had been hurt.

She was able to slide off and stand up next to Finn, and a group of worried people pulled up right behind her, Tim on his horse, and Johnny, Sean, and Tommy in the golf cart. Their first concern was for Nora, but she assured them that she was scared but fine. Tim started to look over Finnbar and found blood on his left flank. They weren't sure if the bullet was meant for Nora or Finn, but either way, it could have had disastrous results. If the horse had run into the wire at full speed, Nora and Finn would likely have had severe injuries.

Nora explained how she had remembered Uncle Cy's secret command that got Finn to slow down in time. Johnny couldn't help but laugh at the idea of the famous Irish drinking toast being the secret word that would control this giant animal. Nora thought that it sounded like something Uncle Cy would think up. Tommy once again enveloped Nora in one of his bear hugs and thanked God that she was not hurt. Oh, if only he could get his hands on whoever was trying to hurt her.

They realized that they were going to have to get back to the hall quickly so that they could make their plane, so they phoned Dr. and Mrs. Duffy and explained the situation to them. Chief Herlihy arrived in his jeep, and they repeated the story to him. Tim led Finnbar back to the stables so that he could treat his wound. Nora gave Finn a final hug and promised to be back to see him soon.

The Duffys and Father Ahearn gave thanks to the entire staff for all that they'd done to make their stay so pleasant, and the family fondly embraced Aunt Lavinia and promised to see her soon. Tim Taylor assured Nora that he would take good care of Finnbar and the dogs until she returned.

Tommy had a difficult time finding a seat on the same Aer Lingus plane as the Duffys, but eventually they worked it out so that his prior reservation was canceled and a new reservation for Nora's flight was confirmed. Old Tim drove them back to Dublin. The roads were packed with tourist cars and buses since it was a gorgeous day.

They encountered a coterie of reporters and television cameras at Dublin Airport and they did answer a few questions, but they explained that they were in a hurry to catch their flight. They were relieved that they had time to check in and get to their flight, which left at 4:00 p.m. for Chicago.

The stewardesses in their attractive green and blue outfits were excited to have such celebrities on their plane, and they showed them copies of the latest newspapers that highlighted the events of the last few days with many pictures of Duffy Hall, Uncle Cyrus, and Nora, and a number of articles with questions about what this would mean for her and for the company. The headlines in the papers they showed her read, "Nora Duffy, Instant Billionaire." A gossip newspaper's headline read, "Was Cyrus Duffy Murdered for His Money?" Another paper had a headline that portrayed Nora as "The Mighty Rich Midget."

The stewardesses gave them copies of the papers to peruse, and Nora delighted in reading the many complimentary stories about Uncle Cyrus and his company, but she also could hardly believe the negative stories about how he made his money and who might have "bumped him off." Thank goodness she hadn't known about his death until after it had happened or the story might say that she was responsible for it. They still might stoop to that.

Dr. Duffy, Eileen, and Father Ahearn passed the time by playing gin rummy and ruminating on the events of the last few days. The flight home was a little bumpy but not too bad, and as they crossed Lake Michigan, the stewardesses asked Nora how she was feeling after having such a huge shock. She assured them everything was in the early planning stages and she wasn't sure what this would mean for any of them. She told them that she would likely be making more frequent trips to Ireland, and they assured her they would look forward to seeing her more often.

During the flight home, Nora received nine letters from fellow plane passengers. Three just congratulated her and wished her good luck, but six were from people with hard luck stories who were seeking money. Nora wondered what would happen when the news of her fortune really got out.

As soon as they landed, Nora called Tim Taylor at Duffy Hall to inquire about Finnbar, but he assured her that her horse friend had just a minor wound and was healing nicely. Chiefs Herlihy and Brennan were in the midst of another investigation to see who might have done this latest shooting.

Monday, September 17
Chicago, 10:00 a.m., CDT

The Duffys and Father Ahearn completed the required processes of those arriving back on US soil, and they started toward the baggage court at O'Hare to procure their luggage. They saw two sets of people, one that delighted them and another that annoyed them immensely. Many family and friends were waiting for them, but so were the media and television cameras.

The reporters stood in front of the Duffys and told them that they had just a few questions to ask them. Nora briefly thought about making an end run around them but realized she would have to face them sooner or later.

Nora said she hadn't had a chance to greet her family yet and asked them all to come up around her. She introduced her mother and father, Tommy, Father Ahearn, and all her siblings and their friends: Jim and his fiancé, Trish; Jack and his girlfriend, Sally; Mary Ann and husband, Al, and expected baby; Maureen and boyfriend, Tim; Siobhan and boyfriend, Mick; Kevin and girlfriend, Jill; Brian; and twins, Molly and Caitlan. In the background stood hordes of aunts, uncles, cousins, neighbors, teachers, priest friends, Sister Kathleen Ryan, and their beloved housekeeper, Mrs. Jesse Meyers. Nora petted the dogs and explained, "This handsome wolfhound is Reilly, and his little friend is Billy."

Nora's little sisters, the twins, Molly and Caitlan, looked rather terrified of the media and their cameras, and they held on to Nora's hands, one on each side of their big sister. Nora turned to the girls and explained that the reporters were paid to find stories that would have something sensational to say about the person they are interviewing to drum up interest for their readers or TV watchers. "Don't be scared, girls. I think I can handle them, and Uncle Frank, who's a senior law partner, is here if I need help."

A reporter yelled out the first question, "Some people say that you knew that your uncle was sick, so you went to Ireland and talked him into giving you his money. Is that the case?"

"Oh, it's going to be that kind of session," growled Nora. "In that case, I need to get more comfortable. I've had these heels on for more than twenty hours straight and my feet are killing me." Nora asked her mother for her flip-flops in her bag and put them on. "Okay, I'm now going to draw myself up to my full imposing height and I'm ready to answer your questions.

"But let's back up for a minute. I assume that I'll be seeing quite a bit of you in the future and I do want to have a good relationship with you. My mother tells me that I was born with an agreeable personality…up to a point. Judging by what you've just asked, I presume that many of your questions will be coming from what I call 'group gossip.' I'll do my best to answer you, but I'm going to stick to the facts.

"When I graduate from Loyola next summer, I'm going to have a medical degree in addition to my degrees in business management and hospital administration. Perhaps the best thing I've learned during these past four years is that sticking to the facts, rather than gossip or innuendo, is the best protection for all sides. As to the rumor that I knew that Cyrus was sick and talked him into giving me his money, here are the facts." Nora enumerated on her outstretched fingers:

"Fact 1: It's not true on so many levels.
"Fact 2: Cyrus and his wife, Emily, were never able to have children. I first met Uncle Cy when I was five-years-old, and he told me several times over the years that he thought of me as the daughter he never had and mentioned that again in his will. I believe that is the primary reason he left me his money.

"Fact 3: I talked to Uncle Cy every Sunday by phone, but we never discussed his will or his money, so I had zero input into his decisions about his estate. His sister, Aunt Lavinia, told me that he had been planning to make me his heir for years, and she knew him better than anyone. The officers of Uncle Cy's company, Duffy Medical, helped him to draw up his will and said he knew exactly what he was doing.

"Fact 4: Uncle Cy was vital and healthy until the last three days of his life. No one, including me, knew that he was terminally ill.

"Fact 5: I was as surprised as anyone about his legacy to me, but he was the smartest person I knew. If he thought it was a good idea to leave me his money, then I'll accept it.

"Fact 6: Uncle Cy was a hardheaded Irishman. No one talked him into doing anything he didn't want to do. We loved each other, and that's the bottom line.

"Fact 7: We'll be passing out copies of Uncle Cyrus' will to all of you. You can read it yourselves."

"Why is someone trying to kill you on two continents?"

"I have no answers to that question at all. I can tell you that the police here and in Ireland are still investigating, and there could be some involvement of the FBI and Interpol since the man who tried to push me onto the subway tracks was a foreign national who was a known terrorist. It's a mystery to me and to my family, and it's frightening."

"You will now be one of the richest women in the world. What will you do with it all?"

"Again, I have no answers to that yet. Many pieces of the puzzle need to fall into place. Right now, I'm still a struggling intern, and payday isn't 'til next Friday."

"What will be the first thing you'll buy?"

"Not sure yet, but it will likely be something that will enhance our family's life or Holy Savior Hospital. One thing I know for sure is that I'm not going to buy even a candy bar until I know that the tax situation is taken care of in both countries, and that will take a while.

I have lawyers and financial advisers here and in Ireland and I'll rely on them for their help."

"You're going to be a brain surgeon, which sounds like a busy job, so how can you also be the head of a major company?"

"Again, no answers yet, but I'll be heeding sound advice from many people."

"I'm sure you've heard before that you look a lot like the red-headed girl in the Disney movie. Just so we don't misreport, how tall are you? Why are you so short?"

"I'm four feet, five inches tall, and I weigh about seventy-five pounds. That's been the same since I've been in high school. I've only seen pictures of her, but my great-grandmother, Alice O'Connor, was supposed to have been short like me. The other females in our family are not very tall, but I'm the only one who inherited the very short genes. It's not usually a problem for me, and I keep several step stools and grabbers handy."

"Some people say you're going to replace all the Irish people on your uncle's company board with Americans."

"That sounds like another 'anonymous sources' question and is so very false. First, it would be stupid to replace dedicated, competent, and experienced Irish officers with Americans who know nothing about the business. Second, there is a clause in the will that says I can't make any binding decisions for the first year unless they are unanimously approved by the board. I'm sure that such a foolish proposal would be unanimously turned down, and I am not foolish. If the company decides to do more business in the US, perhaps there will be Americans on the board, but that scenario lies far in the future."

"The rumor is that you don't drink anything alcoholic at all. That seems to be rather extreme, especially for someone so Irish. Why is that?"

Nora put her hands on her hips, a sign to those who knew her well that her dander was up. She stared at the questioner and said, "I really do want to have a good relationship with you folks, but that doesn't mean I'm going to be a doormat for your comments that I perceive as out of bounds. I believe statistics show that the Irish do indeed like to drink, but if comparisons were done, some other nationalities might well give them a run for their money. While studies on the subject are mixed, any alcohol seems to have some negative effect on the brain. The short-term effects usually mitigate fairly quickly, but I don't even want to experience those.

"On the plus side for alcohol, it seems likely that cave people may have figured out how to make alcohol by mistake and liked it so much they got better at doing it over time. Jesus' first miracle was to turn water into wine for the young couple's wedding at Cana. St. Paul mentions that you should take a little wine for your digestion. I also stay away from carbonated drinks. Most of the people in my family love an occasional beer or glass of wine. My aunt and uncle have a winery in California, and Tommy's parents run a pub. It's a personal preference for me not to enjoy it. Chicago has some of the best water in the world, and that's fine for me. And, before you ask, I want absolutely nothing to do with drugs, unless it's a medical emergency."

"Where did you and Tommy meet?"

"We originally met in high school, but I thought he was a stuck up north-sider in those days. We would see each other in some classes, but that was about it. When I was in college, my friends and I went to Barry's Pub on spring break, and Tommy made it a point to say hello to us. I thought he had improved a lot since I first knew him, and we dated a few times. We've been going out seriously during most of my time in medical school and we got engaged last Christmas."

"Your dog is almost as tall as you are. What kind is he? And does he ever threaten you?"

Nora took Reilly's leash and led him next to her side. "This lovely Irish wolfhound is five years old and his name is Reilly. He is very protective of me. Their sheer size makes wolfhounds look fierce, but they're not very good as guard dogs, because their nature is to be gentle and sweet. Now if you were to make a threatening gesture toward me, then his ancestors' fighting nature might come to the fore. They were bred to hunt wolves. I'm not sure how he feels about pesky reporters. You may have heard that my wolfhound in Ireland is Liam, and he's even taller than Reilly."

Nora yawned and said, "Ladies and gents, I can't answer any more questions today. I've been up for about twenty-four hours, my head hurts, and I'd like to get home and lie down. Thanks for your interest. By the way, my family and Tommy's have a Ceili band, and we'll be playing at Barry's Pub on Irving Park, Wednesday night at seven o'clock. I won't be answering any more questions then, but you're welcome to come and watch."

The reporters continued to call out more questions, but Johnny shepherded Nora and party away from the podium so that they could get their luggage, and they left the airport.

On the way home, Nora suggested that they stop at her favorite pizza place on Taylor Street behind St. Ignatius High School. She had a taste for their unusual pizza and tiramisu, and they ordered it ahead of time on their phone. Soon the car was filled with the delicious scents of pizza and accompaniments. Nora loved being at Duffy Hall, but it felt so good to see the familiar sights on Chicago streets. They made their way down the Dan Ryan Expressway without incident and soon pulled up into the driveway of the old Duffy home.

They made their way quickly through the pizza and dessert and visited with Jesse, the family, and the pets. They looked through the mail that had accumulated while they had been gone, but it appeared to be just the usual mixture of bills and catalogs, except for a letter to Dr. Duffy from someone with a return address in Maine.

Dr. Duffy opened the letter, glanced through it, and said that Eileen and Nora had to hear this. He read it to them:

> Dear Dr. Duffy,
>
> I saw the news about your daughter's inheritance and wanted to say congratulations and good luck. I also wanted to apologize to you for my terrible behavior when I left Savior. I was bitter and hurt and didn't know what to do since medicine was all I knew.
>
> As often happens, a good woman was my salvation. I had a friend who lived in Maine, and

he asked me to come and visit him. He had a beautiful sister, and we took a liking to each other right away. Paula is very wise, and she helped me to admit, eventually, that everything you said about me was true.

She had a dream to open a farm-to-table restaurant, and she asked me to join her. La Table Rouge, named for our red tablecloths, has been open for eighteen months now, and we have been very successful. Our restaurant is in an old whaling city where the B & B's are in the Victorian style, and our French fare fit right in.

Paula and I plan to marry in the summer, and I've never been happier. I'll always miss medicine, but I feel that God led me here through you. If you're ever in Maine, please stop and visit. I didn't know Nora very well, but I imagine that having all this notoriety could be very difficult for her.

I wish you all the very best, and again, I apologize for my past bad behavior.

Sincerely,
Ben Durant

Eileen and Nora looked at Michael who had a sheepish grin on his face. "Well, I never claimed to be a Hercule Poirot. I had talked myself into believing the killer might have been Ben, but I guess we'll have to look elsewhere for our culprit."

Eileen said that it almost seemed like a Dickens' invention that because Michael had fired Ben, he ended up in Maine and met a great woman and had a new career, and he was now contacting Michael because of Nora's inheritance. Perhaps it is true that "there are no coincidences." They all agreed they were happy for Ben, and if they ever had the time, it would be fun to visit Maine. Eileen remembered visiting Ogunquit, Maine, as a child and she'd never forgotten what a wonderful time her family had on the huge beach.

They watched some television, sent some texts, and tried to fight jet lag, but their eyes were drooping, and it wasn't long before they went upstairs for a nap.

Tuesday, September 18
Chicago, 11:00 a.m., CDT

Lieutenant Braxton called and said he would like to come to the house to give them a report on the investigation. Jesse met him at the front door and handed him his jacket that had been sitting in their closet. She explained that things were a bit chaotic today.

"Choose your entertainment, Lieutenant. The children are off from school today. Brian and the St. Ignatius debate team members are practicing their speeches about gun control in the living room. Jim, Jack, and their friends are watching rugby in the study. Ed and his crew are repairing the dance floor in the basement for the Irish dancers. Kevin and his friend, Jeff, are practicing a new solo on their bagpipes, and we've exiled them to the sun porch. Ellen is helping me to make decorations in the kitchen for the charity event for disabled children on Sunday for 125 women. Tonight will be the 'Six months to St. Patrick's Day' event at church, and we're baking and preparing outfits for it."

"Jesse," opined Lieutenant Braxton, "you're amazing. You seem so calm in the middle of all this activity."

"I thrive on it, Lieutenant. It's all so interesting, and it keeps me young. I've been a widow for a long time. I've been taking care of these children for twenty-five years, and we love each other. Dr. and Mrs. Duffy won't be home for about an hour. I think Nora could use some moral support for your conversation. I'm going to extricate

Jim and Jack from their rugby watching, and you and Nora can join them. I'll ask Kevin and Jeff to move upstairs so you can use the sun porch for your discussion."

Nora came in to join them on the sun porch, and the friends, Larry and Keith, said they had to go home. Lieutenant Braxton shook hands with Jim and Jack and asked how the rugby was going. "Not too good for us," replied Jack. "Killarney is losing badly, so we're just as happy to take a break. Can we get you something to drink?"

Lieutenant Braxton assured them that Jesse had asked him to stay for lunch.

Nora's brothers inquired as to whether the police had found out any more about the man who tried to kill her.

"About the only progress we've made is to confirm the man in black's name. All three driver's licenses he had on him when he died were fakes. Interpol says that his real name was Dimitri Plavich. He originally came from Russia and was a well-known killer and terrorist. Many countries were looking for him on a variety of charges and were happy to hear of his demise.

"That still doesn't answer the question as to why someone like him would be in Chicago attempting to kill Nora. We've put out feelers to some of our underground contacts, but so far, we have no more information than we did on that first night. One thing we do know for sure is that someone must have been paying him a lot of money. We understand that he commanded a high price whenever he was planning a hit."

Lieutenant Braxton then told them what they had learned about the Popovs, which astounded the Duffys. He told them that they had taken Mrs. Popov to a safe house and were continuing to question her, but she had not yet revealed any more information to them. Lieutenant Braxton told them it was his opinion that Mrs. Popov was more afraid of the terrorists than she was of the police. They were continuing to look for "Nick," the terrorist contact from the hospital, but so far, there was no sign of him.

"We'll keep the investigation open longer, especially since another attempt was made on Nora's life in Ireland. The two incidents certainly appear to be connected. I want you to know that

I continue communicating with Chiefs Herlihy and Brennan in Ireland. If you find out any new information, please let me know. Do you have any other questions for me?"

"Will you continue to provide protection for me and my family?" queried Nora. "This is very frightening for all of us."

"Yes, we'll keep a policeman at your front and back doors," answered Lieutenant Braxton.

Jesse served lunch, which today consisted of Shepherd's pie, salad, and brownies which, as usual, was delicious and served so artistically.

When Dr. and Mrs. Duffy arrived home, Lieutenant Braxton updated them on the results of their investigation. When Nora inquired about Sergeant Belsky, he told her that Laura had a bad case of the flu but seemed to be getting better. He would tell her that Nora had inquired about her. Lieutenant Braxton thanked them for their hospitality, waved a goodbye to them, and left.

That evening at an early dinner, Michael and Eileen Duffy talked to all of their children about what receiving his bequest from Uncle Cyrus could mean for them. They didn't have the money yet, but he thought it would be good to be prepared. First, he would have to pay for the new roof, but he asked for their suggestions about the rest. Siobhan took notes, and the suggestions broke down along gender lines.

The older girls wanted to buy season tickets to The Goodman Theater, the Symphony, and Lyric Opera as well as for some rock concerts. The older boys wanted to invest in the stock market. The younger boys wanted to buy season tickets for the White Sox, the Cubs, the Bears, and the Blackhawks. The eighth-grade twins said they thought that they should start a family charitable foundation for the homeless and get tickets to the Bono concert in Ireland.

Nora wanted to provide pro bono law services and medical treatments for some of her more seriously ill patients and their families. She'd also like to purchase a black Steinway for their living room and get new instruments for the Ceili band. Mrs. Duffy would like to make contributions to the many charities she supported. Dr. Duffy said he'd promised Father Ahearn that he'd pay to have the renovations done to St. Mary's school gym.

All agreed that they would like to rent or buy a large enough vacation house for the whole family in New Buffalo, Michigan. Eileen would also like to buy a home in Sonoma, California, near her sister, Janet. Nora reminded them that she and Tommy were also looking for a home for themselves. They would also be spending quite a bit on their wedding, especially now since they'd have to invite so many more people than originally planned. She would be handling those things out of her share of the money once she received it, and she had some ideas for how to handle contributions to the homeless.

Dr. Duffy continued, "So all of those goals are good, but we won't be doing them all at once until we're sure how much money we have to work with. What should we do first?"

They all agreed that the piano, the new band instruments, buying some tickets for concerts and football tickets, and the contribution for the gym renovation could be done now, and the other things could be researched. Jim offered to keep track of the money, and they all agreed that it was a good idea. He reminded them that their supposedly modest requests would already come to a tidy sum.

"While we're on the subject of money," said Jim, "there's something we want to talk to you about, Nora." Hearing Jim call her by her real name rather than the usual Bitsy got Nora's immediate attention. Jim looked determined but most uncomfortable.

"We older siblings feel cheated that Uncle Cy left all his money to you and none to us. We know you had this special relationship with him, but he was our great uncle too. We realize that you would likely give us the money if we asked you for it, but we'd like to have a share of the money for each of us independently, say, $100,000 each? It sounds like you'd still have plenty to spare. You seem happy to be like Mother Teresa and just continue on as you have been, but some of us have different plans in mind, and we need money to make them happen."

The twin girls, Molly and Caitlan, always on the lookout for anything hurtful happening to their big sister, put their arms around Nora and glared at Jim, but he pressed on.

Jim raised his voice a notch and continued, "Cousin Johnny from Sonoma called me last month and said he'd just gotten a job in Silicon Valley, and his boss said he needs several more people. I'd like to go, and Jack does too, but we'd need new cars and a place to live, and you know how expensive it is out there. We have some savings, but not enough. Now don't start crying. I know you're worried that having money would corrupt us, but it's not as though we'd be gambling or buying drugs. Mom and Dad raised us to make our own decisions, and we'll be smart about them. What do you think?"

"Are you finished?" responded Nora, brushing away tears. "I'm sorry I didn't talk to you about this earlier. I guess I assumed you'd know that the first thing I'd do would be to take care of my family. You've read the will, and you know that Uncle Cy did mention that I should give each of you a share of the money. True, he didn't mention all nine of you by name, but he often told me he regretted not knowing you better. It's not having money itself that worries me but the divisive effects it has on people. When have you ever talked to me in that tone of voice before, other than to protest that I'd gotten more cookies than you when we were little? One of the first things I did after I got home was to talk to Mr. Abbott about giving each of you $200,000, and that's in the works. It does scare me that you apparently talked to each other about this rather than coming to me directly."

Michael and Eileen Duffy watched the interchange among their children with fascination but resisted the impulse to intervene.

Nora continued, "You're grown men and don't have to tell us about your plans, but we've had a habit in this family before of talking over important decisions with each other. I'm sure you're aware that working in Silicon Valley has some panache, since only the smartest people get hired there, but it's hard on people's emotional and physical health, and there are very few affordable places to live. Aunt Janet would be thrilled to have you closer to her. When is this move supposed to take place? And what about Trish and Sally?"

Jack responded that they were still discussing things with Johnny, but it probably wouldn't be for a few months. Their girlfriends were worried about being so far from their families, and they hadn't yet talked them into going with them. "Bitsy, we're sorry about this, but we didn't know how to bring it up to you. Guess we didn't do a very good job of it."

Nora reminded them that she was not going to use any of the money she was supposed to receive until she was sure the taxes had been taken care of in the US and Ireland, and that wouldn't be for a few months. She would let them know when she received that clearance.

She continued, "I think we can survive this, but we're going to have to work hard to stick together, wherever you go. Tell me right away if you don't think things are going well. By the way, I'm flattered to be compared to Mother Teresa in any capacity, but she would have been very uncomfortable in my high heels. We can talk more about your California dreamin' plans later, but now we'd better get ready for the celebration across the street."

Jim and Jack gave Bitsy a hug and thanked her for her understanding. The other siblings seemed as though they were still trying to process what had just happened. Nora squeezed the twins' hands and smiled at them, but she couldn't help thinking about the scene in Matthew where the devil tempted Jesus three times with great wealth and told Jesus he could have it all if he would just bow down and worship him.

"Well, Jesus told the devil to get away from him, and I'm going to do the same," Nora said with renewed confidence. "I guess this conversation had to happen eventually. The love we've always had for each other is worth fighting for and more important than any amount of money."

The family got ready to attend the "Six Months Until St. Patrick's Day" party at St. Mary's. They would all be involved in playing a musical instrument of some sort, and Jack would be leading off the event with his friends in the Beverly Bagpipers. There would be a dance and a raffle where the first prize was $25,000, so they expected a big crowd at the gym. Tommy and his brothers would be leading the singing of the old St. Patrick's Day songs, like "The Wild Colonial Boy," "Toora, Loora, Loora," "When Irish Eyes Are Smiling," "The Black Velvet Band," and more.

The drawing for the $25,000 had the happy result of being won by a couple with five young children. The chair of the evening, Kevin Donnelly, gave a report on the plans for St. Mary's involvement in both the south side and the downtown parades in March and asked for more volunteers. The food table was groaning with stews, sandwiches, and desserts, and the dancers and sing-along made everyone feel great.

St. Mary's had as one of its missions publicizing the life and mission of St. Patrick, and Nora believed that he would be proud of them. St. Patrick's personal *Confessio* could be found at Trinity College in the *Book of Armagh*:

> My name is Patrick. I am a sinner, a simple country person, and the least of all believers. I am looked down upon by many. My father was Calpornius. He was a deacon; his father was Potitus, a priest, who lived at Bannavem Taburniae. His home was near there, and that is where I was taken prisoner. I was about sixteen at the time...

Nora recalled that Patrick was captured by Irish slave traders and brought to Ireland about 432 AD. He learned how to pray as he spent six years herding sheep on the hills of Ireland amidst conditions of cold, hunger, and pain. A miraculous vision told him to go to the coast where he would find a ship to take him back home, which was successful. However, he kept having dreams where he was called by the people of Ireland to come back to them and tell them about Jesus. His family tried to dissuade him, but he was finally appointed a bishop and was able to get back to Ireland to carry out his dream.

One of the first things Patrick did was to light a bonfire on the hill of Tara to attract the people, but the druids and the king of that region told him he had violated a sacred law by lighting the Easter fire before the druids' own fires. Patrick held out a shamrock and used the three leaves of the plant to explain the concept of the Trinity, the three-in-one God. He might well have been killed that night, but instead, God protected him, and the people embraced him. Before he died forty years later, he had converted almost the entire island to Christianity.

St. Patrick had inspired generations of Irish monks to go out across the world to continue his mission, which continues today. There was even a legend believed by many that St. Brendan and his monks may have been the first Europeans to reach America in a leather-bound boat, centuries before Christopher Columbus.

The Duffy family and so many others at St. Mary's did what they could to follow St. Patrick's inspirational courage and love. When the St. Patrick's mass occurred six months later, it would be preceded by the lighting of a cauldron of fire in remembrance of Patrick's sacred night.

Nora mused that the Irish people today had become more liberal in their religious beliefs, but the image of Patrick with his shamrock was still popular. However, the powerful image of Patrick pointing his staff at the snakes of Ireland and sending them slithering into the sea was just a legend. Scientists said that Ireland was one of the few places in the world where there were never any snakes to begin with. It made a great picture, though!

The next day, Nora kept an appointment at Holy Savior and had more X-rays to confirm that her concussion had not gotten any worse since the shooting at her, and it seemed fine. Nora went to work afterward at the Cancer Clinic and joyfully greeted the staff, parents, and patients. Everyone wanted to talk to her about the dramatic events of the past week, but she asked them to wait for a few days until she had regained her composure.

When she finished her shift, she was accosted by news reporters wanting to find out more news about her and her latest wounds. She told them there was nothing new to report and reminded them that they could come and watch her and her family at Barry's Pub the following evening.

Wednesday, September 19
Chicago, 7:00 p.m., CDT

Nora and most of her family traveled to Barry's Pub for their weekly musical production on Wednesday night with their instruments and music stands. Nora had invited the media to attend the session when she talked to them the previous weekend, and two tables were filled with the representatives from newspapers and TV stations at the back of the room. The family stopped to say hello to them and posed for a few pictures.

The restaurant was crowded with patrons, most of whom were regulars. Green, white, and orange decorations adorned the walls and tables to celebrate "Six Months to St. Patrick's Day." Everyone appeared to have ordered large portions of the delicious food and pints of beer.

At the stroke of 7:00 p.m., Tommy's father came out on stage and made opening remarks.

"Hello, everyone. I'm Patrick John Barry, and this is my lovely bride, Kathleen Barry. We want to thank you for being here tonight, and we hope to see you again soon. If you're here for the first time, you'll see that we take a break from eating and drinking for a few minutes while we unfurl the colors. We'll have our usual Wednesday night musical in a few minutes, but before we begin, I'd like to introduce you to my future daughter-in-law, Miss Nora Duffy, who would like to say a few words to you."

The crowd applauded loudly, which encouraged Nora to take to the microphone.

"Hello, everyone. You regulars at Barry's know that I'm Nora Duffy, and this handsome gent next to me is my fiancé, Tommy Barry. Unless you've been living in a cave for the last few days, you've probably seen a few things about me and my family in the news lately."

The remark elicited laughter from the audience.

"I wanted to clarify a few things to you. I've quickly discovered that some members of the press embellish the facts. I'm sure those sitting at the tables in the back of the room tonight would not do such a thing," Nora said with a grin, "but that will likely continue, whether I like it or not. One very silly story asked if there would be a romance for me with the nice young man who stayed with me during the funeral for our Uncle Cyrus. Neil is the son of a company officer, and I met him for the first time just an hour before that picture was taken." Nora held out the newspaper to the crowd, showing a picture of her being escorted up some stairs on the arm of Neil. "Tommy and I had a good laugh about it, but Neil's fiancée probably didn't think it was very funny.

"So whatever you may see or hear about us, I ask you to take it with a large grain of salt. Our family is pretty boring if reporters are looking for gossip, but I'm sure that won't stop them. As to being one of the 'most powerful and wealthy women in the world,' that seems like a scary burden to me rather than a blessing."

Nora continued, "In order for me to inherit my uncle's business and estate, it means that Cyrus J. Duffy is now dead, and that's a very sad thing since he was such a wonderful man, and we will all miss him so very much. As to being very wealthy, my occupation puts having a lot of money into stark perspective. If you came to me and said, 'My daughter has been diagnosed with a large brain tumor and I'll give you a million dollars to make it go away,' you know that my response would have to be 'We'll try very hard, but we can't promise anything.' Your health truly is your wealth."

Nora said, "Most people tell me how lucky I am to have all this money. I won't have access to it for a while, and at the moment,

I'm still a struggling intern. I guess it will be nice to have some extra money. We live in a big old Victorian house, which we love, but something always needs fixing. Dad, maybe we'll be able to fix those clanking pipes next to my bedroom now. I will likely set up some kind of foundation once I have more details, but all that is in the future.

"I ask you all to pray for us that we will make prudent decisions. Tommy and I will be getting married on St. Patrick's Day, just a few months away now. I don't anticipate that we'll change our plans much, but we'll probably invite a lot more people now and maybe even upgrade the food." Nora chuckled. "We'll keep you posted as we find out more. We're just trying to get through one day at a time. Now, I ask you to wish Tommy a very happy birthday!"

The crowd sang the traditional birthday song to Tommy, and he blew out the candles on a huge cake. He thanked everyone and said, "Let's get on with having fun as we always do at Barry's!"

Mr. Barry continued, "Barry's is always pleased to feature new young artists. Our good Jesuit friend, Father Mike O'Hara, introduced me to three young Native Americans who sing and play like angels. You know that we open these sessions with 'God Bless America,' and Robin Raintree and her brothers, Josh and Sam, will sing that wonderful song for us tonight. Let these talented young people sing the verses first, and then you can join them. First, please stand for the color guard."

The bagpipers sounded the opening notes, then the younger Barry's carried in the Irish flag and the American flag while the band members followed. Robin and her brothers were at the end of the line. She stood straight and tall and was dressed in a blue and white print dress with moccasins on her feet. Her brothers were dressed in white shirts, black pants, blue string ties, and big smiles.

The band and bagpipers joined in playing "A Nation Once Again" while the Irish flag was placed in a holder on stage and many in the audience sang along to the stirring melody. The American flag was placed in a holder on the other side of the stage.

Robin was the lead singer, Sam accompanied her, and Josh played the violin, and they began to sing "God Bless America." As expected, the young people did sing like angels, and the entire audience broke into a rousing chorus of the beautiful song composed by Irving Berlin and made popular by Kate Smith during World War II.

The Ceili band musicians began to play, and there were many instruments involved. Jim and Jack Duffy played the uillean pipes, Kevin the bagpipes, Brian the bodhran, Nora, Lucy, and Kat Barry the fiddle, Bunny Barry the tin whistle, Maureen and Trish Morgan the Irish accordion, Maeve Barry the flute, Paul Barry the drums, Tommy played the guitar, while Neil and Pete Barry joined Molly and Caitlan Duffy as dancers. Nora and Tommy were the lead singers.

All the patrons resumed eating, drinking, and talking, and the noise was deafening. About 10:00 p.m., Mr. Barry announced that the pub would close in half an hour, so it was time for last call.

The Duffys thanked the Barrys for their hospitality. Nora and Tommy spent a few minutes of alone time, and then the family made the return trip to Beverly in several vans. They all agreed that this evening had helped their spirits rise considerably. Nora recalled a theology class about the "Communion of Saints," a combination of the prayers of the deceased and those still on earth, but she felt like an evening like they'd just had was a concrete example of how enriching it was to have many communities of friends.

Sunday, September 23
Chicago, 10:00 a.m., CDT

Nora couldn't wait any longer about finalizing some plans for their upcoming wedding, and she decided to have as many bridesmaids as possible. "In for a penny, in for a pound," as Grandma Peg always said. She spent a good deal of time in the next few days calling potential bridesmaids and getting their acceptances. The current number was five from her family, four from Tommy's, four neighbors, three from her Irish dancing team, four from high school, four from college, and five cousins each from both their families for a total of thirty-four. That seemed like a huge number, but it should also be fun. Nora accepted Connie Carroll's offer to be her wedding planner since she'd always been so organized. Now it was up to Tommy to find an equal number of groomsmen, which might be more difficult.

Later that day, the female Duffy family members drove north to Barry's Pub to meet Tommy's grandmother, Clare O'Sullivan, whose business was making Irish dancing and wedding dresses. Clare had told Nora that she and her staff would be glad to make all the dresses for the March wedding. She would need to know what Nora wanted now since they would soon be busy making outfits for the upcoming dancing competitions.

Eileen Duffy had not yet met Clare and she was a bit apprehensive and wondered if they wouldn't be better off going to a professional bridal shop. She expected to see a little woman bent over from years of sewing, but the reality was that Clare O'Sullivan had a great figure with a personality to match. Her bright blue linen dress fit her perfectly with nary a wrinkle. Clare's stylish look was her best advertisement for her tailoring business.

Clare had a heavy Irish brogue and spoke quickly, so they had to sometimes listen carefully to understand her. She told them that she was thrilled to be involved with her darling grandson Tommy's wedding and she was eager to get started. The Duffys and Barrys had a quick dinner in Barry's restaurant, and then they got right down to business. Clare told them that her husband, Eamon, was the O'Sullivan; she was a Fitzsimmons. They came to Chicago forty years ago, and she'd been making Irish dancing costumes and wedding dresses ever since.

Clare asked Nora if she had some definite ideas of what she *didn't* want first. Nora responded the one thing she didn't want was to have formfitting dresses, because she'd seen dresses like that start out looking great, but as the girls moved and bent, the dresses became wrinkled even before they made it to the reception.

At the moment, there would be thirty-four bridesmaids, but she was still waiting to hear from a few cousins in Ireland, so there could be a few more. Most of the girls were thin, but a few of them were pregnant or still had not lost weight they'd gained during pregnancy. Nora explained that she'd like the dresses to have at least thin straps so that the girls wouldn't have to worry about their strapless dresses staying up.

"Good," responded Clare. "Give me some ideas of what you *do* want. Have you been looking at bridal magazines?"

"The magazines show some elaborate dresses with elaborate prices, and I've looked at suggestions on Pinterest too, but I'd like to hear what your suggestions are," said Nora. "It will be St. Patrick's Day, so at least some of the bridesmaids' dresses should be green, but green is not my favorite color. Thirty-four is a lot, so I'm not sure what to do about colors, and there will be some junior bridesmaids too. I want my dress to be white and full and sparkly. Every County in Ireland has a crest. I'd like my dress to have a long train with the crest of Chicago's Cook County at the top and then the crests of the thirty-two Irish Counties alternating with shamrocks along the edges. I'd like white roses and leaves, either real or ones that look real, around my head and a long veil."

Clare nodded her head and said that all sounded doable and she was glad that Nora had seriously thought things through. Mrs. O'Sullivan's assistant, Gloria, jotted down notes while they were talking. Clare then turned her attention to Eileen, Nora's mother.

"Eileen, I'm sure you'd be interested to know that we'll charge you about half of what it would cost if you ordered the gowns from a bridal shop, and they will be made better. And will we be making the dresses for the mothers and little kids as well? And how many are there?"

"I believe so. There will be the two mothers, six grandmothers, twelve little girls, six little boys, and two girl toddlers."

Clare explained that she had been doing this so long that she could generally figure out a size just by looking at people. She asked Nora to stand up and turn around. "Well, Nora, *a stor*," Clare said with a grin, "I think your size would fit right in with the ten to eleven year olds with a bit extra in the chest. Do you have some general guidelines for how you want your dress to look?"

Nora responded that she would like her dress to be really full and sparkly. "I'm too short to do sophisticated, so I may as well go for the fairy princess look."

"Now, all you ladies stand up one by one and turn around," directed Clare. As she looked at each girl, Gloria jotted down Clare's guesses about their sizes.

"What do you think, Eileen? Would you rather order your own dress?" Clare questioned Nora's mom. Eileen had a change of heart after seeing how professional Clare was, so she told Clare to guess about her too. They thanked Clare for her advice, and they agreed to wait to see her proposals for the dresses.

Then the Duffy family headed to Aunt Betty Gear's house for the family September birthdays event in Oak Park. As their families continued to grow, they had decided on the monthly group birthday parties, which made so much sense. Today they were celebrating the birthdays of six people, so the house was crowded, and the food was plentiful and delicious.

Much of the talk concerned the inheritances that the Duffys had received and what it could mean for all of them as far as being harassed by the media. Nora said the one thing she'd learned so far was to give the media little bits of information just to keep them temporarily happy and to not show signs of hostility toward them. She hoped that she could follow her own advice.

Wednesday, October 3
Chicago, 7:00 p.m., CDT

Nora had a busy day at work and arrived home about 7:00 p.m. She ate a quick dinner and then remembered that she had promised to attend the McIldowney's anniversary party. She felt like just staying home, but the McIldowney's had a rough year, so she decided to go. She heard the doorbell ring, and Jesse told her that Mrs. Graber was here to see her.

Nora got up from her comfortable spot on the divan and warmly greeted Gloryann Graber, her neighbor. She detected a feeling of nervousness emanating from Gloryann who asked if she could talk to her about something important. "Of course," responded Nora. "Please come into my dad's study."

Gloryann said she had a favor to ask her, and she was just going to launch into her story before she couldn't do it at all. Nora called to Jesse and told her to call the McIldowney's and tell them that she would be late getting to their party. She recognized the signs that Glory needed someone to lean on.

"Now," Nora said, "please tell me what you want to say."

"As you know, Greg was killed last July, and the union has been good about helping us with some expenses. I know that the high school entrance exam will be on December 1, which is not that far away. Marcie loves going to school with your young sisters and their friends, and I would very much like for her to attend Mother McAuley, especially since she loves music so much, which is one of their specialties. The truth of the matter is that I just don't make enough money at my job to pay the tuition. Marcie would be devastated if I had to tell her she couldn't go with her friends, so I'm swallowing my pride and asking you if you could loan me the money. I would pay you back, but with my limited income, that would take some time." Gloryann was wiping away tears by the time she finished her request.

Nora had listened to Gloryann without making a comment, but now she flashed a smile at her and told her that she would be glad to pay the tuition for Marcie since she was such an accomplished and smart young woman with a bright future. Gloryann jumped out of her chair and gave Nora a hug, but Nora asked her to sit down again.

They chatted for a moment about the girls, and then Nora told her she had a favor to ask of her. She said that she was going to ask Glory a series of questions that might seem too personal, but she assured her they were necessary. Nora told Gloryann that the media was relentless in their pursuit of anything negative around her, so she would like to head that off if there were any issues.

"I would have to have you investigated for my idea to work, so please tell me the truth right away. I don't know much about you, other than the fact that you are very pretty, you dress well, you work hard to keep your home looking so nice, and you have raised a caring and intelligent daughter. You produce a very professional-looking school newsletter, so I'm assuming you're good at the computer. I have a good feeling about you, and Reilly, my wolfhound, is sitting on your feet, which he only does when he likes someone.

"I've been trying to think of a way to keep track of the many requests like yours for money and what to do about them. I believe that God sent you to me today. Who do you work for again?"

"Gordon Engineering as a secretary."

"Do you like your work? And would you ever consider working for someone else?"

"I like the work well enough, but the salary is small, and I'm always on the lookout for other opportunities."

"Have you been in trouble with the police?"

Glory responded that she had once had a ticket for going the wrong way down a one-way street, but that was all.

"How are you at handling stress? Do you think you could handle aggressive questions from the media?"

"My mother trained me and my sisters from an early age to realize that stress is part of life, and I've managed to deal with the stress around Greg's death, so I think I could do that."

Nora continued, "As you know, I've been willed this enormous amount of money from my Irish uncle. I find it to be a burden. Ever since the news about my fortune has become public, requests for money come in every day. I really don't want to have to deal with those requests any more than I have to. Would you consider quitting your current job and coming to work for me? We'd have to look at your current salary and benefits, but I would likely increase them substantially. I would have to appoint an experienced financial person with a proven track record as the director, but I would give you a nice title to go with the job. I don't have an office for you to work in yet, but I would ask you to help me find one pretty close to our homes."

Nora explained that she envisioned Glory's tasks as helping to prepare an application form that requestors would have to use, treating everyone with a lot of respect, but not actually promising them anything, prioritizing the requests as to which ones she'd need to pay attention to first, sending responses to people, and using a financial program like QuickBooks to keep track of the budget.

"I haven't had a chance to think through all the aspects around this, but my focus would be on those who need emergency medical or financial help. I would have to decide on an annual amount that would comprise the budget. I believe most applicants would be told that this is a long-term loan and they would have to pay a small amount of interest, which would be a way to replenish the funds in the account. Occasionally, we could waive the interest, but you'd have to tell me more about those cases.

"If the person isn't known to me, you'd have to do a background check on them. I wouldn't want to finance criminals or terrorists. Once I get around to disbursing money, I would also have a require-

ment that the recipient would have to agree to do some kind of veri-
fied good deed, such as volunteering at a home or helping a neighbor.
I've been thinking it would be nice if we asked for a picture of them
doing that work. I can't give you an idea of the amount of work all
that would entail, but that would be a huge help to me. Would you
consider taking this on?"

Glory looked pretty shell-shocked, but she also was nodding
her head. "Oh, Nora, I've always admired you, and I think we'd work
together well. I promise you that I would be honest and trustworthy
with your money, and I think I could do what you've mentioned. I
do have one reservation about taking the job. I've heard about the
would-be killer and I wouldn't want to expose Marcie to any danger."

Nora assured Glory that she couldn't guarantee that there
wouldn't be any danger, but so far, it had been concentrated on her.
She asked Glory if she could start work for her at the end of the
month, and Glory agreed that she would. She gave Nora a huge hug
and said she just couldn't believe how God worked in mysterious
ways. "I'll tell Mr. Scanlon that I'll be leaving my current job, and
then you can tell me more about what you have in mind. God bless
you, Nora!"

Gloryann left, and Nora quickly ran upstairs and dressed for the
McIldowney party. This now felt like a much better day!

40

Thursday, October 4
Chicago, 1:00 p.m., CDT

M any observant members of the media contacted Nora
and told her that it had been three weeks since Nora was
promised her inheritance, and they wanted to know if she
had it and what she planned to do with it. Nora wanted to tell them
that it was none of their business, but she knew that would be futile
since they would just keep pursuing her.

She explained that she had received a preliminary report from
Duffy Hall and could have access to large amounts of money if she
wanted it, but she told them she would leave it alone for now until
she was sure that all the taxes had been paid in the US and Ireland.

Nora explained that she and her family had some thoughts about
what having a fortune could mean for them, but it was so overwhelming that they hadn't done anything about it yet. A Duffy Foundation
was being established in the US, and she had hired an Assistant
Director to monitor all requests for money. Her two young brothers
would act as computer geeks for the office, and she was in the process
of hiring a CPA as the Director. That's as far as she had gotten.

She also explained that she was still in the process of sorting out
how much of the money would be hers personally and how much
would belong to Duffy Medical, so in effect, nothing had yet been
done and would probably not be done for several months yet.

When the media said that they found it hard to believe that
she hadn't spent any of the money, she posed in her now-recognized

defiant stance of hands on hips and told them that what she's said is the truth and it's all she'd be able to tell them for several months.

They didn't seem happy, but they finally left after snapping a few pictures.

Nora's young cousin, Aunt Honey and Uncle Joe's daughter, Beth, called the Duffys and asked to speak to Nora. She said that she and her younger sister, Maeve, needed some answers to a question and would like to come and see Nora and her mother. Nora thought it was an unusual call, but she encouraged the girls to come and talk to them, after telling them to make sure that someone at home knew where they were going.

Beth, nine, and Maeve, seven, came to the door of the Duffys home rather formally dressed in dresses and party shoes. Beth had the Irish "gift of gab," and she started right in to explain their visit. "Aunt Nora, we've heard that you give away money for worthy causes, and we believe we have a very worthy cause. Our mother and father's tenth anniversary is coming up next month. They're so busy with us they never get a chance to do anything nice for themselves. They went to Mackinac Island in Michigan for their honeymoon, but we've often heard them say they regretted that they weren't able to stay at the big hotel since it was too expensive. We've looked everything up on the Internet, and we'd like to ask you for $1,000, which would be enough for gas to get them there, two nights at the Grand Hotel, and several meals."

"Aunt Eileen," they turned their attention to Nora's mother, "you'd have to help us out too. We'd like to stay at your house while Mom and Dad are gone. We could stay in Mary Ann's old room, and we'd help Jesse cook all the meals and clean up. Molly and Caitlan could help us get to school on Friday and check our homework. We don't think they'd mind.

"Nora, we've also heard that you want people who accept your money to do something nice for others. We think we could help Grandma Dee by organizing all her quilting and knitting supplies, and Grandpa Conor could certainly use his books organized. We were at their house last week, and they were a mess. What do you think?"

they said with such serious expressions on their faces. "Would you like us to sign something?"

Eileen and Nora were trying not to smile at their sweet request, and Eileen marveled at the many things that young children could do on their own in today's world. Nora told the girls that the first thing she'd have to do would be to check with Honey and Joe to see if they were free that weekend. If they were, Nora said she would be glad to make reservations for them at the Grand Hotel.

Nora asked the girls if they wouldn't want to go along, but they both looked at her with astonishment. "What kind of second honeymoon would that be to bring us along?" queried Maeve. "Besides, a town with only horses and no cars doesn't seem very nice to us."

Nora agreed with the girls' assessment of their great-grandparents' needs and said their proposals would be a be a big help to them. They gave the girls a kiss and told them to go straight home, and Nora would let them know about the hotel tomorrow.

Nora called Honey and said there was something she had to talk to her about, and she asked her to stop in at their house in the morning. When Honey arrived, Nora explained the visit they'd had from their girls. "Gosh, that's very sweet of them to think of it, but we were just going to go to dinner downtown," said Honey. "And that would be a lot of money to spend for a weekend."

Nora told her that it would be nice for them to accept for their girls' sake, and she thought it would be great for them to revisit that beautiful place.

Honey left with a smile in her heart. She knew that Joe would be so proud of their beautiful daughters.

Nora called the Grand Hotel at Mackinac, and she could tell that the woman at the reservations desk was stifling a laugh about getting a room there two weeks from now. "We have nothing available at all for at least three months," the supercilious woman assured her. When Nora pressured her more and asked if they didn't have a very nice lake view room available, regardless of the cost, she said she did have one room, but it would be $2,000 a night. Nora surprised her and said that she would take it and gave her all the information she needed for a two-night reservation.

Of course, Nora wouldn't tell Beth and Maeve that the cost was a little more than they had planned. She found it gratifying that even a nine-year-old was aware of her requirement that money given out required the recipient to help someone else, and she thought that Uncle Cy would be pleased to know that his money was causing a cascade of good deeds to occur around the world.

Friday, October 5
Chicago, 7:00 p.m., CDT

Nora and friends, Therese Cummings from the clinic and neighbors, Connie and Jean Carroll, drove down to Greek Town to celebrate Therese's birthday. Their senses were immediately assaulted by bouzouki music, delicious aromas of wine, lamb, garlic, cheese, and animated conversation the minute they opened the door of the Greek Islands Restaurant. The charming host led them to the table where they met up with Therese's two sisters, Karen and Nell.

Therese found it unbelievable that she was now twenty-eight years old, but her older sisters assured her the best was yet to come. The six young women shared stories, gossiped, and reminisced as only longtime friends could while they enjoyed wine, flaming saganaki, and then moved on to fragrant entrees and birthday cake. Therese gratefully acknowledged their generous gift certificate. Nora and Connie showed off their engagement rings, and Jean thought that she and her boyfriend, Olly, were next. Karen and Nell proudly shared pictures of their smiling toddlers on their phones.

Nora knew they were dying to talk about her recent news, but she begged them not to tonight. For two whole hours, she laughed and cried and gave all her attention to these sweet friends and didn't think about money or the would-be killer at all, which was a blessed relief.

At the beginning of October, Mrs. Jean Carpenter, their real estate agent, tried hard to find Nora and Tommy a home but without much luck. They looked at many city and suburban properties and saw a number of possibilities, but they weren't able to find just the right thing. After a few weeks of looking, they decided to just have a house built for them, and they settled on buying three lots near the Duffys house. One lot was empty, one had an unoccupied old house, and one had an occupied house they had to buy. They gave those homeowners a large fee to obtain their property, which was a win-win situation for both sides since the homeowners had been wanting to move to Florida.

Tom and Nora wanted to build something big enough to accommodate their large families and friends in a traditional style, but more open and with all the latest electronic gadgets. They want a big backyard. They wanted to start construction by the end of October and hoped to have at least the bulk of it ready before their mid-March wedding.

They hired a renowned architect, Mr. Jack Kamin, and stipulated that they would use Uncle Joe Flaherty's construction firm's union workers to ensure that the home would be built very well. They met with both men and found it hard to contain their enthusiasm as they explained their thoughts so far. One of their primary desires was that it would be a "smart house" with as many features as possible controlled by technology on their phones for doors, lights, security, furnace, appliances, blinds, and anything else they might think of.

They knew they could rely on Mr. Kamin to present them with a variety of attractive plans for the exterior of the home and said they would like to be surprised, so they'd wait to see his suggestions.

They had a lot of things in mind for the interior of a three-story home. The first story would have a spacious oval-shaped entrance hall with the walls covered with a wallpaper motif of old Beverly; their talented cousin, Lex, said he would hand paint the wallpaper for them. The floor of the hallway would have the crests of Duffy and Barry imprinted on it. There would be curved double stairways to the second floor, and a large window at the top would flood the hall with light. A large living room and dining room would be spacious enough to accommodate fifty people. The kitchen would run the length of the back of the house with plenty of floor-to-ceiling storage cabinets, an extra-large pantry, and an eating area surrounded by a bay window. A combination laundry and mud room would lead out to the backyard. Also on the first floor would be the master bedroom and en suite bathroom. "A room devoted only to file cabinets for all our papers would sit next to the mud room; this is one of our primary 'must-haves.'"

Nora saw Mr. Kamin's grin as she mentioned the many specifics, but she plunged on. "The second story would have five bedrooms with adjoining bathrooms. The third story would have a large bedroom on both ends and two full bathrooms. The area in between the two bedrooms would be an open family room. The finished basement would have a family room, another bedroom/bathroom, the laundry, and mechanics."

Tom continued, "The fenced-in backyard would have space for a garden, an outdoor kitchen and patio, a basketball court, and plenty of room for Reilly and Billy to play. Hopefully, the dogs will soon be joined by babies, so we'd like everything out there to be as kid-friendly as possible. We won't need such a big house for a while, but since we both have such large families, one never knows when we might have overnight guests. Oh, and don't forget a three-car garage and driveway."

Uncle Joe and Mr. Kamin said with a smile that they would try hard to accommodate their extensive wish lists. They promised to present plans to them soon and they thought that most of the house could be ready before the wedding, if all went well and the winter was mild. They told them to be thinking about their many choices for each of the rooms. They agreed that Nora and Tommy would be able to make periodic visits to the house while under construction.

This should have been a period of great joy for Nora and Tommy, but Nora continued to receive occasional threatening notes from the would-be killer that kept her off-balance. The notes continued to hide any clues as to the gender, identity, or motive of the person who was doing this. Each time, she had passed these notes on to Lieutenant Braxton who now had quite a file of them.

Sunday, October 7
Chicago, 1:00 p.m., CDT

Mrs. O'Sullivan had e-mailed Nora an agreement about the dresses for the wedding, and a week later, Nora and Eileen met with Clare to review her suggestions. Clare showed them drawings of what the dresses would look like. The maid of honor would wear an emerald green dress. The remaining dresses would be in the primary colors of green, red, blue, orange, yellow, and purple, and graduated pastels within each of those colors. There would probably be more dresses in blues and pinks since there were so many varieties of those colors.

Nora told Mrs. O'Sullivan that her cousin, Una, in Killarney had called her yesterday and said she would love to be a bridesmaid too, so that would bring the number to thirty-five. Una was the same size as Nora's sister, Siobhan, so Clare could use those same measurements for her.

Clare laughed and said that would be fine. She showed Nora a sketch of what her magnificent white and sparkly dress would look like, and all she could say was, "Wow." Nora said it looked even better than she had envisioned, and she thought that Cinderella would have been jealous. Clare reminded Nora that she should order her own shoes since she was not familiar with a shoe company that made such small sizes.

Clare explained that her proposed design for the top of the bridesmaids dresses would be an iridescent material, covered in beads and crystals styled to resemble flowers, with a sweetheart neckline, and thin straps covered in crystals. It would be March and probably chilly, so Clare suggested having a matching short jacket that could be used when needed. Clare said she would use a stretchy material for the backs of the dresses, in case there would be a need to make last minute adjustments for weight gain or loss. The bottom of the dress would be a puffy tulle material and floor-length in a matching color.

Each dress would be accompanied by satin sandal shoes dyed to match the outfits, so Clare would need exact shoe sizes for each girl.

"For the mothers and grandmothers, I propose making them long dresses with a tiny train with matching satin jackets. I think gold will match Mrs. Duffy's hair, champagne for Mrs. Barry, and the other colors to be chosen by the grandmothers. They may want a darker color.

"The junior bridesmaids and little girls will have plainer white dresses with rose trim. Perhaps you might want the little boys to wear green velvet pants with white shirts and matching green vests."

The Duffys and Barrys were excited by the proposals and said that it all looked wonderful. Clare said she was still looking into obtaining the crests of the various counties of Ireland, but she should be able to arrange it.

All the female members of Nora's wedding party then met at Barry's for the measuring of the dresses. Clare O'Sullivan and her team were so experienced that their first guesses as to the sizes of the bridesmaids appeared to be spot on, and only two bridesmaids would need a small change in size. It all got done very quickly, except for the very small kids who didn't much like standing still, let alone being measured.

Clare told Nora that they had what they needed and they would gradually start ordering material and then start to make the dresses. Everything would be ready by the middle of January in case anyone had a problem that needed to be fixed.

Monday, October 8
Chicago, 8:00 a.m., CDT

Mr. Jenson and his crew showed up to begin tearing off the very large roof of the Duffys' house. Several areas had a high pitch, so they brought along plenty of safety gear for the men. Dr. Duffy had met with Mr. Jenson earlier about the replacement roof, and they discussed several options and colors. They decided on black slate tiles, and Mr. Jenson told them it would take about a week to get things done. As long as they would be fixing the roof, they also agreed to install copper gutters and downspouts.

Mr. Jenson told them he'd heard about several homes in the neighborhood where the copper gutters had been stolen, so he suggested they ensure that their security system also extended to the exterior. The crew covered the surrounding shrubs and trees so that the old asphalt tiles would not damage anything when they were thrown down from the roof.

Jesse was not pleased about the ensuing dust since they had just washed the windows last month, but they would start again as soon as the roof people finished with their work.

Wednesday, October 31
Chicago, 7:00 a.m., CDT

Gloryann Graber started in her new role as Assistant Director for the Duffy Foundation. She had found an office for them in an attractive building and had transformed the basic space into a classic-looking professional office. She and Nora had agreed on a salary for her role that would enable Gloryann to pay her bills, send Marcie to her preferred high school, and live comfortably. The nearby location to her home was a blessing too. Many requests for money were pouring in all the time, so Nora was able to pass them on to Gloryann, which was a big relief to her. Nora had to find an experienced financial person as the director, and she thought she was close to hiring Ed Buck who was a CPA and had worked as a CFO at a large company.

Gloryann had alerted Nora that five people who requested money were particularly desperate since they were going to be evicted from their homes. Nora directed that enough money should be funneled to them that would stop the evictions for now. Gloryann told Nora that she thought it might be more efficient to hire another person just to do the computer work while Gloryann tried to prioritize which requests were more immediate. Nora said she would consider that and put pressure on Ed Buck to join them as the director. Nora thought that Uncle Cy would be happy to know that his hard-earned fortune was being put to such good use.

Duncan Lloyd told Nora that many people in Ireland were also submitting requests for financial help, and he suggested that he could begin the process of starting up a Duffy Foundation, Ireland. Nora asked him to get it started and to let her know how it was progressing as soon as possible.

Grandma Dee had sewn Halloween costumes for the Duffy twins to wear to school. St. Mary's had encouraged the children to dress up as their favorite saint and write a corresponding essay about the person. Molly chose St. Lucy since she'd always found the picture of her holding a tray with eyes fascinating, and Caitlan chose St. Therese the Little Flower whose motto was "Do small things with great love." Molly and Caitlan also brought Fannie Mae candy to share with their classmates that they had bought out of their allowances.

After school, the twins handed out trick-or-treat candy at the Duffy home, and hundreds of kids came to the door wearing creative costumes and carrying large bags to receive their treats. As always, the toddlers were adorable as they tried to articulate "Trick or Treat."

Barry's had a Halloween night, and all the siblings were invited. There were many creative costumes in the audience, and waiters and waitresses dressed up in costumes as well. Tommy and Nora dressed as the Headless Horseman and his horse. The prize for the best costumes went to Jack Duffy and Sally Doerr who dressed as a lion tamer and his lion. Sally's creative antics as the lion sealed the deal.

The Ceili band and dancers were joined by the night's guest musicians, members of the Irish Heritage Center, the north side center for Irish arts. Many members of the Chicago PD were there for protection, and they also shared in the corned beef and cabbage dinner.

The Duffys headed back to Beverly to spend some time with the younger siblings at their party. Trish Morgan, Jim's fiancé, looked a lot like Maureen Duffy with her long blond hair. Trish is a junior at Northwestern University as a physics major and had taken fencing lessons since she was a little girl. Today she dressed in a costume that made her look like the ancient Irish heroine, Grania, the Pirate Queen, and her sword or foil was real. Fencing had long been part of the Olympics, and Trish's grandfather was an Olympic fencing champion.

Trish left the Duffys' party a little early so she could get back to her family's home for the end of their party. She had five sisters, and her father, Paul, insisted that all six girls take self-defense classes every few years. Trish had never had occasion to use any of the safety tips she learned at these classes, but they made her feel safer.

Trish walked down the street to her car, pulled out her phone, and put it into the dashboard holder. She started the car and attempted to pull out into the street but became aware that an old black car with dark tinted windows had pulled up right beside her car and stopped, blocking her exit. Trish looked in her rearview mirror and side mirrors and didn't see any other cars near the stopped car. The driver of the black car stepped on the gas every so often, which made a menacing sound. He also aimed some type of flickering laser light right into her eyes. A frisson of fear started in Trish's gut. How concerned should she be?

Trish had her fencing foil on the seat next to her, but she realized that when you get scared, you get somewhat paralyzed. A fencing foil wasn't much use if the other person had a gun, but try as she might, she couldn't see into the black car. What did this guy have in mind?

She recalled the warning she'd heard at her classes: Don't take chances; call the police first. She called out to her phone to call Jim. She wasn't sure he would hear her call since there was so much noise at the Duffys home, but he answered right away. Trish tried to control the timbre of her voice and yelled out to Jim that she was in danger so he should ask Andy the cop to run down to her car in front of the Murray's driveway and bring his gun, just in case. Jim assured her they would be right there. A throng of people ran out of the Duffys' front door and rushed toward the Murrays'.

Trish grabbed her phone, turned on the camera, and aimed it at the black car's side window and flashed a picture. At that, the car sped off, and she took another picture of its license plate as it roared down the street. She realized she was shaking, and just then, Andy, Jim, and several other people from the Duffy's came running up to her.

Trish showed Andy the pictures she'd been able to take, and he hurried back to the CPD District 22 headquarters. It didn't take them long to discover that the license plate on the black car belonged to a young man who had reported his car stolen last night. They put out an APB on the black car and found it several hours later next to an abandoned lot. The young man who said the car belonged to him was questioned, but it was pretty clear that he had not been involved. He was given a ticket for having such heavily tinted windows, and they told him to get them changed. He said he had gotten the car from a friend in another state, where such windows were legal, and promised to get them fixed. The police tried to enlarge and brighten the picture Trish took through the side window of the black car, but the visuals were not clear enough for an identification.

Jim ushered Trish back to the Duffys' house, and she called her parents and told them about her experience and that she would be delayed. She also told Jim that she was very surprised at her reactions in an actual emergency. She thought she would be much braver, but such was not the case. Everyone at the Duffys commiserated with Trish and told her how glad they were that she wasn't hurt. Jim said goodbye to everyone and drove Trish to her home a few miles away. Jim wiped away Trish's tears, and they hugged each other and thanked God that nothing more had happened. Trish was finally able to smile and said that she thought it was time for her to retake her safety class.

The police lab tested the black car for fingerprints but, not surprisingly, every surface seemed to have been wiped clean. Lieutenant Braxton was notified, and they assumed that Trish had been mistakenly targeted since she looked so much like Maureen as part of the continuing war of assaults against the Duffy family.

Nora wondered if the would-be killer was branching out and threatening other people she loved. All Saints Day was the next day, and Nora asked the unseen heavenly throng of holy men and women to protect them all.

Monday, November 15
Chicago, 4:00 p.m., CST

Tom and Nora's new house construction had been moving along well, and the first story flooring was almost completed. They had made a lot of progress on Monday, but as it neared dusk, there were still some last-minute details to finish up. One of Uncle Joe's workers, Dave Delaney, agreed to stay behind and work on them so the crew would be ready to move ahead tomorrow.

Dave was standing near the top of a very tall ladder when he heard something heavy hit the floor. He looked down and could see a large rock with something tied to it that looked like a bomb with a lit fuse. Dave had been in Afghanistan and knew that if you could see the fire, it might be too late already. The fire extinguisher was right below him, but he figured he didn't have time to carefully climb down each rung. He decided to just hang onto the ladder handrails on each side and slid all the way down as fast as he could. He grabbed the extinguisher and sprayed foam all over the rock, and whatever was burning went out. It wasn't until he saw red dropping on the white foam that he realized his arm was torn open and was dripping large drops of blood very fast. He got out his phone and called Joe and told him to call an ambulance, the police, and the Duffys in that order because he thought he was about to faint.

He remembered from a first aid class that he should put his arm up as far as he could so the blood couldn't flow so fast. Dave called for help repeatedly, just in case anyone could hear him.

Dr. and Mrs. Duffy had taken Reilly out for a walk, and they suddenly felt the wolfhound pulling them forward as fast as he could run. Eileen still had her heels on and had trouble keeping up, but Dr. Duffy ran ahead with Reilly. Soon he heard Dave's calls for help and found him slumped over the ladder. One glance told Dr. Duffy that Dave was losing blood quickly. When Eileen caught up to him, he asked her to remove her pantyhose so he could put a tourniquet around Dave's arm. He used his cell phone to call the house and told Molly to get over to Nora's new house right now with his medical bag. He had time to do some first aid, but they soon heard the ambulance's siren and saw the blinking blue lights of several Chicago PD squad cars.

Dave was able to tell them that he didn't know what was strapped to the rock, but he thought it might be some kind of bomb. He advised them not to go near it, just in case. The policemen called the bomb squad who came out to look at things. They told them that it was a stick of dynamite. If it had exploded, it would certainly have destroyed the construction and would have injured or even killed Dave. It was miraculous that Dave had seen it and was able to disable it so completely.

Dave told the paramedics that he wasn't sure how he had cut himself so badly. He must have caught his arm on something sharp on the ladder as he slid down. After a few hours in the ER and some stitches, Dave was released. He was unable to tell the police anything about who could have thrown the rock. He had been tightening bolts up on the ladder and was preoccupied with that. The police talked to the Duffys and Uncle Joe and advised them to put a construction fence around the property and have CCTV cameras installed.

They questioned a few neighbors at nearby homes, but no one had seen anything, not even Mrs. Hilda Brown. She was known as the neighborhood watcher—some would say busybody—but she had been out in the backyard at the time.

Nora and Tom could only assume that the would-be killer was trying a new tack to harass them. Whoever it was seemed to have thrown caution to the winds and was now just trying to hurt them however he or she could. Uncle Joe assured them they would halt construction for now and put up a high construction fence around the property.

Lieutenant Braxton and Sergeant Belsky were getting frustrated as well that with all the effort they'd been expending on this case, they still didn't know who the perpetrator was. They said they would find a way to have police protection placed around the construction site.

Father Ahearn talked to the police and said that Monsignor Callahan's room had an excellent view of the construction site, and they could put cameras outside his window too.

Nora told Tommy that she thought she knew what the proverbial mouse felt like as it was repeatedly attacked by a very big cat who was deciding how to permanently dispose of her.

Thursday, November 22
Chicago, 6:00 a.m., CST

Sometimes Chicago Thanksgivings required going "through white and drifted snow;" however, this year, the dawn brought only cold temperatures but clear skies. Thanksgiving morning started out for the Duffys at the 10:00 a.m. mass with all the Duffy children playing an instrument or singing. The afternoon was spent providing a meal for people who were alone or sick in the neighborhood at a dinner served in the basement of St. Mary's school. Everyone in the family helped out. Mrs. Rita Marshall from the parish organized the dinner every year, which was always well-attended.

They made several turkeys at the Duffys', and many other families roasted a turkey and brought it to the dinner at 2:00 p.m. Other people provided potatoes and vegetables, cranberries, and desserts. Volunteers from other churches in the area helped with set up and cleanup. They made an effort to decorate the tables and to use china plates and cups so the participants would have a pleasant experience. Nora and her siblings and friends provided music, and after dinner, they first played games and gave out prizes, and then they invited everyone to sing. A big Christmas tree had been set up, and participants could help to decorate the tree if they wished. Each person received an envelope containing a gift certificate for the County Fair market.

The media heard about the dinner and wanted to televise it and interview some of the participants. They seemed surprised that the

"Mighty Rich Midget" and her family would be spending their holiday in this way, but Nora told them they'd been doing this since she was a little girl. She told the reporters that they were welcome to help out too, but most of them had an excuse as to why they couldn't stay.

Everything closed up about 7:00 p.m., and then the Duffy family went back to their house to watch television, snack, and visit.

The Barry family had Thanksgiving dinner at the restaurant with their patrons, but they had provided generous contributions of food for the St. Mary's dinner.

Nora had to be on call at the hospital at 5:00 p.m. The hospital had a turkey dinner for the kids and their parents, which was very popular. Nora took a break about 8:00 p.m. and went to the cafeteria where she saw her friend, Bob.

"Bob, you look bedraggled. Bad day in the ER?"

"Hi, Bitsy. Oh, just the usual share of holiday fun with people cutting and burning themselves and inflicting food poisoning on their relatives. Had one guy who may have blinded his mother-in-law in one eye by popping a plastic champagne cork at her face. I'm waiting for ophthalmology to take a better look at it.

"I've heard of this, but I've never actually seen it until today. Some genius dropped a frozen turkey into his deep fryer that was sitting on his outdoor deck. He and three of his friends were splashed with burning grease when the turkey exploded, so they are being treated for those painful burns now. He set the deck on fire, which also spread to his house. His wife is here, and she is not thrilled with him. I'm sure the only dinner he'll be getting will consist of turkey fried rice.

"We also had a couple of heart attacks and the usual car accidents with people who had too much to drink. A motorcyclist broke both his arms. Basically, it's a zoo down there. How's your day going?"

"Not too bad today. The kids and parents enjoyed the dinner. No one is critical, so that's a good day for us. We're due for three new admits tomorrow, so that's always hard. How's your mom doing, Bob?"

"She seems better today and was looking forward to having dinner with the family, but she's having a heck of a time walking after that leg surgery. She's got Victor for a physical therapist, so hopefully he'll get her back on her feet soon. So how's it going being a woman of wealth and property?"

Nora responded with a dismissive wave of her hand, "It's more of a pain in the neck than anything. They've given me some idea of what the money is going to look like. I've got the government of both countries hungrily licking their chops for a share of it. Think the financial advisors have figured out that if I just get paid a decent salary as an employee of the company and leave the rest of it in the bank, it will work out better for me and all involved.

"You hear that people who win the lottery get approached by all the people they've ever known and asked for money, and it's true. This week I got a letter from a guy who says he sat next to me in seventh-grade English—I very vaguely remember him—and he needs $50,000 to start his restaurant. The lawyers have been helpful about how to deal with these letters, and they've advised me to hire people who do nothing but read through these requests, verify who the people are, and then judge the need of the person.

"Some people's needs are more immediate, like a neighbor who is about to be evicted because he lost his job and can't pay the rent. I've hired a neighbor to keep track of these requests, and she sends on the urgent requests to me. You can be sure that the Church wants their cut too. I've got the lawyers working out deals with our parish, St. Mary's, and Catholic Charities, plus the charities of the other churches, mosques, and synagogues in Chicago who have suddenly discovered that I'm their good friend.

"I made the big mistake of telling some reporter that my car was eleven years old, and now I get calls and mailings from every car dealer in the Chicago area. I suppose I should think about getting a new car, but I feel like I'm being harassed and I worry that some reporter would be following me around at the car dealers.

"All in all, it's like having another business, which I don't have the time or energy to deal with. Some financial planners suggest starting a business and hiring these people who are asking for money to run and work in it. That sounds like a possible solution, but then I'd have to hire somebody to start the business. It was nice of my uncle to do this for me, I guess, but I'm still trying to figure it all out. I'm used to having no more than $100 in my pocket at any one time, and that's how I plan to keep things. I hope no robber approaches me looking for money, because I won't have it with me."

"Isn't this the time of year when your little sisters get so involved with the Irish dancing?"

"Yes, they left tonight with my mom and my aunt and are driving to Louisville, Kentucky, for the Midwest Championships. They have multiple outfits and wigs and shoes and other paraphernalia and their suitcases, so the car was bursting with stuff. It's a long ride, but they should be there about 1:00 o'clock this morning. They don't compete until the day after tomorrow, but they wanted to be there in enough time for more practice and to check out the competition.

"Molly and Caitlan and our cousin, Lizzie, will be competing with about 150 other thirteen-year-olds. It's very stressful for the kids and their parents since the numbers get whittled down until there are only the top ten left. Their teachers are excellent, so I think they'll do well, but the competition keeps improving. I would have loved to go with them, but I'm on for the clinic all week. Our other cousins, Maisie and Orla, are going too, but they are in the fiddle competition. These competitions are a whole subculture that most people have never heard of, but you wouldn't believe how many people are involved."

"I hope they do well after all their work. You used to dance too, didn't you?"

"Yes, I did for years and I still miss it. I keep practicing with the girls, though, since it's great exercise for the whole body. It's a lot of fun, and I love the music."

"Well, I've got to get back to the zoo," said Bob. "Who knows what other ways people can find to injure themselves before the day is done?"

The Duffy family gathered on Friday and had their own Thanksgiving dinner. Everyone made their specialties. Nora made the breakfast soufflé that they all loved, and Maureen took advantage of her time off to make her delicious apple cinnamon coffee cake. They all gathered to watch either football or movies. Dr. Duffy made it home from the hospital in time for the early dinner, and they sat down in the beautifully decorated dining room to enjoy several large turkeys, many trimmings, pies, and homemade cookies. Grandma Marie reminded them that in the "old days," they wouldn't have been able to eat meat on Friday. Kevin and Brian said they were happy they didn't live then.

Ed and his helpers had put out most of the exterior Christmas lights around the house last week, but Michael and Eileen had gone shopping to the Christmas store in Long Grove and purchased some additions, which they put out after dinner. The new front door wreath and Santa's sleigh for the front porch looked just right.

The giant Christmas tree in the living room had been put into place in the bay windows, and after everyone got a second wind, they gathered to start the decorating. Most of the ornaments were old and represented special occasions that had impacted the Duffy family. Jesse prepared a variety of Christmas treats, and they made short work of those. Siobhan played the piano, and everyone joined in singing the old Christmas carols. Nora accompanied her on her violin, but she had the night shift at the clinic and had to leave by 7:00 p.m.

Nora talked to Tommy, and they agreed to meet the next day at Macy's in Water Tower Place to start their Christmas shopping. They decided to give everyone a gift certificate, plus they would buy each of them one nice gift. They wanted to save going to the Walnut Room at Macy's downtown for Christmas Eve, so they went to the Italian Village for lunch and ordered their delicious chicken parmesan.

The Duffys heard from Eileen that it had been a stressful dance competition, but Molly, Caitlan, and Lizzie all qualified to go to the World's championships next April. The fiddlers did well too, and Maisie and Orla would be joining them for the trip. They will be driving back today and would reach home by dinnertime.

The Sunday after Thanksgiving was always reserved for Dr. Duffy's Holy Savior Hospital Christmas gathering at the house. For the past few years, Nora had also invited her colleagues from the cancer clinic to attend. There were so many people expected that they ordered catered food from a number of local restaurants, and Jesse and her crew supplemented by providing a delicious array of appetizers and cookies. It was a festive gathering, and Dr. Duffy acted as Santa and gave out presents to all.

Lieutenant Braxton had heard about the planned party and told Dr. Duffy he would provide extra security for it. Lieutenant Braxton had been working with Mrs. Samuels at Holy Savior Hospital about employees who could have had regular contact with the suspected terrorist contact, Nick Chernoff, while he was employed there. A few employees remembered talking to Nick in the smoking area, and all of those people had been questioned. Lieutenant Braxton relayed that two of the questioned employees were from Dr. Duffy's office, Jason Reynolds and Sue Bonner.

"We haven't learned much new yet, but we don't want to take chances when you have a large gathering at your house," said Lieutenant Braxton.

The resulting party was a happy and successful affair, and nothing threatening occurred, but Dr. Duffy was relieved to know that the Chicago PD, dressed in plain clothes, were circulating among the guests.

On Monday morning, Nora met with her financial advisors in Chicago who confirmed their information with Duncan Lloyd in Ireland. Nora would receive a yearly salary of 300,000 euros or about $350,000 for her services as the chairman of the board of Duffy Medical. She asked for clarification from John and Duncan about their expectations of her, and they said they were putting together a report for her. There would be an immense amount waiting for her in the bank, and she could request more if she needed it. Mr. Lloyd said he would forward the formal report to her by e-mail and by express mail.

Her Chicago lawyer, Mr. Paul Abbott, was also finalizing the process of setting up the Charitable Foundation, which would make it easier to process the requests she received for money. This should be ready before Christmas. Ed Buck had also agreed to become the Director of the Chicago Duffy Foundation, and he had already had a briefing with Gloryann Graber. This much progress made Nora feel much more comfortable about things, and she breathed a sigh of relief.

Saturday, December 1
Chicago, 7:00 a.m., CST

December was filled to the brim with meetings, events, and parties. Today was the high school entrance examination for Molly and Caitlan and their friends. They had all been studying for weeks now, and although they were nervous, they felt well-prepared and seemed to make it through the lengthy test fine. The twins were especially tense taking the test at different schools since this was the first big thing they'd done apart from each other. They wouldn't know the results of the tests until mid-January, but they needed a stress break. They met many of their friends at Portillo's Restaurant in Oak Lawn for hamburgers and shakes and shared their thoughts about the test. It was a relief to have it over with, and they could now focus on making plans for the various Christmas events.

On December 5, Chicago was hit with one of her early snowstorms, and by evening, six inches of snow covered the streets and sidewalks that looked pretty for a short time. Chicago had always been known as "the City that works," and an army of dedicated workers with their snow plows soon had most of the snow removed. That was a good thing, because the annual December 7 memorial of Pearl Harbor was coming right up.

On December 7, "a day that will live in infamy," as President Franklin Roosevelt had proclaimed, the entire Duffy family attended the mass at St. Mary's to remember Mrs. Duffy's great uncle who was one of the unfortunate men among the 1,177 sailors who lost their lives on the USS Arizona destroyed by Japanese bombs on that fateful day. The ship sank almost immediately and lay at the bottom of Pearl Harbor with the memorial above it. It was easy to imagine the agonies that those men went through as the ship was sinking.

The Duffys invited all the WWII military survivors in the Chicago area to attend, and a good contingent of them and their families did come. These brave men were dying at a fast rate now since they were in their mid to upper nineties. Representatives from many churches, synagogues, and mosques across Chicago attended, and the church was packed. Eileen's cousin, Evelyn, was Uncle Bob's daughter and was happy to greet the family and thank them for not letting her dad be forgotten.

Father Ahearn gave an inspiring homily about the evils of war and the sting of hatred and mentioned the irony that about one-third of all cars sold in the US today were Japanese. That would certainly have surprised Bob and his buddies in 1941.

Nora prayed that the sting of hatred would also be removed from the heart of whoever had been trying to kill her.

After Communion, Evelyn thanked everyone for coming and said that it was somewhat of a comfort to her as she was growing up to have people remember her dad as a hero, but she would have much preferred to have heard his voice reading her a story or felt his hand holding hers. That was always the way after a war with so many people and their potential lost.

When Evelyn finished, a midshipman played "Taps," and then the choir sang the stirring sailor's song, "Eternal Father, Strong to Save," which was based on the dangers of the sea as described in Psalm 107.

At the conclusion of the mass, the entire congregation joined in singing "America the Beautiful." Everyone then went to the basement of the church for a delicious brunch. Evelyn and many others then went to visit at the Duffy home.

On December 8, Nora and Tommy went to a paper goods store to pick out their wedding invitations. *Should the invitation be modern and minimalistic, traditional, or antique and flowery? Should it have something Irish on it for St. Patrick's Day?* They looked through many sample books and were almost ready to forget the whole business when Tommy came across one that he thought would be unique and a good compromise. It was a talking card, and they could record what they wanted it to say. The cover was oval shaped and had a beautifully magnified picture of white roses and lily of the valley. The writing on the card could be in whatever script and color they desired. They wanted a note on the card to say that no gifts were desired, but donations could be made to Catholic Charities. In his usual way when he felt like they'd devoted enough time to this enterprise, Tommy said, "There. Done."

They ordered 2,000 invitations, but then the owner reminded them that they were not quite done. "I assume that you'll want a QR (Quick Response) symbol that tech-savvy people can use to respond, but you should also include a card and stamped envelope for those who don't know how to do that. Also, you may want to include a stamped envelope addressed to Catholic Charities so the invitees don't have to look that up." Mr. Nolan told them that they should come back tomorrow to make the final arrangements and record what they wanted the card to say. He assured them that the invitations would be ready two months before the wedding. He told them that he also had a service that would address the cards and mail them out seven weeks prior to the wedding, if they would like. They did like it and they made those arrangements and promised to get the list of invitees to him in a few weeks.

They couldn't forget about sending out Christmas cards too, so they went to the Hallmark store and found perfect cards and spent several nights writing out greetings, addressing cards and stamping them, and dropping them off at the local post office. Many of their friends just sent Christmas greetings through their e-mails or phones, but Nora still enjoyed the process of sending out cards and loved to see the many artistic cards they received in return.

The family attended various Christmas celebrations all through December at their offices and schools and helped Jesse make various candy treats for Christmas presents. On December 15, they attended the big Christmas party at Barry's. It was energizing to be involved in so many celebrations, but they were beginning to lag a bit by the time that evening was over. They were revived the next night when they joined a huge throng singing the "Do-It-Yourself Messiah."

Monday, December 24
Chicago, 10:00 a.m., CST

Everyone in the Duffy family made the necessary arrangements with work so they could have Christmas Eve off. Michael and Eileen Duffy had been bringing their large brood with them on Christmas Eve morning to eat under the big tree in the Walnut Room at Marshall Field's/Macy's since Nora was a baby. The big tree's decorations changed yearly, and this year, the tree was covered in giant multicolor ornaments and ribbons. The topper for the big tree, when it was owned by Marshall Field's, used to be stuffed representations of Uncle Mistletoe and Aunt Holly, but now it was just a star, beautiful though it might be. The children always looked forward to having one of the beautifully dressed fairy princesses tap them on the head with her magic wand, sprinkle them with fairy dust, and encourage them to make a fervent wish with their eyes closed.

Waiting for a table is easier now that they could just talk to a young woman with an iPad to reserve their spot. In the "old days," someone had to stand in the long line the entire time so that their place wouldn't be given away.

Some things on the menu kept changing, but Mrs. Field's Chicken Pot Pie had been part of the fare since 1890, although it'd had various iterations over the years. Grandpa Conor always ordered the Special Sandwich, which consisted of a half-head of lettuce, some turkey, bacon, cheese slices, and olives—all covered in thousand island dressing. Molly always said it looked like a tomato brain.

Tommy and other friends joined them too, and they had about fifty people in their group. They inevitably saw other families that also had made it part of their family traditions to go to the Walnut Room on Christmas Eve and stopped and said hello to them.

After lunch, those couples with little kids went to see Santa while others did a little last-minute shopping. Nora's favorite place to visit was the bookstore, which long ago was on the third floor but had been in the basement for a long time now. In 1993, a break occurred in the old transportation tunnels under the Chicago River, and the entire basement was flooded and had to be abandoned for weeks, the bookstore included.

Nora had a number of favorite authors, so she asked the clerk to search for them on her computer to see if they had a new book out. Nora settled for another mystery book by Donna Leon. This prodigious author had written so many stories about Inspector Brunetti that Nora felt as though she knew him, his co-workers, and his interesting family, and she always learned new things about the magical city of Venice. Nora had heard that another Winston Churchill biography had come out, and the clerk showed her where she could find it on the shelves. She admired his visionary grasp of history and what he had done for the world.

If the weather wasn't too terrible, the whole family then enjoyed walking around the store outside and admiring Macy's windows and their amazing dioramas.

This year, Nora would be joining Tommy at his parish's midnight mass, so she said goodbye to her family.

Before they went back to the Barry's, Nora and Tommy drove over to Irving Park Beach and gave each other their Christmas presents. Tommy had ordered Nora an antique gold ring that had once belonged to an important Chicago socialite from the nineteenth century. The ring had an impressive ruby in the center and diamonds on the sides. The setting was antique style and would just need a few adjustments to fit her perfectly. Nora gave Tommy a pair of cufflinks with the Barry crest of a shield with red and white stripes and an armored head. They were both delighted with their gifts and the joy they'd given to each other.

They drove to the Barrys and were warmly welcomed by Tommy's mom and dad and all the brothers and sisters—Lucy, Maeve, Kat, and Bunny, and Paul, Neil, and Pete. They were both too full to eat much, but they snacked on cheese and crackers and grapes and watched a delightful version of *The Nutcracker* on television.

They got ready to go to midnight mass and thanked God for the fair weather that had enabled them to drive about the city pretty easily. Monsignor Conway said the mass and gave an inspiring homily. The decorations around the church were impressive, and the choir performed brilliantly. At the conclusion of the mass, the entire congregation joined in singing the hallelujah chorus from Handel's "Messiah." As they were leaving, the church bells rang out "It Came Upon the Midnight Clear," and snowflakes were lightly falling.

The Barry family returned to the house, and Mr. Barry made pancakes for everyone. Afterward, Nora shared text messages with her family, and she received a text from her mom saying that everyone had gone to midnight mass at St. Mary's, and they announced that Mrs. Weber, who had been sick so long, died that afternoon. Nora had such good memories of this charming woman who was so generous to all the kids in the neighborhood, and she knew they would be going to that funeral in a few days. Life was a constant confluence of happy and sad events.

Nora then settled down in an extra bed in Lucy and Maeve's bedroom and caught up with their news. Kat and Bunny joined them for some girl talk. Lucy was pretty sure that her boyfriend, Kevin, would be giving her a ring the next day, and she was so excited. Maeve had been accepted by the Boston Ballet and hoped to be dancing with them the next summer. Nora was happy that these energetic girls would soon be a part of her family too.

She was especially happy that she hadn't heard anything lately from the killer, and after a while, she fell asleep. She wondered if perhaps the killer had given up and prayed that might be the case.

Tuesday, December 25
Chicago, Noon, CST

Tommy and Nora headed back to the Duffys, and they were glad to see that the snowfall only amounted to a few inches. Dedicated Chicago Streets & Sanitation workers had been busy overnight clearing streets, so it was no problem to drive on the Dan Ryan Expressway and get to the house easily. Tommy told Nora the good news that his sister, Lucy, wanted her to know that her boyfriend, Kevin, was now her fiancé, and Nora was thrilled for her. One of the best things about having a big family was that there was always something new happening now and in the future. It was exciting to know that there would now be another wedding to prepare for. Lucy would make a beautiful bride.

They arrived at the Duffys, and they saw that Molly, Caitlan, and their friends had managed to eke out a respectable snowman from the few inches of snow and had decorated it with a Duffy plaid scarf and hat. Nora and Tommy were greeted with many hugs and kisses, and their hearts were warmed to hear the sounds of Christmas carols in the background. Reilly, Billy, and Cheshire also greeted them and waited to be petted. The girls updated them on the caroling party for the seniors last night, which was so much fun. The family decided to open gifts now and have dinner later.

First, they called the folks at Duffy Hall in Sneem and wished them a Happy Christmas. Everyone at the hall thanked the Duffys for their very generous presents. They told them that the Christmas

Eve release of Cleary's Holly & Ivy perfume, colognes for children, and Danny Boy for men were all huge sellers. Everyone there was doing well, and they hoped to see them soon.

The family did their best to give each other perfect gifts according to the recipient's tastes. Jack acted as Santa and handed out the many packages under the enormous tree to each person. Tommy received tickets to two Cubs games in the spring, even though the Duffys were die-hard White Sox fans. Nora received Lyric Opera tickets from her mom and dad for one of her favorites, *Tosca*. Her sisters pitched in and bought her a new pair of Jimmy Choo shoes, open toe heels in black with blue trim. Her other siblings gave her tickets for Shakespeare in the Park's presentation of *A Midsummer Night's Dream*.

Nora revealed that her gift to the whole family was a large vacation home she bought in New Buffalo, Michigan, one of the family's favorite places. The house was near town, and it was being completely rehabbed. It would be ready for them to use by early March. It had a panoramic view of Lake Michigan, was steps from the beach, and there was a pool in the backyard. There were six bedrooms and a finished basement where more sleepers could be accommodated. It was a year-round house with heating and air-conditioning, so they could use it whenever they had free time. It would be much closer to Notre Dame in the fall. There was much clapping and dancing around, and everyone was thrilled by the news.

They thought they were finished opening their gifts, but Jack noticed that there was still a small box way under the tree wrapped in brown paper and addressed to Nora. The return address said it was from Santa's Workshop at the North Pole, which seemed charming. Nora shook the package with a smile and started to open it, but Dr. Duffy suggested that she bring the box with her and talk with him out in the hallway. "Nora, I think we should call Lieutenant Braxton about this box. We don't know how it got under the tree or who it's from, and I don't think we should take any chances. Let's put it out in the garage for now, just in case."

Nora shakily agreed with his assessment, and Dr. Duffy brought the mysterious box out to the garage. Eileen tried to keep everyone else happy by playing a game to distract them, but she was very much aware that something frightening might be going on. Dr. Duffy called Lieutenant Braxton, explained their problem, and asked if he'd come and take a look at the package.

Eileen didn't want to alarm the rest of the family until they knew more, so she encouraged them to adjourn to the beautifully decorated dining room to enjoy the delicious food that Jesse had prepared for them. Nora was unable to eat much, but she kept up her end of the conversation so that the younger siblings wouldn't be frightened. The dogs and Cheshire were given their treats too, and there was almost a natural atmosphere of hale and hearty family togetherness.

Lieutenant Braxton had been at Sergeant Belsky's family home on the north side, but they rang the Duffy doorbell in about half an hour. They must have flown to get there so quickly. Dr. Duffy and Nora showed them the small package, and Matt agreed that it did look suspicious. They brought a protective bag with them, so he inserted the package, wrapped it up tightly, and drove it to the police lab. One of their experts began the analysis of the package immediately.

The lab discovered that the package did not contain an explosive, but it was filled with a white powder. It could be baby powder, but it could also be something more sinister. More testing revealed that the powder contained anthrax spores. If Nora had opened it, it could have infected the whole family with disastrous results. Militarized anthrax was very deadly. If that's what it was, the person who put the box under the tree must have had powerful connections to have obtained it.

Lieutenant Braxton notified the Chicago PD chief and the FBI of the results of their test, and several of their representatives showed up at the Duffy home in about an hour. They were somewhat amazed that this small young woman and her family seemed to be caught up in something very sinister, but they were not surprised by much. They got more details from Nora and her parents and from Lieutenant Braxton and Sergeant Belsky, and they left with a warning that whoever the perpetrator was, he or she was getting much more aggressive. They encouraged the family to be even more vigilant about anyone or anything strange they might observe and they doubled the police guard around the Duffy home. They were concerned not only about the Duffys, but also about their neighbors.

Dr. Duffy was hailed as a hero for taking the initiative on this, but he was just so grateful that the package wasn't opened in the house. Nora tearfully suggested that she'd better move out until they find out who's doing this. She didn't want to expose the family to any more danger. She was furious with whoever was doing this, because they had ruined what had started out as a lovely Christmas Day.

Grandma Marie, with her usual perspicacity, reminded Nora of a saying she had heard from her mother: "An idle mind is the devil's workshop. When you allow your mind to dwell on evil thoughts, they can lead to evil deeds." They all feared that whoever was doing these things had passed the line between mischief and insanity.

Nora packed a bag and left with Sergeant Belsky so she could sleep at her house tonight until they figured out what to do. She put on a brave face for the family, but Nora was feeling traumatized. She gave Tommy a piece of paper with Laura's phone number, but they warned him not to call her unless there was an emergency. Nora bade a quick farewell to her family and told them the same thing. She didn't even want to put anything in writing in a text since they don't know if someone might have access to her messages.

Nora had hardly been willing to think about this in the light of day, but she was also wondering if she and Tommy should even go ahead with their wedding plans. She didn't want to put him in danger just because he was associated with her.

Unfortunately, the reporters who had been watching the house astutely noticed the extra police presence at the Duffy home, and they tried to get interviews. Dr. Duffy asked them to respect the sacred time of Christmas, and they were put off for now.

Wednesday, December 26
Chicago, 9:15 a.m., CST

On December 26—St. Stephen's or Boxing Day—Lieutenant Braxton brought Nora, her parents, Jesse, and Tommy down to the police station to talk to their expert in criminal profiling. He introduced them to Mrs. Manuela Torres, a small but determined-looking woman who said she would like to speak with Nora alone first and she'd wanted Lieutenant Braxton and Sergeant Belsky to come along since they knew the case so well. She ushered them into a small room with a whiteboard that covered one whole wall. She also introduced them to her assistant, Sergeant Lisa Scott, who would be recording their conversation and taking notes. She asked them to call her by her nickname, Manny.

"Nora, I feel as if I know you since your story is everywhere. I understand that neither you nor the police have had any luck in identifying who it is that has been attempting to kill you. I'm sorry that you're having to go through this and I hope that I can help you. I've asked to see you alone at first because quite often, a family member is the person who is the culprit."

When Nora started to protest, Manny pleaded with her to just keep quiet and listen to what she had to say. Manny told her that she had been doing this work for more than twenty years, so she had a lot of experience that could be helpful.

"I've received your basic information from Lieutenant Braxton and Sergeant Belsky, so we'll skip over that for now. I'd like to start by having you tell me some information about your family."

Nora began. "My name is Nora Eileen Duffy, I'm twenty-six years old, and I've lived in the same house on the south side of Chicago all my life. My parents are Dr. Michael Duffy, a heart surgeon at Holy Savior Hospital, and Mrs. Eileen Duffy, his head nurse. My parents are kind, funny, and smart, and they've passed those genes onto us kids. I have nine brothers and sisters, all younger than me. All ten of us were born within fourteen years, so we're very close.

"The two oldest brothers and the oldest sister next to me live elsewhere. Jim and Jack share an apartment in Bucktown, and Mary Ann is married and lives not far away from us. All the rest of us still live at home, including two more brothers and four more sisters. I have many relatives that live in the Chicago area. Our family travels to Ireland a few times every year to visit relatives, and a few times, we've taken side trips to visit other countries. I went to elementary school at St. Mary's school, high school at St. Ignatius, and college at Notre Dame University. I'll graduate soon from Loyola Medical School. I currently work as an intern at Holy Savior Hospital in the Children's Oncology Unit, and I plan to be a pediatric brain surgeon."

Nora continued, "I'm engaged to Mr. Thomas Barry who lives on the north side, and we plan to be married on March 17, St. Patrick's Day. Tom is a lawyer for a large downtown law firm, and he also has a large family. I'm an experienced musician and I play many instruments, but I specialize in the violin. I'm a dancer and a runner. I've recently inherited billions of dollars from a great uncle who died and left me his estate in a town called Sneem in Ireland. I was almost pushed off a subway platform, I've been shot in the head twice, and someone put a present under our Christmas tree that contained anthrax spores. I have no idea why this is happening or who could be doing it. That's the gist of things so far."

Manny took off her glasses and stared at Nora. "It will be difficult to develop a profile quickly for you since you have so many people, places, and events in your life, but we'll give it a try. I'm sure you've done some of this thinking before, but perhaps I can help synthesize what we know.

"I believe the first time an attempt was made on your life was when a large man in black clothes tried to push you onto the subway tracks. You survived with some injuries, but that was just days before you found out that you were to inherit your uncle's estate. Lieutenant Braxton tells me that you've made the assumption that someone knew you were going to inherit all this money and didn't want you to have it. Why would that be? If you had died, what would have happened to the money?"

"I believe it would have just reverted back to the estate. I can check that with Mr. Duncan Lloyd, the lawyer for my uncle."

"The second attempt on your life occurred at your uncle's castle where a rifleman shot you in the head and the arm. You survived, again with minor injuries. In between these attempts, you received several threatening letters from the would-be killer that didn't reveal very much about his or her identity.

"The third attempt on your life and your family just happened yesterday on Christmas Day when you received a package of white powder laced with anthrax spores, which could have killed all of you. So let's see what we have so far. Although we don't know who the killer is, we do know a few things. For purposes of our conversation, I'm going to refer to the killer as *he* or *him*, but it could well be a woman too. He must either be wealthy or at least had enough money to hire an international assassin. I believe that title 'international assassin' has been a major stumbling block in making progress in this case.

"The killer wants to protect himself from being identified and has been extremely careful in how he's approached this. He must be very smart. He leaves no clues in his letters as to his gender, what his relationship is to you, or why he's doing this. The only clue we have is that he is trying to take revenge on you and now, presumably, your whole family.

"The killer started out cautiously, but the anthrax powder means that his thought processes are rapidly deteriorating. He had to know that using anthrax would result in federal agencies being called in. I believe that his need for revenge is overcoming his need to protect his identity.

"Let's move on and try something different. Nora, I want you to think about what your prejudices are. We all have them. Is there anyone you can think of that you hate?"

Nora responded quickly, "Yes. Tall girls with long straight hair."

Manny did not appear amused. "I assume that was a joke. Is that your usual modus operandi when you feel pressured? To distract people by making jokes? By the way, was that a joke? You are very short with extremely curly red hair. Does that bother you?"

"Yes, that was a joke. Two of my sisters and most of my cousins are blonds with long straight hair. I came to terms with my appearance long ago and I rather like it. People usually react very positively to me."

"Let's go about this a different way. Are there people that you do not feel comfortable being around? You're very white, and I'm a Latina. If we were in a social situation, would you feel uncomfortable having dinner with me? Or with African-Americans or Muslims? You're very Catholic, and I suspect that your politics are conservative. Perhaps you've antagonized someone of a different ethnicity or race or religion or political viewpoint?"

Nora attempted to remain calm but felt that Manny was going over old ground that she herself had thought about repeatedly. She assured Manny that she had tried to think along those same lines for many weeks now. "Although I probably do feel most comfortable with people that look like me—but then, who does look like me?— my parents have always surrounded us with a diverse set of friends, and that is certainly the case at the hospital where I work. Before my freshman year at Notre Dame University, I heard that my roommate would be an African-American girl. I had been hoping to room with my cousin, Lesley, so I wasn't too happy at first.

"When I first saw Jessica, it was obvious that she was 'Vogue Magazine tall and beautiful,' and then there was me. We were both a little scared of each other, but then we just started laughing at the foot-and-a-half discrepancy in our heights, and that broke the ice. I believe that laughter smooths over a lot of difficulties. We were good for each other in so many ways, and today we are best friends. And as my mother, the nurse, always says, once you get under our skins, we all look alike. Our outer covering is just the result of millennia of DNA."

Manny had another thought. "What if you are a secondary target? Perhaps the killer is angry with your father as a surgeon or your mother as an important nurse and thinks that he'll punish them more by killing you?"

"Yes, I've thought of that too, but it still hasn't led me any closer to figuring out who it could be. Dad must have made some enemies over the years among the hospital staff, and there are likely patients or family members who weren't happy with their treatment. But again, I just don't know who it would be."

"Before I bring your family in, are you sure that you can't think of any of them who might hold a grudge against you?"

"I'm absolutely positive about my parents, and I've helped to raise all my brothers and sisters and know them very well. Our housekeeper, Jesse, is like a second mother to me. I also have complete faith in my fiancé, Tom."

Lieutenant Braxton called in the rest of the family and Jesse since she was always around the family so much. The conversation with Manny continued, but no more revelations occurred.

Manny asked about the small brown package under the tree and how it had gotten there. "Is there any information anyone can think of that would shed any light on who put it under the tree?"

Everyone looked at each other but no one could recall seeing it before. Nora explained that dozens of people had been in and out of house since Thanksgiving with all the events that had gone on all during the month of December. Jesse said that a few packages had come in addressed to various family members, and she just put them under the tree, but she didn't recognize that particular package.

"That adds a new dimension to the puzzle since the killer must be someone who has access to your house."

Lieutenant Braxton relayed that he was still working with the head of Human Resources at Holy Savior Hospital about anyone who could have had contact with Nick Chernoff (if that was his real name), the suspected terrorist who had worked at the hospital. Two employees from Dr. Duffy's office were among that group—Sue Bonner and Jason Reynolds—but it didn't appear that they knew anything about where Nick went after he left the hospital. Both of those people attended Dr. Duffy's hospital Christmas party at the Duffy home on the Sunday after Thanksgiving, so they had to be on a list of possible suspects. Lieutenant Braxton assured them that the investigation was ongoing.

Manny assured the family that she would continue to think about things on her end and asked them to call her immediately if there were new developments.

After speaking with Manny, Nora decided to return home to her family since there didn't seem to be any imminent progress in discovering the identity of the would-be killer. She was happy to sleep in her own bed, but long-term stress had left her uncomfortable and nervous.

Chicago's weather didn't always cooperate on New Year's Eve, but tonight, the streets were clear, and the sidewalks were walkable. Nora and Tommy and their parents put on their "fancy duds" and went to the Chicago Symphony to hear the "Salute to Vienna." They followed up with dinner and dancing at the Drake Hotel's Grand Ballroom, a golden venue that never failed to impress. Nora didn't always eat dessert, but she couldn't resist their delicious Baked Alaska.

Dr. Duffy heard his phone ring and told Eileen and Nora that he would have to leave right away to get to the hospital. He handed Eileen the parking garage ticket and said he would take a cab since the bypass patient he worked on yesterday had taken a turn for the worse, and Dr. Marlowe thought it was important that he should come. Medical personnel were used to having the best of celebrations cut short.

Eileen and Nora chatted with the other people at their table and then made their way home. Dr. Duffy didn't get back home until about 4:00 a.m., but he was pleased to report that they were able to get the patient back into a good heart rhythm.

On New Year's Day, they called Duffy Hall and spoke to Aunt Lavinia and a number of others at the castle to wish them a very happy year. They told the Duffys that their weather was pretty terrible with an unusual North Atlantic gale, so no one was going anywhere, but they were doing fine otherwise. The twins at the castle assured them that the horses and dogs were doing well too. They would be glad to see Nora the next time she came their way.

The Duffys went to early mass, watched the beautiful Rose Bowl Parade in wonder—how did they manage to construct those marvelous creations out of flowers?—had brunch with the family, and then watched various football games. Some of the women preferred to watch the Hallmark movies, which Brian called chick flicks. They put some effort into talking about their New Year's resolutions, but most people realized that after a few months, the resolutions were forgotten.

Nora and Tommy worked on their lists—again—of invitees to their wedding. The invitations would be sent out soon, so they tried to finalize the list so they could get it to Mr. Nolan at the card shop. Nora's usually ebullient personality should have been at its zenith, but she felt beaten down at the thought that the killer was still unknown.

Lieutenant Braxton and Sergeant Belsky had checked with the local post office and Ryan, the usual carrier, to see if they could determine any more information about the brown paper-wrapped package and who delivered it. The killer was getting bolder and using more vicious methods, but they didn't seem to be making much progress in finding out who it was.

Wednesday, January 9
Sneem, Noon, GMT

Valerie Carroll and Ellen Jordan, wives of Duffy Medical board executive members, met for lunch at the Sneem Hotel restaurant and agreed that they were sick of seeing Nora get so much praise and the money that should have been theirs. Ellen said that she didn't know what they could do about it, but Valerie revealed that she'd been thinking about a plan that might work to get rid of Nora once and for all. Valerie opened her purse and took out a piece of paper that she said could change the future for all of them. She'd written a letter that said it was from Nora to Aunt Lavinia and explained that Nora had been planning to get rid of all the current board members and replace them with Americans.

"Oh my God, she is?" Ellen asked Valerie with a horrified look.

"No, silly, I'm just saying that she plans to do that in the letter I wrote. Fred is so gullible that he'll believe me if I tell him that I found the letter by mistake."

"OMG," replied Ellen, "you are a cunning minx if ever I saw one," replied Ellen with a giggle. "Let me see." Ellen glanced through the clever letter surreptitiously as though anyone nearby would know what she was looking at. She found it very believable:

1 January 2019

Dear Aunt Lavinia,

Thanks for your hospitality. We are busy at home, and I may not see you for some time. Our weather has been terrible, and we've seen nothing but grey skies. I wanted to talk to you a little more about the conversation we had before I left for Chicago.

I have access to all the money now, but I'm waiting to spend anything until I know for sure how much the US and Ireland tax systems are going to want to take out. Then I can begin to put my plan into place. We can replace most of the board members by buying them out. I figure about 100,000 dollars each would do the job. I hate to spend that much, but it will be worth it in the end. I'll make up some excuse about why we're getting rid of them. I'll likely keep John and Duncan in place, just because they know the company so well.

I'm going to ask them to just fire those two men and their snarky wives that have caused such trouble, Fred Carroll and Ben Jordan. Then we can begin to bring in more Americans and mold the board as it should be. No offense to you, but most of those Irishmen just aren't as smart as Uncle Cyrus was about business. When I replace them with people from the US, Duffy Medical will make more money than ever before, and we'll be even richer.

I'll let you know when I hear more. Don't say anything about this to John or Duncan until I'm sure we can make this work.

Love,
Nora

"I think this just might work if the board thinks it's real," Ellen said with a frown, "although I'm not so sure that Ben will go along with it. You know what a conservative stick in the mud he is, and he did have so much regard for Cyrus and Lavinia. And I don't know that I like being described as 'snarky.' Your plan kind of scares me. What if they find out that you wrote the letter and Nora had nothing to do with it?"

"Leave it to me," said Valerie. "I've spent weeks copying Nora's handwriting and thinking about just the right words to say. I didn't go to acting school for nothing. I'll convince Fred and Ben that the letter is genuine, and then they'll do the rest with the other board members. Some of them don't like Americans much, so it won't take too much convincing."

Fred arrived home from work about 6:00 p.m., and Valerie had prepared an unusually nice dinner for him and had purchased a better than average wine to accompany it. Fred was surprised but pleased by the meal and was in a receptive mood for conversation. Valerie engaged him in small talk and then told him that she had something unpleasant to talk about.

She told him that she was sorting through some mail at the castle earlier and found a letter in their pile of mail that apparently got there by mistake. "I glanced through it and was just shocked to see what Nora Duffy had written to Aunt Lavinia."

She gave Fred a copy of the letter and saw the look of incredulity on his face. "I just can't believe this. Nora told us all when she went back to Chicago that she thought we'd been doing a good job of keeping the company going well, and you know how much Cyrus loved her. And Lavinia is a charter board member. I can't see her going along with this."

"Well, I think that little miss has been deceiving you all along. You should take steps to stop her before she does something to actually make her plan a reality. Lavinia has been getting forgetful lately and she seems to have been completely taken in by that ugly little girl."

Fred called Ben and asked him to come over to the house right away. He revealed the existence of the letter that Valerie had discovered and asked his advice. Fred said he didn't find the letter very credible and suggested that they call Lavinia and Nora to ask them about it. Valerie convinced him that it would just give them a way to put their plans into place sooner. She suggested that they call an emergency meeting of the board and ask them for their advice. Finally, Fred and Ben agreed to do that. "What about Lavinia? She is on the board too."

"We'll just tell her that a very serious matter has come up that affects all of us, and everyone on the board needs to be aware of it."

Fred and Ben called in John and Duncan and told them about the letter. John and Duncan said they wanted nothing to do with this and they believed in Nora and Lavinia.

"Leave us out of this, but you can call for a board meeting the day after tomorrow."

Kitty, Nora's assistant, was supposed to type up the invitation to the board members, but first she made an excuse that she had to go on an errand. She ran as fast as she could to tell Lavinia about it. Lavinia was a little shocked but not surprised since she had been suspicious of Valerie and Ellen all along. She called Nora and told her that it was extremely urgent for her and her parents to come to Duffy Hall the day after tomorrow for the board meeting. Nora could hear the fright and desolation in Aunt Vinnie's voice and she told her not to worry and that they would be there. Nora was supposed to be attending an important conference at the hospital, but she canceled that. She told her parents about the disturbing news, and they quickly made the decision to leave for Duffy Hall. They made the necessary arrangements at home and at work and booked plane reservations for tomorrow afternoon.

Lavinia called her lawyer friend, Fiona Finnegan, who handled legal matters for Cleary's perfumes and was one of the smartest people she knew. She asked her to come to the hall and meet with her urgently. She said she would explain it all when she got there, but basically, the future of Duffy Medical was on the line so she had to come prepared for battle.

Lavinia called in John and Duncan and told them that she was retaining her own lawyer. She trusted them both, but they had to represent Duffy Medical while she was being personally accused, so she needed her own solicitor. Duncan gave her a hug and said he understood and wanted to get this cleared up as soon as possible. Not for the first time, he wished that Cyrus Duffy was still here. This would certainly not have happened if he had been at the helm.

Friday, January 11
Sneem, Noon, GMT

Fiona Finnegan arrived at the hall, and Enda, the receptionist, was impressed by her determined aura, flawless makeup, and silver fox fur coat. Fiona demanded to be taken to Lavinia immediately and said that they would need a pot of very strong tea and some brown bread, because they were going to be very busy for several hours. Kitty Condon introduced herself and asked her to wait a moment until she could fetch Duncan Lloyd, the chief solicitor for Duffy Medical.

Duncan welcomed Fiona to Duffy Hall and told her that he had heard about her for years and was very glad to make her acquaintance. Fiona's aggressive persona scared even Duncan a bit, and he began to feel more positive about the resolution of Lavinia's and Nora's challenges.

Kitty took Fiona to the small conference room adjoining Lavinia's bedroom, and Lavinia greeted her warmly. Lavinia presented Fiona the basics of the story of how she and Nora were being accused of wanting to buy out all the Irish members of the board and replace them with Americans. Lavinia assured her that none of it was true and she believed they could prove that it was a complete falsehood. Fiona pulled out her notebooks and started to make notes. She was accompanied by her assistant, George Conroy, who summarized their conversation on the whiteboard behind them.

Lavinia expected to see Fiona shocked that people would think up such a cruel plot, but Fiona told her that when money is involved, she had come to realize that anything was possible. The first thing they needed to do was to get all the facts straight.

Lavinia had made arrangements to have Chiefs Herlihy and Brennan meet with them, and when they arrived, she asked if their investigations had uncovered any more facts.

It turned out that, indeed, there had been some unexpected developments. The Gardai had fanned out to all the surrounding properties around Duffy Hall, and they found an eyewitness who had seen the rifleman hiding in the willow trees and shooting his rifle the day Nora was shot. The witness thought at first that the gunman was aiming at pheasants, but it's very possible that he was the one who shot at Nora. The witness recognized the man as Jim Boyle, a man of known weak mental faculties who lived with his family just north of the castle grounds.

The Garda had gone to Jim's home and questioned him, and he broke down and told them the whole story. He had been approached by a "fancy woman," as he called any woman who came from the castle, who told him that there was a "wicked girl" at the castle who needed to be taught a lesson and frightened into leaving. If he scared her away, he would get $500 to use in whatever manner he wanted. He also had shot at Nora's horse, Finnbar. Jim had been angry with Uncle Cy because he wouldn't let him shoot the pheasants on the castle grounds, so he agreed to do the shooting.

Jim told them he didn't think Nora looked very wicked when he saw her, he had tried to miss hitting her, and he was sorry now that he had agreed to any of it. He hadn't spent any of the money. He showed Garda Lenehan that he'd hidden the $500 away in an old boot in his closet. He was very happy when he found out that Nora hadn't been seriously hurt and was glad to hear that Finnbar was recovering.

Chief Brennan explained to the group that they'd taken Jim into custody and, based on Jim's description of the "fancy woman," were about to question Valerie next. By the end of the afternoon,

Fiona and Lavinia agreed that they should have more than sufficient evidence to prove their case.

When Nora and her parents arrived that night, they were introduced to Fiona. Nora felt better as soon as she shook hands with this self-possessed and competent young woman who was wearing a pair of Louboutin heels Nora would love to have. Nora hugged Lavinia and said she was so sorry that she had to go through this. Fiona outlined the results of their afternoon's work for Nora and Dr. and Mrs. Duffy and said she thought they would have no problem proving their case, especially now that the Garda had arrested Jim Boyle who had confessed to shooting at Nora.

Mrs. O'Hara served them some Irish stew and bread pudding for dinner, always accompanied by Nora's favorite brown bread. Nora went out for a run with Liam, the wolfhound, and stopped at the stables to talk to Finnbar and the bog ponies. The family was tired out after their travels and more stress and they went to bed early.

Saturday, January 12
Sneem, 8:00 a.m., GMT

In the morning, they had a quick breakfast, and then Nora went for her run and waved to Uncle Cyrus and Aunt Emily at their tombstones. She then returned to the hall so she could change into her formal black suit and favorite white lace blouse and prepared for the board meeting to begin.

Lavinia brought in her counsel, Fiona, and her assistant, George, and showed them where to sit. Nora saw the assembled board members and wondered which of them was friend or foe.

John and Duncan called the meeting to order, welcomed everyone, and explained that the reason for this unexpected meeting was to hear from Fred Carroll and Ben Jordan about a letter they'd discovered.

Fred passed out the letter to the board and explained that his wife, Valerie, found this letter by mistake and brought it to his attention with the sole purpose of protecting the future of Duffy Medical and everyone on the board. He asked them to read it for themselves and said that, in view of this, he suggested that Nora should be removed as chairman of the board, and Lavinia too for conspiring with her.

Nora and Lavinia sat quietly and observed the board members as Fred told them this story. They saw some puzzled faces, but a few members seemed to be nodding yes.

When it appeared that Fred was finished, Lavinia stood up and asked to be recognized. She looked sad as she introduced them all to

Fiona and George and said she thought the quickest way to resolve this issue was to hear directly from Nora first.

Nora walked confidently over to the podium and waited until she had everyone's attention. Her many years of debate team tactics had trained her well for how to deal with a hostile audience. She walked back and forth a number of times on her black and white high heels but didn't say anything until she was assured that the audience had finally stopped talking to each other and their eyes were on her. When there was silence, Nora began speaking in a loud and assertive voice.

"God bless all here, and I ask him to help us find the truth today and help move Duffy Medical forward to its rightful place in the world. That can only happen if we're united, but it appears that is not the case today. I wish I could say it was a pleasure to see all of you, but there are very serious and uncomfortable accusations floating about. I had no intention of coming to Sneem at this time, but Lavinia told me about the existence of a letter that was going to be distributed to all of you and asked me to come and talk to you. I've analyzed that document, and I assure you that the entire letter is a fabrication, and we can easily prove that to you. Aunt Vinnie's solicitor, Ms. Fiona Finnegan, and her assistant, George Conroy, have put together a PowerPoint presentation so that you can see various points on the screen."

Nora gestured toward the audience, "First of all, the letter does not reflect in the slightest what my real 'plan' is. I told you when I left here that I thought you had all done an outstanding job of running Duffy Medical, and I wanted you to continue to do so. I'm a bit hurt that you would just believe the worst about me, but then you really don't know me too well yet. But I am outraged that you would believe that Lavinia would do anything to injure Duffy Medical or all of you, Cyrus' dear friends."

Nora couldn't help but notice that Fred and Ben looked quite uncomfortable now. Nora revealed the existence of hers and Vinnie's secret code as the first proof that the letter was a fake. "If it were genuine, the letter would have been addressed to 'Dear Mortimer Lear' and signed by 'Cordelia.' This was the code that Aunt Vinnie and I had agreed to for our communications since she was wise enough to realize that it might be necessary. Also, someone who is not an American wrote this letter. The date is the first thing. If I had written it, it would have said January 1, 2019, not 1 January, 2019. It's true that Chicago skies are often gray, but I would not have spelled the word as *grey*. Duffy Medical's money is accounted for in euros, not dollars, so I would not have used a dollar amount.

"Secondly, Lavinia and I agreed to keep our code arrangement a secret, and I know that the document we both signed is kept in Lavinia's safe above her fireplace. The key to Lavinia's safe is hidden under the unicorn in the rose garden." Nora sent George to get the key and open the safe, and he returned with the document detailing the code arrangements that Vinnie and Nora had agreed to months ago. She said that anyone who wanted to see this agreement could get a copy.

Nora continued, "I believe that Valerie Carroll and/or Ellen Jordan wrote the letter you're holding in your hands."

A collective gasp was heard from the board members.

Nora revealed that Chief Brennan had discovered that Valerie had met with the rifleman from the adjoining property and told him to shoot at her. Chief Brennan stood in the back of the room and told them that he had taken Jim Boyle into custody and was about to take Valerie Carroll and Ellen Jordan into custody for questioning.

Fred Carroll and Ben Jordan were flabbergasted. They were willing to go along with the plan to remove Nora to keep control of the company, but they'd known nothing about the plan to possibly murder her. They could see their efforts of a lifetime on behalf of Duffy Medical slipping through their grasp because of the crazy plotting by their wives. They should have looked into their claims more carefully. Fred whispered an apology to Cyrus profusely for all that had happened.

Valerie screamed out to the group that she was only trying to protect them all from the ambitious Americans. "I hired Jim from the house next door to do the rifle shooting because I thought it was the only way to protect Duffys and all of you who had worked so hard for the company! Nora was going to have all that money, which should have been ours, and I was trying to scare her off. I didn't realize that the stupid guy would actually shoot her! When that didn't work, I had to find another way, so I wrote that letter saying that it was from Nora to Lavinia and that Nora was going to buy out our board members and replace them with Americans. Again, I just wanted to protect you, and I thought it was a good way to get rid of that damned American girl. Why should she get all that money when we've worked so hard for Cyrus all these years?"

Duncan Lloyd reminded Valerie that Nora had received the money as a result of a legal will made by Cyrus Duffy and said she had made quite a false interpretation of the facts. The other board members were understandably horrified by Valerie's words, and they all apologized to Lavinia and to Nora and her parents. John O'Malley, the CEO, told Fred and Ben that it was unfortunate that their wives had done these things, but in view of what they've just heard, they would likely be asked to resign from the board.

"This has all been a horrible mistake," Valerie blubbered. "I wish I could turn back the clock. Fred, I thought I was protecting you," she cried out to her husband.

"I never realized before how far you would go to hold onto power," responded Fred while holding his head in his hands. "I told you last year that we should have retired, but you were always plan-ning how we could get even more money. Now you won't have any money at all," he cried.

Ellen yelled out that Valerie had been responsible for the whole thing. "Ben, you know that I would never have had the brains to think of such an elaborate plot. Valerie made it seem like such a good idea, and she talked me into going along with her!"

Ben quietly responded to her that he had warned her not to become involved with Valerie's schemes for a long time, so he was not surprised that she had gotten into such trouble now. "You've always just gone along with whatever plots she hatched, and now you're going to receive the rewards for your labors. Now Fred and I will likely have to resign, and we should have been smarter about trusting either of you."

The two hysterical women were led away from Duffy Hall by Chief Brennan.

Fred and Valerie decided to separate after this catastrophe. There was still a suspicion that perhaps Valerie could have had a part in the first attempt on Nora's life in the subway, although that didn't seem plausible. Chief Brennan and Lieutenant Braxton would continue to investigate.

Ben stood behind Ellen and blamed himself that he didn't look more carefully at her allegations. She had been rather a silly person over the years, but now that very unpleasant reality had set in for her, she was going to need his support.

John O'Malley asked the board for a unanimous show of hands that they supported Aunt Lavinia and Nora, and every hand went up. Nora thanked Aunt Lavinia, Fiona, George, and the board, and she and her parents promptly returned to the US. She promised to keep in touch with the board members via e-mails and hoped that this unpleasant episode would have served a purpose by making them more unified.

52

Friday, January 18
Chicago, 5:00 p.m., CST

Nora's young sisters were excited to receive the letters from their prospective high schools and were thrilled that they were accepted. The letters gave the details of the courses they would be taking and told them to look over the list of elective activities they could choose. Molly signed up for the advanced music program at Mother McAuley, and Caitlan chose science electives at St. Ignatius. Many calls to friends ensued as they talked about their future plans. They also marked off all the dances, plays, and recitals that would be occurring during the school year on the big wall calendar. This was going to be fun!

Kevin received his letter of acceptance from Notre Dame, although he was strongly advised to consider signing up for a tutor for chemistry. He was planning to try out for the position of leprechaun mascot for the football team. His short stature and bright red hair should have given him some preference. The family was thrilled that they would have yet another member of the group to visit in South Bend.

End of January
Chicago and Sneem

Now that the Duffy Medical board had reaffirmed their confidence in Nora, she felt comfortable implementing one aspect of her plan for the company. She sent a one-page letter to all employees that had been approved by John and Duncan, laying out what she planned to do at Duffy Medical and what she would expect of its employees. The letter said that it was an honor to continue the great work started by Cyrus, Emily, and Lavinia Duffy, and John O'Malley and the board.

She explained that she would request the board to give approval for an increase of the staff's salaries and benefits because they had been working hard for years to make Duffy Medical the excellent firm that it was and because it was the right thing to do. She wanted to create a code of conduct for all Duffy Medical employees, and she requested their ideas about it before it was finalized. Nora wondered how the nonprofessional employees would feel about wearing uniforms, either suits or shirts and pants, emblazoned with the Duffy logo.

She asked each person to submit a letter to her with their suggestions and also asked that they would sign their names so she could respond to them. Her one request was that they confine their suggestions to a one-page letter. Winston Churchill had that rule for his generals when he was fighting WWII so they should be able to think about things logically and clearly in that format. Putting their ideas in bullet point format would be even more ideal. Her hope was that working together, they could make Duffy Medical—with its dedicated workers, superior products, and beautiful buildings—a shining city upon the hill for all of Ireland and the world.

Nora had requested that she receive responses by mid-February, and the employees must have liked what she had to say, because responses started to pour in. The twins categorized the responses into various columns and prepared a report for Nora and the board. So far, the increase in salaries and benefits was universally applauded, while the idea of uniforms received a tepid approval. Much more work would be required to make these things a reality, but Nora felt it was a good start.

Jim and Jack called the family together and told them that after more analysis, they had decided to call off going to work in Silicon Valley. Cousin Johnny had started to work there and very shortly realized that he was miserable, and he thought they would be too. "We actually like our jobs here a lot, despite the Chicago winters, and Trish and Sally had been having second and third thoughts about moving so far away. So, apologies to you, Bitsy, for the foolish way we talked to you earlier."

The family applauded their decision. Nora gave them the thumbs up sign, mumbled a silent prayer of thanks, and realized that time and patience could often work wonders.

February
Chicago, CST

Maureen and Siobhan organized a surprise baby shower for big sister, Mary Ann, on February 9 at Barry's Restaurant. Mary Ann's nickname was Merry since she was usually laughing, and a huge crowd responded that they would be delighted to attend. Mrs. Duffy was finally able to give Merry the many gifts she'd been accumulating for months. Many of the husbands and boyfriends of the family gathered at the Bar while the gift-giving was going on and watched basketball. Merry and Al didn't want to know whether it would be a boy or a girl, so most of the gifts consisted of baby products and furniture, although there was a fair smattering of baby clothes as well.

Nora and Tommy gave them a pledge of babysitting whenever their schedules would allow. Barry's provided the food, and many of those who came brought tasty desserts. Merry and Al were thrilled with the gifts and especially the friendship of all these people, and they looked forward to their new wee one.

On February 16, Tom and Nora attended a Pre-Cana Conference, which was a requirement to get married in the Archdiocese of Chicago. They heard wise and humorous talks on a variety of subjects by a knowledgeable married couple and shared stories with the other engaged couples at their table. There was also time for Tom and Nora to talk to each other to ensure that they were ready to get married and committed to their partner. They felt that their long experience with their large families and their older age probably had already prepared them well, but they embraced anything that would assure their success as newlyweds. They met a couple, the Carters, at the conference and felt an instant bond with them, and each couple invited the other to their upcoming weddings.

Nora had been attending classes at the oncology clinic that would help her to deal with the parents of kids with cancer. The class was taught by Professor Eleanor Barrett, and she told her students that it was impossible to predict how the parents would act when they received the bad news that their child was now going to have to undergo treatments for cancer. All they could do was to keep improving their own education and trying to maintain an empathetic attitude with them.

Nora could attest to that the next day when she met with the parents of a beautiful four-year old, Christina Thomas. Christina had gone through initial testing, and now Nora had to tell them that they'd discovered that Christina had leukemia. She stressed that many strides had been made in treating leukemia and it was good that they had discovered it early.

Nora watched Christina's parents carefully. The mother looked terrified but stoic and just wanted to know what they had to do to make this go away. The father, on the other hand, was hysterical and accused them of making this up. He wanted to leave right away, but Nora talked him into listening. She outlined the near-term course of action and explained what they could expect during the tests and treatments. She wished she could make things easier for them, but the chances were that all of their lives had been changed forever. While it was true that the five-year survival rate for children with leukemia had significantly improved, each case differed.

They saw a long stream of babies and young children of all skin colors and parents at all emotional levels. The work could get overwhelming, but they felt good that they would provide comfort to all and many would be saved. Nora was the assistant to Dr. Christopher Whiteside, the premier doctor for children's cancers at Holy Savior, and he tried hard to keep his staff motivated and healthy.

On the wall over the desk in the reception area where the parents checked in was a reminder:

Some people live for an hour, some for 100 years, most of us in between. What are you going to do today to maximize the time you have?

February 17

Clare O'Sullivan called for the members of the wedding party to come to Barry's for a final fitting for the dresses. Nora's dress was perfect, and of the thirty-five bridesmaid dresses, only two needed adjustment, so that was great news. The dresses for the mothers and grandmothers fit very well and looked perfect on them. The little girls' dresses fit well too, although little Lindsey grew an inch since she was first measured.

Dr. Duffy talked to Nora about whether she should have a pre-nuptial agreement now that she had so much money to be concerned about. She assured him that she and Tommy had already discussed it with their lawyer. The part of the money that was attributed to Duffy Medical was being held in a trust so that was nothing to be concerned about. They had each made a will, and their remaining "regular" money would be inherited by the surviving spouse, except for some additional specific bequests to family and friends. Mr. Abbott, their lawyer, had all the details.

On February 24, there was a wedding shower for Nora, organized by her five sisters at St. Mary's hall for about 500 women. At first, there was some confusion about what to get Nora since she now had enough money to buy the best. What do you get for the woman who has everything? Something that money can't buy. Everyone was asked to bring a favorite recipe or a photo and a memory of something about either Nora or Tom.

Merry had saved a photo of Nora in the famed yellow Chanel dress with Tommy looking very handsome in his black blazer, and they had a painter blow this up and paint over it in oil paints. The three-by-five-foot painting would be a remembrance for them all the rest of their lives. Jesse and her crew made delicious foods and supplemented them with a cake from Weber Bakery. The Barry girls provided a variety of fun games, and the winners received spring plants. Nora thoroughly enjoyed the party, although she was always wary that the would-be killer could be lurking nearby.

Ash Wednesday occurred on March 6 this year, and Father Ahearn called Nora and asked her if she could play for the early morning prayer service since the organist had developed a case of the flu. Nora said she'd be glad to do it, but she wouldn't be able to stay long since she had early rounds at the hospital. Ash Wednesday memories were special to Nora. She recalled the ashes being created from burning blessed palm fronds from the last Palm Sunday. The congregation was asked to come forward, and Father Ahearn and other assistants dipped their thumbs in the container of ashes as they made a dark sign of the cross on each person's forehead while reciting the admonition, "Remember you are dust, and unto dust you shall return."

Many people gave up various foods for Lent, but Nora preferred to do something positive. She resolved to say a rosary every day for cancer victims everywhere and made a generous contribution to the cancer clinic in her family's name.

The wedding rehearsal was scheduled for the evening of March 15 with dinner to follow at Bourbon Street restaurant. Unfortunately, there were monsoon-like rains, which was better than snow, but it still made for a most uncomfortable night. A group e-mail was sent to everyone in the wedding party saying that they should not worry about wearing anything nice but they should leave in enough time so they could get to St. Mary's by 6:30 p.m. Surprisingly, everyone but Siobhan arrived in plenty of time. She sent a text saying that she was stuck in traffic on I-80 and would be there as soon as she could.

Connie acted as the wedding planner and had an Excel sheet that she consulted to tell everyone how they should line up at church. There was some chatter back and forth about the terrible weather, but each girl found her boy, and they were lined up and ready to go by 7:00 p.m. Father Ahearn greeted them and took his place, and just as the organist was about to start the processional, Siobhan came running in and met her partner, Neil.

Connie gave instructions to the girls about how to hold their bouquets at the waist so the bouquet wouldn't hide the tops of their gowns, and plastic flowers were handed out for the practice. The organist began the processional music, "Ode to Joy," and the little girls and boys started to walk down the aisle. Two five-year-old girls would have baskets of rose petals to throw down on the white carpet, but tonight, they settled for newspaper pieces that would be easy to pick up. Two toddlers were brought up in a wagon, and only one of them cried.

Connie had brought along a copy of the movie *High Society* and had the bridesmaids watch how Grace Kelly had walked down the aisle one graceful step at a time. The ladies met their appropriate partners who were lined up in the front. Connie had assigned her sister, Jeanie, to act as the person who showed them where to stand and sit. Tommy walked down the aisle with his parents on either side of him, and then it was time for Nora to start, shepherded by her mom and dad, and the organist switched to the "Trumpet Voluntary." Father Ahearn guided Nora and Tommy through the parts of the wedding mass and advised them when to sit and stand.

At the end, Jim and his bagpipers sounded the opening notes of "Amazing Grace," and they led Nora and Tommy back down the aisle. Everyone else marched down the aisle in the reverse order of how they came in to the strains of "The Lord of the Dance."

They did so well that everything was done by 8:00 p.m. They then drove over to Bourbon Street Restaurant for dinner and celebration, although they had to make at least one detour due to street flooding. Nora hoped that St. Isidore, patron of weather, would help to ensure that the rains would cease by the seventeenth.

Saturday, March 16
Chicago, 7:00 p.m., CDT

Most of the out-of-town wedding guests, including the invitees from Duffy Hall Castle, were staying at the Oak Lawn Hilton, but Aunt Lavinia and the twins, Kitty and Maryann, were staying at the Duffys'. Nora and Tommy brought their families and the Duffy Hall group together for dinner in a conference room at the hotel the night before the wedding. Delicious food and tasty drinks were served, but the emphasis was on sharing humorous stories and looking forward to a very happy wedding day. The evening took on a magical atmosphere when Tommy's cousin, Sean Hanrahan, a marine posted in Germany, was able to make a surprise appearance.

54

Sunday, March 17
Chicago, Early a.m., CDT

St. Patrick's Day celebrations usually lasted months in Chicago, although many of them had little to do with the holy man himself. Some places celebrated the "six-months before" day, princesses were selected, floats were constructed, and parade arrangements were finalized. "Tons" of corned beef and cabbage and "rivers" of beer were sold as well as green merchandise of all kinds to wear to the parades. Churches had special services, and businesses and stores had parties. The Chicago River was dyed green. Irish dancers and musicians were in popular demand at many locations. There were large parades in downtown Chicago and other parts of the city, and most suburbs had their own celebrations.

By St. Patrick's Day, the major festivities were over, so it seemed like a good time to have the Duffy wedding and keep the party going.

When the big day for Nora and Tommy's wedding arrived, the weather cooperated beautifully at sixty degrees and no rain. The mass was scheduled at St. Mary's Church at 1:00 p.m., and the reception was scheduled at the downtown Conrad Hilton at 5:00 p.m. for 2,000 people.

Nora woke up before dawn and listened to the birds singing outside her window and to the quiet that enveloped the house before the chaos that would soon begin. She wanted to get married and to start her life with Tommy, but it was also sobering to think that her home of the last twenty-six years would never be the same for her again.

Nora was very excited as she thought about today's events, but that was muted by her fear that the would-be killer might decide to try to ruin their day. Lieutenant Braxton had a phalanx of police organized to try to prevent any such fears becoming a reality, so that helped her feeling of security.

She tiptoed down to the living room, snuggled up with Reilly on the couch, and dozed until she heard her mother's familiar footsteps coming down to find her. They'd had their mother-daughter talk about what it meant to be married last week, so today they just smiled at each other, held hands for a moment, and said a prayer that all would go well. Eileen told Nora to stay on the couch while she got them a cup of tea. It wasn't long before they heard alarms ringing, showers running, and many voices chattering, and then it was "off to the races."

Nora joyfully greeted Aunt Vinnie and the twins from Duffy Hall Castle when they came downstairs, and Connie escorted them to the dining room so they could partake of the wide variety of treats before they had to leave for the church. Vinnie seemed to be enjoying herself immensely and had no trouble fitting right in with the rest of the happy group. Lavinia had bought a new dress for the occasion and looked lovely in pale green and gold set off by a pendant necklace with a large emerald.

The large wedding party was scheduled to meet at the Duffys' at 10:00 a.m. The outer porch and inside rooms were awash with fragrant white flowers, and various wedding day music alternated in the background. Mrs. Duffy and Jesse had imported food from several local restaurants, and everything was set out in the dining room and available for the group to eat whenever they liked. Long paper bibs were also available so they wouldn't drip anything onto their clothes.

Tommy and his family had stayed overnight at the Oak Lawn Hilton so they wouldn't have to drive so far in the morning. That meant they thought it would only take ten minutes to get to St. Mary's, but they hadn't counted on the 95th Street traffic, so they arrived at the Duffys' with no time to spare.

It was an exciting sight to see several large tents set up in the St. Mary's parking lot to accommodate anyone who was unable to fit into the church, the hall, or the school basement.

Maggie and several of her beautician friends arrived at the house to make final fixes to hair and nails and to apply makeup. There were plenty of bottles of Carol Cleary's perfume available for all. An occasional cry from a toddler occurred, but even the young children seemed to get into the spirit of the day.

Nora was assisted by her mother and her sisters, and they all had to suppress their tears so their mascara wouldn't run. She did look like a princess from a fairy-tale in her lovely dress, and Nora was especially pleased that the long train was lined with the badges from all the counties in Ireland. When she added the diaphanous veil, all of them spontaneously clapped.

Everyone started to get into their wedding clothes, and then suddenly, it was 11:30 a.m., the final countdown hour as directed by Connie. There was some nervousness, but everything had been planned so well that even Grandma Dee felt reassured that all was going to be fine. Everyone was called into the living room for a final inspection, and Connie checked them off her list as she felt they were ready. Colorful wrist corsages were given out to the mothers, grandmothers, and Aunt Vinnie.

Meanwhile, at St. Mary's, the bouquets of roses, peonies, lilies, and lily of the valley were delivered, and Jeanie checked that they were all labeled with the correct names.

They looked out the windows about noon and could see that people were starting to arrive at the church already. At 12:15 p.m., Dr. Duffy asked everyone to say a prayer of thanks for the good weather and that they would have a happy and successful day. Everyone then walked the short block to the church, and they waved to the people who were arriving. The large wedding party made a wonderful sight in their colorful dresses and formal tuxedoes.

As people were waiting at St. Mary's for the ceremony to begin, the orchestra played some of Nora's favorites, Mozart's "Eine kleine Nachtmusik—A Little Night Music," and then Vivaldi's "Four Seasons." Tommy's brother, Paul, and Nora's sister, Maureen, teamed up to sing "Nessun Dorma" from the opera *Turandot*. It was one of Puccini's most-loved arias, and the music was glorious. Paul and Maureen were not Pavarotti, but their rendition was certainly heartfelt.

Then the choir sang Schubert's "Ave Maria" followed by Jim and his bagpipers and drummers who led a procession around the church playing "Amazing Grace." The groomsmen in their formal gray tuxedoes gathered at the front of the altar.

Finally, the orchestra played "Ode to Joy," and the female wedding party members began to step off. It was a glorious sight to see all the women in their gorgeous dresses in so many colors, and the children looked enchanting. Lindsey and Alice took turns throwing various colored rose petals on the white carpet and looked proud and happy. The ring bearer, Sean, had a slight dance step to his walk down the aisle, and his impish smile was camera-worthy.

Tommy sported a red sash across his tuxedo decorated with the Barry crest and looked like a prince as he was escorted down the aisle by his parents. When Nora was ready, the organist and five trumpeters began to play "The Trumpet Voluntary," and the entire congregation stood to see her in her fairy-tale wedding dress. The bagpipers joined in too. Nora was so happy she couldn't stop smiling at so many people she recognized.

Father Ahearn and twelve other priest friends were on the altar to lead them through the prayers for the wedding mass. Nora and Tommy had picked hymns that complemented the Old and New Testament readings they'd chosen.

When it came time to exchange their vows, Nora and Tom joyfully took each other's hands to formalize the union that had existed between them for a long time now. They could have written their own vows, but they felt that the Church's words used for weddings over the centuries were most appropriate and not something they could improve upon:

"I, Nora, take you, Thomas, for my lawful husband, to have and to hold, from this day forward, for better, for worse, for richer, for poorer, in sickness and in health, until death do us part."

Tommy reiterated the statement as he looked at his beautiful bride. They gave each other the beautiful rings they'd chosen and were thrilled to hear Father Ahearn say that the bride and groom had declared their consent to be married. He prayed for God's blessing on the newlyweds, and declared, "What God has joined, let no one put asunder."

Father Ahearn gave a stirring homily and explained how he had seen this young couple grow in love and maturity and asked everyone in the congregation to continue to support them with their prayers.

During Communion, a dozen assistants helped the priests distribute the consecrated hosts, and the same process occurred at the remote sites. The orchestra and choir played and sang the famous hymn written by St. Thomas Aquinas, "Panis Angelicus," and then they switched to "I Am the Bread of Life."

Near the end of the mass, Tom and Nora walked over to the shrine to our Blessed Mother, and they placed a large bouquet of white lilies and pink roses in a Waterford vase on the altar. Then Tom and Nora took the microphone and joyfully sang one of their favorite hymns, accompanied by a trio of harpists, and they asked the congregation to join them in singing to the Irish Madonna, "Our Lady of Knock, the Queen of Peace."

Finally, Father Ahearn introduced Mr. and Mrs. Thomas Barry to the congregation, they kissed each other happily, and there was a huge round of applause for this young couple who had endured so much heartache already.

Maureen asked the congregation to join in singing "The Lord of the Dance," and the wedding party almost danced down the aisle. The happy couple, their families, and the wedding party stood at the back of the church and greeted their guests. After about half an hour of this, Connie reminded Nora that they needed to speed things up a bit to get down to the hotel on time. The photographers gathered the entire wedding party at the front of the church again for many posed pictures. Reporters and television cameras were also encouraged to snap some quick pictures.

Finally, everyone entered their limousines and cars and made the drive downtown to the Conrad Hilton. They savored walking up the ornate steps that had seen many celebrities over the years, and they entered the Grand Ballroom where the walls had been decorated to look as though they had just entered a very large thatched cottage. Neil acted as the disc jockey, and he played a variety of popular songs as everyone entered. On the floor below, guests from nursing homes and the homeless joined in the celebrations and watched the action on big television screens.

Many ushers with iPads escorted the guests to their assigned tables, which had been decorated with colorful St. Patrick's Day-themed flowers. Snacks of nuts, fruits, and cheeses were at each table, and waiters took their drink orders. The large wedding party was fanned out at the tables that stretched across the walls of the room, which made a beautiful tableau. The entire event was streamed to the cancer clinic, Holy Savior Hospital, and to Duffy Hall Castle in Sneem so that those friends could also see the party. Reporters and television cameras sat at the back of the room and were busily writing stories and snapping pictures.

Champagne was served, and when it seemed as though everyone had been seated, many toasts to the newlyweds were made by the best man and maid of honor as well as by a number of other people who'd known them all their lives. Most were serious, but Tommy's brothers told "secret" stories about him that had the whole crowd laughing.

Then Tommy and Nora stood up and thanked everyone for being there, and they toasted the crowd. Tommy said that they were a very lucky and unusual couple in these days. "Both sets of our parents are still married. Even more remarkable is that all four sets of our grandparents are alive and still married. That equates to almost 300 years of marriage wisdom." Tommy grinned. "And we asked them what their secret was. The most consistent things they said were that you should start out really liking the other person and wanting to spend time with them. You should continue to know what makes them happy as the years turn. Support each other in good times and in bad, and learn to pray together. And before you know it, thirty years goes by in a blink. They've been such good examples for us, we can't help but follow their advice." Everyone clapped loudly and wished them good luck.

That was the signal for Father Ahearn, and he led the group in asking God's blessings on the meal they would share, for those who wouldn't have a meal today, and for all those who are sick in body or mind, and he asked God to send them angels.

The food was then served by an army of waiters. Each plate contained a medley of ribeye steak, sea trout from the Sneem River, turkey breast, with mashed potatoes, asparagus, and a berry compote. Irish soda bread and cinnamon rolls graced each table, and waiters served wines and soft drinks. While people were eating, a string quartet played a variety of tunes from Broadway shows. Two-thousand people talking and laughing made a happy noise.

After the meal, Tom and Nora cut the magnificent twelve-tier cake, which had been sculpted to look like Duffy Hall Castle, adorned with a welter of colorful flowers. Atop it stood a plastic statue that had been molded to be the image of Tom and Nora. The cake layers consisted of chocolate, vanilla, and strawberry, filled with custard, and topped with lemon icing. The cake was taken away to be sliced, and shortly, the waiters served the many guests a generous slice of the delicious cake with coffee or tea.

When the meal was about complete, Nora noticed her two young sisters signaling to the waiters and to some children who appeared behind a curtain. In a few minutes, chairs were put into place on the dance floor, and Nora recognized some of the members of the St. Mary's Band who came in with their instruments. She shrugged when Tommy asked her what was happening.

Caitlan Duffy took the microphone and announced that in honor of the World War II veterans who were sitting in the first row, she asked everyone in the room to stand while her sister, Molly, made her debut as an orchestra conductor. Mr. Andy Mullen, the band director, was there to support Molly, but he let her take the lead. Molly made sure that all the band members were ready. She raised her baton and gave the downbeat, and then Jack and his bagpipers and drummers started the parade into the huge room while the band members played "God Bless America" and invited everyone to sing along. The WWII vets saluted the flag, and everyone clapped loudly.

Caitlan announced that the St. Mary's Children's Choir had been practicing (just) two songs as a surprise for Nora and Tommy, and they were going to begin with something quiet. Molly waved her baton, the band members played the introduction, and then all the younger children sang along to the Louis Armstrong hit, "What a Wonderful World."

Uproarious applause exploded from the crowd as the adorable children finished.

Then Molly gave a signal, and the older members of the children's choir joined the younger ones. Caitlan explained that they knew that one of Nora's favorites had always been the Beatles' song, "Hey Jude." She and her fellow choir member, Matt Conway, were going to start, but she invited everyone in the audience to sing along whenever they wanted to. Molly pointed to each one of band members with her baton and then brought in the choir, and the iconic song reverberated throughout the huge hall.

Many of the guests had turned on their phones and waved them back and forth as though they were at a concert. Tom and Nora had gotten up from their chairs and danced in place, which prompted a barrage of people taking pictures. By the time they got to the "na na na" part, the entire room had joined in. This was a fabulous way to begin the celebration.

Tom and Nora both left their seats and embraced their talented sisters and thanked all the band and choir members. Molly and Caitlan explained that they had practiced all this after school for a few weeks. Nora was glad that she'd told the makeup ladies she didn't want mascara since she had a feeling that she'd be shedding quite a few tears today.

When it came time to begin the dancing, members of the orchestra began to play "The Blue Danube Waltz," and Nora and Tommy showed off the steps they'd been practicing. Then Nora and Dr. Duffy and Tommy and Mrs. Barry danced to "I Could Have Danced All Night." Eileen Duffy and PJ Barry joined in. Then all the wedding party members took to the floor and invited everyone to join them. The orchestra members played many traditional waltz, rock, and polka favorites for the first hour, which was Nora's way of being sensitive to the needs of the many senior citizens who were present since many of them thought about leaving once the music became noisier.

Nora and Tommy went down to the floor below and visited with the nursing home residents and the homeless they'd invited. They had previously made arrangements with the hotel to provide them with appropriate assistance. As they were about to leave that room, they heard the sound of loud voices and dishes crashing to the floor. Tom moved himself in front of Nora in case there was trouble. Several policemen walked over to the area and told them that two homeless men had been arguing over who was going to take home the leftover rolls. They began throwing punches at each other, and one of them picked up a steak knife and stabbed the other in the arm. They were about to take them both to the hospital. It had seemed like a good idea to invite them last month, but Nora realized they hadn't counted on the acquisitive nature of some of the homeless when extra food was available to them. The rest of the people there assured them they were having a wonderful time and thanked them for inviting them.

Then they proceeded upstairs to greet their guests at each table. As Nora joyfully greeted each person, she couldn't help but wonder if one of them could be the killer, which somewhat dampened her spirits.

Irish singers and dancers came up to the stage for about half an hour, and Nora removed her train and veil and joined them. Tommy hadn't had experience with Irish dancing, but it looked like they were having so much fun, so he attempted to join them. He discovered that it was harder than it looked and finally gave up. Then Neil took over as the disc jockey for the rest of the night, and the crowd enjoyed dancing to the usual funny songs like "The Chicken Dance" and "The Hokey-Pokey" before switching to tunes by artists like Taylor Swift, Katy Perry, and Justin Bieber. The hotel finally told them that it was time for the party to end, so they started to reluctantly leave the ballroom.

"Good night, good night! Parting is such sweet sorrow. That I shall say good night till it be morrow."

The wedding party members stayed overnight at the hotel, and the party continued for a long time. In the morning, a few people slept in, but most of the wedding party partook of a fabulous breakfast buffet in the hotel dining room. Then Nora and Tommy got ready to go out to O'Hare Airport so they could travel to Ireland for their honeymoon. The long-planned day had lived up to all their expectations, and they thanked God that the would-be killer had not made an appearance.

Tuesday, March 19
Feast of St. Joseph
Dingle, Ireland

Tommy and Nora had looked at so many possible places for their honeymoon and were still undecided a few weeks before the wedding. They now had the money to go anywhere in the world, but the lack of privacy that they'd experienced in recent weeks made them shy away from destinations where the media was likely to be waiting for them. They looked at warm and beautiful places like Florida, California, Hawaii, The French Riviera, Italy, Spain, or Bora Bora. Tommy liked to ski, but Nora wasn't fond of the snow and didn't want to risk breaking a limb.

They finally decided that privacy was their number one priority, so they made reservations in Dingle Town on the tip of the Dingle Peninsula in Ireland. They were about a month too early for the ferry boat rides to the Blasket Islands and Skilling Michael Island, but they talked to the locals, enjoyed the magnificent views of the ocean, and discovered an ancient cemetery with tall Celtic crosses.

At night, they went to the pub, enjoyed the food and the band, and joined in the singing. When they were in town, there was nothing Nora could do about her height, but she kept her hair under a hat so it couldn't be seen, just in case the media was around. The cold temperatures were a natural spur to lovemaking, and they felt totally relaxed and wonderful.

They arrived on Tuesday morning, but by Thursday night, they looked at each other and knew that they were getting bored with all this relaxation. They were so used to being constantly on the go and missed their families. Hopefully, they would have many years to come to be alone with each other, but it would be so much more fun to share this beauty with them.

They agreed to call both families and ask them to come to Ireland on Saturday. Nora called the twins at Duffy Hall and asked them to find a place large enough for all of them to stay in the Wicklow Mountains outside of Dublin. They made some calls home, and it turned out that most of their extended families could come, except Al and Mary Ann because of her pregnancy. They asked Jesse to come along, and she was thrilled. Nora also called Elsie Young, the young woman who had taken the pictures in the subway of the terrorist, and she was delighted to accept. Nora asked close aunts and uncles and the twins from Duffy Hall, Johnny Moreland, the security guard, Chief Herlihy from Duffy Hall, and Lieutenant Braxton and Sergeant Belsky from Chicago to come along too so they could share in the fun. Dr. Duffy invited his office staff, and Nora invited several people from the cancer clinic. All in all, there would be about 100 people. The Duffy Hall twins were able to rent out almost the entire hotel. Nora and Tommy were excited and looked forward to seeing everyone.

Unfortunately, an intrepid Chicago reporter noticed that the whole Duffy family was about to go traveling from Chicago and followed them to O'Hare Airport to try to get a statement. Jim headed them off by telling them that they were going on a vacation, but he knew they would still be looking for them.

John Cahill picked up Nora and Tommy in Dingle Town and drove them across Ireland to the Wicklow Mountains south of Dublin. They stopped along the way to see famous towns, castles, and shops, and then they met the family at the hotel and rejoiced at being together.

Grandpa Burke said it best for all of them: "Jesus, Mary, and Joseph, we thought we'd gotten rid of ye for a while." And then he laughed uproariously and gave Nora and Tommy a bear hug.

They enjoyed an afternoon of sightseeing at the Wicklow Mountains National Park and visited the monastic ruins at Glendalough, the valley of the two lakes. St. Kevin had lived there in the sixth century. They saw seven ancient churches, several tall stone crosses, and a round tower that was 1,000 years old. At the top of a breathtakingly beautiful vista, four of them got out their instruments—Nora on her fiddle, Jim on his uilleann pipes, Maeve on her bodhran drum, and Brian on his tin whistle—and the strains of "The Wearing of the Green" echoed across the lakes and mountains. The haunting music and the ambience at this very holy site gave them all goosebumps, and they found it hard to leave this enchanting place.

After an afternoon of hiking and taking pictures, everyone was tired and ready for an enjoyable meal and entertainment at the hotel. Jet lag caught up with the family and their guests, and they went to bed fairly early so that they would be ready for the trip into Dublin the next day.

The next morning, their drivers brought them into Dublin, and they checked into their hotel for an overnight stay. They all took the hop on/hop off tour buses that enabled them to see the various destinations and determine the ones they wanted to visit.

Some of the men went to see soccer/football in Croke Park, the famous sports venue. The crowd on both sides of the stadium waved their flags and sang along with various chants. Dr. Duffy was not a fan of soccer or Irish football. According to him, nothing seemed to happen very much in the hours they were there except a lot of running back and forth with almost no scores to show for it. He was told that he just didn't appreciate all the strategy that's going on. He could appreciate the runners' athleticism and strength, and many thousands of people there disagreed with him and seemed to be having a grand time.

Most of the women went shopping in Grafton Street and enjoyed the street musicians and shops and restaurants of all kinds. One particularly talented group stood near the statue of Molly Malone and sang that famous song in harmony:

In Dublin's fair city,
Where the Girls are so pretty,
I first set my eyes, On sweet Molly Malone,
As she wheeled her wheel barrow, Through the streets
broad and narrow, Crying cockles and mussels,
Alive, alive, o! Alive, alive, o! Alive, o!
Crying cockles and mussels, Alive, o!

The Duffy's gave them a generous tip. There used to be a statue on O'Connell Street of the "floozy in the jacuzzi," an eponymous depiction of the River Liffey that resembled a woman in a bathtub, but it had been replaced by a tall column called "the stiletto in the ghetto." Dubliners loved to manipulate the English language and often did so.

Chief Herlihy warned them that Molly and Caitlan should never be left alone since they could easily become a kidnapping target. The Irish media couldn't seem to get enough news about the "Mighty Rich Midget" as Nora was being described in their press. The twins were unhappy about being watched so closely, but Jim and Jack were assigned to accompany them wherever they went, and Maureen and Siobhan stayed with them too in case the twins needed female assistance.

They saw the old post office, which still bore the scars of bullet holes where the rebels from the 1916 Easter Rising began their quest for independence.

Mrs. Duffy insisted that they make at least a brief stop at Trinity College where she went to university many years ago. She wanted the family to see where she and Dr. Duffy met. They also got to see the most impressive collection of medieval manuscripts in the library and today's page in the *Book of Kells*, the famous illustrated manuscript of the Four Gospels that could only be viewed in its glass case.

Mrs. Duffy suggested that they visit St. Mary's Cathedral, which she remembered as being very beautiful. Their guide told them that the story of St. Mary's Pro-Cathedral mirrored the convoluted story of Ireland's religious history. The "Pro" designation meant that it was an "acting" cathedral for the Catholic Church. The Cathedral of the Holy Trinity, or Christ Church, was the original cathedral in Dublin, dating back to 1030. When Henry VIII in England decided he wanted to have his own church in the 1530s, he took over all the churches in England and Ireland. The Catholic Church refused to accept that Christ Church was no longer their cathedral, because it had been originally designated that way by the Pope, so when St. Mary's was built in 1825, it became known as the Catholic Pro-Cathedral. There was another Cathedral too, St. Patrick's, which was the national church of the Church of Ireland and the tallest and largest church in Ireland.

The Duffy's found the church's history confusing, but they enjoyed seeing St. Mary's Romanesque architecture. The exterior looked more like a courthouse than a church, but it was very beautiful inside, and they agreed that it was well worth a visit. They would have loved to see the other cathedrals too, but they were running out of time.

Dr. Duffy whispered to Eileen that the guide forgot a rather important detail. After Henry VIII took over all the churches, it was considered a crime for either priest or peasant to attend a Catholic mass, and it was punishable by death. This continued to be the case for hundreds of years from 1536 until 1829.

They continued on the tour and found the Museum of Natural History fascinating. They liked the exhibit that showed how well-preserved a body could be in the Irish bogs. They saw a young man still wearing a golden circlet around his throat who had been in the bog for hundreds of years and was likely a victim of human sacrifice. Both the gold and the body looked as though they were just placed there recently.

The Duffys loved going to the Museum of Art and admired the many beautiful paintings, and they bought a number of small copies for their living room. Nora bought several prints that she planned to use in the dining room of their new home. The knowledgeable woman at the register told her she'd be better off buying the framed copies since it would be difficult to find frames in the US to fit the paintings that were measured in centimeters rather than inches. There was so much to see in Dublin, but they had to speed up their sightseeing so that they would have enough time to get back to Duffy Hall tomorrow.

They took the tour of the Guinness factory and heard interesting tales like the factory was started in 1759, the founder, Arthur Guinness had twenty-one children, and their slogan was "Guinness is good for you," although the current owners stress responsible drinking. They walked the crowded streets and ended up in Temple Bar, an area similar to Rush Street in Chicago. They were told that the area once had a dubious history of crime and prostitution, but that had been fixed long ago, and now it was a destination for those who wanted to enjoy good food and drink and have fun.

They stopped in at a pub, which was so crowded that they had to sit near the back next to an ancient fireplace that was burning peat turves. They ordered Irish stew made with Murphy's Stout accompanied by pints of Guinness. The ambience of delicious food, attractive surroundings, and being able to share it all with the people they loved best overwhelmed them with joy. The band started to play, and later, the Irish dancers came on stage and entertained the crowd.

One of the members of the dance troupe recognized Nora, and they asked her to come up and dance with them, and she brought her sisters with her as well. The troupe supplied them with shoes, and the familiar music gave their feet a boost. They were soon flying across the stage. The Irish girls complimented Nora and her sisters on their dancing, and the audience gave them a rousing reception. Afterward, they returned to the tables and struck up a conversation with a couple who was there on vacation from Amsterdam. There was a bit of difficulty understanding them, but music was the universal language, and they all laughed and sang together.

Siobhan, Nora, their parents, and some of the Barrys went to the Abbey Theatre to see *The Country Girls* by Edna O'Brien, a coming of age story of two teenage girls, which was banned and even burned in the 1960s when it was first published. Siobhan had a similar look of awe on her face when she first walked into the Abbey Theatre as Dorothy did when she first entered the Land of Oz. Siobhan was thrilled and got to meet some of the actors backstage. She could see herself being part of this noble profession, and from what she'd seen so far, she loved Dublin. She promised to come back for more of their productions.

Dr. Duffy finally reminded them that they should return to the hotel and get some rest, because they would be leaving early for their trip across Ireland to get to Duffy Hall the next day.

They met Ann O'Shea, the reporter from the *Ennis Tribune*, at the hotel and explained to her that this large contingent of their family and friends had added enormously to Tom and Nora's enjoyment of their honeymoon. Ann appreciated that they were giving her "first dibs" on their story.

They had difficulty relaxing after their jam-packed day. Much laughter and many stories were exchanged before they drifted off to sleep.

In the morning, they had a delicious brunch at the Shelbourne Hotel, which was built in 1824. They were told that the Irish Constitution was drafted there. They then drove west across Ireland back to Sneem. They stopped at various places along the way, like Blarney Castle where they kissed the Blarney Stone so they would have the "gift of eloquence," and then went to the ancient Rock of Cashel where they walked through the ruins and the graveyard filled with tall Celtic crosses. They arrived in the beautiful city of Cork and saw the harbor where many of those who left Ireland to come to America began their journeys.

They arrived in the town of Kinsale eventually, but drivers had to be careful as they traveled over the bridge that led to this delightful town since the "Irish mist" could produce a fog so thick that it was hard to see the front of the car, let alone the road. Kinsale was where the bodies of hundreds of people were brought who were drowned during the horrific sinking of the *Lusitania* during WWI near Old Head. Today, the town of Kinsale has a picturesque harbor filled with fishing boats and lined with colorful shops and restaurants.

They drove over to Galway and spent some time at the famous Cliffs of Moher, 700 feet high above the Atlantic Ocean. Nora had been warned about the effects of the weather at the cliffs by her friend, Ann Maloney. It was such a blustery day when she and her family had stopped there that she was knocked down and needed stitches in her face. That was not the case today, and they enjoyed perfect weather and spectacular views, although Mr. Duffy warned everyone to stay far back from the edges. They stopped at the orphanage Uncle Cy had supported for many years and gave presents to all the kids.

The family and guests finally arrived at Duffy Hall and brought presents to everyone on the staff. After a warm welcome, they were shown to their attractive rooms where peat fires were burning. There weren't enough rooms for everyone to have a room to themselves, so some people had to double up. Jesse and Sue Bonner, Dr. Duffy's scheduling secretary, shared a small room in the annex close to Lavinia's suite; and Amanda and Diane, the charge nurses, shared the room across from them. Everyone else found a room somewhere in the main part of the hall.

Nora and Tommy enjoyed showing their guests around the castle and the grounds of the hall, including the deer park and the chapel. They were impressed by the size of Liam, the wolfhound, and Finnbar, the racehorse, and they loved watching the tiny bog ponies. They could see why Nora loved this place so much.

After the tour of the grounds, the entire party enjoyed cocktails and appetizers in the spacious living room area and then moved to the impressive dining room where they were served a delicious dinner prepared by Mrs. O'Hara and her staff.

After dinner, the party shared more drinks and stories. Dr. Whiteside sat next to Nora and said that he had heard tidbits about the medical research building that might be built on the property and said he'd like to know more about it. Nora and Tommy filled him in on their proposed plans, but they told him that many things had to happen before it could become a reality.

Nora said she'd been investigating the possibility of researching "orphan diseases," diseases that are so rare that the medical community and the drug companies paid little attention to them. Dr. Whiteside said he thought that would be a wonderful way to spend her money. His sister's child had been born with a rare disease that affected her muscles, and the only known medication was prohibitively expensive. He asked Nora to keep him updated, and he offered to help if he could.

Dr. Duffy asked Eileen to join him, and he asked the members of his office staff to informally join them for a chat. Lieutenant Braxton had asked the Duffys to keep an eye on their people, since Jason and Sue were among the Holy Savior employees who had been seen talking to Nick, the suspected terrorist contact at the hospital.

Dr. Duffy began by asking Amanda, Diane, Keisha and her husband, Calvin, Sue, and Jason if they'd had a good time and what their favorite part of the trip was. Amanda and Diane, never at a loss for words, said they loved the food they'd had at the Dublin pub, and there were an awful lot of good-looking guys there. "If I could have just had a little more time, I think I would have had a date with the guitar player in the striped shirt," laughed Amanda.

Keisha said she'd loved the shopping, and she had bought her daughter, Chelsea, a leprechaun doll she thought she'd love. Calvin had bought several decals for his motorcycle at a shop in Kinsale. Sue said she was surprised at how ancient castles were sometimes right in the middle of the towns, and she liked the appearance of the stores that were each painted a different color.

Jason had a faraway look in his eyes as he said he thought the Cliffs of Moher would be an ideal place to set a mystery story. "If a murderer wanted to get rid of someone, it would be the perfect place to just walk toward the edge, and while the victim was preoccupied with the view, a good shove would send him 700 feet to the rocks below." When he felt the eyes of the group looking at him strangely, Jason said that he was merely talking about a hypothetical situation.

"On a happier note," Jason said, "I stopped in at a jewelry store on Grafton Street and bought a ring for Belinda. "Mind you, it's not an engagement ring, but Bel loves sapphires, and I know she'll really like the antique setting. If this goes well, maybe a diamond will be the next step."

"Wow," exclaimed the ladies, "we never thought that bachelor Jason would fall so easily. Ireland must have worked its charms on him!"

Dr. Duffy and Eileen were pleased with most of their responses, but the fact that Jason had talked about pushing someone off the edge of the cliffs made them wonder if he could have been involved with Nora's "accidents." He always seemed pleasant, but he was young and strong and would be physically capable of violent actions. They resolved to watch him more carefully.

As the travelers started to wilt after their very busy day, Siobhan played the antique piano, and many of the group joined in singing some of the old Irish and American tunes. Finally, they had to admit that they couldn't keep their eyes open and all drifted off to their rooms.

Nora and Tommy agreed that they could not have wished for a more perfect honeymoon. That was a good thing since the events of the next few days made them almost forget what a good time they'd had.

Monday, March 25
Sneem, 10:00 p.m., GMT

Everyone started to get settled down and hoped for a good night's sleep. Jesse, the Duffys' trusted housekeeper, had never warmed up to Sue Bonner, her roommate for the night. Sue was Dr. Duffy's scheduling secretary, and Jesse thought that she seemed to have a surly personality and face to match with poorly dyed blond hair. Jesse tried to be polite as they readied themselves for bed and asked Sue how she had enjoyed the trip through Ireland.

Sue surprised her by saying that she thought they'd seen some nice scenery, but Dr. Duffy could have provided them with more spending money.

Jesse thought that was an odd thing to say since the trip had been entirely paid for by the Duffys. Jesse tried to switch the conversation around by asking Sue how she liked working for Dr. Duffy. "It sounds like your job must be challenging."

Sue didn't respond to that comment but instead asked Jesse how she could stand working for the Duffys and taking care of all those kids. Jesse responded that it could sometimes be tiring, but she loved it all. Sue said that it seemed to her that the Duffys were just using her as a slave to do all the things they didn't want to deal with. "Dr. Duffy is good at using slaves to do his dirty work," Sue said with a sneer.

Jesse wanted to respond that the Duffys gave her a generous regular salary, paid for all her insurance, and treated her like a loved member of the family, but something told her to back off and not respond. "Well, I don't agree with you, but I'm going into the bathroom now to get ready for bed. All that walking around today tired me out."

Jesse slipped into the bathroom, shivered, and locked the door. Little alarm bells had started to tinkle in her brain and were getting louder all the time. In the twenty-five years that she'd worked for the Duffys, she'd never known anyone who actively disliked them. Yet, this young woman who worked with Dr. Duffy every day seemed to almost hate him. Jesse knew that the would-be killer had not yet been identified, and she began to wonder if it could be Sue. She had nothing to back up that assumption except a gut instinct and Sue's remarks about being a slave, but after Sue fell asleep, Jesse heard her mumbling things that sounded like, "I'll get you."

Jesse asked St. Brigid for her help, but she was exhausted from all the activities of the last few days, and after a while, she came out of the bathroom, got into bed, and fell sound asleep.

Sometime during the early morning hours, Jesse was awakened by the powerful smell of honeysuckle and the sound of whispering that seemed to come from the curtains right behind her bed. She couldn't make out the words, but she thought a voice was telling her to "get up right now."

Jesse was frightened at first since she'd heard talk of a ghost that sometimes whispered in the hallways, but then she thanked whoever it was that had alerted her that Sue had gotten up and was tiptoeing out of their room. Anyone who was trying to protect her beloved Nora was fine with Jesse, ghost or not. Jesse had her robe and slippers handy, and she followed Sue to see what she might be up to.

Jesse saw the back of Sue's plaid pajamas as she surreptitiously opened Aunt Lavinia's bedroom door and went in. "Holy Mother of God," whispered Jesse. *I have a very bad feeling about this. There's no reason why she should be bothering Lavinia so early in the morning. Maybe my suspicions were right*, she shakily thought to herself. *I'm no hero and I don't have one of those phone gadgets like all the young people do.* Nora and the family members were too far away for her to alert them. *St. Brigid, show me what to do.*

Jesse peered into Lavinia's room and watched Sue tiptoe over to a large green velvet box on the table across from Lavinia's bed. Lavinia had also had a bad feeling that something threatening would happen tonight, so she was only half asleep. Her alert spaniel, Lady, raised the alarm, and Lavinia turned on her light and challenged Sue as to what she was doing there.

At first, Sue tried to talk her way out of a confrontation and said she couldn't sleep. She'd heard about Lavinia's jewel collection by looking her up in Ireland's Who's Who and just wanted to see her jewels.

Lavinia responded, "You thought it was acceptable to just come into my bedroom so early in the morning to do this? I don't believe you. Did you think I would be stupid enough to leave the jewels unguarded? The chest is glued down to the table, and the latch can only be opened by a special key. Those jewels are precious to me since they were a gift to me from my fiancé many years ago, and someone like you is not going to have them. I suppose you are also the person who has been trying to hurt my Nora?"

Sue then dispensed with all pretenses and told Lavinia that she had a connection in the underground world who told her that not much was known about Lavinia, but anytime she appeared in public, she wore magnificent jewelry. Sue then pulled out a gun from her pocket and laughed at her maniacally. "What would an old witch like you need with a fabulous collection of jewels?" asked Sue. "No wonder the English defeated you people so easily. Ireland is supposed to have so much charm, but all I can see is old people and sheep. As soon as I get rid of the Duffys, I'm heading to New York with your jewels."

Lavinia turned her back on her, walked over to her telephone, and said she was going to call Chief Herlihy. Sue warned her not to pick up the phone, but Lavinia wasn't about to be deterred. Sue saw the heavy Waterford punchbowl sitting next to the jewel box, picked it up, and smashed it onto Lavinia's head, and the old woman dropped to the floor like a stone with blood spurting out of the top of her head.

Jesse saw all this from behind the door and stuffed her hand into her mouth to prevent herself from screaming. She watched as

Sue put some kind of device on her gun, fired at the lock on the jewel case, and then scooped a cluster of glittering jewels into a bag she had brought with her.

Jesse waited until Sue left Lavinia's suite, and then she ran to the room where she knew that Mr. John O'Malley was staying. She frantically tried to tell him what she had just seen and screamed out that she thought that Lavinia was dead. "Sue is also likely the person who's been trying to kill Nora," Jesse stammered out. "She has a gun with her and knows how to use it."

John helped the distraught Jesse to sit down, and then he called Chief Herlihy, relayed what had happened, and directed him to call the Garda immediately. Duncan Lloyd had heard the interchange between Jesse and John, and he comforted the sobbing Jesse. John told them he'd check on Lavinia, and Duncan led Jesse to the kitchen where she could stay with Mrs. O'Hara and her crew.

Meanwhile, Sue ran to Dr. and Mrs. Duffy's room and pointed her gun at them. She motioned for the startled couple to get up and head for the lobby of the castle. The front of Sue's blouse was splattered with Lavinia's blood, and her scarlet-stained clothes and crazed visage made a frightening appearance. She jabbed the gun into Dr. Duffy's ribs and forced the couple to walk through the lobby, then down the hallway to the basement door where they proceeded down the ancient flagstone steps.

When Dr. Duffy inquired what this was all about, Sue told them her wild story of hatred and revenge because Dr. Duffy had operated on her fiancé, Jimmy, did a terrible job, and ended up killing him. "I've been trying to get back at you by trying to kill your Nora, but she keeps escaping my plans. So now I'm going to kill both of you instead," she screamed as she waved the gun at them with a horrible grin on her face.

Dr. Duffy and Eileen realized that Sue was exhibiting signs of an extremely disordered psyche, but she also was very determined. He tried to gain some control over the situation by explaining to her that Jimmy was in such very poor condition that he probably would have died that night anyway. "We'd been waiting for a heart transplant candidate, but that hadn't worked out. I agreed to go ahead with the operation because I thought there might be a very slim chance to keep him alive longer, and I felt sorry for you. I prayed for a miracle, but it didn't happen. Once we opened him up, we realized that his heart was in even worse shape than we had thought. My partners and I tried as hard as we could to keep him alive, but we couldn't get his heart to pump."

Sue responded that they hated Jimmy because he was a Latino. "If he'd been white, you would have tried harder to stop the bleeding."

Mrs. Duffy replied in as calm a voice as she could muster that no matter what ethnicity or color we were, underneath our skin, we all looked alike; but Sue was beyond thinking logically.

Dr. Duffy tried to keep Sue talking about her plans of the last six months, asking her how she was able to conceal her hatred while still coming to work every day and getting her work done. His calm and authoritative manner had helped many a patient overcome their fears, but Sue was having none of that today. She just kept spewing out hatred for them and for their children, especially that phony "sweetness and light" pretender, Nora.

Dr. Duffy wondered if he had any chance of distracting Sue enough so that he could knock the gun out of her hand, but she was too far away, and nothing came to mind. He tried to think of movies where the hero was able to make that happen and how he did it, but then, they were just movies. The muzzle of the gun pointed right at them was beginning to take on the appearance of a cannon, and he and Eileen automatically reached for each other's hands.

They were trying to keep Sue talking while they prayed for a miracle that someone would realize they were down here, but their chances of being rescued seemed to be getting slimmer by the minute.

Tuesday, March 26
Sneem, 7:00 a.m., GMT

Nora had been visiting the stables with Tim Taylor and had just come from riding Finnbar who now welcomed her with a lick of his long tongue. The huge horse's back was so wide, it made for uneasy riding for Nora at first, but Tim had created a special saddle and extra-long straps for the stirrups, so she managed to feel comfortable enough on him. Nora had discovered that Finnbar felt more secure when she whispered encouraging words to him and petted his head, so she did that frequently.

Chief Brennan pulled his car up in front of the stables and told Nora that he had some interesting information for her about Valerie. She had called him in and said she wanted a lesser sentence in exchange for more information. She told him that she knew things that could potentially save Nora's life. The chief told her he couldn't guarantee anything, but if her information was really helpful, they could probably make a deal.

Valerie told him that she didn't actually make that up about Nora wanting to replace the Irish officers at Duffy Medical with Americans. The young woman who worked in Dr. Duffy's office, Sue Bonner, told her that. Chief Brennan continued that Sue had told Valerie that she hated Dr. Duffy and his family since he operated on her fiancé who died after the operation. Sue was the one who suggested that Valerie find someone to shoot at Nora, and Sue said she would give her $5,000 to have him do it. Valerie knew about Jim

Boyle—the retard, as she called him—at the neighboring farm, and she told Jim she would give him $500 to shoot at Nora. Then Valerie would still have most of the money for herself.

Chief Brennan said, "So it appears that mousy little Sue has been behind these shenanigans that have been getting more and more serious."

Whenever Nora got nervous or worried, she became as still as a statue until she figured out what to do. She now sat on Finnbar's saddle as still as the steel leprechaun after hearing what Chief Brennan had to tell her. One by one, the tumblers of pattern recognition clicked into place!

No wonder the killer always knew what their plans were! Sue was an organizer and a listener, and she was around Dr. Duffy almost every day. All she had to do was keep track of his schedule and ask him a few questions to find out all she needed to know about where all the members of the family would be.

"We've been thinking of the motivation of the killer all wrong!" Nora realized. "Apparently, Sue didn't care about my inheritance at all. She just wanted to punish Dad in any way she could. Now that I think of Sue in that context, everything that happened to us makes sense."

Nora whistled for Liam, and Johnny appeared with him. "Johnny, make sure you stay close to me and bring Liam along." It must have been Sue all along who had been trying to harass and kill her, and who knew what she might be doing now to her parents? She recalled that her parents had decided to stay behind at the castle, and Sue and Jesse were there as well. "Security guard, Johnny, is here with me, but there's probably no guard at the castle."

Nora yelled to Chief Brennan to follow her, and she turned Finnbar around and rode him like the wind the two blocks back to Duffy Hall. The huge horse felt the tension in Nora's body and acknowledged her shouted words to him by running faster than he ever had before. She couldn't help but think of the tune the cavalry bugler played as they rode to the rescue. They were soon at the front door of the hall, and Nora jumped down from Finnbar's saddle and took the twenty-eight steps as fast as her short legs could carry her to the lobby with Chief Brennan, Johnny, and Liam in hot pursuit.

"Enda, where are my parents?" she shouted. Enda didn't know and said she had left her desk for a minute, but she'd seen Sue's back with her parents in front of her going down the hallway toward the basement door. The group soon saw with horror that bloody shoe tracks led right to the studded basement door.

Nora ran flat out toward the enormous door and pulled on it, but it was securely locked, and she couldn't budge it open. Nora asked if there was an exterior entrance to the basement, and Enda said there was, so they ran outside. Nora and Johnny tried to pull open the exterior door to the basement, but it was securely locked too. They realized there was no other way into the basement except through the large window around the corner.

They cautiously walked around the edge of the hall and spotted the window. If it was locked, they planned to smash it open so that Liam could jump through the opening. Johnny realized that the window was not locked and he was able to push it open. The screeching sound of the window opening distracted Sue, and she turned her attention away from Nora's parents and fired at Johnny, Nora, and the dog, but her gun had momentarily jammed.

Nora instructed her huge dog to jump through the window opening and prayed that his normally friendly nature would remain submerged so that he would knock Sue down. Liam let out a huge bark and jumped on Sue who did fall down while shooting wildly.

Chief Brennan and the Gardai had managed to get into the basement from the first floor, and they shouted out to Sue to drop her gun. Sue kept shooting and, unfortunately, one of the bullets found Chief Brennan's guard dog, Dusty, who whimpered and fell to the floor.

Sue had discovered the circular stairway that led all the way up to the roof, and she frantically ran up the metal stairs with the speed and strength of the desperate quarry being pursued by the intrepid hunters. She reached the top and was able to open the door that led to the roof of the hall, followed by a contingent of Gardai.

Sue had a second gun hidden in her boot and aimed it at the officers who had followed her. One of her bullets found the unprotected leg of an officer, and he screamed in pain. The Gardai insisted that Dr. and Mrs. Duffy and Nora stay behind, and the family clung to each other in terror but in joyful recognition that they were alive.

Tommy had been out taking more pictures of the deer enclosure and didn't realize the drama that had been taking place on the roof until he got closer to the castle and heard the gunfire. What a frightening sound that was! "Now what?" he yelled out as he raced toward the castle and Nora.

58

Tuesday, March 26
Sneem, 8:00 a.m., GMT

Meanwhile, Lieutenant Braxton and Sergeant Belsky of the Chicago PD had been admiring the artwork in the main hall of the castle. They heard gunfire and didn't realize at first where it was coming from, but they thought they'd find out quicker if they could get to the nearby roof of the portico that overhung the front doors of the castle. They had just recently completed another "active shooter" course, so they thought that training would come in handy now. They were pretty sure now that the gunfire was likely coming from the very top of the castle.

Lieutenant Braxton asked Enda if there would be a rifle handy, and Enda showed them a gun case in the little lobby near the front door. Lieutenant Braxton grabbed a rifle and bullets and handed them off to Sergeant Belsky who had the reputation of being a crack shot. She could also try using a handgun, but the likelihood of a bullet from a handgun traveling up to the roof accurately was extremely limited.

Enda directed them to the wide window that opened out just above the portico that was a story below the roof of the castle. They jumped down to the portico roof, and Laura looked up and could see that the shooter appeared to be a woman whose long blond hair was blowing in the wind. Her back was exposed as she stood next to an opening in the crenelated stones at the very top of the castle. They could hear repeated warnings from the Gardai for the woman to drop her gun, but she kept firing. It would be a tricky shot, but Laura thought she might be able to bring down the woman who was so preoccupied.

Sue was busy screaming and trying to shoot as many people as she could on the roof and was unaware of the danger below her. Laura took careful aim with her rifle, fired, and saw the blond hair disappear from view. Laura would have preferred just wounding her, but judging by the wildness in the shooter's voice, she had taken her best shot so that the woman couldn't shoot anyone else. Laura didn't even know who the woman was, but Chief Brennan yelled out that the shooter was down and seriously hurt.

Dr. Duffy, Eileen, and Nora finished climbing the steps to the roof, and they first worked on the injured police officer and stabilized his leg wound. Another officer had been shot in the lower arm, and they stopped the bleeding until an ambulance arrived. They then turned their attention to Sue who was stretched out on the floor in her plaid pajamas, surrounded by Aunt Lavinia's many jewels that had fallen out of her bag and were brilliantly twinkling in the sun. They worked on her for a long time, but they were unable to stop the bleeding.

Sue gasped out to them that she was so very tired and she had been in such misery that she couldn't think straight. She told them she'd been behind all the attempts on Nora's life since she'd wanted to inflict the maximum pain on Dr. Duffy.

Dr. Duffy asked Sue if she was the one that put the brown package containing the anthrax spores under their Christmas tree. Sue said that his name held a lot of clout at the laboratory they often used, and she told them that Dr. Duffy was doing research on the effects of anthrax. "They sent a good sample to me within a few days, and I fixed the package and pushed it way under your tree during the Christmas party you had at your house." Sue panted out, "I'm glad that you figured it out before it could kill your family."

Sue asked them to pray for her, and then she took a final breath and lay still.

Father Tooley had heard the gunshots and saw the Gardai around the back of the castle. He followed the Duffys up to the roof, and he now said the last rites over Sue's body. He said it was a good thing that Sue expressed some sorrow for what she'd done, and they could only pray that a loving God would take her into his arms.

Tommy finally made it up to the roof and cradled Nora in his arms. Nora understood James Joyce's stream of consciousness better as the tears flowed down her cheeks. She had been with Sue on so many occasions but never thought of her as the possible killer. She was so "ordinary" that it didn't seem as though it could be her.

So many thoughts ran together concurrently in Nora's mind: *You stupid girl, why did you put yourself and us through such misery? Vinnie died because of her connection with me. Sue had no wolf man exterior to gradually shed, but I hope the transformation happened for her on the inside at the moment of death. No one should die awash in such hatred. Who knows what evil lurks in the hearts of men? To sleep, perchance to dream…ay, there's the rub. We're safe! Pray for us now and at the hour of our death. Life always matters so much. May the road rise to meet you. Tommy will be so happy. Cy and Lavinia, help this mixed-up girl. Rest in peace! We're safe, safe at last. I'm so tired of death. I am the Resurrection and the Life!*"

Nora felt her mother's gentle touch on her shoulder. Eileen helped her Bitsy to stand up and took her into her arms. "That's enough now, Nora, *a stor, a stor.* You've done your best. Now let God take over."

Tuesday, March 26
Sneem, 9:00 a.m., GMT

Sergeant Belsky said to Lieutenant Braxton with tears in her eyes that she felt terrible since she'd never killed anyone before. "Oh, Matt, it's one thing to do it in target practice, but it's another to see a human being fall down dead because of me," cried Laura. "I don't think I want to do this anymore. I understand Steve McQueen's girlfriend's comments better now in the movie *Bullitt*. After seeing the dead body of a murdered young woman, she said to him, 'You're living in a sewer day after day.' Steve responded to her, 'That's where half of it is.'"

Laura told her partner and friend, "I don't want to live in the sewer anymore."

"Laura, dear," Matt responded, "I don't know what happened to that poor woman, but she had obviously become insane. You had no choice, Laura. A bunch of Irish policemen up there are very glad that you're such a good shot."

Matt held Laura in his arms and said, "Don't you think it's about time for us to stop this pussyfooting around? When things calm down today, why don't we take a drive in this beautiful countryside? I'll tell you how I've been feeling about you for a long time." Matt and Laura kissed tenderly and looked forward to a happy future. First, they had to find a way to get down from the portico roof, and Chief Herlihy found a ladder so they could climb down where they were roundly hugged and congratulated.

The Duffys could hardly believe that their nightmare of the last many months was finally over, and they thanked everyone for helping to end things, especially Laura. It seemed impossible that she could have found a way to make the shot that she did, but they thanked her profusely for saving them.

Nora and Tommy stayed with Aunt Vinnie's body until Mr. Dowling arrived from the village and took her away. It seemed impossible that this could have happened, but Nora envisioned Uncle Cy, Emily, and Mort waiting for her. What a loss Vinnie's death was to Nora, Duffy Hall, and the world!

Nora and Tommy comforted dear Jesse and thanked her for her vigilance. Jesse grabbed Nora in her arms, cried over her, and told her how grateful to St. Brigid she was that she was safe.

They returned to the dining hall, and Mrs. O'Hara served them a restorative lunch after they promised to tell her "all the gory details of the excitement." Nora then went to Aunt Vinnie's room, looked through her papers, and found a letter to her that said in case anything happened to her, she wanted to tell her a little more about her long-dead fiancé, Mortimer O'Brien.

> Mortimer was a talented artist and painted many pictures of people at festive occasions. You'll see his better paintings throughout Duffy Hall. Two of my favorites are the one in my bedroom of children rejoicing when school is out for the summer and a magnificent large painting in the dining room of the men and women in the fields during the potato harvest. One of his quick paintings hangs over my fireplace, the one of the sheep whose hind quarters are painted pink or blue to indicate which farmer they belong to.

> Mort's main occupation was as an architect, and he built many famous homes in Killarney. My cousin, Blanche, lived in one of the houses designed by Mort, and she never stopped praising his vision for an ideal home. It was traditional

in exterior design, but the flow of the rooms and the modern appliances made things much easier for the homeowners.

Mort had wavy blond hair and piercing blue eyes, and we met at a fair in Killarney. We fell in love quickly and spent a wonderful year planning our future together. Unfortunately, Mort was an avid fisherman, and he took his boat out on a blustery North Atlantic day and drowned just a month before we were to be married. I grieved for him for a long time, but I thanked God for the time we had together. I never found another man who attracted me as much as Mort had, so I never married and devoted myself to caring for Cy. I've had a satisfying life, but every so often, I feel Mort's presence and realize how much I've missed him all these years.

I hope that you and your Tommy will have better luck in life than we did, and I pray for you every day. I thank God for bringing you into my life, and I think you know that I consider you as my daughter.

Love, Mortimer Lear

Nora put the letter back into the box of treasured documents that Lavinia had left to her and smiled at her signature. She grieved that she would not now be able to get to know this fascinating woman better, and she vowed to keep her memory alive.

The Duffy family and their guests adjusted their schedules to stay in Sneem for a few more days. The staff at Duffy Hall were sadly experienced now and familiar with all the processes they had to follow to notify everyone about Lavinia's death and to make arrangements for her wake and funeral.

Nora and Tommy brought their guests to the town of Sneem for some much-needed diversion, and they had dinner at Dan Murphy's Bar and brought the owner up to date about the latest news at Duffy

Hall. "You've had enough of sadness and death there, and that's for sure, so," he said. He served them a delightful meal and said he hoped they would come back again in happier times.

Two days later, they again gathered for a wake in the chapel behind Duffy Hall and then went to Lavinia's funeral mass at St. Joseph's in Sneem. Nora told the congregation that she considered Aunt Vinnie to be a martyr since she likely knew that Sue would kill her, but she distracted her to keep the rest of us safe. Once more, Nora enlisted the help of many of the musicians who had played at Uncle Cy's funeral mass and she used her violin to honor Aunt Vinnie by playing "Movement IV" from Beethoven's 5th Symphony. Hearing this incredibly stirring music made the congregation feel glad that they had been privileged to be a part of Lavinia's life rather than being sad. The resulting exuberant applause was only partly for the musicians; Nora had made sure that Aunt Vinnie's many accomplishments had been well-publicized.

Then Lavinia was returned to the grounds of Duffy Hall where she was buried next to her old fiancé, Mort, on the hill behind the hall.

Nora had a hand in picking out the tombstone for Vinnie:

> Lavinia Mary Duffy
> 1931–2018
> LOVER OF LIFE
> I will arise and go now to Innisfree

Nora thought the phrase would please Aunt Vinnie who had always loved the lyrical poetry of William Butler Yeats. She hoped that Vinnie was with Mort now and singing the famous poem with him:

> I will arise and go now, and go to Innisfree,
>   And a small cabin build there, of clay and
> wattles made;
>   Nine bean-rows will I have there, a hive for
> the honey-bee,

And live alone in the bee-loud glade.

And I shall have some peace there, for peace comes dropping slow,

Dropping from the veils of the morning to where the cricket sings;

There midnight's all a glimmer, and noon a purple glow,

And evening full of the linnet's wings.

I will arise and go now, for always night and day

I hear lake water lapping with low sounds by the shore;

While I stand on the roadway, or on the pavements grey,

I hear it in the deep heart's core.

Nora hoped that they would all "have some peace there in their deep heart's core," in their new home once it was ready.

Friday, March 29
Sneem, 10:00 a.m., GMT

The next day, the group bade a fond farewell to the staff at Duffy Hall, and they boarded an Aer Lingus plane for the flight back to Chicago. They've had such dizzying days, it would take some time for them to unpack it all. They shared many memories, and Nora dozed on and off and thought of the lines from the Robert Frost poem that now seemed to have a good chance of becoming a reality:

> The woods are lovely, dark, and deep
> But I have miles to go before I sleep
> And miles to go before I sleep.

Nora and Tommy looked forward to some tranquility, but with all the people they interacted with at home and at work, there was always the possibility of another exciting adventure in their future. They could only hope the next one would be less dangerous.

Nora had fond memories of one of her teachers, Sister Nicolena, who told them that God had given them the abundance of beauty in the natural world for their pleasure and their learning. "Just by looking around, we can see that God gives us pointers for how we should think and act. Birds fly in a V-shape and exchange leaders during flight to conserve their energy, an excellent example of cooperation. Flowers always bend toward the light because it's life-giving.

It's always up to you to lean toward the light and life, because if you don't, well—" Nora could hear her saying it—"you might just end up dying violently on the roof of a castle in Ireland."

The Duffy's thought afterward that they should have suspected Sue Bonner earlier, but she was always so mild-mannered and good at her job that they hadn't realized that a frantic desire for revenge had destroyed her ability to think rationally. They also found out when they got home that Sue's parting "gift" to Dr. Duffy was to mix up all the schedules for the hospital and patients for the next two months before she left. They hired an experienced scheduler to take Sue's place, and eventually, she got things under control.

Dr. Duffy had talked with Mrs. Samuels in HR, and they organized a monthly seminar about how to handle grief for staff and patients. They weren't sure if having something in place like this would have helped Sue, but they resolved to give it a try. How could such a small woman have caused such a huge amount of turmoil for so many people?

Sue's body was eventually returned to Chicago, and Nora paid for the funeral and burial. Father Ahearn gave an inspiring homily on the meaning of salvation and redemption. Nora and Tommy were very grateful to everyone who had helped them bring this dreadful episode to an end, although the painful memories would linger for a long time.

Despite the many efforts of the police, Nick, the suspected terrorist who had worked with Sue in her attempts to kill Nora, seemed to have disappeared, but they were keeping the investigation open.

Dr. Duffy and Eileen felt they needed some extra time to recover from the trauma of being so close to death in the basement of Duffy Hall. They realized more than ever that time was fleeting, so they took an extra week and went back to Italy where their honeymoon had been spent so many years ago. There was nothing like attending mass at St. Peter's Basilica in Rome, perusing the grand ceiling in the Sistine Chapel, visiting the glories of the Uffizi Gallery in Florence, and listening to the serenades of a gondolier while floating through the canals of Venice to cure melancholia and rekindle romance.

Tommy and Nora temporarily moved into the Duffy home after returning. Their new house was almost ready, and they found the prospect of filling up some of those extra bedrooms exciting. They tried to be realistic as they faced the future. They'd seen the best and the worst of human nature and were aware that they shared the same tendencies. They knew it was usually the little things you don't pay attention to that caused problems, but they had faith in God and in each other. Starting their life together feeling safe had taken on the glow of promises made and kept. Surely God wouldn't want them to go through anything like their trials of the last few months again, would he?

Nora's natural inclination to a positive disposition carried her through the coming days. She often found herself humming the seventeen-note glissando opening clarinet solo in "Rhapsody in Blue" and imagined herself and her family being carried up and up to wonderful things she couldn't even imagine.

> We are such stuff as dreams are made on;
> and our little life is rounded with a sleep.

EPILOGUE

D r. and Mrs. Duffy's first grandson was born at the end of March to Mary Ann and her husband, Al O'Rourke. Dylan Michael was named after Al's grandfather and Dr. Duffy. Dylan had curly red hair, and at nine pounds, it wouldn't take him long to catch up to his Aunt Nora. The entire family rejoiced in this latest member of the clan.

Mr. Karner asked Tom Barry to become the head of his firm's international division, and Nora was another step closer to her goal of becoming a brain surgeon. Dr. Whiteside suggested that she continue her training at the hospital for another six months, and she happily agreed.

Lieutenant Matt Braxton and Laura Belsky became engaged and planned their wedding for the fall. They were thankful to Nora and her unmitigated good humor that made them realize how much they had not seen in each other earlier. Laura had decided that police work was not for her anymore. She had been leaning in that direction all along, but the shooting of Sue solidified her decision. She had gone to work for Tommy's law firm and had been taking classes at the Art Institute.

Nora had a special display case prepared for the library at Duffy Hall to hold Aunt Vinnie's jewels, and their brilliance added even more light to that special room. An expert appraiser examined the jewelry and stones and estimated their value at $5 million. Nora was surprised by that and agreed with Fiona Finnegan that while they were adding high-speed Internet to the building, they should also equip the entire castle with a high-quality security system.

Tim Taylor had been so impressed by how fast Finnbar ran when he galloped back to the castle with Nora that he had contacted a horse trainer. He thought they could likely enter Finnbar into the Galway races in the summer. Nora was thrilled to hear that Uncle Cyrus' handsome horse would be able to show off his beauty and talent, and she and Tommy hoped to be there for his big race.

Without Cyrus and Lavinia at Duffy Hall, it could become a lonely place. Time had revealed that Kitty Lloyd and Sean Duffy had more than just Duffy Medical business in common. When they got married in the summer, they would be delighted to accept the invitation to live at the hall and act as its caretakers.

Nora submitted her short and long-term plans for the renovation of Duffy Hall Castle to the board, which were quickly approved. She would hire an expert restoration firm to analyze how best to renovate the castle, inside and out. Dangerous things would be taken care of immediately, but the remaining renovations could take place gradually. The old part of the castle had only been partially excavated to date, so she would ask the restoration firm to research how to maximize that space too and to look for any lost treasures.

A team of architects had drawn up plans for the start of construction of the state of the art medical research building behind Duffy Hall. The suggestion for a store on the grounds that would sell products produced from the grounds of Duffy Hall was still being investigated, but early opinions seemed to be positive. The investigation of Duffy Medical being traded on the New York Stock Exchange had also been moving forward, and a number of experts in Ireland and the US were analyzing this exciting plan.

Nora acquired the approval of the Duffy Medical board to make a movie about Duffy Hall and its founders, Cyrus, Emily, and Vinnie. A knowledgeable director and producer had begun the project and promised to include artful portrayals of the castle, grounds, and animals as well as to highlight Sneem and the other towns on the Ring of Kerry.

Jesse was thrilled that everything had turned out so well for Nora, and she would always be grateful to the Duffy Hall ghost for her help. They all had to endure a lot of suffering, but she'd always believed, "It's an ill wind that blows nobody good."

Bridie the Beautiful, the aforementioned ghost, smiled as she received her official Badge of Completion and Promotion to Angel from Angel Christopher. He commended her on her interventions at just the right moments that had protected Nora and the Duffy family. Christopher also told her that she was done with the whispering. She and Brendan would now be members of the angelic choir, so she would have to use her "outside voice" loudly while singing "Glory to God in the Highest, and Peace to Men of Good Will." She would also be wearing her new silk gown trimmed with Irish lace.

Bridie was then ushered to the place where she could be reunited with Brendan, and she uttered a good west of Ireland sigh of contentment. It was very gratifying to know that she had helped Nora to survive, and she thanked God for his faith in her. "It took me an extra-long time to figure this all out," Bridie realized, "but my Angel status will be even sweeter now. By the way, thanks to all of you who have been on this journey with me for your good wishes and prayers. They worked!" Bridie elatedly said with a wink.

About the Author

Babs is from Chicago and had been reading a number of Irish mystery stories on her Kindle and looked for one centered around Sneem, the hometown of her fraternal great grandfather. When she didn't find one, she decided to write a story about this magically beautiful place on the southwestern coast of Ireland, one of the towns on the famous Ring of Kerry.

Murder at Duffy Hall Castle is Babs' first book. Almost all the places and people in the book are fictional, but the relationships of the characters were inspired by people she has known. She has been a life-long writer for work, school, church, and family. Babs has a degree in English Literature and continues to learn from the masters such as Shakespeare, Joyce, Dickens, and the plethora of British mystery authors like Agatha Christie or P.D. James.

She has had a variety of managerial roles in her working career and is an organist and piano teacher. She is a wife and mother, which she feels is good training for any other role and has been a volunteer caretaker for several family members.

Babs loves anything from astronomy to zoology that stimulates her curiosity to learn more about our wonderful world and its fascinating people. She is interested in big "why" questions: Why are we here? Why is the universe so big? Why are wars still happening? Why can't we find a cure for cancer? Why do people see the same thing so differently? And so many more.

She has been a musician since she was four years old and is grateful that she can play most anything by ear. She enjoys watching the interactions of musicians to produce food for our souls, whether it's a symphony or rock concert. She admires the abilities of artists to capture our inner emotions and marvels at what we can learn from movies and television programs. She appreciates the efforts of so many in the technology field that have made the process of writing so much easier. She loves to travel to near and far places, especially when it's to see a loved one.

Babs likes to learn from people who are different than those she encounters on a regular basis. She finds inspiration and courage from the Bible and the encouraging words of many historical figures. She enjoys hearing personal stories from those who spend their lives serving others. She regularly reads nonfiction biographies and histories and always loves a good mystery novel. She has been a book club member for most of her life and has learned as much from the other members as she has from the books. She loves to pray, decorate, cook, shop, and enjoy good food, especially with her circle of long-time friends.

Babs first met her tall husband when he was kind enough to reach for a book about dinosaurs for her that was on a high shelf in the university library (rather than the metaphysics book she was supposed to be reading). She delights in seeing babies grow and develop. Babs receives the most joy when she is able to spend time with her large family but takes advantage of social media platforms to see and hear them when she can't give them a hug.

Babs is a "glass is half-full" person and shares the perspective of Gerard Manley Hopkins about us and where we live: "The world is charged with the grandeur of God. It will flame out like shining from shook foil." If anyone needs a physical reminder of this truth, she tells them to go to the Cliffs of Moher in Ireland at dusk and watch the sun gradually sink into the ocean. God is in charge!

CPSIA information can be obtained
at www.ICGtesting.com
Printed in the USA
LVHW111304290722
724664LV00004B/35